Pregna

Expecting…or her wedding day!

Pregnant Brides

THE FATHERHOOD AFFAIR
by
Emma Darcy

EXPECTING HIS BABY
by
Sandra Field

DR CARLISLE'S CHILD
by
Carol Marinelli

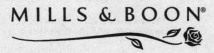
MILLS & BOON®

*MILLS & BOON and MILLS & BOON with the Rose Device
are registered trademarks of the publisher.
Harlequin Mills & Boon Limited,
Eton House, 18-24 Paradise Road, Richmond, Surrey, TW9 1SR*

PREGNANT BRIDES © by Harlequin Enterprises II B.V., 2004

The Fatherhood Affair, Expecting His Baby and
Dr Carlisle's Child were first published in Great Britain by
Harlequin Mills & Boon Limited in separate, single volumes.

The Fatherhood Affair © Emma Darcy 1995
Expecting His Baby © Sandra Field 2001
Dr Carlisle's Child © Carol Marinelli 2001

ISBN 0 263 84076 X

05-1104

*Printed and bound in Spain
by Litografia Rosés S.A., Barcelona*

Initially a French/English teacher, **Emma Darcy** changed careers to computer programming before the happy demands of marriage and motherhood. Very much a people person, and always interested in relationships, she finds the world of romance fiction a thrilling one and the challenge of creating her own cast of characters very addictive.

**Don't miss the last instalment of Emma Darcy's
exciting trilogy:
THE OUTBACK BRIDAL RESCUE
Book Three of *Outback Knights*
Out *this month*, in Modern Romance™!**

THE FATHERHOOD AFFAIR
by
Emma Darcy

CHAPTER ONE

A GREAT deal could be done in two months.

The thought brought a feeling of satisfaction to Natalie Hayes as she walked from the foyer of the Regent Hotel and up the grand staircase leading to Kable's Restaurant. Today she intended to show Damien Chandler precisely how much could be done in two months, and how much could be made to happen.

This luncheon was the ideal occasion to let Damien know she didn't need him as a watchdog any more. She could take care of herself. Damien's sense of duty—or was it guilt?—could finally be laid to rest.

She was back to her best weight. The bold orange dress was light-years away from any suggestion of lingering bereavement. It hugged her curves and highlighted both her recently acquired tan and the artful blonde streaks in her radically restyled hair. Damien couldn't call her a pale ghost of herself today.

Her face had colour. She no longer had hollows in her cheeks. She had played up her light amber eyes with a subtle shading of brown and gold. The shorter, softer, brighter hairstyle suited her face much better than the long and rather lifeless fall of honey-coloured hair she had simply let grow in the past twelve months. Natalie was satisfied she looked quite pretty again, younger, and certainly up-to-date in every fashion sense.

She had felt absolutely confident about walking into this hotel, one of the classiest hotels in Sydney. She looked like a new woman. She felt like a new woman. She *was* a new woman.

There was a buoyant lilt of anticipation in her step as she reached the landing that led to the highly reputed restaurant. She was going to enjoy the surprise in Damien's eyes. He would have to realise, must be made to realise, that she no longer required a crutch or a spur or advice or criticism. All these things he had supplied in abundance over the past year. It was time to bring it to a halt. A dead halt.

She saw him seated on the sofa beyond the receptionist's desk. He was hunched forward, apparently contemplating the drink in his hand. Despite an air of weariness, probably from jet lag, he looked as impressive as he always did. A three-piece grey suit had the expensive sheen of silk in the fabric. Tailored for him in Hong Kong, Natalie surmised.

He glanced up and saw her.

The shock of recognition on his face was not the reaction Natalie had expected. Surprise, yes. She had

hoped to surprise him. She had not expected a reaction that arrested all movement, dulled even further the light in his eyes, an outright withdrawal
away from her into himself.

It was too extreme for Damien. It mangled the
smile that had been hovering inside her. It sent an
odd tingle of apprehension down her spine. She
stopped walking. She was assailed by the sense of
having a comfortable familiarity forcibly taken away
from her.

Natalie had never seen Damien Chandler completely thrown by anything. He was always in
charge of himself. He was always in charge of everything and everyone within his ambit. It was nigh
on impossible to tell what went on inside the man.
He revealed that to no one.

In the space of a few seconds, she saw total shock,
followed by a twist of anguish, a jaw-clenching look
of determination, veiled anger, then a plainly visible
relaxation of his features into a smile of forced,
lukewarm pleasure as he put his glass down and rose
to his feet.

'Natalie...' He managed to inject both surprise
and delight into his voice, although what he really
felt Natalie had no idea. He moved to meet her.
'What a joy to see you looking so brilliantly alive!'

Damien was a master of such blandishments.
Natalie had heard him do it to every woman he had
met over the years they had known each other. It

sounded right. It was what she had wanted to hear. But something was missing. That *something* was approval. She couldn't see it in his eyes.

Not that she needed Damien's approval. It was simply that...why were his eyes full of questions instead of recognising she had answered all the criticisms he had angrily impressed on her at their last meeting?

Then he took hold of her hands as though it was the most natural thing in the world to do. But it wasn't. Not with her. She had seen him perform the same welcoming gesture with other women, making a flirtatious intimacy of it and often accompanying it with a light kiss. He had never tried it with her. Never! Not even when she was Brett's bride and Damien was best man at their wedding.

Her shoulder muscles stiffened as electric prickles ran up her arm. She didn't understand what was going on. Damien wasn't supposed to step out of the mould he had established in her mind as Brett's closest friend and business partner. She did want him to drop the role of self-appointed guardian to Brett's widow, but...his uncharacteristic behaviour was ruining everything.

It was a relief that he didn't try to press any closer. If he had, she would have recoiled, unable to prevent the reflex action. As it was, she was acutely aware of the warmth and strength of the fingers enclosing hers, and the caressing graze of his thumbs across her knuckles.

'I leave you a pale shadow of yourself, and I come back to find you glowing,' he said in light bemusement, his tone belying the intense probe of his eyes. 'You benefit from my absence. Is there some special reason behind the change?'

Natalie shrugged. 'Lots of reasons.' He was one of them. She forced a smile. 'Wasn't it your intention to jolt me into getting on with my life?'

'The result is stunning.'

'But you don't like it.'

'I prefer to have more time in which to make a judgement.'

He looked at her in a way he had never overtly looked at her before. Raw, jungle hunger. Natalie was stunned by the sudden blaze of uncloaked desire in his eyes. It burnt into her, making her feel naked and exposed. It bore no relation whatsoever to the kind and supportive business friendship they were supposed to be having. It sizzled with unrepressed sexuality.

She felt her heart catch. Her mind jumbled chaotically around the thought that Damien now saw her as different from the unexciting *hausfrau* she had been. And he was letting her *know* it. Without hesitation, he was jettisoning all of their past. The years of keeping his distance from her had just winked out.

He meant to have her. No doubt about that. Knowing Damien as she did, Natalie realised she would have her hands full trying to stop him. The charge of animal electricity coming from him had her nerves leaping like fire-crackers.

He released her hands. Natalie's relief was short-lived. He smoothly moved to link one of her arms around his for escorting her into the restaurant. His eyes didn't leave hers. 'Hungry?' he asked.

She wondered what type of hunger he had on his mind. 'Yes,' she said lightly, trying to fight the un-settling effect of his closeness.

Taking her arm was an ordinary enough courtesy. It was absurd to have this skittish feeling of wanting to shy away from him, to put more distance between them. He couldn't seduce *her* into taking him as a lover. It would be like involving herself with Brett all over again. She wouldn't consider it. Not in a million years. Damien had better put it out of his mind or this luncheon would come to a very abrupt end.

He gestured their readiness to the *maître d'*, who smiled and set off to lead them to their table.

Natalie registered that the smile was a typical fe-male response to Damien. Most women would clas-sify him as outstanding in the tall, dark and hand-some category. Add to that the charisma of keen intelligence, a charm of manner based on rock-solid self-assurance, and the attention he drew was perfectly reasonable.

As they passed tables where women were seated, interested looks were cast his way. Damien Chandler commanded a second glance from everyone, men included. He carried the air of being *someone*. He stood out from the general run. People noticed him, remembered him. Such attributes were both social and business assets. Objectively, Natalie had recognised this long ago.

She would never have believed that the simple act of having her arm linked to his would make anything different, but it did. The looks directed at Damien slid to her, looks of envy and assessment, matching her against him as a couple. It did nothing for Natalie's self-confidence.

All the same, Damien was not going to sweep her off her feet. She didn't care how many women fancied him or how fanciable he was. She knew better than to lay her head on his chopping-block. Easy come, easy go. She had seen it too many times to be even faintly interested. That he could be turned on by her new image was virtually an insulting demonstration of how facile his sexual urges were.

Damien would never marry. Of that she felt certain. He had done it once, in his mid-twenties before they had ever met. From all accounts, it had been his wife who had walked out on him. Which carried its own message to Natalie.

She was glad to reach their table and be seated. She concentrated on laying her shoulder-bag beside the leg of her chair, smiling at the hovering waiter, ordering a champagne cocktail, smoothing the table napkin across her lap. The actions gave her time to recover some of the sense of well-being and purpose with which she had started out for this meeting.

She felt Damien's gaze on her and glanced up to meet it, determined on acting naturally. 'How was your trip?' she asked.

'Successful.'

That was normal. Damien was a powerhouse of energy and inspiration. She smiled. 'Does this mean you'll be back and forth to Hong Kong for the foreseeable future?'

'No.'

His thick black lashes swept down. Combined with deeply set eyelids, they had the effect of making his eyes look dark from a distance. Their silvery-grey colour came as an intriguing surprise. When he looked up his expression was flint-like and purposeful.

'I've sold the company, Natalie. It's being taken over by a Chinese consortium that wants to spread its interests out of Hong Kong. If it's allowed to do so.'

She was dumbstruck. Changes were coming thick and fast today. She could hardly put two thoughts together. Concern for him slashed through her mind, prompting the question, 'Were you in financial trouble, Damien? Did paying me Brett's share...'

'No,' he answered curtly. 'As I told you before, and as cruel as it may seem, Brett's death...' He didn't go on.

'...was my financial solution,' she concluded for him. The solution to several other problems as well, she thought bitterly. But the cost of it was still difficult to bear.

'I never wish to refer to the matter again,' Damien said, a hostility in his voice.

'You're not selling the company because of me,' Natalie protested. 'You can have the money back if you need it. I haven't touched it.'

'It has nothing to do with money, Natalie. I simply want to be out.'

'Why? You're so good at what you do. Surely...' Her mind clicked on to another path. Was it because Brett was gone? Damien was superb at selling conversions for computer programs. He was brilliant at working out what was required by the clients, but Brett had been the force behind delivering what was promised. His was the genius that had put it all together and made it work.

'It's not the same without Brett,' Damien said flatly. 'The company has the personnel and expertise to carry on. It's still a viable business, Natalie. But I miss Brett's quick understanding of what's needed.

I'm reminded of him all the time. It was something we shared.'

'Yes. Yes, I know.'

They'd been as close as, if not closer than brothers. That wasn't to say they never fought over issues. They did. Like cats and dogs. In the end, they always stood together, no matter what. Their loyalty to each other was so strong that it overrode the loyalty owed to her.

The waiter brought their drinks and handed them menus. Natalie stared blindly at the printed list for several moments, realising for the first time that Damien's grief had probably been as deep as her own. Worse, in the sense that he had been abseiling on the cliff, a helpless witness as first Ryan, then Brett, trying to save their son, fell to their deaths. At least she had been spared that.

Natalie fought back tears. She had to put her dead child behind her. She had to put the misery behind her. She had let grief swallow up her life long enough. She was not going to let her resolution slip now. She selected the Caesar salad as an entrée, and the Atlantic salmon for her main course, then set the menu aside.

Damien was watching her.

She raised her eyebrows. 'So what do you plan to do?'

He relaxed. 'I'm obliged to stay on with the company for six months to ease the change-over. There's a three-year exclusion clause from taking on any similar type of work.'

'That's quite a lot of time to fill in.'

'I have a project in mind.'

'What is it?'

He looked intently at her, as though there should be some intimate understanding between them. 'Don't you have any idea?'

'None whatsoever,' she answered airily.

'That makes everything a little more difficult.'

He paused a minute, reassessing the situation. She gave him no encouragement. She kept an expression of bland curiosity pasted on her face.

'What are your plans, Natalie?' he asked, deciding to approach his purpose from another angle. 'Did you come to this meeting with a definite idea as to its outcome?'

An appalling thought struck her. Had Damien interpreted her new image as an attempt to attract him? Natalie burned with embarrassment. How could he entertain such an implausible idea? Perhaps, though, that was why he had looked at her in the way he did. The need to rectify any misunderstanding caused her amber eyes to glitter with fiery golden sparks.

'Yes, I did.'

'Well?'

'I wanted to tell you certain things.'

He smiled encouragement, confident of holding his influence over her thoughts and actions. 'Go ahead and tell me,' he invited, gesturing with open hands.

'For one thing, I don't want you guarding me like a watchdog any more.'

His smile turned rueful. 'It was only for your protection, Natalie. You were…rather lost and defenceless.'

'Well, I've found my defences again.'

'Fine!'

'And I never want to hear another word of criticism from you. It's my life and I'll live it as I see fit. Not as you see fit.'

That sobered him. His eyes went still and wary.

Her chin lifted in defiant self determination. 'I don't want you to ever mention Brett again in my hearing,' she added strongly. Her flow of thought then faltered under his hard, relentless stare.

'Is that all?' he asked tersely.

'More or less,' she answered. 'But I'll think of more if you press me.'

'In other words, you want *me* out of your life.'

'Yes.'

'As a business advisor and as a friend?'

'Yes.'

He left her no alternative if he wanted to mix sex with friendship. Her gratitude for what he *had* done for her didn't extend that far. Nevertheless, she did feel a certain hollowness burrowing through her stomach. He had been like a cog around which her life had turned for a long time. A mainstay. Her head swam a little with the enormity of cutting free from him. Did she really want that?

'Is there another man?' His harsh tone of voice verged on the critical.

Natalie's eyes flared. 'Not yet. But there will be.'

He returned a steely challenge. 'What do you really want, Natalie?'

Had he somehow read her mind? Sensed the doubt? The fearful uncertainty in severing all ties? Natalie focused hard on the question. If she was going to be her own woman, she had to know the answer. It came to her in a burst of bright clarity.

'The best thing that ever happened to me was Ryan. I can't replace him. He was a unique and wonderful child. But I can have another child who can be just as unique and wonderful, Damien. That's what I intend to have.'

Damien sat back abruptly in his chair. Once again his face reflected shock. He stared at her as though he had never known her, an unseeing blankness in his eyes, all the clever intelligence frozen, or turned inward.

It sent a chill through Natalie's heart. He had left her. The impulse to draw him back surged through her so wildly, words were spilling off her tongue before she could stop them.

'Aren't you glad to be rid of me? Aren't you glad to have any responsibility to me set aside?'

The taunt succeeded. His eyes refocused on hers. 'No.'

The stark negative gave her nothing to work on. Damn the man and his self-sufficiency! Why couldn't he reveal what was going on inside him?

'What purpose is there in our ever seeing each other again?' she pressed. 'Give me one good reason.'

'Your husband was my friend,' he said slowly, picking his words with care. 'However much you think he loved you, I believe he was no friend to you.'

The import of those words was not lost on Natalie. She sat very still, holding her breath. Damien's loyalty to Brett was cracking. Would he now speak the truth about her husband, reveal the infidelities he had helped to cover up? Did Damien even suspect how much she already knew, or was he still convinced he and Brett had artfully concealed everything?

He leaned forward. As though he had flicked a switch that flung open the windows of his mind, his eyes once more blazed with naked desire.

'The reason I sold the company was to have the time to prove to you—conclusively and forever—that you married the wrong man, Natalie.' The low throb of passion in his voice gathered a deep soul-shaking conviction as he added, 'The man you should have married was me. Not Brett. *Me!*'

CHAPTER TWO

MARRIAGE? To Damien?

Natalie felt as though she had been pummelled in the solar plexus. Her mind was blown into whirling confusion. She stared incredulously at Damien, struggling to connect what she knew of him to the words he had spoken. He held her gaze, relentlessly reinforcing what he'd said with compelling intensity.

She supposed she should feel flattered…a man of his many attractions wanting *her*. She wondered what influenced his choice. He hadn't mentioned love. She wasn't the first woman he'd wanted, and wouldn't be the last. So why her?

Natalie's shell-shocked mind finally grasped the motive behind Damien's statement.

Brett.

She felt sick.

And angry.

She leaned forward, her eyes a golden shower of blistering sparks. 'Even now, with Brett in the grave, you can't help competing with him, can you? You can't let go. You want to take me over to prove to your insatiable ego that you were the better man.'

He grimaced in frustration. 'That's nonsense! Why are you avoiding the obvious?'

'The obvious is that Brett's still on your mind,' she retorted. 'You began and ended your ridiculous claim with Brett. After I'd specifically asked you never to mention him to me again.'

'So it still hurts that much, does it? Goddammit, Natalie, I've waited long enough! Will you recognise me for what I am?'

'That's the problem, Damien. I do recognise you for what you are. You told me straight out that you sold the company because it wasn't any fun without Brett. It was something you *shared*. So what's the new project? *Me*. Something else you can share with him in some tormented, twisted, perverted way.'

'I'm not sharing you with anyone,' he declared indignantly. 'When I saw you today...'

'You thought the *fun* could begin.'

From somewhere inside her came a billow of outrage. It activated a burst of adrenalin. She reached down, snatched her shoulder-bag from the floor, opened it, and grabbed her wallet.

'I thought you had finally put your grief behind you,' Damien continued.

'I will not be beholden to you for anything, Damien.' She found a twenty-dollar note and slapped it on the table. 'That will pay for our drinks.

I don't want to eat with you. I don't want to be with you. I will never, in any circumstance, *sleep* with you. Do you understand what those words mean?'

'So the brave new front is just a charade,' he mocked angrily. 'You can't face up to a different reality.'

'What's different?' She returned her wallet to her bag and stood up, casting him a look of contempt. 'If you want to prove you're a better man than Brett, you can run after all the women he had on the side.'

'What?' He looked astounded, incredulous. 'You knew?'

'Of course I knew. And your part in it, as well.'

'I played no part in it…'

'Don't lie to me, Damien. You covered up for Brett. He deceived me. You betrayed me.'

Disdaining to glance at Damien again, Natalie set off down the length of the dining-room to the exit of the restaurant.

'Natalie…' It was both a protest and an appeal.

She ignored it. She heard Damien coming after her, brushing past hovering waiters, but she neither turned her head nor slowed her pace. She felt utterly deflated and cast down. She should never have trusted the feeling that he meant well by her. It was a sham so he could win out in the end. Against a dead man.

As she stepped into the reception nook outside the restaurant, Damien caught her arm, forcibly halting her. She gave him an intimidating stare of icy rejection.

'What did you want from me that I didn't give?' he demanded. 'Tell me one thing.'

'Approval. As in a-p-p-r-o-v-a-l. APPROVAL as in block letters. *Approval* as in italics. Simply approval. That's what I wanted from you, Damien. That's what you never gave me. Not even today.'

'You've always had that, Natalie.'

'Never.'

He dragged in a deep breath. 'I'm sorry I was impatient with your grieving for Brett. Terribly sorry.'

'I was grieving for Ryan, not Brett. Brett had whittled away my love for him. There was none left.'

'How was I to know that? You never gave any indication. I never realised you were disillusioned with your marriage.'

'Who parades private pain in public?'

His eyes narrowed. 'How would you have reacted if I'd come running to tell you about Brett's affairs? You would have hated me for it, Natalie.'

'It would have destroyed your friendship,' she mocked.

She wrenched her arm out of his grasp and headed for the staircase. What he said hurt. It bit painfully into her psyche. The deep-seated sense of rejection, the sense of failure, of being a discard, inadequate.

Damien fell into step beside her. 'What makes you think I covered up for him?'

'I know.'

'Give me one example.'

'You slipped up at the funeral.' She paused at the head of the stairs to face him with bleak derisive eyes. 'The woman who went on the camp with you and Brett that weekend…it was reported that she was your companion, Damien. She wasn't.'

'She was,' he insisted.

'Don't think I'm ungrateful for your discretion. If the media had latched on to the fact that adultery was mixed up with the death of my son and my husband, they would have had more of a field day than they did.'

'Natalie, I swear before God she was with *me*. I invited her. I took her there. She shared my tent. Brett had Ryan with him.'

She shook her head. 'It doesn't add up, Damien. She wept copiously at the funeral. You didn't go near her. Not one word or gesture of comfort.'

'I didn't leave *your* side,' he asserted with passion. 'She meant nothing to me. She was keen on abseiling. I asked her on the trip to make it a foursome instead of a threesome. I wasn't to know you were going to be too sick to come. We were already there at the campsite when Brett arrived without you.'

Was he speaking the truth? Had she misread the

situation? 'How did Ryan get so close to the edge of the cliff? Why wasn't Brett watching him? Ryan was a sensible little boy. He would have obeyed his father.'

'Natalie, for God's sake! Accidents can happen so quickly. Don't torture yourself like this.'

'It doesn't matter any more,' she said dully. 'Nothing can bring my beautiful little boy back.'

She started down the staircase. She had to get away from all this. It wasn't doing her any good, raking over the miseries of the past. She had to look to the future, break with Damien now, start a new life. That was abundantly clear.

Damien wasn't a friend. And that hurt, too. In his way, he had acted honourably towards her. Yet she had known he had the same attitude towards challenges as Brett had. They were two of a kind. She simply hadn't anticipated that he would see *her* as a challenge.

He was matching steps with her, still not prepared to let her walk away from him. 'Why didn't you leave Brett?' he asked.

She didn't answer. She couldn't imagine any man would understand. Trapped by a pregnancy... making excuses. Trapped by wanting the best for her baby...making compromises. Hoping things would change. Wanting to believe in renewed promises because the sense of failure was too hard to face.

Brett wasn't all bad. Mostly, but not all. She had fallen in love with his joy in living, his wit, his charm, his exuberant personality, the athletic body he made master of any physical challenge, the mind that thrived on solving problems few others could. She had thought herself the luckiest woman in the world that Brett Hayes had fallen in love with her.

She had never considered herself anyone special. She was averagely pretty, helped along by a better than average figure that had been very firm and trim when she had met Brett. She had been working then as a bush-walking guide, supplementing an irregular income from the paintings she sold to the tourists who flocked to her hometown. Noosa was a very popular seaside resort on the Sunshine Coast of Queensland, and Brett had been one more tourist, indulging his love of the outdoors, and sweeping Natalie into a marriage that had seemed idyllic. At first.

She had come to realise, painfully, that Brett saw women as a challenge, too. All of them. He couldn't resist testing himself, over and over again. Natalie he had put in a completely separate category. She was his chosen wife. The mother of his child.

Ryan…always Ryan stopping her from taking that final step away from Brett. He was indisputably a loving father, proud of his son. Ryan had adored his Daddy. She simply hadn't been able to bring herself to deprive them of the relationship that was naturally theirs. In the end, it would have saved Ryan's life—both their lives—if she had. She shook off the torment of 'if only's.

'Brett felt inadequate,' Damien declared. 'He…'

'Don't be absurd,' Natalie answered coldly.

Brett was the most gifted, talented individual she had met in her life. A bright golden god among other men. *Brett made other people feel inadequate.* People like Damien. People like herself.

Damien touched her arm to try to draw her attention back to him. 'If you knew about his infidelities, why didn't you divorce him? What stopped you?' he asked, exasperation creeping into his voice.

They had reached the foyer. It didn't really matter what she said to Damien. Whether he comprehended it or not was irrelevant. She was not going to see him again. She glanced at him with determined finality and gave him the one reason that had kept her with Brett.

'He was the father of my child.'

She didn't pause to gauge his reaction to that bare statement. She had no intention of explaining or embellishing it. She took a direct line towards the doors that led out of the hotel. This meeting with Damien had been a disaster from start to finish. She was ashamed of having been deluded into thinking he actually cared about her as a person.

Of course, she had realised that to Damien she was an extension of Brett, but there had been thoughtful gestures from him which she had believed were for her sake alone. She had thought he cared about her interests, suggesting ways of developing and extending her creative talent. She had no idea he was so…well, almost deranged…in his obsession about Brett.

Tears blurred her eyes. She had looked forward to telling Damien about the commission to illustrate a children's book. Damien had taught her creative graphic design. She had imagined him being pleased for her. She had actively gone after the job and got it, an achievement she was sure would earn his approval. Finally.

She had tried so hard to get her life moving again in order to please him. She was proud of her efforts over the past two months. She had wanted Damien to be *proud* of her.

Disappointment wrenched her heart. This was her second bad mistake, letting another man like Brett get close to her. At least Damien wasn't pressing any more questions on her. She was grateful for his silence as he accompanied her out to the covered driveway that serviced the hotel. As far as she was concerned, there was nothing more to say. Except goodbye. Forever.

'Taxi?' the doorman asked.

'Please,' Natalie answered.

'We need to talk this through, Natalie,' Damien

murmured as the doorman moved forward to summon the first cab from the rank in the street below.

'No point,' she demurred.

'You have some serious misconceptions…'

'Mine have already been sorted out. Yours haven't.'

'Look at me!' he commanded in exasperation.

'I don't want to.'

She kept her gaze steadfastly locked on the taxi turning slowly up the duel driveway, taking the lane closest to the hotel entrance. She couldn't bear to see that blaze of desire in Damien's eyes again. It reduced her to nothing but another potential conquest.

'I've a lot to say to you,' he burst out.

'I've heard enough.'

'You can't dismiss five years in five minutes and reduce it to nothing, Natalie.'

'Watch me.'

'Give me the chance to explain. You owe me that.'

'I didn't ask you for anything, Damien. You gave it.'

'You accepted it.'

'Call me stupid. I didn't understand what my role was,' she said bitterly. 'I didn't realise I was supposed to become another bed partner.'

'You're the woman I want in my life.'

'For the present.'

'Give it a chance.'

'So you can play and lay while I have your children?' She turned derisive eyes to his as the taxi halted in front of her. 'No, thanks, Damien. I've been through that once. Perhaps the next woman you feed that line to will be more accommodating. Goodbye and good luck to you.'

The passenger door of the taxi was held open for her by the hotel employee. She stepped forward and swung herself into the back seat.

'Natalie...'

She ignored the urgency in Damien's voice, but she couldn't ignore the strong bulk of his body.

'I'm coming with you.' His powerfully muscled thigh pressed against hers.

She hastily scrambled to the other side of the seat. 'No, you're not,' she protested.

'Otherwise we will never see each other again.'

'That's what I want.'

He closed the door. The inside of the car suddenly seemed filled with his presence. It pulsed with an energy that clutched at her heart and caused her senses to sharpen alarmingly.

'It's over!' she cried, feverishly desperate in her need to convince him.

'It never started,' he replied, a rough edge of passion in his voice.

'It wasn't meant to be.'

He turned to her, his face stripped of any civilised

veneer. Raw, jungle hunger leapt from his eyes and impaled her.

'I won't accept you judging me by your experience with Brett.'

Her mind swam with the realisation that she had underestimated Damien. She shouldn't have likened him to Brett. He was as dark in nature as Brett was bright. Dark and deep and intense, and with all his unleashed energy, indefinably dangerous.

For years she had wondered what went on inside him. What restraints he had…and, if all his secret longings were bared, what would a woman experience? The thought had intrigued her. She was getting more than a glimpse of the answer now, and it both fascinated and frightened her. She saw a primitive male hunter, relentless in his determination to track down his quarry, unstoppable.

She shivered. 'I don't want you, Damien. I don't want you.' She heard the wary, almost excited note in her voice, and didn't care as long as he got the message.

'What would happen if I took you in my arms, Natalie?' His eyes burned down to the agitated rise and fall of her breasts as she took quick breaths to calm her pulse-rate. 'If I were to kiss and caress you…'

'Stop it! I won't listen! Go away!'

But the images evoked did have an insidiously seductive power. Damien might be the hunter, but as a woman she knew if she tossed over the traces, threw everything upon the wind…anything and everything was possible. There had been solitary, vulnerable moments when she had fantasised… Damien wild, irrepressible, adoring her, approving of her, being proud of her. They had been some kind of solace at the time when Brett was entertaining himself with some other woman.

She had sternly repressed such wicked thoughts. That they should focus on her husband's best friend made them even more reprehensible. They were not fitting for a married woman who considered herself moral and decent. It dragged her down to Brett's level. Natalie had been ashamed of herself that they had occurred at all.

Now Damien wanted to do what she had forbidden herself to think about. More. Natalie felt there was some key to her mind and heart and body, and if some man was to unlatch the lock… Brett had had the key for a while but he had thrown it away.

Damien probably had the key, too, but it would not last. The experience would be wild and wonderful and dangerous, and in the end, as with Brett, would cost her too much. She had to stop this now, not let Damien tempt her into something she knew would lead to more hurt and disillusionment. Men didn't seem to understand how it was for a woman: the giving of more than her body.

She felt for the handle of the passenger door on her side. If Damien wouldn't get out of the taxi…

'You've always avoided touching me, Natalie,' he said softly, suggestively.

'You avoided it, too,' she flung at him.

'*We didn't dare touch one another for fear of what would follow*,' he taunted her.

'I feel the same way now.'

'I *don't*.'

There was too much truth in what Damien was suggesting. Natalie felt an urgent need to escape from it. She found the handle, lifted it, and flung the door open. Before Damien could stop her she leapt out of the taxi, plunging away from him.

She heard the shout, ignored it. The screech of tyres gripping the road surface in protest she didn't ignore. She didn't see the car in the other lane. She didn't feel it hit her, and she didn't feel any pain. Violet, purple and red colours merged momentarily on her retina. She felt an impact. Then nothing, nothing at all.

CHAPTER THREE

NATALIE'S mind was definitely fuzzy. She had the sense of being disembodied. She was in a bed. It wasn't her own bed. How she knew she wasn't quite sure, but she knew.

She tried to reason out where she was and why. Nothing surfaced. Her memory seemed to have disintegrated into a jigsaw where the pieces needed to be sorted out. She gave up the effort. The thought came to her she should open her eyes and look.

She did so with some trepidation. It was a hospital bed. Tubes looped to her arm. She shut her eyes again. She'd seen enough to identify where she was. It was an intensive care unit.

Someone was talking nearby.

'...severe concussion. Brains are a bit scrambled at the present moment. Nothing broken. Nothing that won't heal properly.'

It was an affable voice, speaking with confident authority, but how dared he speak of her brains as if they were a pastiche of broken eggs!

'So the prognosis is...?'

A different voice, deeper, warmer, richer, more passionate.

'Fine. There'll be some memory loss for a short period. That will return quite naturally.'

'How long?'

'Somewhere between a few days and a few months.'

'But her memories, all her recollections, will return?'

'Without fail. Everything.'

Natalie forced a wary eye open. Who were these people who appeared to be discussing her quite openly in front of her?

The light wasn't too bad. She opened the other eye, as well. Two doctors stood at the foot of the bed.

'Ah, she's awake again.'

That was the affable voice. It belonged to a short, slightly built man with sandy hair and spectacles.

'Do you know your name?' he asked.

'Of course, I know my name. It's Natalie.'

'Natalie what?'

'It's not Natalie Watt at all.'

'Can you tell me your second name, Natalie?'

The persistent questioning made her feel very uncomfortable. She knew she knew the answer but it didn't come to mind.

'Natalie Something,' she responded irritably. They wouldn't be able to argue with that.

'That's good. Very good,' the affable man soothed.

Natalie dismissed him. She turned her attention to the other man, the one with the passionate voice. He was tall and broad-shouldered and so good-looking Natalie bet all the nurses swooned in his wake. He moved around the bed and sat on a chair beside her. He had riveting eyes, grey, with double rows of thick black lashes.

'You've had a nasty knock on the head. Seven stitches. Everything is going to be fine,' he assured her.

'I know that, Doctor,' she assured him back. She'd heard the other one say there was nothing that wouldn't heal properly.

'I'm not a doctor.'

'Who are you then?'

'I'm… Damien.'

He looked anxious, uncertain, so she smiled to put him at ease. 'Hello, Damien.'

He relaxed and took her hand in his. 'Hello, Natalie.'

He had a beautiful voice. His fingers gently stroked her palm. Her skin tingled. It was a pleasurable sensation, soothing in one way yet oddly intimate, as though he was imparting some of his own energy through his fingers. She could feel little rivulets of warmth travelling up her arm. She wondered if he had healing hands.

'I like your touch,' she said.

His face broke into a smile. His lips gave it a rueful twist but his eyes simmered with a warm approval that seemed to zing right into her heart. There was something very special about this man.

'Are you some kind of therapist?' she asked.

He looked at her helplessly, seemed to come to some decision. 'I'm your lover,' he explained. There was a blaze of determination in his eyes, as though he wanted to sear that claim indelibly on her mind.

Natalie stared at him in consternation. How could she mislay a memory of that magnitude? What was she doing with a lover anyway? Then she recollected she was in an intensive care unit. Only family was allowed there. Had he lied to get in? If so, who had sent him? And why?

She looked sharply at the doctor who still stood at the foot of the bed. Did he accept this man as her lover? He didn't look suspicious. He seemed to have adopted the role of interested spectator. Natalie decided to get some facts straight.

'Where is my mother?' she demanded.

The doctor gestured to the man called Damien. Natalie swung her gaze back to him, her eyes sharply watchful as she waited for answers.

'Your mother's in Noosa, Natalie.'

'Did the ambulance take me to Brisbane?'

'No. You're in Sydney.'

'What for?'

'Do you remember what happened to you?'

'I had a fall in the gym. Tried a double somersault over the vault.' She frowned, not quite sure she had that right. 'Maybe it was a triple.'

'You've been floating in and out of consciousness for two days, Natalie.'

She'd lost two days of her life. No wonder they were dripping something into her arm! She couldn't comprehend why they had flown her to Sydney.

'Can I go home now?' she asked.

'If you tried to stand up you'd probably fall over. Try sitting up.'

Natalie tried and gave up without a struggle. It was easier to lie still.

'You had an accident. Your memory will come back. So will your strength.' Damien fondled her hand, pressing reassurance. 'It will simply take a little time.'

She had a very uneasy feeling about those statements. 'What's wrong with my memory?'

'What happened in the gym must have occurred years ago, Natalie. You're here because you were knocked over by a car.'

Years ago?

Her mind whirled. That couldn't be right. She stared at him, looking for some waver in his steadfast gaze. There was none. The grey eyes had more than caring concern in them. They poured a message straight into her bewildered mind. *I'm here for you. I'll look after you. I'm the rock for you to lean on.*

'How old am I?' she asked, feeling that he knew. She should know, too.

'Twenty-eight,' he said without hesitation.

He squeezed her hand hard—or did she squeeze his? Twelve years lost! She had been sixteen when she had taken that fall in the gym. What had she done with her life since then? She remembered her ambition to become an artist, as well as a great gymnast. She suspected she hadn't been much good at either.

'What kind of work do I do?' she asked, feeling an urgent need to fill in the gaps.

'You're very creative. You do graphic design on a computer. At the present moment, you've signed a contract to illustrate a children's book.'

'I must be good at it, then,' she said in surprise.

'Your work is stunning.'

The admiration in his voice gave her a deep sense of pleasure.

'Keep telling her everything that will prompt recall,' the doctor encouraged. 'The patient is doing fine. I'll leave you to it.' He gave Natalie a smile, Damien a man-to-man nod, and made a brisk departure.

The doctor's confidence was comforting. Natalie did her best to relax. She rolled the name 'Damien' around in her mind, trying to find echoes of it to patch together into a meaningful picture.

Nothing.

Yet his hand and eyes said she belonged with him, and the feeling he evoked in her suggested the same thing. She looked at him wonderingly. She was twenty-eight. He looked to be in his mid-thirties. What precisely was their connection?

'How long have you been my lover?'

His eyes were unflinching, steely, unrelenting. 'Many years. But in all that time we never made love physically.'

'Why not?'

'You were married.'

Another shock! 'Who was I married to?'

'A man named Brett. Brett Hayes.'

His eyes were searching hers.

She looked away, disconcerted at not remembering. How could she possibly forget a husband? And a lover! She glanced down at her left hand. No rings. The hospital staff might have taken them off. She stared at her ring finger. The golden tan of her skin was unbroken by a pale band. She couldn't have worn her wedding-rings.

'Am I divorced?'

'No. Widowed.'

She felt a glimmering of memory...something coming back...something important. Her heart filled with a rush of maternal love and pride. She swung her gaze to Damien, feeling a sense of triumph. 'I have a son. A beautiful boy.'

He nodded gravely. 'His name was Ryan.'

'Where is he now?' she cried eagerly. 'Why isn't he here?'

It was Damien's turn to be discomfited. He lifted her hand and kissed her fingers, transmitting his healing warmth and a deep caring. Then he looked at her with a sad compassion that chilled the warmth. 'I'm sorry, Natalie. There was another accident a year ago. Ryan was...killed.'

As soon as he said it, she knew it was true. The happiness drained out of her heart, leaving an aching, senseless void. Her beautiful boy was gone. Like the years he had occupied in her life.

Damien must have seen or felt her distress. 'That's why you want to have another child,' he said, the intensity in his voice drawing her attention back to him.

'Do I?' she asked listlessly.

'Yes. More than anything else,' he asserted. 'And I want very much to be the father of that child.'

His passion poured into the empty spaces inside her and stirred a consideration of the future. She didn't understand how he was her lover, yet they still hadn't made love together. He looked a very virile man. It must be she who was holding back for some reason.

Damien's fingers grazed longingly over hers,

wanting a response from her, not demanding, but she could feel the wanting reaching into her, finding a deep chord of harmony that assured her he was speaking the truth.

She didn't know why, but the thought of this man being her lover felt…familiar. A sense of rightness, of contentment, swept through Natalie. Yes, she did want another child. And what better man could she choose as the father? Most women would gladly line up to have such a man as their mate.

'We're not married,' she half-queried.

'I don't think you wish to marry again.'

'Why not?'

'Your first marriage…' He hesitated. She could see it pained him to talk about it. He shook his head. 'It wasn't all you wanted it to be, Natalie.'

So that was the problem. She was wary of commitment. It wasn't exactly fair on Damien to load him with the damage caused by another man. If he had loved her for years, he had been waiting a long time for her acceptance. She should know…

'Chandler,' she said. 'You're Damien Chandler.'

'That's right.'

'And I'm Natalie Arnott.'

'Before you were married you were Natalie Arnott.'

Whatever had happened in her marriage was over, Natalie thought. Damien must be more important to her now. She had remembered his name.

'Thank you for being a nice and very patient lover, Damien,' she said warmly. 'Thank you for…for looking after me.'

His smile irradiated sunshine. 'I'd do anything for you, Natalie.'

She sighed, deeply moved by his devotion to her. The talking had made her very tired. Her eyelids closed of their own weight. She could feel the light tingling of his strong hands. It forged a bond of trust.

'I like your touch,' she reaffirmed.

Of one thing she was certain. Whatever she had been like before the accident, her instincts had been very good at choosing a lover.

CHAPTER FOUR

DAMIEN came to see her every day.

No one else did.

He brought her flowers, chocolates, fruit, magazines, highly expensive and beautifully perfumed toiletries, everything she might desire to make the hours in hospital less burdensome. She was moved out of Intensive Care after the danger of a cerebral haemorrhage subsided. In the more relaxed atmosphere of a ward, Damien's attention to her excited curiosity and speculative gossip.

That was all very fine, but Natalie wanted her memory back. Once she was out of her drug-haze from the initial trauma of the accident, it weighed very heavily on her mind that she had a twelve-year gap in her life, and she was increasingly frustrated in her efforts to recall it.

Why did there appear to be only Damien in her life? That troubled her more and more. She tackled him about it on her fifth day in hospital.

'Not one person has come to visit me except you. Do other people know I'm here, Damien? I can't remember so I don't know whom to call, but I must have some friends in Sydney.' She accepted now that she did live in Sydney, New South Wales, and not at Noosa, Queensland.

'You shut everyone out of your life when Ryan died,' he explained. 'This past year…there were friends and acquaintances who did try to draw you back into their social circle. You rejected every invitation. After a while they stopped trying and drifted away.'

She could understand their withdrawal, however regrettable she found it now. 'You're saying I isolated myself.'

'Completely.'

'Except for you.'

He gave her a dry smile. 'I persisted.'

She wondered why. She had looked at herself in a mirror. Admittedly the stitched gash on the side of her scalp didn't help her hairstyle. She did have nice eyes and a good figure, but she was not the type of woman who would automatically create a sensation wherever she went. Damien only had to enter the ward and general conversation faded out as every eye swivelled to follow him.

On the other hand, all she had to do was look into Damien's eyes to know he wanted her. Very much.

And she wanted him.

Every time she saw him she felt the strong kick of response inside her. It wasn't so much how handsome he was or how splendid he looked in his tailored suits. There was more to Damien than superficial charisma. It was what happened between them, the tug of feeling, a response that was evidently grounded in a long knowledge of each other.

'I must have been a trial to you,' she stated flatly.

He shrugged. 'You were grieving.'

For her son.

But what about her husband?

Damien wouldn't talk about him. She supposed that was natural if he wanted her for himself. Why remind her of the man she had married? Nevertheless, it made Natalie feel as though she was trapped in a dark area, unable to move forward with the confidence she should have.

'You have a faraway look in your eyes,' Damien observed. 'What are you thinking?'

'Speculating about the future.'

'Am I in it?'

Her eyes danced teasingly. Perhaps it was a female instinct to like him being a little bit uncertain of her, but she quickly chided herself for being unkind in the face of his unswerving devotion. 'How could you not be,' she said lightly, 'in some form or other?'

She expected him to smile. It surprised her that he didn't. 'You could cut me out of your life like this,' he said, using his finger to demonstrate the action of a guillotine. 'You've done it to…others.'

She winced. 'Was I so bad, Damien?'

He took her hand. His eyes were hooded as he fanned his fingers over her knuckles, arousing the sensitivity she always felt at his touch. 'We all carry some emotional baggage which turns out to be garbage, Natalie,' he said. 'At the moment, you're free of it. When your memory returns, it will colour your reactions and responses.'

'To you, as well?'

'Yes, certainly. To me.' He lifted his gaze and seared her heart with the agonised conflict that raged inside him. 'I don't want it to happen, Natalie. But it will.'

'Will it be a...bad...reaction? To you, I mean.'

He paused fractionally, then gave a firm answer. 'Yes. It will be a bad reaction.'

'So what does that mean?' she asked, perplexed.

She couldn't imagine why she should turn on this man. There did not seem to be any reasonable explanation. She waited expectantly for Damien to give her an answer. When his reply came, it was nothing she could possibly have anticipated.

'It means,' he said slowly, as if he had an infinity of pain, 'that I have limited time ... maybe ... between one or two days and a couple of months before your memory is fully restored. In that period of time I have to fulfil my life.'

The blaze of purpose, resolution and desire coming from his deeply recessed eyes lent such impact to his words, Natalie was struck by the need for an instant response, an assurance to him, a defence of the fair-minded person she felt herself to be. Through whatever eyes she had seen him before, the man she saw now was a man she wanted in her life.

'I don't know what you're talking about, Damien, but I promise you this. I won't forget what you've done for me, nor the way you've stuck by me through everything.'

She had hoped he would relax, look reassured.

All that stared back at her was total disbelief.

'What did you do to me,' she whispered, 'that I should respond to you…in such a negative fashion?'

'Nothing,' he said mockingly. 'Maybe I should have. I don't know. What I can declare with absolute conviction and honesty is that I did nothing to you at all.'

It chilled her.

'Then what kind of person does that make me?'

'Essentially you are the finest person I've ever known. But you were hurt, Natalie. Dreadfully hurt.'

'And that's what I've got to recollect?'

He nodded. 'All the doctors state definitely that you will have total recall.'

'I don't know that I want those memories back.'

'It's inevitable. It must be accepted.'

'What will happen to us…when I do remember?'

The alarm and concern she felt must have been written plainly on her face. Damien moved, sitting on the edge of the bed where she was propped against the tilted backrest. He gathered her into his arms, holding her close to him, tenderly, as though he treasured her.

She slid her hands around his neck and lay her head on his shoulder. They were broad and strongly muscled shoulders, made to lean on, to weep on, to rest on. As she nestled her breasts against his rock-solid chest, and breathed in the wonderful, unique scent of him, Natalie felt a comforting sense of homecoming…relief, pleasure, the sweet promise of all that was missed, and the magic of finding it waiting to be taken up again.

His fingers caressed the nape of her neck. His mouth brushed over her hair, and she was glad it was soft and silky from having been washed today. She wanted to feel perfect to him, as perfect as he felt to her. She was tempted to press her lips to the warmth of his throat, but realised this wasn't the time or the place for such an intimacy.

She felt the tension in his body, the restraint with which he was holding her, and knew he was thinking of how to answer her question about their future together, even as he imparted the comfort that he would never change.

'You will hate me, Natalie,' he said gently.

No equivocation. Forthright. Blunt. Honest.

His certainty jolted her. 'Even worse than I hated my husband?' She didn't know how she knew she had hated her husband but she intuitively suspected she had.

'I think it will be worse,' he murmured. 'Far worse.'

'Why?'

'You suspect something of me which isn't true.'

'What is it?'

'It's not a memory I want you to recall.'

'You won't tell me?'

'No.'

She lifted her head, deeply perturbed by the deadly barriers he saw coming between them. She wanted to push them away, decry their existence, but one look at the grim bleakness on Damien's face told her he had spoken the truth, a truth he hated, but one that was inescapable.

Natalie's mind suddenly latched on to the most recent event in her life. 'The accident, Damien? Why was I knocked over by a car?'

He did not flinch. 'You did not look where you were going, Natalie, because you were running away from me.'

She stared at him, thunderstruck. It was proof of what he said, yet it was in direct contradiction of the feelings he evoked in her. She struggled to make sense of it. People ran away in fear and confusion. Or when they were dreadfully hurt.

She drew back from him, instinctively reacting to fear and confusion now. Damien did not try to hold her in his embrace. He gently eased her on to the pillows, then tenderly stroked her cheek.

'I am trying to prepare you, Natalie,' he said, pained at the need, yet clearly determined not to hide behind a curtain that might be ripped aside at any moment.

He was right to do it. Yet his honesty was devastating. It gave Natalie a miserable feeling of isolation. Total isolation. Without Damien, her life would be barren of any meaningful human connection.

Where could she go?

What could she do?

CHAPTER FIVE

NATALIE fretted over her situation long after visiting hours had passed and Damien had gone. There was too much she didn't know about herself. She had to relocate her identity. It was not healthy to be so dependent on one person. She had to broaden her world.

She thought of her mother. On impulse she rang her. It was a strangely unreal conversation to Natalie. It didn't serve its purpose at all.

Her mother chatted on about what had been happening in the boutique she managed in Noosa. She told her the same kind of news Natalie had heard in her adolescence. Nothing had changed. They were simply echoes of a past long gone.

Even when Natalie mentioned her accident and the loss of memory resulting from the concussion, it was readily apparent that no help would be forthcoming in her quest to find herself. Her mother represented love and care and support, but she was too far away in more than physical distance.

Natalie ended the call, accepting the fact that her years in Sydney formed a different phase of her life, a phase she would not have confided to a parent. It was easy to share happiness and achievements. Failure was naturally hidden. Natalie was in little doubt that she must have considered herself a failure. Perhaps even as a mother. Was that why she had grieved so long, so excessively over Ryan, shutting herself away from everyone?

She searched her mind for something positive about herself.

The answer finally came to her.

It was in her handbag.

The one concrete fact connected to both her past and future was the signed contract for her work on the children's book. She didn't know why she had been carrying it with her on the day of the accident, but it represented something she had achieved.

Natalie took it out to look at it again. The contract contained her home address and the publisher's address. Attached to it was a covering letter from an editor who wrote enthusiastically about Natalie's work. The name signed at the end of the letter was Sharon Kippax.

Surely she must have met Sharon Kippax if they were doing business together. It might be worthwhile meeting her again, talking to her. It would be an opportunity to gauge another person's reaction to her, even if it was only that of the slimmest acquaintance.

Resolution formed in Natalie's mind. Tomorrow

she would release herself from the hospital and pay her publisher a visit. Although she was bruised and sore, and a little shaky on her legs, she was not so weak she couldn't manage to get around by herself. There was nothing really wrong with her, except for the intimidating gap in her memory.

The fearful thought struck her that she might not be able to fulfil the contract. Had she forgotten the skills needed to produce what she did? Would her work still be as 'stunning' as Damien said it was?

She fought the fear down with an even firmer resolution. There was no point in worrying about it. She would find out tomorrow. It was time to take a step by herself, for herself. No running away. No sheltering behind Damien's devotion to her. She had to go out and meet the world she occupied head on.

The next morning Natalie discovered that signing herself out of hospital was a tedious business. They didn't think she was ready to leave, so every obstacle was put in her way.

She had the feeling that Damien could have achieved the same result in half the time, but Damien was at work, and she couldn't call on him for *everything*. Besides, she took some pride in proving herself capable of handling and overcoming the difficulties she met.

When she was dressed, packed and ready to leave, she did call the number Damien had given her. A secretary informed her, 'Mr Chandler is at a business meeting.' Natalie left a message for him that she had left the hospital, then set off to accomplish what she could alone.

The taxi from St Vincent's Hospital deposited her outside a tall office building in North Sydney. The directory in the foyer listed her destination as the fourth floor. She caught a lift. When the number four flashed up, she picked up her suitcase, ready to step out. The doors opened.

A woman was waiting to step in. She wore a striking yellow suit with black accessories. Her hair was black, her eyes dark, and she was beautiful.

I know her, Natalie thought with a little spurt of excitement. The sense of triumph was dashed when the woman stepped briskly into the lift and pressed a button, giving Natalie no more than a cursory glance in passing. There was not the slightest flicker of recognition in her eyes, no smile of fellow acknowledgement.

Natalie quickly propelled herself out of the compartment, embarrassed by her expectation and the dismissive manner of the other woman. Yet her inner certainty that they were not complete strangers made her turn to glance questioningly at the woman again. Did she know her or didn't she?

The woman returned a preoccupied look. The lift doors closed, putting an end to the odd encounter. It niggled at Natalie's mind as she walked over to the receptionist's desk, and continued to niggle throughout her meeting with Sharon Kippax.

The editor was in her twenties, cheerful in nature, and immediately sympathetic to Natalie's plight. She showed Natalie a portfolio of what she had submitted. Natalie couldn't help feeling a thrill of pride in the striking flights of fantasy she had produced. She really did have talent!

Sharon went through what had been planned for the children's book. She was kind, patient and as helpful as she could be, but she struck no chord of recollection in Natalie.

It wasn't that Sharon had a nondescript appearance. She had friendly hazel eyes, a mass of curly brown hair, and an attractive, expressive face. Natalie instinctively liked her.

'Have I been difficult to deal with?' she asked bluntly.

'Not at all,' Sharon replied reassuringly. 'You've been as eager about the project as I have. I love your work. It's creative. I truly don't think you have anything to worry about. Once you sit in front of the computer again...well, it's like reading. You haven't forgotten how to do that.'

Natalie hoped it was a valid point. 'Have we met often?' she asked, fiercely wishing she could remember.

'No. Only three times.'

'I'm sorry I can't recall you. The doctors do say it's only a matter of time.'

'Please...don't distress yourself. I'm sure it will all come back to you.'

'There was a woman getting into the elevator. She wore a yellow suit. Very smart...'

'My boss. Project manager.'

'What's her name?'

'Anne Smith.'

Natalie sighed. It didn't mean anything to her. 'It's hardly possible to get a more prosaic name than that,' she remarked ruefully.

'Believe you me, Anne Smith is not a prosaic person,' Sharon said, rolling her eyes at the comment. 'She's a human dynamo. She's not only on the ball all the time herself, she expects everyone else to be. In fact, it was Anne who spotted the work you submitted. Instant decision. ''Get this person under contract,''' she mimicked, then smiled. 'She has a great eye for spotting talent in every form.'

'She wore black when I met her,' Natalie said with gathering certainty.

Sharon frowned. 'But you've never met.'

'We've *never* met?'

'My orders were to handle this project myself. Completely. Anne's kept right out of it. You've never met.'

'That's extraordinary! I was so certain...' Natalie

dismissed the idea for the time being. Perhaps her memory was playing tricks on her.

Sharon, she thought, might become a friend in time. She felt the liking was mutual. Apart from that, she did have something to do, and something she did well. What Sharon had shown her of her work had convinced her of that. It gave her a pleasant sense of satisfaction and autonomy.

She caught another taxi to her home address at Narrabeen. It was a beach suburb on the north side of Sydney Harbour, which probably explained her tan, but Natalie felt cold inside when she saw the house she lived in. A double garage faced on to the street. A high brick wall hid the rest, giving the place a shuttered, unwelcoming appearance.

She found the key to the locked gate in the brick wall on her key-ring. She walked slowly down a side-path that led to a covered porch protecting what was obviously the entrance to the house. Natalie automatically chose the right key for the door.

She stepped into a large open-space living area, very modern, and furnished in a style she knew instinctively was not her taste. She eyed with a sense of disbelief the glass and chrome tables, the leather sofas and chairs, the lack of any colourful character.

She dropped her suitcase and shoulder-bag in the entrance foyer and walked over to the glass doors at the far end of the living-room. Beyond them was an extensive patio and a swimming-pool. No lawn.

No garden. A few landscape-designed areas with palm trees and ferns for shade.

An expensive house in an expensive location, she thought, and wondered about her finances. Was there a heavy mortgage on this property or was it paid for? Had her husband been a high-income earner? Had they led a very social life throughout their marriage?

She trailed slowly through the house, room by room. The furnishings were basically neutral, smartly fashionable, ultra-modern, without any striking individuality. Show-rooms, she thought, finding it difficult to accept she had lived here without wanting to change anything, or at the very minimum add some personal touches. Hadn't she cared about her surroundings? Had Brett insisted on this sophisticated but soulless lifestyle image?

Why had she continued with it after his death? Why hadn't she sold the house and made a different home for herself somewhere else? Had she simply stopped caring about anything? Even the study where she obviously worked on the computer was functional rather than personal.

What must have been Ryan's room had been stripped of any evidence of childish occupation. No nursery things. No toys. No remembrances at all. Maybe they were shut away in the cupboards. Or had she been unable to bear reminders of what was forever lost and given it all away to a charity?

Natalie found her tour of the house unutterably depressing. If this represented her past, she felt no kinship with it. Perhaps, if she opened the cupboards, went through the drawers, some sense of familiarity might return. There had to be mementoes of her life here somewhere. But she didn't feel capable of continuing her search. The purpose that had fired the day's activities drained into a flood of exhaustion.

Her legs finally carried her back to the master bedroom where she flopped weakly on to the king-size bed. She managed to work off her shoes and drag some pillows out from under the quilted cover. She was trying to settle herself comfortably on her side when she saw the photograph.

Her heart lurched.

Ryan.

A golden little boy framed in gold.

The photograph stood on the bedside chest of drawers, turned to face where she lay. Natalie's hand automatically reached out to bring it closer to her.

He was laughing, his sherry-brown eyes sparkling with delight. He had a soccer ball clutched in his arms, and he wore a red tracksuit and navy blue sneakers. The background was a park she didn't recognise, but she remembered how Ryan loved playing with balls and balloons: kicking them, catching them, throwing them, bouncing them.

A happy child, giving happiness. Poignant memories flashed into Natalie's mind: Ryan splashing joyfully in a bath, squealing excitedly as she swung him out and bundled him into a towel, holding him close, smelling the sweet clean freshness of his skin and hair; Ryan uninhibitedly snuggling up to her, saying, 'I love you, Mummy.'

Natalie hugged the photograph to her as she lay back and closed her eyes, savouring the pictures that slipped into her mind. Ryan, taking his first steps towards her, the surprise, the glee that he could do it shining from his eyes; the joy of riding his tricycle on his second Christmas; the pride of achievement when he learnt to swim... 'Look at me, Mummy!'

I couldn't have been a bad mother, Natalie thought with heart-lifting conviction. My boy meant the world to me. My son...Ryan...

Chimes echoed through the house, insistently calling for her attention, too many chimes for it to be a clock. The doorbell, she realised, shaking herself out of the doze she had drifted into. The doorbell could only mean Damien. She had shut everyone else out of her life.

The framed photograph of Ryan slid off her stomach as she pushed herself up from the pillows. She picked it up, gazed sadly at the laughing little boy, then reinstated the golden memory where it had sat on the chest of drawers. It wasn't a piece of celluloid she needed to hold, but a live flesh-and-blood child.

The door-chimes called again.

She fumbled her feet into her shoes, raked her fingers through her hair, then made her way out to the foyer to let Damien in. She opened the door and was instantly subjected to a concentrated scrutiny from caring grey eyes that bored into her soul, filling the emptiness there.

'Are you all right, Natalie?'

She nodded. 'Come in, Damien.'

His glance fell on her suitcase and shoulder-bag as he entered. 'You haven't been here long?'

'Long enough.' She closed the door, then gestured sweepingly at the living rooms open to view. 'This...doesn't feel like home to me.' She searched his eyes, anxious for the answers she needed. 'What was I like...as a person?'

'On the day you were married you were filled with joy and love and laughter, brightly anticipating all the good things in life. You were...' his voice softened, deepened '...the most desirable woman in the world.'

'You were there...on my wedding-day?'

'Yes.' His mouth took on an ironic twist. 'That was when I met you for the first time.'

'What did I become, Damien?'

'Withdrawn, introspective, unresponsive. No smiles for anyone...except Ryan. This past year you've been sullen, morose, isolated and alone. People could talk to you and were ignored. I doubt you knew they were talking to you, myself included.'

'Why did you put up with it?'

'Who wants to see a candle snuffed out? A flower that fails to bloom?'

She shuddered at the images evoked. 'I don't like this house,' she cried. 'It's…it's sterile. It isn't me, Damien. If it was, I don't want it to be me any more.'

'What do you want, Natalie?' he asked softly.

She went to him unhesitantly, her hands resting lightly on his chest, her eyes imploring his for understanding and acceptance.

'Take me away from here, Damien.'

His arms came around her, drawing her closer. 'Yes,' he said simply.

She leaned on his wonderful strength, laying her head contentedly on his shoulder. She felt his chest rise and fall. A long breath wavered warmly through the short waves of her hair. She didn't know or care where Damien would take her. She wanted the candle to burn brightly, and the flower to bloom, and she wanted to be with the man who believed it was possible, who had cared enough to wait to see if it would happen.

CHAPTER SIX

DAMIEN took her to his apartment.

It overlooked the ocean at Collaroy, not far from Narrabeen, yet the moment Natalie stepped into Damien's living-room she was in a different world from the one she had once inhabited.

Warm, welcoming, earthy and sensual were the words that sprang to mind. The carpet was the colour of candied honey. Big squashy sofas were upholstered in a fabric that combined green and orange with leopard and zebra prints. The parquet top of a large square coffee-table fascinated with its unique design. A smaller mobile table supported a television set.

Set into a recess was a cabinet for stereo equipment. A rack displaying a range of compact discs rose above it. Bookshelves holding an extensive private library stood beside a nook accommodating a well-stocked bar. Oak and brass dominated. Wooden stools were softened by tan leather seats.

In front of the floor to ceiling windows overlooking the sea views was an informal eating area: a round cane and glass table with four tub chairs softly cushioned in the same fabric as the sofas. The adjacent kitchen featured oak cupboards, polished granite bench-tops, and a luxuriant potted fern spilling its long fronds over the divider from the dining setting.

Natalie was intrigued by what was revealed of Damien. He enjoyed comfort, liked a touch of the exotic, and was used to pleasing himself. He was methodical, tidy, had a place for everything, and everything in its place, yet that did not detract from the welcoming atmosphere. This was very much a home, a highly individual one, and Natalie felt a sense of privilege at being invited into it.

'Have I been here before?' she asked.

'No. This is the first time,' he said softly, as though it was a momentous occasion for him, the end to years of waiting and wanting.

Natalie's heart contracted at all she had put him through, however unwittingly. She swung around to face him. He had set her bags down near a hallway and was observing her reaction. She smiled her pleasure at being in such a user-friendly place.

'Was it because I always refused any invitation? Was I being remiss?'

He shook his head. 'You were never invited.'

So bringing her into his home was a decisive step for him, laying himself open to her as he had never done before. He didn't look vulnerable in her opinion. There was an air of lonely pride about him as he waited to see how receptive she was to the situation. It was as though he was saying to her, This is the man I am. I want you to stay but the choice is yours.

'I'm happy to be here,' she assured him, 'and your sofas look very inviting.' She gave a rueful sigh. 'I'm afraid I'm about ready to wilt.'

He visibly relaxed and gestured her forward. 'Make yourself at home. Have you had anything to eat?'

'No. I didn't think of it.'

'I'll get you something in a moment.'

While he took her bags to another room, Natalie slipped off her shoes and gratefully sank into the deeply cushioned corner of one of the sofas. She lifted her legs up and settled herself comfortably. Her body ached. She was exhausted. Too much in one day, she thought, although she did not regret any of the steps she had taken.

Damien returned, divested of most of his business suit. His shirt collar was opened, his sleeves rolled up. Clearly he intended relaxing with her. He gave her a smile of approval as he passed by, leaving her to rest quietly while he went to the kitchen and set about making coffee and sandwiches.

Natalie watched him, marvelling that *she* had some special appeal to him. Many women must have crossed his path over the years, and he was far too attractive not to have been pursued by some. It seemed unreasonable to her that he should have reached his mid-thirties without forming a serious attachment to anyone else. Yet she looked around her and saw entrenched self-sufficiency. There was not one sign of female companionship present.

He brought her a plate of ham and cheese and lettuce sandwiches. Natalie found she was hungry and ate with appetite. Damien settled into the sofa opposite her, content to sip his coffee and wait until she was ready for conversation.

'All the time I was married...you couldn't have remained celibate, Damien.' She was curious to know more about him.

'I tried to get you out of my mind,' he said drily. 'I wasn't notably successful at it.' There was a hungry look in his eyes, softened by the prospect of the intimate togetherness her presence in his apartment promised.

'What about before that?' Natalie asked.

'I was married.'

It surprised her. She felt uncomfortable with the idea of Damien's having a wife, a woman he must have loved and lost. She sternly reminded herself that she had lost a husband. Had Damien's wife died, too?

'What happened?' she asked.

He shrugged. His expression changed to a world-weary cynicism. 'I suppose you could say everything or nothing. We ended up wanting different things. As it turned out, divorce was the only thing we shared. Or had in common.'

He must have been hurt by it, Natalie reasoned. No one could fail to be hurt by the crumbling of a commitment that was entered into with deep emotional involvement. 'I'm sorry,' she said with sincerity and sympathy.

He shrugged, as though that segment of his life no longer had any relevance to him.

'How long were you married?' Natalie asked, slightly disturbed by his apparent nonchalance to the severing of vows that, to her mind, should never be taken lightly.

'Three years.'

'Any children?'

The hungry look swept back into his eyes, sharper, more intense than before. 'None.'

Was that an intrinsic part of her attraction for Damien—her love for Ryan and her desire for another child? He had made no secret of his desire to be a father. It was a natural biological urge. Natalie certainly had no quarrel with it. She knew intuitively she would have little in common with a man who didn't want a family. Damien wanted what she wanted. She breathed a sweet sigh of contentment. It was a relief to know there were no children hurt by his divorce.

'Where is your ex-wife now?' she asked, wondering if the past was completely cleared away for him.

'She's the feature editor for a national women's magazine.'

He made it a simple factual statement, without any trace of judgemental opinion in his voice. Not that Natalie expected any from Damien over a woman's career.

'Are you on friendly terms?'

He toyed with his coffee-cup, then looked at Natalie in the most direct fashion. 'Lyn was a lovely person. Later, she changed. I deeply regret what happened between us. It was unnecessary, ineffectual, and in a word...stupid. But it did happen.'

'I'm sorry. I didn't mean to intrude on something so private and personal...'

'I rarely see Lyn any more,' he continued, determined on answering the questions she had raised. 'The difference between us was one of priorities. She now has a live-in relationship with a made-to-order television journalist. It seems to suit her. They've been together for a few years. On the surface they appear to be happy. If that's what she wants...I'm content to let the matter rest.'

Two journalists involved in demanding careers, no time for children, Natalie thought. Everyone was entitled to their choice of lifestyle, and if being free and unencumbered suited them best, that was fair enough. Damien was right. He accepted the separation between himself and his wife and whatever pain he had suffered at the time of their divorce was long since gone.

Natalie wondered how she'd feel when she remembered her own marriage, then quickly shuffled the thought aside. She had no right to judge Damien on whatever hurt she had suffered through another man. She felt a strong surge of conviction that Damien was the right man for her, right in every way. She didn't want her present opinions clouded by what was best forgotten.

She frowned over this last thought.

'Something wrong?' Damien asked.

'It occurred to me that I might have a subconscious wish to block out my memory of Brett.'

He said nothing. His face tightened fractionally. His wife might be in the distant past but clearly the spectre of her husband stirred raw feelings.

'Can you respond to me as I feel now?' she appealed, wishing she had not reminded him of Brett.

'What do you want?'

She laughed at herself. 'I'm too tired to move, yet there's a restless urge inside my mind. I feel I want to go somewhere but I'm not sure where it is or why I want to go there.'

'Well, we could try looking for it tomorrow,' he said obligingly, but she sensed his disappointment that she was not content to simply remain here with him.

She leaned forward impulsively, wanting him to know she cared, wanting him to understand, searching her mind to explain more clearly what she felt. 'Let us go somewhere together. Somewhere…to start afresh.'

The desire that flashed out at her was hot and urgent and barely controlled. She was suddenly, painfully aware of how sorely she had tried his patience, how frustrated he must be in still finding her elusive. A flush of guilt and shame pulsed into her cheeks and she looked away, struggling to justify her decision to follow her own instincts instead of considering his needs.

'Whatever you want, Natalie,' he conceded gruffly. 'You are like a will-o'-the-wisp…'

His voice trailed away. She understood perfectly what he meant. She could not afford to keep him waiting too long without running the risk of forfeiting everything. Her gaze flew back to his in apology.

'It sounds so selfish after all you've done for me.'

He shook his head. 'I did what I wanted to do. You owe me nothing.'

The self-mocking look in his eyes hurt. How many rejections had he suffered from her?

'You look worn out,' he said flatly. 'I'll show you the bedroom. Let you get some sleep. Tomorrow is another day.'

He pushed himself up from the sofa, rounded the

coffee-table, took her hands and helped her onto her feet.

Tomorrow, she thought. Will I be different tomorrow? Will I remember things that appear to be best forgotten?

He led her into what was obviously the master bedroom. Her bags were already there.

'You'll find the en-suite bathroom through that door,' he said matter-of-factly, pointing it out to her.

'Where are you going to sleep?' she asked, turning to him with anxious eyes, not wanting to disappoint, ready to agree to whatever he wanted even if she wasn't fit to do much more than lie in his arms.

'There's a divan in my study.'

Her hand fluttered to his chest in both appeal and protest. 'I don't want to turn you out of your bed, Damien.'

He touched her cheek tenderly. 'You need a long rest, Natalie. You wouldn't get it if I were in bed with you.'

His hand dropped to her shoulder and trailed slowly, caressingly down her arm, transmitting a need to touch that quivered through her skin. She saw the conflict rage in his eyes, felt the tension of fiercely imposed control.

'This may not be very appropriate action right at this moment,' he said huskily, 'but I've been waiting a long time.'

His hands enclosed her waist with a steady, sure, purpose. His eyes were locked on to hers, compelling her acceptance. The powerful force of his desire stirred a turbulent restlessness inside her. She didn't know if she moved towards him or he towards her. Her hands slid over his shoulders, around his neck. Her head tilted back. She felt her body poised for what was coming, every nerve alive with anticipation. Her lips parted.

His mouth seemed to explode into hers with a hungry passion, wild for the taste of her, demanding a response that matched his need. From deep inside Natalie came an overwhelming surge to satisfy him, to please herself, to lose herself totally in the excitement of knowing all they were capable of feeling together.

Fatigue was forgotten. If there was pain from her bruises when Damien pressed her closer to him, she didn't feel it. She was completely possessed by the yearning to feel his body against hers. She revelled in the hard strength of him, the power that embraced her, enveloped her, kept her captivated in absolute thrall to the sensations he aroused.

Her head swam with the intoxication of a kiss that was no mere mingling of mouths. It was a fierce claim on all that she was, a driving, heart-pounding, unbridled search for what was, and what could be between them, a giving and taking that sent streams of exultation bursting through her. Yes, she wanted this. Yes, she wanted him. All of him. Yes, it felt wonderfully, beautifully, gloriously right. He was the man for her, the man who could share this with her and so much more. She wanted everything.

Natalie was still awhirl in her vibrant inner world when Damien started to draw away from her. Not abruptly. His lips lingered over hers. His arms relaxed to a gentle hold. His hands caressed, no longer pressing her to him. He lifted his head and she heard his fierce intake of breath, felt the swell of his chest.

It took her several moments to realise he didn't intend to go on. Dazedly she opened her eyes. She had no idea what he saw in them, but in his was a look that seared her soul, compelling recognition and acknowledgement of what had just happened between them, and for which he had been waiting all these years. She belonged with him. To him. He would not accept anything less, and from the response he had drawn from her, the response she had ultimately and uninhibitedly given him, he had every right to expect it to be the same in the future.

He *knew*. The knowledge blazed in his eyes.

He said nothing.

Natalie could not find her voice to speak.

There was no need for words anyway.

He *knew* and she *knew*. The knowledge throbbed between them, irrefutable. They were in intimate accord in wanting each other. There could be no going back to whatever their relationship had been before the revelations of those last few moments.

He stepped away from her, his arms dropping to his sides. She stared at him, realising he meant to leave her alone in his bedroom to rest, to wait for tomorrow. She almost cried out for him to stay, yet in some strange sense the knowledge was enough for now.

She watched him go, watched the door close behind him. The last door, she thought. Tomorrow they would go away somewhere together and there would be no doors between them.

Except the door to her memory.

But it wouldn't matter if that opened or remained shut, Natalie decided confidently.

Damien Chandler was the man for her, and nothing could shake or change that decision.

CHAPTER SEVEN

'NORTH or south?'

Damien's question was accompanied by a smile. It was evident he didn't care where they went. His eyes glowed with anticipation for what would come at the end of their journey. In the meantime, they were together, sitting side by side in his car, ready to leave for whatever destination Natalie chose.

She wasn't quite sure what prompted her reply. It did not come from any urge to be contrary. 'West,' she said decisively, answering some strong intuition that no other direction would serve the need she felt to find a special place.

'You want to go to the Blue Mountains?'

Was it surprise that wiped out Damien's smile, or did he dislike her choice?

'Do you mind?'

His eyes quickly scanned hers. 'Of course not.' He dismissed the question.

She shrugged. 'I don't know why, but it feels right.'

'Whatever you want,' he said, nodding agreement as he started the car.

Natalie relaxed contentedly as the powerful engine thrummed into action. The lambswool seat-cover was heaven to sink into. The Jaguar SL suited Damien, she decided. Sensual comfort and high-level performance. A ripple of excitement spread through her at the thought of how he would translate both those aspects of his character into lovemaking. Or would the wild passion he had briefly unleashed yesterday slip out of his control?

She looked at the hands guiding the steering-wheel, strong, capable, yet so knowingly sensitive in their touch. Her gaze drifted to his muscular fore-arms, left bare by the navy and cream T-shirt he wore, then dropped to his powerful thighs where the denim of his blue jeans was tightly stretched. Was it the casual clothes that made her more physically aware of him, or was it the memory of how his body had felt pressed to hers?

She studied his profile. What woman wouldn't find him attractive? How was it possible she could have been unmoved by his pursuit of her before the accident? Natalie shook her head in helpless be-musement. She must have been a blind fool.

It was a beautiful day, brilliant sunshine from a cloudless blue sky, a day befitting the start of some-thing new. Natalie sighed her satisfaction. She might not know precisely where she was going, but she was certainly in the right company.

'Is being with me causing any problem with your

business, Damien?' she asked, struck by the realisation he would normally be at work since this was a weekday.

He laughed. 'I wouldn't care if it did.'

'That's rather a cavalier attitude for the boss of a company, isn't it?'

'*You* are more important to me.' He slanted her a sizzling look that made Natalie's skin tingle with heat.

There were years of frustration behind that look. With fulfilment of his long repressed desires in the offing, Damien was not about to let anything get in his way. Natalie couldn't blame him for the attitude. Patience did have its limits, and Damien felt pressured by the threat of her hating him when she remembered all there was to remember.

Was she being reckless in taking this plunge with him now?

Natalie squashed the thought, angry with the doubt, determined to trust her feeling for him no matter what eventuated. Damien had sworn he had done nothing to deserve her animosity and she believed him. She must have been dreadfully twisted up inside to have misjudged him so badly. She would get the misunderstanding sorted out when her full memory returned.

The choice to head towards the mountains should indicate something about herself. She searched for a memory that made sense of it. She suddenly recollected being a tourist guide at Noosa, taking people on bush-walks through the national forest and…yes…to the Glasshouse Mountains, so named by Captain Cook because of their conical shape. She had always enjoyed those day-trips.

The Blue Mountains to the west of Sydney were a long way from south-east Queensland, but Natalie was sure the peaks and cliffs and valleys would have a similar appeal to her. It definitely felt right to go there.

Satisfied she had made a relevant connection, Natalie was smiling happily to herself when other images of the past flashed into her mind: painting in her spare time, mostly landscapes that were readily saleable at a price most people could afford. She had been quite good at capturing a scene, although far from being an outstanding talent. Of course, it was much easier to experiment with colours and different palettes on the computer. It was marvellous how the whole aspect of a picture could be changed and polished in a manner no traditional artist would attempt.

It surprised and delighted Natalie that these last thoughts followed on so naturally. It boosted her confidence in her ability to fulfil the contract with her publisher. Sharon Kippax was right. The knowledge was there in her mind to be tapped when she was ready to start again.

'Have you met Sharon Kippax, Damien?'
'Never.'

'Do you know anything about children's books?'

'Only what I remember from my childhood.' He gave her a reminiscent smile. 'My mother used to read to us every night. Bedtime stories were a ritual. I think they're great for kids.'

The warmth in his voice reminded her of his desire to have a child of his own...with her. She formed a mental picture of Damien reading a book she had illustrated to their children, pointing out Mummy's vision of the story with pride and love. It tugged on her heart, making it ache with longing.

She could not remember her own father. He had been killed in a cyclone trying to help other people to safety. She had been only two years old at the time and her mother had never remarried. Natalie had envied her friends who had fathers and brothers and sisters. It was no fun being an only child and she now recognised that her mother had not found it easy being a single parent.

'Do you come from a big family?' she asked.

'Three boys, two girls.' He grinned at her. 'I was the youngest, but we were all close. Most of the kids in the neighbourhood came to our house to play. I had a great childhood.'

'Tell me about it,' Natalie prompted.

He recounted a series of wild adventures and outrageous mischief. It seemed that his parents had adopted a policy of free rein, occasionally pulled in with some salutary discipline when the line of acceptable behaviour was flagrantly overstepped. They were an achievement-orientated family, seeking to stretch their horizons and go wherever their interests took them.

Damien's amusing anecdotes kept Natalie interested and entertained through the trip across the city to the foot of the mountains. He fell silent as they started the climb upwards.

Natalie was hard-pressed to keep the conversation flowing. She found out Damien's oldest brother was a pilot working for Singapore Airlines. His other brother was a marine biologist, based in Tasmania. One sister lived in London, having gone to England on a working holiday and found employment as a nanny for the children of a widowed stockbroker whom she subsequently married. The remaining sister had gone to New Zealand, become involved with the women's movement, fallen in love with a sheep farmer, and had settled happily into farm life, breeding Galloways as a sideline.

Damien's parents had retired to the Gold Coast of Queensland years ago. They now enjoyed a life of leisure in the sun.

'So you're the only one left in Sydney,' she mused.

'Yes.'

'You must miss them.'

'We keep in touch. Mostly when Christmas comes around.'

Christmas was for families, Natalie thought, and especially for children. It was now the month of March. By next Christmas she would be twenty-nine.

'How old are you, Damien?'

'Thirty-four.'

If they were to have a family together, their first child could be born by next Christmas. Natalie was about to act on impulse and reach across to Damien when a familiar landscape caught her eye.

'Oh! Take the left turn before the overhead bridge,' she urged quickly.

Damien gave her a sharp and penetrating glance. 'Does this mean something to you?'

'Yes...no...I don't know.' The question flustered her because she had no ready answer to it. 'I just feel this is the way to go.'

He took the turn. 'The road leads to Leura.'

It meant nothing to her. They had left the outskirts of Sydney some considerable time ago and she had only been vaguely aware of travelling up the freeway to the mountains since then. Whether they had reached the top of the range or not she had no idea.

They approached a fork in the road. A signpost to Leura pointed to the right. 'Keep left,' Natalie said automatically.

Damien frowned at her. 'You remember being here before?'

'Not really. I don't understand it but I feel sure this road leads somewhere I want to go.'

It was a long road. They passed signs to two vacation resorts, one longstanding, one new. Damien gave her a run-down on their facilities. Neither of them had any instinctive pull on Natalie. They passed golf links. Then she saw the row of pines, thickly clustered to close out the rest of the world.

'That's it!' she cried excitedly.

'What?'

'There's a gateway between the pines. It has an arch. You'll miss it if you go quickly, Damien.'

He slowed down. He turned the car into the driveway and brought the car to a halt. On the arch was printed the name of the property, 'MERLINMIST'.

It had to be a magical place to be called that, Natalie thought, feeling certain it had the special quality she had been seeking.

'What does Merlinmist mean to you, Natalie?' Damien asked, his eyes fastened intensely on hers, almost accusing. The tension emanating from him bewildered her.

'Does it mean something to you?' she countered.

He made a visible effort to relax. 'I've never stayed here.'

'But you know of it.'

He nodded. 'It's listed as a boutique guesthouse. *Haute cuisine*. Four guest suites, each one uniquely decorated. Very exquisite. Very exclusive. Very expensive. Very, very expensive. The gardens and trees were planted forty or fifty years ago by Hildegard, a famous landscape artist. I believe the outlook over the Jamieson Valley is quite spectacular, something any artist would want to paint.'

'You must have been here before to know all that,' Natalie said, disappointed he had already shared it with someone else.

'No, I haven't,' he repeated. 'I've heard about it. Many times.'

Her heart lightened. 'Is it too expensive for us?' she asked warily.

'Not for you.'

'I'd like to stay.'

'Natalie...' he seemed to struggle with some inner conflict '...you said you wanted a fresh start together.'

'This is the place, Damien,' she assured him. She must have seen it before, gone past it perhaps, and been so drawn to it that the wish to stay had lingered in her subconscious memory, a special place for a special occasion. 'Every instinct I have tells me it's right,' she added with conviction.

'Instinct...' A look of savage irony flitted over his face.

'What's wrong, Damien?' she asked anxiously, aware that her choice did not meet his wholehearted approval.

'You're the only one who can make the decision.

If you say it's right, it's right,' he said decisively, shrugging aside whatever doubts he'd had. He gave her a rueful smile as he reached across and took her hand. He interlaced his fingers with hers. 'We're together. Nothing else is more important to me.'

Natalie was intensely relieved at his surrender to the compulsion that had selected this place above all others. Yet she could not easily dismiss the tension flowing from him. His fingers gripped hers tightly, impressing his need for her. She wanted to say nothing else was important to her, either, but it wasn't true. For some inexplicable reason, she needed Damien to share Merlinmist with her.

He withdrew his hand, and with an air of determination drove into the parking area for guests. The house was large, solidly built in red brick, two-storeyed, many-chimneyed, and with an impressive pillared portico protecting its entrance. It gave the sense of having stood the test of time, built to last against adversity. It had an instant and deep appeal to Natalie, as though it represented all she had lost, or all she was looking for in her new life.

Damien nodded to the three other parked cars as he helped Natalie alight from his. 'We could be disappointed,' he warned. 'They might be fully booked.'

'Fate wouldn't be so unkind,' she declared, her eyes alight with confidence as she curled her arm around his.

He smiled at her but he was still tense. She wished he would relax and enjoy the moment. The air was crisp and cool and invigorating. She felt brilliantly alive. Nothing could possibly go wrong. They were going to have a wonderful time together.

A honeymoon, she thought.

Merlinmist was the perfect place for a perfect honeymoon.

CHAPTER EIGHT

THEY were lucky. There had been a late cancellation. One suite was available until the weekend. Three days and nights in this marvellous place, Natalie thought triumphantly. It was more than enough.

She loved the smell of beautifully polished furniture, loved the glorious floral arrangement in the foyer, loved the grand mahogany staircase that led upstairs, loved the dignified and gracious atmosphere that came with tall ceilings and panelled walls and richly patterned rugs and carpets.

Her eyes sparkled with excitement as she was ushered into the bedroom she would share with Damien. Her gaze was immediately drawn to the magnificent half-tester bed that dominated the décor. Its yellow drapes looked stunning against a padded bedhead upholstered in a striped floral pattern. The detailed designer fabric was repeated in the valance below a white quilt on which were piled a liberal adornment of yellow and white cushions.

The night-stands on either side of the bed were matching Victorian sewing tables on graceful three-legged pedestals. They held tall brass lamps with yellow shades. Natalie swung around to see what balanced this splendid grouping of furniture. Facing the bed was a majestic chest of drawers with a large mirror, reflecting it all, giving double the visual pleasure.

She turned to look at Damien, hoping he was favourably impressed. She saw only the back view of him as he followed their hostess past the green velvet armchairs flanking a wide hearth. At the end of the sitting area, a log fire was set behind a glass-fronted fireplace. Damien adopted a listening pose as he was told how it worked, then crouched down to open the door and set the logs aflame.

Natalie's attention wandered to the far wall where an elegant *chaise-longue* was placed in front of the windows. It provided casual relaxation for the viewing of winding valleys and spectacular red and yellow ochre cliff-faces that stretched as far as the eye could see.

A shiver ran down Natalie's spine. The sheer stone cliffs looked so stark above the blueness of the eucalypts massed below them, stark and... unforgiving. She frowned over that fanciful last word. It was silly to attach any emotion to a geographical phenomenon.

She quickly responded to their hostess's invitation to inspect the en-suite bathroom. Damien stayed behind to watch the progress of the licking flames, apparently intent on ensuring that the fire, which was rendered unnecessary by the air-conditioning system, made adequate progress.

Natalie had the feeling that Damien did not know what to do with himself, but any activity, no matter how intrinsically useless, was preferable to doing nothing.

The bathroom was as splendid as everything else. Walls of gleaming white tiles were topped by a blue and green ceramic frieze, making a highlighting feature of the blue and green and yellow towels. The floor inside the shower stall repeated the colours in foliage tiles to match the frieze. A spacious spa bath added the ultimate touch of luxury.

Natalie made appropriate comments to their hostess who nodded her satisfaction and waved Natalie back to the sitting-room. A porter brought up their bags. A maid carried in a tray holding a crystal bowl of sultana grapes and strawberries, a bottle of champagne in a silver ice-bucket, and two fine flute glasses. She placed it on the table near the armchairs. Their hostess informed them lunch began at one o'clock should they wish to use the dining-room. The business of getting settled was finally completed, and Natalie and Damien were left alone in their suite.

Damien stood with his back to the fire, as though he needed warmth. There was a strained look about his face, a watchful reserve in his eyes. He made an effort to smile. 'A fine room,' he said.

He seemed to be waiting for her to take the first step. It was her choice of setting, her insistence that had brought them to here and now. Natalie wondered if she had made a mistake in taking the initiative away from Damien. Did he feel she had her priorities wrong? Was he keeping himself aloof in expectation of another rejection?

She recalled him saying as he acceded to her wish to stay at Merlinmist that the decision was up to her. This was decision time, too. He had told her what he wanted with her. He could not have spelled it out more clearly. Only she was important. The surroundings meant nothing.

'Thank you for indulging me, Damien,' she said softly, dismissing the attractions of this unique guest house as she walked across the room to him, her eyes locking with his in compassionate understanding of the dilemma he faced...whether or not to take what he most wanted while she was willing to give herself to him. The temptation must be tearing him apart, aware as he was she might hate him for taking advantage of the present situation.

'I want you to be happy with me,' he said with heart-tugging simplicity.

'How could I not be when you give me so much?'

There was anguish in his eyes.

Natalie lifted her hands to his chest. She could

feel his heart thumping madly under her palm. She tried to impart reassurance, confidence. 'I trust what I am now, Damien, not what you tell me I might become. If I'm going to change, I want you to feel fulfilled with me now. Let this be my gift of love to you. Forget all that's gone on in the past. Feel only this.'

She slid her hands up to draw his head to hers and she pressed her lips fervently to his, wanting to give flesh-and-blood reality to her words. His arms came around her, crushing her to him as his mouth began to move over hers in a yearning kiss that ignited a flood of desire.

She felt the tense urgency in his body, the need that strained against the soft pliancy of her stomach, stirring an ache deep in her womb. She opened her mouth, inviting the passionate force she had tasted yesterday, exulting in the wild mutuality of their hunger for each other.

Kissing wasn't enough. Holding wasn't enough. She rubbed her breasts against the hard muscles of his chest, wishing it were flesh to flesh. Damien's hands slid to her buttocks, squeezing them possessively as he thrust her closer to the pulsing surge of his need.

His mouth left hers. His chest heaved for breath. She opened her eyes, hot liquid amber, burning with the fiery mission to complete what had been started. Somewhere in the back of her mind was a sense that it had started a long time ago, started but been kept rigidly hidden behind doors she had locked. Whatever had simmered so long between them was loosed now, free to find the satisfaction it craved, and she fiercely wanted what Damien promised her, the ultimate height and depth and breadth of intimacy that was possible for a man and a woman...this special man and herself...together.

She saw the leap of recognition in his eyes, a wild glitter of elation at her uninhibited desire for him. He released his physical hold on her. It wasn't needed. There was another stronger bond pulsing between them, an elemental certainty. There would be no turning away from this final revelation of all they were to each other.

Damien tugged her shirt free of her jeans and began unbuttoning it.

'Take yours off first so I can touch you,' she said huskily.

He did so with a happy chuckle. It was the first sound of happiness she had heard from Damien. It swelled her heart and made it pump faster. She grazed her fingertips down the cords of his throat, across his broad shoulders and down his strongly muscled arms. He was beautifully made. Her man, her mate, she thought with such primitive satisfaction that it made her acutely aware of the basic drive that brought men and women together.

Damien peeled off her shirt, removed her bra. His

hands cupped her breasts and he gazed down at them as though enthralled by their womanliness. Was he thinking they were made to give succour and comfort, to pleasure him in the ways men found pleasure in their shape and softness? She felt her nipples harden. Damien inhaled deeply and lifted his eyes. Natalie's breath caught at the look of tenderness in them.

'You touch my needs more deeply than anyone I've ever known,' he said softly, then bent to take her breasts in his mouth, sucking them in turn, sending deep shafts of pleasure through her body, tapping a well of love so strong she found herself cradling his head, stroking his hair, wanting to hold him to her forever.

But he slipped away from her, kissing her stomach as he knelt to remove the rest of her clothes. That gave her a different pleasure, both shivery and molten, the soft, warm brush of his tongue stroking her naked flesh, the sensual caress of his hands on her thighs, behind her knees, her feet.

She reached for him as he rose upright, her hands feverishly ready to strip his manhood bare, to make him feel valued and cared for and cherished. His skin quivered under her touch as she freed him from constriction. His fingers twisted convulsively through her hair as she trailed her lips over the swollen life force of his flesh, cupped and gently squeezed the potent pouch that held his seed…for fathering a child.

He moaned her name in an ecstasy of longing and she rejoiced in his need for her, his pleasure in what she was doing. She drew rippling patterns over the powerful muscles of his thighs, feeling them tighten to rock-hardness as she cleared them of the clinging fabric.

Then he was helping her, freeing himself so he could scoop her up and hug her body to his, his mouth invading hers with urgent passion as he carried her with him to the bed. He hurled the quilt aside and laid her on the cool sheets. He loomed over her, then pulled himself back, arching in anguish as he realised what had been forgotten.

'Natalie…'

'Throw caution to the wind, Damien,' she urged, wanting him to embrace their union in all its totality, flesh to flesh, pulsing life to pulsing life.

'Yes…' He expelled the word with a violence of feeling that expressed a turbulent inner world of pent-up emotion. She saw his control disintegrate, torn asunder by a raw blaze of male possessiveness.

He drove himself deep inside her and she wrapped her legs around his hips, rocking with him in a rhythm that beat into her mind and heart and soul, a pounding crescendo of ecstatic fulfilment as they claimed each other in a mating ritual as old as time. She loved the solid strength of him plunging to her womb, tried to hold him clasped there, to restrain the passage of his withdrawal, exulted as he thrust forward to fill the waiting void again. Her whole being centred on the sensation, and the excitement of it multiplied, peaked, and burst into a molten mass of exquisite pleasure.

She heard Damien cry out, felt the wild strain of his body still pulsing inside her, then his climactic release spilling another flood of warmth, mingling with hers, forging the ultimate completion. His arms burrowed under her, hugging her close, carrying her with him as he rolled on to his side, enveloping her in a cradle of intimacy that held them joined together.

His hands moved caressingly over her in a blind fervour of touching. He kissed her hair, his lips skimming sensually over its soft silkiness, savouring the freedom to taste and feel in the blissful knowledge that she belonged to him as wholly and solely as he belonged to her.

Natalie lay contentedly in his embrace, her head upon his shoulder, basking in the vibrant warmth of their intimacy, feeling an incredibly sweet sense of security. We were meant to come together, she thought in languid pleasure. She had been right to abandon the past and take the future Damien offered her. Everything felt right with him.

She had no inclination to speak. The silence was beautiful, peaceful, imbued with a harmony that words couldn't express. Eventually she had to move to ease her leg. Damien was quickly solicitous of her comfort, piling pillows for her head, dragging the quilt over her to ensure she didn't become cold.

His eyes were soft, telling her how special she was to him. She smiled and trailed her fingers down his cheek, wondering if he was as sensitive to her touch as she was to his. There was still so much to learn about him.

'Tell me what you feel,' she said impulsively.

'Joy.' He grinned. 'I am literally tingling with a wild effervescent pleasure I can barely contain.'

She laughed from sheer elation that he felt the same fulfilment she did. 'You don't have to contain it, Damien. We can do whatever we like.'

'What would you like?'

It was typical of him to consider her feelings first. Natalie thought for a moment, wanting to please him. 'Let's have some champagne. I think we should celebrate.'

'That certainly suits my mood.'

'Stay here.' She stopped him from moving. 'I'll get it. We'll drink it in bed.' Her eyes danced wickedly at him. 'I love this bed. Especially with you in it with me.'

He laughed, his exhilaration bubbling over.

Natalie flung the quilt aside and sashayed down the room to the sitting area, deliciously aware that Damien's eyes were glued to every feminine curve of her body. It was highly stimulating to know he found her so desirable and Natalie was proud of the fact she had kept her figure in good shape. She took immense pleasure in his watching her. It was a measure of her sense of security with him that she could feel so uninhibited about her nakedness. Not only uninhibited, she found herself revelling in it.

She carried the ice-bucket back first, nestling it in the quilt beside Damien. He was propped up on one arm, a delighted grin fixed on his face, his eyes sparkling with happiness.

'You could busy yourself with the cork,' she admonished.

'I can't take my eyes off you.'

Natalie had no argument with that. She made a return trip for the glasses. The way Damien's eyes feasted over her breasts and hips and thighs was very tantalising. She decided they would forget about lunch altogether. Champagne and grapes and strawberries were fine. And seductive. And exciting. And fun.

She set the glasses on the closest night-stand and started back for the bowl of fruit. 'We might as well be totally decadent,' she declared. 'You can feed me strawberries while I'll arrange little morsels for you.'

'I feel my appetite stirring,' Damien said, the tone in his voice clearly intimating food was not on his mind.

Tucked into the side of the bowl of fruit was a grey card embossed in gold. 'MERLINMIST' was printed on it in Roman calligraphy. It was so beautifully done, Natalie automatically picked the card up and opened it to look at what was inside. '*Compliments of the house*' was printed in the same script. Her eye, however, was drawn to the hand-written message underneath.

'*Thank you for staying with us again.*'

It was signed by the manager.

Natalie frowned over it.

'What's the matter?' Damien asked.

She looked quizzically at him. 'You did say you hadn't stayed here before.'

It arrested Damien's full attention. 'That's true.'

'But I have?' It was more a statement than a question. Memories were starting to come back.

Damien looked like a man who had discovered a treasure at the end of the rainbow, only to see it summarily snatched away.

'Tell me the truth, Damien,' she demanded, but she already knew the truth. As he did, too. 'When did I stay here before?' she asked accusingly.

His face tightened into grim resignation. His eyes dulled with weariness. 'On your honeymoon,' he replied, each word a heavy drip of despair. 'On your wretched honeymoon with Brett.'

Natalie shuddered as the apt description struck home, stirring all the memories of painful confusion and disillusionment that summed up her honeymoon with Brett. The revelations rebounded on the intimacy she had just shared with Damien. She suddenly felt dirty and shamed and hurt and wounded.

The compulsion to cover her nakedness was compelling, overwhelming.

She whirled and almost ran to the bathroom, remembering the robes hanging behind the door. She couldn't bear to hunt the floor for her clothes. Such a reminder of her utter abandonment to Damien Chandler was humiliating. In *this* place...of all places! How could she have chosen it?

'Natalie...'

She ignored the imploring call, plucking a bathrobe from its hook, frantically pulling the belt apart, thrusting her arms into the long floppy sleeves, wrapping the heavy towelling fabric tightly around her in a fierce need to be properly covered.

But there was no hiding from the man who had brought her here, the man she had shared a *honeymoon* bed with, the man whose influence was so pervading and inescapable. She stepped out of the bathroom, her head tilted high, her hands thrust into the deep pockets of the bathrobe.

'Yes,' she said bitterly. 'It was a miserable honeymoon with Brett. As miserable as any woman could have. And apart from Brett himself, you had more to do with it, Damien, than any person alive.'

She glared at him, her mind flooded with black resentment of the perfection he had promised. 'How can you ever be forgiven?'

CHAPTER NINE

DAMIEN'S expression underwent a profound change. His eyes kindled with fiery determination. He rose from the bed with all the bristling pride of a man whose honour had been challenged. He was totally unconcerned by his nakedness as he strode down the room. He scooped his jeans from the floor and drew them on as though girding his loins for battle. Steely grey eyes pinned Natalie to where she stood by the bathroom doorway.

Not that Natalie wanted to move any closer to him. Damien Chandler had a lot to answer for. Outrage burned through her stomach, turning the desire she had felt for him to blistering bitterness. He had known what memories Merlinmist held for her, and he had let her make the decision without saying a word to stop or discourage her. Had there been some lurking subconscious thought that she would regain her memories in such a horrible fashion? What kind of man did that make him?

'Now, tell me, Natalie…' he stood with his arms hanging free, his torso bare, aggressive in its raw muscular power '…what possible blame can you lay at my door for what happened on your honeymoon with Brett? I wasn't here. I am not responsible for...'

'You *were* here,' she cut in fiercely. 'Every minute of every day you were here. It was because of you Brett chose this place for a honeymoon. Not to please me, but to best you, Damien. He beat you so he could boast about it to you.'

'That is not...my...fault,' Damien bit out, his eyes as sharp as scalpels, intent on slicing to the heart of her retreat from him.

She gave a bitter laugh. 'I hated you before I came to know you.'

'What did I do to deserve such prejudice?' he demanded.

She stared at him, her mind tunnelling back to her wedding-day... Brett's best man...his best friend and business partner...Damien Chandler...charming, courteous, faultlessly correct in his behaviour towards her, yet holding an aloofness that denied her entry into his personal world. That hadn't worried her at the time. She had had Brett. At least, she'd thought she had Brett. She didn't know then that Damien was the centrifugal force around which Brett's life spun, that she was a pawn in a competition, giving Brett a leading edge over Damien.

'You knew all about it, Damien,' she stated with

unequivocal conviction. 'You knew Brett a lot better than I did.'

'What a man knows of another man is not what a woman knows of him, Natalie,' he argued. 'From what Brett told me, you were the perfect woman for him, and from what I observed on your wedding-day you were very much in love with him.'

'But that wasn't all you observed, was it?'

There was a flicker of evasion in his eyes. 'What are you referring to?'

'You knew what a womaniser Brett was. He didn't even have the discretion to keep by my side at the wedding reception. The only time you engaged me in conversation, at length, was when Brett went missing with one of your married friends. You should remember her, Damien,' she said with biting sarcasm. 'I asked you her name. It was Rhoda Jennings.'

'She was...the wife of a friend,' he replied stiffly. 'A gushing flirt...particularly after a few drinks. She meant nothing to Brett.'

'You covered up for him. You deliberately moved in and covered up for him while he...*bonked* is the word, isn't it?...another woman on our wedding-day.'

His head jerked in a pained negative. 'I couldn't believe he'd do it. I still don't know if he actually did. Why would he do such a thing when he had you?'

'You stopped me from looking for him.'

'I wanted to protect you from any needless upset. Brett had finished with Rhoda months before. Slipping off with her could have been a stupid impulse he'd quickly think better of. I hoped…it worried me…but I didn't know for certain, Natalie.'

'You protected him. Or tried to. You were two of a kind…'

'I disagreed violently with some of the things Brett did.' Damien was clearly disturbed by the course the conversation was taking. 'But I don't feel I have to disown someone because I violently disagree with them.'

'When Brett undressed that night, the musky smell was unmistakable and pervasive. He explained it away, saying it was desire for me. I wanted to believe it…'

'For God's sake! Why not believe him? Why on earth would he want anyone else?'

'No doubt it gave him a kick, a perverse pleasure, leaving you on Best Man duty while he lived dangerously. Thanks for looking after my bride, Damien. I'll be having her for seconds. Is that what he said to you when he came back?' Natalie couldn't keep the scorn from her voice. 'I married a creep who didn't have one faithful bone in his body.'

'You married a man with a serious problem. The way he was brought up by his father after his mother deserted them…it was an ingrained attitude, Natalie.

He never learnt how to relate to women except in the most basic biological fashion. I thought once he had a wife...'

'You saw him go with that woman. You helped him all the way.'

A flush of anger speared across Damien's cheekbones. 'I knew *you* meant more to him than any other woman who'd crossed his life. I gave him the benefit of the doubt. I didn't ask what he'd been doing, and he didn't tell me. He was very attentive to you when he returned. I thought everything was all right.'

He sounded sincere. Passionately sincere. Natalie hesitated, wondering if she was doing him an injustice. Perhaps he hadn't realised Brett had been using her in a game of one-upmanship with his best and oldest friend. Yet how couldn't he know? The cruel game must have been going on for years...women, places, sporting activities, business...nothing was excluded.

Natalie wondered if Brett had deliberately kept her away from any contact with Damien while he courted her, always flying up to Noosa, never asking her to visit him in Sydney. Was getting himself a wife some kind of coup over Damien, who had lost his through divorce? Or had Brett been ensuring there was no competition over the woman he had chosen to marry?

The first time she and Damien had laid eyes on

each other was in the church, moments before the marriage ceremony had begun. She remembered thinking what a contrast they were, Brett with his golden good looks and sky-blue eyes, his best friend darkly handsome, thick black lashes shadowing deeply set eyes. They had looked so striking, standing together. Then Brett had smiled at her, a bright dazzling smile, and Natalie had forgotten the man at his side.

She didn't know then she would be endlessly reminded of Damien throughout her honeymoon, that he was ever-present in Brett's psyche, dominating what should have been an exclusive sharing with her.

'I wasn't enough for Brett,' Natalie stated bluntly. 'Apart from whatever he did with Rhoda Jennings, we were no sooner here than he started eyeing the wife of another guest, playing up to her, openly flirting. He had to be the king-pin, organising outings, making each night a party. And your name was a constant accompaniment to everything that pleased him. Damien will be green with envy when I tell him about this. Damien, Damien, Damien…'

Her eyes flashed intense bitterness. 'You were more important to him than I was. Everything was more important to him than I was. It was as though he had won a cast-iron possession so he didn't have to work at giving me his undivided attention any more.'

'I'm not clairvoyant, Natalie. When I saw you walking up the aisle to Brett, I thought him a very lucky man. I thought he'd appreciate his luck.'

'So you helped his luck along,' she mocked. 'Was it a score to you when you told him you'd saved his marriage from being over before it started?'

'I've explained why I did what I did,' he snapped.

'But you called my honeymoon with Brett *wretched*, Damien. How would you know it was *wretched* if you truly believed everything was all right between me and Brett? Brett would never have told you it was *wretched*, and I would never have admitted it. Especially not to you.'

'No, your loyalty to Brett was absolute,' Damien retorted savagely. 'You never admitted anything. You shut me out as though I were a leper.'

'So how did you know?' she challenged.

'Your honeymoon…your honeymoon with Brett…was wretched *for me*, Natalie.'

The pain in his eyes stabbed her into silence. She had been so focused on what had happened between her and Brett that she hadn't considered Damien's feelings about their marriage.

'Because Brett had beaten you?' she asked.

His mouth twisted in disagreement. 'There was no contest in my mind. You had chosen him. You were my best friend's *wife*. I had to accept that. But I couldn't help wishing I'd found you first. I couldn't stop myself from thinking of you…with him...wondering if it was good...and wishing it were me.'

The passion in his voice shattered the defences she had raised, yet still she felt the need to clear the tangle of doubts in her mind.

'Did you think you might get what you wanted without my remembering? Was that it, Damien? You decided to risk staying at Merlinmist to fulfil what you couldn't have before?'

'It was *your* choice, Natalie. I acquiesced. I didn't like what was happening.'

He turned aside, scooped up his shirt, and pulled it on. He picked up his shoes and socks, sat down in the closest armchair and proceeded to finish dressing himself, doggedly ignoring her presence although the tension between them was palpable.

'I asked you what Merlinmist meant to you. You should have told me,' she fired at him, angered by his dismissal, and the truth contained in it.

'I didn't want to remind you.' He stood up, his eyes glittering resentment. 'Why the hell should I remind you of what Brett did to you? What *he* did. Not me. I never did one damned thing to hurt you. Ever!'

'You went along with my choice of staying here, knowing it might hurt me,' she returned hotly.

'What did I *know*, Natalie? *You* directed us here. *You* insisted every instinct told you it was right. I believed in your instinct. This was where you wanted to be with me. To start afresh.' He made a derisive sound. 'What choice did that leave me?'

She had to acknowledge he hadn't liked it, but did that excuse his acquiescence?

'For all I knew,' he continued bitterly, 'you had a need to wipe out unhappy memories, overlaying them with good ones. I was the one who had to stop myself from being haunted by the ghost of Brett. And now you throw him in my face. Well, if this is some twisted revenge for your twisted perception of me, I can do without it.'

She was abruptly presented with his back as he strode towards the door. 'Where are you going?' she cried, suddenly torn by the fear of him leaving her.

'To get some fresh air.' He wrenched the door open, then halted his exit, his gaze sweeping back to her, piercing in its intensity. 'Why you would want to pollute what we just shared together is beyond my understanding.'

Before she could muster any reply, he stepped out of the room and closed the door firmly behind him. As a parting shot it was deadly, sinking home the fact she was destroying the present with a past that could only poison any chance of happiness.

She lifted shaky hands out of the robe's pockets and rubbed at her forehead. What Damien said was true. He had been answering her needs in coming here, doing what she asked. She had urged him all the way. But why had she connected Damien so strongly to Merlinmist? More than that. To a *honeymoon* at Merlinmist.

All those years ago, had she ended up wishing it were Damien with her, and not Brett? Had she been playing out a secret fantasy in bringing Damien here? Or had she felt he owed her the kind of honeymoon she should have had?

She shook her head. What had happened wasn't his fault. Damien was right about that. None of it was his fault. He wasn't responsible for what another man did. Yet somehow she couldn't quite banish the feeling that Damien was some dark Macchiavellian figure behind all of Brett's actions. The dominator. But that might only be the sheer strength of his character and personality. Could he be blamed for simply being the man he was?

Natalie tottered over to an armchair, shocked at such devastating revelations about herself. She sank into the soft cushions, grateful for their support as she tried to sort through the turbulence in her mind.

Damien had predicted this violent reaction to him, the surge of hatred that would be blind to all he'd done for her, all he felt for her. It shamed her that he'd been right. He didn't deserve it. Damien hadn't forced her into anything. He had simply been there for her. Maybe he had always been there for her…throughout her marriage to Brett. Although she hadn't recognised it. Lovers, he had said, but not in the physical sense. How much frustration was there in that?

Her body clenched at the memory of their intimacy, desire so strong it blotted out everything but their driving need for each other, the fulfilment of a wanting that couldn't wait any longer. And it had been good. More than good. Wonderful. Incredibly perfect. Why couldn't she hold on to that and put the past in the past? She had to learn how to let go. Why was she afraid to accept what she had shared with Damien at face value?

Damien claimed he had never done anything to hurt her. She had no real evidence to the contrary. But it sat uneasily on her that he had been Brett's best friend…his business partner…inextricably linked to her rotten marriage. Her hatred of him…was it the other side of love? Had it been her defence against the feelings Damien stirred within her?

If only she could remember more. The years following on from her honeymoon were a grey blur. She couldn't pluck anything out of them except Ryan, the precious child she'd loved and lost.

Ryan… Her gaze drifted to the window…the unforgiving cliffs on the other side of the valley. She felt the blood drain from her face as understanding drove through her mind. Ryan had fallen over a cliff, fallen to his death…and Brett had died, too, trying to save Ryan…but too late…too late…

Damien was mixed up in those events somehow. Damien, covering up for Brett, always covering up. She couldn't trust Damien. She didn't know what went on inside his head, what his real feelings were. He only told her what he deemed it necessary for her to know within the ambit of their relationship. While he might have spoken the truth, was it all the truth?

She didn't know. She simply didn't know. And she was afraid of what she didn't know. One thing she was certain of. She couldn't stay here with Damien now. Merlinmist was too tainted with memories that neither of them would be able to dispel.

She considered what course of action she should take. She needed time to fill in the gaps in her memory. If her perception of Damien was twisted, as he claimed, she wanted to get to the heart of the matter, and she couldn't do that until she knew more.

She didn't feel up to travelling far, didn't want to go back to the sterile house she had shared with Brett. She remembered the name of one of the resorts they had passed on the way here. Fairmont. A few days there might provide some answers. She could hire a car or take a train when she was ready to return to Sydney. Since Brett had been Damien's business partner, she must have some money, although a memory stirred that there had been financial difficulties.

Having made her decision, Natalie pushed herself

into moving. She telephoned the Fairmont Resort. There were rooms available. She booked one for a week. Satisfied she had a place to go to, she showered and dressed. With one last regretful glance around the room that had seemed so warm and welcoming, she picked up her bag and went downstairs. Perhaps one day she and Damien might return and know lasting happiness in the half-tester bed with the yellow drapes. She thought not. The ghosts of yesteryear were not so easily exorcised.

She left her bag at the reception desk in the foyer and went outside in search of Damien. She had to speak to him first before calling for a taxi. She checked the parking area. His Jaguar was still there. She walked around the grounds, barely noticing the artistry of the landscaping, not pausing to read the plaques on the magnificent specimen trees. Damien was nowhere to be seen.

She took the zigzag path that led down to the valley far below. She hoped Damien hadn't gone far. She didn't have the strength for a strenuous walk. She paused at the first bend, watching the mist swirling up from the valley, obscuring the view. What she needed was Merlin's magic to dispel the mist in her mind. If only it could be that easy.

She plodded on with a heavy heart, not anticipating any joy in meeting with Damien, but she couldn't run away from him. He deserved an explanation from her. An apology, as well. She had to be fair. In her ignorance, she might be doing him an unjustifiable injury in not accepting what he held out to her.

He was sitting on the garden bench at the third bend. He was not looking at the view. He was hunched over, elbows resting on his thighs, hands linked between his knees. He didn't hear her approach, too absorbed in his thoughts to be aware of anything outside them. He looked weary beyond measure.

Natalie's heart squeezed with painful uncertainty. Had she tried him too far? Was she a fool to hesitate over joining her life to his? Would she lose what she wanted through doubts that had no substance?

'Damien…'

His head jerked up and snapped around. It was plain he was startled to see her. Not expecting it. Not expecting anything from her. He rose to his feet in a slower movement, gathering his emotional resources to deal with whatever came. She could sense him arming himself and wished it didn't have to be that way. If only they could go back…retrieve the heady freedom of having no emotional baggage from what had previously happened. But it hadn't been that way for him, and now it couldn't be that way for her.

'I'm sorry I acted so…so unkindly,' she offered, feeling hopelessly inadequate to express herself.

'It was always going to happen, Natalie,' he stated

flatly. 'I knew it…yet I can't accept it.' His eyes searched hers for some latitude. 'Are you staying or fleeing?'

No attempt at persuasion. Her choice would tell him all he wanted to know.

'Damien, I'm very attracted to you…'

He made a sound of deep exasperation. 'Is this the overture before I get the "Can we be good friends?" speech?'

She flushed. 'I can't afford another mistake like the one I made with Brett.'

'Can't you trust your instincts, Natalie?' he burst out, his eyes blazing with the need she had fed so recklessly.

'My instincts led me into marrying Brett,' she cried, more in protest at what Damien stirred than with any logic in her argument. 'I need some distance to get everything in proportion.'

'You had everything in proper proportion when you couldn't remember anything.' His hands lifted in a gesture of urgent appeal. 'Stop listening to your mind. Go with what you feel. Come to me.'

'I can't. Not yet. Please…' She stepped back, fighting the strong tug on her heart. 'I'm asking you to wait, Damien.'

'Wait!' His face twisted with feeling. He fought to control it but it throbbed through his voice. 'How long, Natalie? How long am I to wait this time?

Until you have another car accident? Another life-time?'

'Until I believe what you tell me.'

It silenced him. He arched his head back as though she had hit him with an uppercut to the jaw. Then slowly he turned to look out over the mist. 'Will-o'-the-wisp,' he muttered. 'You'll bracket me with Brett until the day you die.'

That could be true. Natalie had no answer to it. She'd had a rotten husband, and for all she knew, Damien had been aiding and abetting Brett in his infidelities, perhaps encouraging him to do what he'd done, wanting her to find out, wanting her to turn to him, wanting to win out in the end. Or was that a twisted reaction from the miserable life she had led?

Who else knew Damien intimately? Who could tell her what he was really like to live with?

The answer came immediately.

His wife. His ex-wife. Lyn. It should be easy enough to find a Lyn Chandler who worked on a woman's magazine.

'Give me a month. I need that to get my bearings, Damien. I promise I'll give you a definite answer then.'

He turned to her with a gaze that seared her soul. 'What if you've conceived our child today, Natalie? Will I be told?'

Her stomach contracted. 'It won't happen. I'm sure it won't.'

'But if it does?' he insisted.

'You'll be told,' she heard herself say. The consequence of throwing caution to the wind was that she could end up with a child whose father she did not wish to marry or live with. 'You'll definitely be told,' she repeated, but her lips trembled.

She turned and headed up the path, trepidation for the future in every step. It was vitally important that she remember everything, vitally important to question Damien's ex-wife. She had to know what kind of husband Damien had been, and why the only thing he and his wife had shared in the end was a divorce.

CHAPTER TEN

NATALIE spent five days at Fairmont. It was a fine, impersonal place for her to rest, eat well, exercise in the heated indoor pool, and take long leisurely walks. The room service was excellent, the amenities first class. She didn't seek company and no one pressed company upon her.

She tried very hard to marshall all the facts she knew and make some consistent order of them. Bits and pieces of her four years of marriage to Brett came back to her, and she tried to take a more objective view of her husband, and why he was the way he was.

He had taken her home to that house in Narrabeen. It had already been furnished by a 'first-class' interior decorator, and Brett was intensely proud of it. No way would he countenance any change.

He had been generous with money, encouraging her to buy 'first-class' clothes and whatever added dignity and status to their lives. She was the woman in his home, his wife, the artist, the mother of his child…all images that reflected well on him.

It was important to Brett to be perceived as a man who had the best of everything.

Damien was right about Brett's not relating to her, or any woman, as a person. She had never connected that aspect of Brett's character to his background as Damien had. She had viewed their upbringings as something they had in common, both of them only children, cared for by a single parent.

Yet hadn't not having known a father influenced her to stay with Brett despite her personal unhappiness? She hadn't wanted Ryan to be without a father, and Brett had been very good with Ryan. Perhaps as his father was to him.

If attitudes and values came from family background, then what of Damien's? Surely, with his happily married parents and an ample number of brothers and sisters, he should be a well-rounded person, confident of holding his own anywhere and in any company. That was the way he came across. Perhaps Brett had seen Damien as the man who had everything, someone to pit himself against to be at the top.

Precisely how did Brett and Damien relate? They had certainly meshed in their computer world. Perhaps it was difficult to find people who could connect compatibly within that specialised type of field.

They both enjoyed the same athletic activities.

They were both popular at parties, though different in the way they performed at them.

Damien tended to have conversations. Brett specialised in witty repartee. Damien engaged people's interest. Brett made them laugh.

Of course, that was why Damien was so good at making deals. He listened. Brett skated over the surface in talking, but he skated it so brightly, no one seemed to notice any shortcoming in depth. It was Damien with the depth.

He and Brett complemented each other in many ways. Alike, yet not alike. That was probably the basis for a strong and lasting friendship, but they were *not* two of a kind. Natalie came to the strong conviction she had been wrong in holding that point of view.

It could very well be that it was only Brett who had been obsessed in competing with Damien, while Damien felt no sense of contest at all, only companionship.

And loyalty.

Not by word or deed had Damien ever indicated he coveted his friend's wife while Brett was alive. Perhaps that was why she had never been invited to his home. On the other hand, not by word or deed had he ever indicated she had good reason to divorce Brett. Not to Natalie's recollection.

She could not make up her mind if this implied his attitude to women was the same as Brett's or not. Perhaps he'd considered Brett's wife untouchable, but he had certainly touched other women, and all of them, to her knowledge, only short-term affairs. Like Brett.

Was it true that none of them had measured up to her in Damien's mind, or was that an excuse for his brief dalliances?

Natalie caught a train back to Sydney on Monday morning, and spent the entire two-hour trip wondering how to approach Lyn Chandler. Over the weekend she had looked through the staff lists of several women's magazines, checking the names of the features editors until she found Lyn Chandler's place of work. It struck her as odd that the woman had not reverted to her maiden name after the divorce from Damien. The more she thought about it, the odder that circumstance appeared.

Somehow she had to persuade Damien's ex-wife to meet her and talk about the marriage that had only lasted three years. It would be a revealing key to Damien's character. Or to Lyn Chandler's. Natalie was sure of it.

She wondered if her graphic design work might interest a features editor. A professional approach might be best. After so many years' separation from Damien, his ex-wife might be totally uninterested in any personal angle that involved him. Although anything could come out in a face-to-face chat. After all, Natalie had been the wife of Damien's business partner. Lyn Chandler had to have known Brett before he married Natalie.

Since Natalie could now relate the house in Narrabeen to her life with Brett, she could walk into it without it worrying her. After unpacking, she hunted through the desk in her office and found a portfolio of her work. She hoped it was impressive enough to give substance to a business meeting.

She telephoned the magazine's office just before twelve o'clock, hoping to catch Lyn Chandler at a free moment. She was in luck. She was put through to the features editor with no trouble at all.

'Natalie Hayes!' a bright voice exclaimed. 'You wouldn't happen to be Brett Hayes' widow by any chance?'

'Yes, I am,' Natalie affirmed, surprised at the other woman's instant connection of her name to Brett.

'Damien and I were talking about you only the other night. You're illustrating children's books now.'

'Yes.' Natalie barely got the word out. Damien had given the impression he was out of current contact with his ex-wife.

'Well, good for you!' Lyn Chandler said warmly. 'Losing both Brett and your son was a terrible tragedy. Must have been devastating. Brett was so full of life. A wonderful man.'

'Yes,' Natalie agreed faintly.

'I dare say you don't want to talk about that but I wanted to express my sympathy. Now, what can I do for you, Natalie? I may call you Natalie?'

'Of course.' Natalie was stunned by the open friendliness being offered. 'I wondered if I might interest you in the kind of work I do. Perhaps run a feature on it as a career choice. If we could set up a meeting...'

'Great! How about four o'clock this afternoon? I'm free then. Does that suit?'

'Yes. Thank you.' Natalie was begining to feel like a gasping fish, stunned by the ease with which everything was being arranged.

'If you're not busy afterwards, perhaps we could follow up with a few drinks and a bite to eat somewhere. I might be able to give you some good contacts for placing your work.'

The offer was so incredibly obliging to Natalie's needs, it raised the question if Lyn Chandler wanted something from her. Nevertheless, it was an opportunity too good to miss. 'That's very kind of you.'

'Not at all. I was very fond of Brett. Great as a party guy. I'm well acquainted with how lonely it can be on your own.'

'Thanks, Lyn. Whatever you suggest is fine by me.'

'OK. I'll look forward to meeting you at four. Just ask at the front desk and they'll direct you to my office.'

'Thanks again.'

Natalie sat in a daze, wondering what was going on. Lyn's friendly attitude couldn't be Damien's doing. He would have no reason to suppose she would get in touch with his ex-wife, no reason to ask any favours for her sake. Lyn had to have reasons of her own for setting up a social get-together.

Which brought Natalie to the loaded question...had Damien deceived her about his current relationship with his ex-wife? What had been going on there, between the brief affairs he'd had with other women?

She frowned, wanting to believe what he had told her. Perhaps their recent meeting was one of the rare occasions he had mentioned. Natalie told herself she would find out soon enough, so there was no point in worrying about it.

Female pride prompted her to dress and groom herself to her best advantage. She was going to meet a woman whom Damien had presumably loved. Not that she was competing, she told herself severely, but she would feel much more confident if she looked good. Professional. The white linen suit was simple and elegant and shaped very nicely to her figure. Natalie was satisfied it was an appropriate choice for the occasion.

At four o'clock she was ushered into a work-efficient office that was crowded with filing cabinets and a large desk loaded with stacks of folders. Lyn

Chandler looked very much at home in a hive of industry. She radiated vitality as she rose to greet Natalie.

She was a chic blonde, her hair cut in a short, fashionable bob that suited her pretty face. Deep dimples in her cheeks somehow made her smile infectious. Her eyes were striking: large and long-lashed, with light green irises ringed with brown. She was tall and slender and looked very stylish in a form-fitting beige skirt and tan silk blouse. Her perfume was more spicy than floral, a sharp rather than a soft scent, perhaps an assertive statement that she was a woman who chose not to conform to others' expectations.

Natalie had no problem imagining any man being attracted to Lyn Chandler. She would light up anyone's life with her smile. She also exuded warmth and caring interest, so much so that Natalie couldn't help thinking it had to be Damien's fault that the marriage had broken up.

Lyn enthused over Natalie's portfolio and asked a lot of questions, drawing her out about previous artwork, training, ambitions, and the children's book she was illustrating. She made notes and expressed the opinion that an article could be worked around unusual art-forms and the women who were creating them. Natalie could expect a follow-up call for an interview when arrangements were made.

Business satisfactorally completed, Lyn invited

Natalie to share a taxi to the Intercontinental Hotel, where they both relaxed in the Cortile, a casual lounge area where both snacks and drinks were served and background music was supplied by a pianist stroking the keys of a grand piano.

Lyn ordered two gin and tonics, two double brandies, and triple vodkas. Natalie swallowed her astonishment and made no protest, although she privately considered so much alcohol excessive. It might, however, loosen Lyn's tongue, which was all to the good.

A dish of mixed nuts on their table provided nibbles. Natalie scooped up a few cashews, biding her time until the drinks arrived, making appreciative comments on the décor around them. The waiter returned with their order. Lyn disposed of her gin and tonic as though it was lemonade. Natalie decided this was as good a time as any to open the conversation she wanted.

'I didn't know you saw much of Damien any more,' she prompted.

Lyn laughed lightly. 'Oh, I saw him as recently as Saturday. Damien always has time for me. I needed a shoulder to cry on. My *ex*-live-in and I had a fallout.'

'I'm sorry to hear that,' Natalie said sympathetically, hiding her unease at the familiarity that apparently remained between ex-husband and ex-wife.

'He is now definitely *ex*,' Lyn said with satisfaction. She smiled. 'It makes a difference to Damien.'

Natalie tensed, unable to control the alarm that shot through her heart. Had Lyn been using her live-in lover as some kind of lever to wring some concession from Damien? She sipped her gin and tonic, refraining from comment, waiting for Lyn to elaborate.

'I could never rely on Julian for anything,' she said, shrugging a contemptuous dismissal of the man she had lived with, 'and I'm tired of always having to manage everything for myself. I now realise I need someone solid and dependable and stable. Like Damien.'

'You mean...financially?'

'That, too. But other aspects have priority now.' Lyn picked up her glass of brandy and sipped it. She looked speculatively at Natalie as though sizing her up. 'I don't mind getting back with Damien,' she stated with cool deliberation. 'There's still that spark of attraction between us. And now that he's selling his business, he'll have the time necessary for me.'

Natalie barely veiled her shock. 'I thought you must have been disillusioned with your marriage to Damien. Wasn't it you who commenced the divorce proceedings?'

'I thought marriage to Damien was going to be

fantastic. It was for a while. Mr Perfect, you know? I was madly in love with him.'

'So what went wrong?'

She laughed easily. 'He had the bad habit of working long hours, and taking business trips at the drop of a hat. I felt neglected. I hated coming home to an empty house. It was miserable and lonely. He defended it by saying he was making money for *us*. But if he rang, and I was out with Brett or some other friends, he'd get testy about it. He wanted the little woman at home waiting for him, and that simply wasn't my idea of bliss.'

'It sounds as though he might have been more considerate,' Natalie volunteered, wondering if Damien had enjoyed the company of *friends* while he was away.

'Considerate!' Lyn rolled her eyes. 'Most people are content to pay off a house over twenty or thirty years. Not Damien. He had his mind set on getting the house paid off as quickly as possible so we could start a family without any debts over our heads. We couldn't *waste* money on having a good time.'

A man who took his responsibilities seriously, Natalie thought, but that could be oppressive if taken too far. 'You never went out together?'

'Only when he could fit it into his schedule,' Lyn tossed off dismissively. 'It was nowhere near often enough for me. Life was boringly dull. Brett spent money as if there was a hole in the bucket. I hated being made accountable for what I spent out of our joint account.'

Natalie looked her surprise. 'I wouldn't have thought Damien was mean.'

Lyn heaved a sigh. 'I couldn't get him to understand that what I made myself simply wasn't sufficient for my needs. We married too early in life. Damien was pouring money into the business, trying to expand it. *Our future*, he called it. Brett was taking money out of the business on some loan arrangement so he could have a good time.'

'It sounds as if you should have married Brett,' Natalie said unhappily.

'You're right about that.'

And she should have married Damien, Natalie thought. *Both women had married the wrong man.* The thought hit Natalie forcefully. Perhaps it was something she had always recognised and sternly repressed in the hope that everything would eventually come right.

'Don't look so glum,' Lyn said with her infectious smile. 'Everything is going to turn out fine.'

'How do you know that?' Natalie couldn't help registering her surprise.

'Damien and I discussed you at some length, and the role you've played in his life.'

Natalie's instincts rose to the fore. There was something very wrong about this conversation, something she couldn't quite put her finger on yet...

'What conclusion did you come to?'

'You missed the boat, Natalie. Happily for me, I fell right into it.' She winked. 'It's called the rebound effect. Damien and I will very shortly be announcing our remarriage.'

Shock hammered through Natalie. It couldn't be true. Unless Damien had decided there would be no happiness with her, no matter how long he waited. She frantically searched her mind for something effective to say. Lyn sipped her brandy with a calm, self-satisfied serenity that left Natalie floundering.

'But...but...you said yourself you should have married Brett.'

Lyn put her glass on the table. The happy infectious smile spread wider. There was no bile in what she said. 'That was then. This is now. Damien can now afford me, and I'm now prepared to make him a father. The deal is done.'

She stood up and tucked her handbag under her arm. 'I wanted you to know,' she said with an air of confidentiality that was somehow insufferably smug. 'And by the way, I will do my best to give your career a boost. I hope it leads somewhere good for you.'

She sauntered off, not looking back, leaving Natalie to pay the bill.

CHAPTER ELEVEN

NATALIE seethed all the way home. Lyn Chandler had neatly sucked her in, drew her out, dismissed the past, and moved in for the kill. She had obviously done the same thing to Damien, though with a different end in view.

Superficially Lyn was glittery gold, just like Brett, but underneath the bright patina was an unremitting core of self-centredness. If Damien thought his ex-wife had undergone a change of heart in regard to her priorities, he was sorely deluded. However, Lyn was undoubtedly clever enough to dress herself in tones that appealed to a man who had just been rejected, and holding out the carrot of having his child was a master stroke.

Lyn wouldn't be a good mother. Natalie was certain of it. Damien would end up being a parent, all right. Full-time. Either that, or hire a nanny. Natalie couldn't imagine Lyn taking kindly to changing nappies or losing sleep over a baby. As for the pampering she would demand throughout a pregnancy, the sky wouldn't even be the limit.

How could Damien be such a fool as to take that

woman back into his life? Hadn't he learnt from his experience with her the first time around? Natalie was strongly tempted to go to his apartment and confront him with what he was inviting upon himself.

On the other hand, Damien was a highly intelligent man. Maybe he knew precisely what he was doing. Maybe he had already counted the cost of a second marriage to Lyn and accepted it as the price to be paid for the family he wanted. After all, Lyn had been his first choice as the mother of his children. His first love. Natalie couldn't be sure the *spark* wasn't still there. She had never seen Lyn and Damien together.

Of course, there was the possibility that Lyn was lying through her teeth about what had gone on with Damien last Saturday. When Lyn had poured out her woes over the break-up with Julian, Damien might have reciprocated with an account of the disastrous *fresh start* with Natalie. Perhaps, Lyn had seized the opportunity today to drive a decisive wedge into the situation between them, leaving the way open for her to inveigle Damien into a second marriage that would provide her with what she wanted.

In which case, she had to be stopped, and what better time than right now? Natalie no longer had any doubts about Damien's integrity. She was ready to make the commitment he wanted from her. She wanted to make it. She hoped she hadn't lost him through not trusting her instincts.

The taxi she had caught from the city pulled up at her house. Natalie didn't get out. She checked her watch. It was well past six o'clock. Damien would probably be home from work by now. If not, she could wait for him. She leaned forward and redirected the driver to Damien's apartment in Collaroy.

Natalie immediately started planning what she would say to Damien. The more she thought about it, the less she liked the various scenarios that ran through her mind. They all revolved around her visit to Lyn, and how could she explain that away without it being offensive to Damien?

'I went to find out what kind of husband you'd been.'

The scorn in his eyes would be spine-chilling. 'I see. Would you like to see my character references, as well?'

Worse was, 'I needed to know if you'd been unfaithful when you were married.'

Utter disgust. 'Still bracketing me with Brett.'

There was no way that Natalie could see where she could come out of it well. Her heart cramped as she imagined Damien saying, 'At least I know what to expect with Lyn. She won't be checking me out with all and sundry behind my back. Nor will she be flinging false and unfair accusations in my face.'

Natalie sagged back in the car-seat and closed her

eyes. She had made a bed of nails for herself in not trusting Damien. How on earth was she going to climb out of it without lasting injury?

She remembered the words she had flung at him at Merlinmist…'How can you ever be forgiven?' When she considered his patience, his caring, his unstinting giving to her, how could *she* ever be forgiven for accusing him of motives that related entirely to Brett?

'This is it, lady.'

Natalie's eyes flew open. She stared out at the block of apartments that contained the home Damien had made for himself. What was she going to do? What could she say?

'Want to change your mind again?' the driver asked cheerfully.

The memory of their parting at Merlinmist came rushing back to her… Damien's concern that he be told if she had conceived…a man who took his responsibilities seriously. She had put such an outcome to the back of her mind, not wanting to think about it or deal with it. But it was a way back to him, a far more effective way than trying to excuse her doubts and fears. If she *was* pregnant, delivering the news to Damien would give her the opportunity to demonstrate she now believed all he had told her.

Hopefully, it would also spike Lyn's guns!

'Driver, I need to go to a chemist shop. Do you know where there might be one open?'

'No problem,' he said, sounding amused.

Natalie flushed. He probably thought she was considering a 'hot date', and wanted to come prepared for all eventualities.

He drove straight to a shopping centre along one of the streets in Collaroy and parked outside a chemist's, engine and meter still running. Natalie rather unnecessarily asked him to wait. The driver was happily aware he was on easy money with this fare.

She purchased a pregnancy test-kit, enquiring of the pharmacist how long after conception would the test give a definitive result. He informed her that the tests were so sensitive now, it was possible to get a result within a couple of days. It would be accurate provided she followed the instructions accompanying the kit. Satisfied with this information, Natalie returned to the taxi.

'Back to the Narrabeen address, please, driver.'

'Whatever you like, lady,' he agreed, grinning from ear to ear.

Natalie felt considerably lighter-hearted herself. Of course, she might not be pregnant, but the test was, at least, a decisive place to start for formulating a plan to recover the ground she had lost with Damien.

Then a terrible thought struck her. If she had conceived last week...and if Damien had slept with Lyn on the rebound...and Lyn had deliberately missed taking whatever contraceptive pill she would probably have been using with Julian…both of them could be pregnant to Damien. The thought of Damien becoming a father twice over at almost the same time made Natalie's hair rise.

It lent an extra urgency to using the test.

She could hardly make Damien's choice for him, but Natalie was not about to stand back and let Lyn make all the running where Damien was concerned. Certainly she could not afford to let a month go by before contacting him, pregnant or not. Somehow, she had to counteract the damage she had done in turning on him as she had at Merlinmist.

Once back at Narrabeen, Natalie paid off the taxi-driver, adding a tip that inspired him to wish her the best of luck. She would need every bit of it, she thought, wondering if Lyn was with Damien right at this moment, giving him *her* version of today's meeting, undermining Natalie's credibility with malice aforethought.

The instructions on the test-kit advised that early morning was the best time to carry out the test, when urine had been stored in the bladder for four hours.

Natalie spent a restless night. Damien's protests kept preying on her mind… 'Do I have to wait for another car accident? Another lifetime?'

She still had no recollection of the day of the accident. She suspected that Damien had revealed his desire for her and she had reacted badly, colouring his motives with Brett's attitudes. Had that come as a shock to him, finding himself put in another man's shoes?

Would she ever have accepted Damien's pursuit of her had she not lost her memory? Probably not. The emotional garbage from her marriage was mountainous. Only by having it cleared away for a while had she been able to see Damien in a different light. It was now paramount she convince him that the return of her memory would not form a running sore between them, a sore which would never heal.

Otherwise, Lyn *could* win.

It was with mixed feelings that Natalie carried out the test the next morning. It was wrong to use a child to hold a man. She couldn't...wouldn't do it. If Damien showed any sign of being unsure about their future together, she would not push for the marriage she now wanted. On the other hand, she could and would let him know where he stood with her.

The result was positive.

Relief and joy were swiftly followed by a sense of wonderment. She was going to have another child. Would it be a girl this time? It would be lovely to have a daughter, although of course a son would be just as welcome. The impulse to share the news with Damien had Natalie rushing to the telephone.

But telling him wasn't enough. She needed to be with him, to watch his face, to see how he responded to the confirmed fact of her having his child. That would tell her more than anything else how matters stood between them.

It was early. She had time to catch him at home before he went to work. Natalie dressed at top speed, rang for a taxi, and was on her way to Damien within twenty minutes. Again she spent the trip to his home planning what to say to him, how best to put it. She couldn't burst out with the simple fact she was pregnant. She needed to tell him much more. Or did she? Announcing their child-to-be might be the best ice-breaker.

Natalie was still in two minds about what approach to take as she stood outside Damien's door, waiting for him to answer the button she had pressed. She doubted she had ever felt quite so nervous in her life. Not even on the day she had married Brett.

The door opened.

Damien looked at her in blank surprise.

She stared back, choked by the memory of the intimacy she had rejected. He wasn't dressed. The short wrap-around robe he wore left a deep V of chest bare, as well as his forearms and lower legs. Whether he was completely naked underneath the robe or not was irrelevant. Natalie remembered him naked, and she was swept by a desire so strong that any words she might have spoken were completely jumbled in her mind. Her heart pumped a flood of heat through her body.

'Natalie?' The need to know what had brought her here sharpened Damien's eyes.

'I…I wanted to see you,' she said, struggling to regain some composure.

To her consternation, he didn't ask her in. An expression of tense reserve set on his face. He stepped outside the apartment, pulling the door almost shut behind him. It was such an unwelcoming stance, it froze Natalie into silence.

His body language was all wrong, stiff and off-putting and reserved. Didn't he want her any more? Was he in a hurry to go somewhere? His hair was damp from a shower. She picked up the smell of his after-shave lotion, except it wasn't quite the same. It seemed to be mixed with some other scent. But she couldn't afford to be distracted by that. The important point was he obviously didn't want to give her much of his time. Which was a total turnaround from his attitude of last week.

'Is there some reason for coming to me at this early hour?' he asked.

The impulse to share the news of her pregnancy was shrivelled by his aloofness. 'I came back home yesterday,' she temporised. 'I was thinking of you. We…we didn't part very well.'

He grimaced. 'It was…difficult…for both of us. If you think I misled you after your accident…'

'No…no…' She shook her head vehemently.

'You were fair. If anyone's to blame for anything, it's me. I hope you don't think too badly of me.'

She searched his eyes anxiously. Had she lost him?

'What you asked was reasonable, Natalie,' he said flatly. 'I apologise for my outburst at the time. A month is not long, considering all that's gone before.'

'Maybe it doesn't have to be a month,' she suggested hopefully, trying her utmost to reach into his mind and heart. Surely he realised she did want him. She wouldn't have come otherwise.

The suggestion made him uneasy. 'I can wait.'

It was like a slap in the face. Was he giving her a taste of what she had dealt him? Was he savagely thinking, Let her wait, too?

She was seriously rattled by the distance he was keeping between them. 'Well, I guess I wanted to be sure of that,' she said slowly, letting him know she had not wiped him out of her life. If he wanted to know.

He nodded, not giving her any extra reassurance. It dawned on her that his nod was a dismissal. He wanted her to go. She stepped back, desperately wanting him to say something to stop her, to keep her with him.

He didn't.

'I wanted to know how you were,' she said.

'I'm fine.'

The brusque answer gave her no opening to go on with the conversation. She nodded. Too many times. Feeling hopelessly foolish, she dropped her gaze to his bare chest. She wondered whether or not it would break the dreadful barrier he had slid between them if she reached out and touched him. She couldn't find the courage to do it.

The thought came to Natalie that he didn't trust her any more. She had acted on impulse in directing him to Merlinmist. He probably thought this early morning visit was another impulse that could all too easily go wrong.

We're going to have a baby, her heart cried, but it was impossible to tell him under these circumstances. Pregnancy could feel like a trap. She had known that feeling once. She couldn't give it to someone else. Maybe Damien had endured enough of her. He might even now be balancing what he felt for her against what Lyn offered him.

Natalie could not bring herself to throw their unborn child onto the scales. It was wrong. Terribly wrong. She was mad to have thought of it.

'I'm sorry for interrupting your dressing,' she said stiffly, chilled by the paucity of his response to her. 'I'll go now.'

'I hope you have a pleasant day,' he said with formal politeness.

'You, too,' she returned, then hurried away from him, miserably embarrassed by the whole scene.

She could feel Damien's eyes burning into her back. She wondered, if she turned quickly, would she see the blaze of desire she desperately wanted to see? No, he wanted her to go. He was watching her go.

She went. She walked straight past the elevator and took the staircase. It wasn't a month any more, she reminded herself. Only another three weeks. The hurt would stop then. On both sides. It had to. She couldn't bear to contemplate anything else.

CHAPTER TWELVE

ON HER return home from the disturbing visit to Damien, Natalie settled in front of her computer, needing to take grasp of some purpose in her life, telling herself she had work to do. It would make the time go faster if she immersed herself in her work.

Concentration eluded her. She sat blankly in front of the monitor screen, unable to summon the necessary will-power to actually strike a key. Her mind kept revolving around the consequences of the decisions she had made. Especially Damien's reaction to her this morning.

The ringing of the door-chimes was a welcome distraction, providing relief, however short, from her tormenting thoughts. She didn't wonder who was calling on her. She was simply grateful for some activity.

Damien stood on her porch.

He was dressed in a business suit, ready for work, but his eyes seared hers with questions. Natalie's breath caught in her throat, rendering her speechless.

Her eyes clung to his, pleading for a change of heart from his earlier stand-offishness.

'Do you want me, Natalie?'

'Yes.' She expelled the word on a rush of breath that emptied her lungs.

'Certain?'

She nodded.

'Is it right for you now?'

A huge well of emotion threatened to choke her again. 'Yes.' It was a bare whisper.

Whatever uncertainties had plagued Damien's mind were summarily dismissed. He stepped forward and swept her into his arms. There was no more talking, no more thinking, no more agonising. He kissed her, and there was no holding back from Natalie. She responded with all the pent-up feeling that had been gathering force since they had shared the bed at Merlinmist.

She craved the warm solidity of him, the passion of his desire for her. She needed to feel it was real, substantial, so deeply connected to her that it could never be taken by any other woman. 'Love me,' she pleaded. 'Love me as I've never been loved before, Damien.'

The front door was shut. He scooped her off her feet and carried her into the master bedroom. She didn't care that it was the bed she had previously shared with Brett. Damien superseded everything she had known with her former husband. He was earth and fire and air and water to her. He was life.

Clothes were discarded in wild haste. There was no sense of discovery this time, only a driving need to have and to hold, to lose all doubts and fears in the ecstatic security of coming together, being as one, their bodies the perfect instruments to bring harmony from the discord generated by the recovery of her memory.

Natalie had never really experienced lust before, yet from the moment she convulsed in sheer bliss around Damien she was gripped by a wild, insatiable greed to know and exult in every pleasure their bodies could find and indulge in. It was as though every fantasy she'd ever had about Damien as a lover sprang to life in her mind, demanding expression and absolute fulfilment...the power, the passion, the sensuality, the stamina, the intense virility of the man unleashed, coursing from his body to hers in tidal waves of sensation.

She wallowed in his lust for her, floated in it, drowned in it, incited it with a wantonness she had not known herself capable of. Perhaps it was inspired by the release of a host of repressions built up over years. Or the fear that she might have squandered the chance to take and know and feel all that Damien was.

Whether he sensed this rampaging compulsion within her and responded to it, or whether he was sating his own frustrated needs and desires, Natalie had no idea. Their feelings melded in a long, tempestuous lovemaking that was intensely mutual, intensely satisfying, and overwhelmingly different from anything she had known with Brett.

Only exhaustion tamed their ardour for each other, and even when their energy was totally depleted, the need to touch, in however a desultory fashion, kept them enthralled with each other. She loved the feel of his firm muscles, the tight smoothness of his skin. She caught a faint scent of his aftershave lotion. Not the one she had smelled earlier. He must have disliked that and washed it off in favour of this one. Natalie liked it better, too. It was enticingly sexy, just like Damien.

Natalie couldn't help thinking back over her marriage to Brett, how devoid it had been of this kind of togetherness. Her mind inevitably drifted to Damien's marriage. Had it been this good for him with Lyn? This...*complete*?

She shied from the idea, but it kept nagging, fraying the edges of her contentment. Damien had been with Lyn on Saturday night. There would have been no grounds for Lyn's words and actions yesterday if there had been no meeting between them. Had Damien succumbed to a rebound effect? Was that why he had been so distant this morning, feeling it wasn't right to resume a relationship with her?

Yet he had come after her.

'Was the sex in your marriage good, Damien?' she asked.

'I thought it was.' His voice was rich with contentment as he added, 'You've revolutionised my thoughts.'

She smiled, happy that he was happy. All the same, she would be happier still to have the matter of Lyn completely cleared away. She couldn't help dreading the thought of what might have happened on Saturday night.

'Did you ever sleep with your ex-wife after your marriage ended?'

'Yes.'

Natalie fought against tensing up. What was done was done. It would be different after this morning.

'I had the crazy idea I could win her back,' Damien went on in a light, self-mocking tone. 'It was soon after the divorce. Lyn indulged me. She liked the power.'

Relief poured through Natalie. She had nothing to worry about. Damien was talking about years ago. Before they'd ever met. Yet his words stirred her curiosity about the woman who'd caused her so much concern.

'You mean she used you to boost her ego?'

'Something like that,' he said carelessly. 'She relished having me run after her, but had no intention of meeting me halfway. Once I realised that, I let go.' His fingers trailed down the curve of her spine.

'It's not easy to accept failure when you've been fully committed. Is that why you never showed you knew about Brett's infidelities, Natalie?'

'Pride,' she answered. 'We had a lot of arguments about it. He'd promise me...' She sighed. 'If it hadn't been for Ryan...but it doesn't matter now.'

She thought of the baby she had conceived, their child, Damien's and hers, then decided there were other things she wanted to tell Damien first, the feelings she had denied for most of the years they had known each other.

'I used to wonder how it might be with you,' she confessed, luxuriating in the freedom from all inhibitions.

Damien pressed a kiss on her forehead. 'You remember actually thinking that?'

'Yes. Sometimes it hurt to watch you with other women. I hated feeling so...affected by you.'

'You hid it extremely well,' he said with a dry touch of irony.

She hitched herself up, wanting him to see the truth in her eyes. 'I saw you as being like Brett. I know that's not true, Damien, and never was. I think it was some kind of defence to shut off the feelings you stirred. I was ashamed of having them. I blamed you for things I had no right to blame you for, because it helped me to push away thoughts I didn't want to have.'

'There was always a current of attraction between

us, Natalie. You buried it so deep I began to despair of your ever acknowledging it. I did not think you could ever be mine.'

'I acknowledge it now. It was there all the time. That polarity. That pull.'

He smiled. His eyes glinted deep satisfaction. 'I think we just proved that.' The smile widened. 'Of course, we could try improving the proof.'

She laughed and rolled on to her back, stretching her body provocatively. 'I'm a limp rag,' she declared, her eyes teasing. 'The energy will have to come from you.'

'I've suddenly discovered vast reserves of it.'

As he was poising his body to demonstrate his rejuvenation, the telephone rang. Damien did not so much as glance at the handset on the bedside table. Natalie was very much inclined to ignore it, as well. She held her breath and focused all her concentration on feeling the marvellous sensation of Damien entering her once again. He did it very slowly, with a sensual roll that was exquisitely exciting.

The telephone stopped ringing.

Natalie sighed with ecstatic pleasure as she felt Damien's full length pushed past the edge of her womb.

The telephone nagged again with a persistent buzzing.

'It might be important,' Damien said with a wicked twinkle in his eyes. 'I think you should answer it.' Holding himself deep within her, he reached out, picked up the receiver, and handed it to her. Then he continued moving them both in a highly erotic rhythm.

'...Kippax.'

The name spoken from the receiver filtered through the delicious bombardment of tingling sensations, snapping Natalie's mind into some alertness.

'Sharon! Help. I mean, hello,' she managed somewhat breathlessly.

'I'm glad you're home.' The friendly voice was warm with relief. 'I've called a few times, but no answer. I was beginning to worry about you. What have you been up to?'

'Many things,' she gasped. Damien was building a momentum that was far too distracting for her to put two thoughts together. 'Stop it!' she hissed. 'It's my editor!'

'Tell her you're receiving inspiration.'

He was an absolute devil but she loved him. She loved what he was doing to her, too. She took a deep breath and tried to be sane.

'I had a few days away,' she explained to Sharon. 'There's no problem with my memory now. I'm about to get back to work.'

'You are at work,' Damien muttered. He was really moving quickly now. She hoped the bed wouldn't start squeaking.

'That's wonderful! I might have another commission for you if you're interested.'

'How exciting!'

'This is just the preliminaries,' Damien promised, his eyes laughing as she squirmed around him.

'Is there any chance of you coming in to my office this morning?' Sharon asked.

'I'll find out.' She put her hand over the receiver. 'Is there any chance of my meeting my editor this morning?' she whispered urgently.

'Possibly…possibly…' He was getting too worked up to concentrate properly.

'Possibly,' Natalie answered.

'I have the manuscript here,' Sharon pressed. 'Another children's book. I'd like to discuss it with you.'

Excitement was swelling through her in waves. Both of them must climax soon. 'Would an hour…from now…be all right? I'll be able…to come then.'

'I expect you to come before then,' Damien put in purposefully.

'Great! Bye for now.'

'Thanks, Sharon.'

Impossible to replace the receiver. It fell from Natalie's hand as she succumbed to the pleasures of the moment, riding a crest of sweet exultation until Damien had delivered all he had promised.

Afterwards they showered together, which was a

splendid way to extend the glorious intimacy they had shared.

Damien offered to drive her to the publisher's offices and took a great deal of pleasure in watching her dress for her meeting with Sharon. Once they were on their way, it occurred to Natalie that they hadn't made any arrangement for getting together again.

'Will I see you later today?' she asked, aware he was dressed for business, as well.

'I think I should take you out to dinner tonight. We mightn't eat otherwise.' The glint of lust in his eyes was an intoxicant in itself. 'Would you be ready by seven-thirty?'

She laughed. 'With bells on.'

There wasn't time to tell him about their child now. But tonight... Natalie wanted to hug herself, her happiness soaring beyond anything she'd ever known... Tonight was going to be the best night of her life!

CHAPTER THIRTEEN

NATALIE breezed into the building that housed her publishing company. She felt on top of the world and full of zest for the prospect of taking on a new creative project. It was only when she stepped out of the elevator on Sharon's floor that her buoyant spirits suffered a slight puncture.

This was where she had seen the woman in the yellow suit. Natalie frowned. She was sure she had recognised that woman. The image of her wearing black was very strong. It vexed Natalie that she couldn't place her. She had the feeling it was not a happy association. Which probably meant that the woman had been one of Brett's side interests.

Natalie brushed aside the cynical thought. It was hardly reasonable anyway. How would Brett get to meet a high-powered lady in the publishing world? Natalie had certainly not introduced her to him. She'd had no connection to this publishing company until well after Brett's death.

There had to be some other answer.

She announced her appointment with Sharon to the receptionist and was waved on with a nod and a smile. Sharon eagerly welcomed her, and they very quickly got down to business. The story submitted by the author was a fantasy adventure, set on a fictional planet far from Earth. The description of its inhabitants and their environment allowed Natalie a great deal of creative licence and her imagination caught fire with what could be done.

Sharon specified the number of colour plates she wanted for the book. She also wanted the cover design to extend over the front and back of the hardcover edition, and be intriguing as well as spectacular. She had the feeling this book could become a big seller.

Satisfied that Natalie's ideas for illustrations would enhance the story, Sharon had no hesitation in moving on to discussing a new contract.

'I expect you'll be wanting better terms on this book.'

Natalie grinned. 'I won't say no.'

'I'll bring up some figures on the computer.'

Natalie watched Sharon's fingers fly over the keyboard. Information flashed up on the monitor screen. It was amazing how much could be stored and so easily retrieved on a computer.

The thought struck her that computers had been Brett's business. Computers were everywhere these days. A publishing company might have very specific needs that were not answered by general purpose software.

'Did this company ever hire anyone to do a computer conversion?' she asked.

Sharon looked surprised. 'Yes, they did. Everything runs beautifully now.'

Natalie's mouth went dry. 'How long ago?'

'It was being completed when I first started here. A couple of years ago.'

'Do you remember the people who did the conversion?'

Sharon's bright hazel eyes sparkled. 'Do I? Two of the most gorgeous hunks I've ever seen. Not that *I* got an introduction. They dealt strictly at the executive level.'

'What was the company name?'

'CCS.'

Damien and Brett. And Anne Smith was executive level. There *was* a connection.

'Is something wrong?'

'No, there's nothing wrong.' Natalie tried to smile, but the floodgates on her last missing recollections were swinging open.

The woman in black.

Black.

The memory slammed into Natalie's mind with heart-stopping force.

The funeral!

Anne Smith was the woman who hadn't stopped weeping, the woman Damien had had no time for, although he should have if their story had been true.

Natalie remembered now. All of it. Ryan and Brett and Anne Smith at the top of the cliff, Damien abseiling down the face of it. Anne Smith...the only witness to what had happened...how Ryan had come to fall...how Brett had failed to stop him from going too close to the edge.

She had said Ryan had chased after a ball. But what had she and Brett been doing in those few critical moments it took for Ryan to run out of reach?

The explanation had never rung true to Natalie. She had brought Ryan up to be careful. He had not been the kind of child who would run heedlessly into mortal danger. Despite his love of playing with balls, he wouldn't follow one over a cliff. He would call out to Daddy to get it back for him.

'Natalie? Are you all right?'

The question roused her out of the dark introspection. She refocused her eyes on Sharon.

'You've gone as pale as a ghost,' Sharon observed in concern.

The ghosts were gathering with a vengeance.

'Just a bit faint,' Natalie excused. 'I was so busy rushing around this morning I didn't have time for breakfast.'

'Sorry. I should have offered you a coffee. How do you like it? Milk and sugar?'

'Yes, please. One sugar.'

'I'll get one for you now. And bring some biscuits, as well.'

'Thank you.'

Sharon quickly rose from her chair and left the office to fetch the offered sustenance. Natalie was relieved to be left to her thoughts. They were too painful and private to share with anyone, and too pressingly urgent to put aside.

Anne Smith. Sharon's boss, who had ordered Sharon to handle Natalie Hayes by herself. It was sheer accident that Natalie had seen her here. Otherwise they would never have met in this building.

It amazed Natalie that the woman had risked giving her a job at all, regardless of talent. Apart from any unpleasantness that might rise out of the situation, surely the woman wouldn't want to have any reminder of a tragedy in which she had been involved? Particularly if she was guilty of negligence. Or worse.

On the other hand, guilt could lead to remorse, to the urge to compensate. Natalie remembered Sharon saying that Anne Smith had taken one look at the work Natalie had submitted—or the name attached to that work—and ordered that she be put under contract to the company. Ryan was gone forever, but perhaps a job might help the bereaved mother—was that how her mind had reasoned?

Or did pride in her position as project manager

take first place? Perhaps her executive status demanded the attitude that talent was talent, no matter who, what or where. Certainly Sharon was impressed with Natalie's work.

Natalie felt a burning need to know the truth of what had happened. But would it serve any good purpose to pursue the past when she had so much to look forward to in the future? Did she really want to stir up again all the pain surrounding Ryan's death? She couldn't bring her beloved son back. She was going to have another child.

Her thoughts shifted to Damien. She had given him her trust. It would be wrong to start doubting him now. He had sworn that Anne Smith had been with him that weekend, not Brett, and Natalie believed him. Nevertheless, Anne Smith had known both men. She might have accompanied Damien on the trip, but was it Damien she had wanted?

Had Damien believed Anne Smith's account of events on the clifftop? Did he have any doubts himself? He had said to her that accidents like that happened so quickly. What made him so sure, particularly when he hadn't been right there to see with his own eyes?

And Anne Smith…what of her? Could she be believed?

Sharon returned with the coffee and a plate of shortbread biscuits. Natalie made the effort to eat one between sips of coffee. Sharon discussed what terms she was prepared to offer on the contract. The thought of Anne Smith simmered in the back of Natalie's mind. She came to an agreement with Sharon but had no idea what it was. She simply accepted the proposals put to her. Sharon promised to have the typed contract in the mail to Natalie by tomorrow.

'That's it, then,' Sharon said with satisfaction.

'I guess it is,' Natalie said heavily.

'Let me show you out.'

'No. I'll be all right,' Natalie assured her. She knew what she was going to do and she didn't want Sharon at her side.

Her meeting with Anne Smith would not touch on editorial responsibilities.

She smiled as she stood up to take her leave. 'Thank you for looking after me. I'll deliver the best work I can.'

'I'm sure you will.'

They parted on that mutual note of goodwill, and Natalie walked back along the corridor to the receptionist's desk.

She expected to be fobbed off. Anne Smith clearly didn't want any contact with her. Natalie was determined to force it, one way or another. She had a right to know how and why Ryan had died.

'I wish to see Miss Smith,' she said with steely resolution.

The receptionist gave an aplogetic smile. 'Miss

Smith has a very busy schedule. You would need to make an appointment to see her. Would you like me to call her secretary?'

'I want Miss Smith informed directly, right now, immediately, that Mrs Hayes is here to see her. The matter will not wait. It concerns her dead child.'

The receptionist's eyes widened in surprise and shock. 'Very well,' she assented.

Regardless of how busy Anne Smith's schedule was, the reaction was swift and decisive. A secretary came to collect Natalie. A few minutes later she was ushered into the project manager's office.

Anne Smith was standing behind her desk. She made no move to come forward to greet Natalie. The two women eyed each other as antagonists with much of personal value lying between them. Natalie took grim satisfaction from the little signs of strain showing on the other woman's beautiful face: the tightness around her mouth, the wariness in her eyes, the sharp tilt of her chin.

She was wearing a vibrant green suit today, a bright lime-green that accentuated her dark colouring. But Natalie remembered her in black far too well to be impressed or influenced by the other woman's power dressing.

'How can I help you, Mrs Hayes?' The polite question was accompanied by a gestured invitation for Natalie to take a chair.

'I want to know the truth about my son's death,'

Natalie stated bluntly, not prepared to sit while the other woman remained standing.

'I said all I had to say at the inquest. I have nothing to add. I'm sorry...'

'You lied.'

Anne Smith raised her finely arched eyebrows. 'That is a very serious allegation.'

'Who retrieved the ball that was supposed to have rolled over the cliff?'

Two hot spots appeared high on her cheeks. 'I didn't know it was retrieved.'

'Don't you consider it strange that it was in Ryan's bag when the police returned it to me?'

'I don't understand...'

'I know you're lying.'

'Perhaps we should leave the conversation there, Mrs Hayes. Knowing and proving are two different things.'

'You could face perjury charges, Miss Smith,' Natalie fired at her, hoping to crack her defences.

The beautiful dark eyes flashed defiance. 'Then I'll face them if I have to, and pay what penalties need to be paid...if I have to.'

'You could go to gaol.'

Her eyes narrowed, calculating the risk. 'And you might never realise how lucky you are,' she said with slow deliberation. 'You have Damien Chandler as a...friend. You might lose him...forever.'

'Tell me the truth, Miss Smith.'

'I can't.'

'What happened on the top of that cliff?'

'Only one person can tell you that.'

'And you're the one.'

'No.'

'Who then?'

'Damien Chandler.'

CHAPTER FOURTEEN

IT HAD proved impossible to draw anything further from Anne Smith on the subject. Natalie was deeply disturbed by her insistence that only Damien could tell her the truth about Ryan's death. It left her with the inference that Damien had hidden from her the truth of where he was at the time of the accident.

It might not be a case of covering up for Brett. Perhaps Damien had been at fault in some way. Perhaps it was Anne Smith's fault. Perhaps they were all at fault, and the agreement had been made that the memories of the dead should wait upon the realities of the living.

Natalie recoiled from that idea. She didn't want Damien to be involved in any circumstances that had led directly to her son's death. Besides, it couldn't be true. Anne Smith had expressed the opinion that Natalie was lucky to have Damien as a friend. It was a very supportive statement on his behalf. She must have had good reason to give it.

Not that Natalie needed to be told by Anne Smith how good a friend Damien had been to her. She was well aware of that herself. He was the most wonderful lover she could ever have. No way was she going to jeopardise her future with Damien. There had to be a reasonable explanation for the course of action he'd decided upon concerning that fateful weekend.

Despite telling herself this, over and over again, Natalie still couldn't let the matter go. She wanted it cleared up, once and for all. Then she could let it rest in peace and concentrate entirely on the future.

The thought of bringing the subject up at dinner was less than appealing. She no longer felt in the mood to dress up and celebrate the end of all that had kept her apart from Damien. She needed to talk to him about Ryan.

Since Damien was to be at her house at seven-thirty, Natalie decided he would probably be home from work by six o'clock. It was no longer of any concern to her if they went out to dinner at all. She felt too unsettled to wait until seven-thirty to see him.

It was six-fifteen when she pressed the bell-button at his apartment. Natalie was not kept in suspense. The door was opened within a few moments. Damien looked startled to see her, naturally enough considering the arrangement they had made. He was clearly in the midst of changing his clothes since he wore the wrap-around robe he had greeted her in this morning.

'I had to come, Damien,' Natalie rushed out apologetically.

'Is there a problem?' he asked, a frown of concern creasing his brows together.

She was momentarily distracted by a waft of the same scent she'd smelled this morning. It struck her as odd because his jaw wasn't freshly shaven. She pushed the irrelevant thought aside and concentrated on what was important.

'May I come in?'

He hesitated, his frown deepening.

A voice floated from his living-room.

'Shall I fix you a drink, darling?'

Lyn's voice!

Another recognition speared into Natalie's mind, shattering in its implications. It was Lyn's perfume she could smell on Damien. It had come from him this morning while he kept her out of his apartment. And now...after he had been with her!

Natalie's heart froze. Her skin chilled. She looked at Damien with wounded eyes. 'Couldn't you wait a month for me?' she cried, stricken to her soul that she had given herself to him so completely while he...what had he been doing? Satisfying a long-frustrated lust for her?

His face tightened. His hand lifted towards her.

Natalie backed away, turned, and ran to the elevator, slamming her hand on the down button. The doors slid open, the compartment not having moved since she'd stepped out of it.

'Natalie…'

Damien's call rang in her ears, harsh and commanding. She whirled forward and hit the button for the ground floor, desperate to escape the situation. She couldn't bear to expose her feelings under Lyn's gloating eyes. She didn't want to hear Damien's justification for his duplicity. Perhaps it was her fault he had turned to Lyn, but that couldn't excuse tonight. Not after their lovemaking this morning.

Damien beat the closing of the doors. He slammed his hand on the button to keep them held open, then confronted her, chest heaving, eyes blazing with anger.

'Be damned if I'll stand still for any more of your false assumptions about me, Natalie!' he thundered at her. 'I am *not* Brett. The woman in my apartment is my ex-wife. She calls all men *darling*. It's typical of the crowd she mixes with.'

Tears of confusion and bewilderment welled into Natalie's eyes. 'But she…you…'

'Come back and meet her for yourself.'

It finally penetrated the emotional chaos seizing Natalie's mind that Damien's anger was the anger of an innocent man who had been placed in a compromising position. When he lost patience with her dumbstruck stare, he took her hand and pulled her

with him, determined that this particular contre-
temps be resolved right here and now.

Natalie followed numbly, her stomach churning,
her head sickeningly awhirl with what might even-
tuate with Lyn. Damien closed the door to his apartment behind them and ushered Natalie into the living-room where her feet faltered to a wary halt.

Lyn was seated on one of the stools at the bar,
sipping a martini, looking very much at home. Her
only garment appeared to be an oversized T-shirt,
probably belonging to Damien. Her hair was ruffled
as though she'd just got out of bed. She gave Natalie
one of her deeply dimpled smiles. Natalie's facial
muscles were too stiff to return it. Although she
wouldn't have returned that smile even if she could.

Damien moved forward to bridge the gap between
the two women. He started an introduction. 'Natalie,
this is Lyn...'

'We met yesterday,' Lyn cut in brightly, putting
down her glass and sliding off the stool with mes-
merising confidence. She stretched with the sinuous
grace of a dangerous cat, ensuring the soft fabric of
the T-shirt outlined every naked curve beneath it.
Her nipples pouted from seemingly perfect breasts
and she rolled her hips as though loosening up tired
muscles.

Damien frowned at his ex-wife. 'You didn't tell
me about any meeting.'

Lyn shrugged and undulated towards him, her

hands lifted in appeal. 'It wasn't good news, darling. I think the only positive thing Natalie said about you was that you weren't mean with money. Now I, on the other hand…' she insinuated her arm around Damien's, cuddling up to him '…extolled all your virtues. And I do appreciate them, Damien. I really do.'

The feline purr made Natalie's hackles rise.

Damien coldly extracted himself from her kittenish hold. 'I don't know what game you think you're playing, Lyn, but I don't appreciate it one bit. Tell Natalie why you're here.'

Lyn was unperturbed. 'Natalie knows I've broken up with Julian, darling. And I told her I came to you. She's well aware of the situation. There's no need to get stuffy about it. She understands.'

Damien's gaze swung to Natalie, piercingly sharp. 'What do you understand, Natalie?'

Lyn had lied to her. Damien had lied by omission, not telling her Lyn was staying with him. But perhaps he had good reason for that. One thing was patently clear to Natalie. There was no intimacy here. Absolutely none from Damien. Lyn's performance *was* a performance. It didn't gell with Damien's reactions.

'Your ex-wife told me you and she would shortly be announcing your remarriage,' she answered flatly.

'Not a chance in hell!' His response was so peremptory and decisive, there was no doubting it.

Damien looked grim. 'Is that why you asked about her this morning, Natalie?'

'Yes.'

'But you didn't believe me.' His eyes seethed with resentment.

'I did believe you, Damien,' Natalie asserted. 'I'm sorry for doubting you just now, but when I heard her voice and smelled her perfume on you…'

'She drowned my robe in it. Spilled the damned stuff all over it. I haven't had time to get it laundered.' He turned a look of icy contempt to the woman beside him. 'You're a bitch, Lyn. An out-and-out bitch.'

'Why? Because I've got the guts to go after what I want?' She tossed her head in defiant pride. 'It was good for us once, Damien. It could be good for us again.'

'That time is well and truly gone, and you know it, Lyn.'

She flicked a sly look at Natalie. 'You let me stay here with you.'

'I felt sorry for you.' His mouth twisted self-mockingly. 'Wasted sympathy. You'll always bite the hand that feeds you.'

'You're wrong, Damien. I'll give you what you want…'

'I don't want it from you. I stopped wanting it from you a long time ago.'

'I'll give you a baby…'

'No damned way!'

She nodded towards Natalie. 'What if she won't have you? I'd give you more than one baby. I'm ready to give you the family you want, Damien.'

A muscle in his jaw contracted. 'Go and get dressed, Lyn. I want you out of my life. Now. And don't ever come back to me again. Not for anything.'

'You're a fool, Damien. If you'll…'

'Move *now*,' he commanded tersely. 'Either that or I'll gather your belongings and you can dress in the lobby outside.'

She shot Natalie a venomous look as she flounced away from Damien and headed off to the hallway leading to the rest of the apartment. She left a silence bristling with tension. Not until a door slammed shut behind her did Damien turn to Natalie. His eyes were hard and glittering with challenge.

'Lyn came here on Saturday night,' he stated flatly. 'She'd had a violent fight with her lover. There were bruises on her upper arms. She asked if she could stay until she found an apartment for herself. She slept in the study if you want to check.'

'I believe you, Damien,' Natalie said quietly.

His mouth thinned. He shook his head. 'Lyn set this up so you would come and catch me with her. And you came.'

'No. It didn't enter my mind she'd be here with

you. I came this morning because...' She didn't want to tell him she was pregnant while Lyn was still here. Her eyes pleaded for his understanding. 'I had a bad night. I realised, after the meeting with Lyn yesterday, how blind and foolish I'd been in misjudging you. And how very much I wanted to keep you in my life.'

He searched her eyes for several nerve-racking moments. 'I didn't know why you'd come. You said a month. And Lyn was here. I thought you'd think the worst...'

'As I did just now.' She made an apologetic gesture.

He shook his head. 'It was stupid of me to open my mouth to Lyn about you. It was a way of letting her know she couldn't use me for consolation. I had no idea...'

'I know,' Natalie broke in gently. 'There's no need to explain. If I'd stayed with you, none of this would have happened.'

'Why did you come here tonight, Natalie? After what we shared this morning, did you still feel driven to check up on me?'

His eyes burned with a need so intense it shamed Natalie for all she had put him through.

'Please forgive me for doubting you, Damien.' Her feet moved of their own accord, impelled to go to him. 'I swear I didn't come to check on you. It never occurred to me that Lyn would be here. She wasn't on my mind at all.' She lifted her hands to his chest, her eyes begging his belief. 'And I don't link you with Brett. Not any more.'

Damien caught her hands and held them still, his eyes deeply pained as he said, 'There has to be trust, Natalie.'

'On both sides,' she reminded him. 'If you'd told me Lyn was staying with you…'

'Yes, I realise that. I…' He heaved a deep sigh. 'When does it end…this feeling that I have to keep fighting what Brett did to you?'

A door slammed again, fracturing the false sense of being alone together. Lyn reappeared, shooting them a look of haughty scorn. 'How touching!'

'Goodbye, Lyn,' Damien said curtly.

She paused on her way to the front door, a malicious little smile curving her lips. 'I had Brett, too. He was a more exciting lover than you, Damien.' Her green eyes stabbed briefly at Natalie. 'You just can't get it right, can you?' she said pityingly.

'Witch!' Natalie retaliated in anger.

'Bitch!' Damien flung at his ex-wife.

Lyn didn't wait for any more. Having put them both down as best she could, she made her exit with another slam.

Natalie felt acutely discomfited by this further revelation of infidelity, and the crude comparison between Brett and Damien. 'It's not true, Damien,' she said, flushing at the need to say it.

'Typical of Lyn, wanting to twist the knife. Another lie,' he said with a snort of disgust. 'Brett never touched her.'

'How do you know?'

'He told me so after Lyn and I had parted. He said she'd made a play for him and he swore he hadn't taken her up on it. He told me because he didn't want her making any trouble between us out of spite.'

'And you believed him?'

'Yes. Brett wouldn't have risked our relationship. Not for an idle screw. And that's all it would have been to him.'

'Yet he risked his relationship with me. Over and over again,' she said with a pang of hurt. 'You meant more to him than I did.'

'Natalie...' He winced. 'Brett needed me. He needed you. Despite the way he used sex as a cover for his inadequacies and feelings of worthlessness, you were *his* woman, the only one who really counted.'

She had come to realise that, although it hadn't given her any satisfaction. But for Ryan, she would have walked away from Brett and nothing in the world could have talked her back into being his wife.

'Yet I came to despise him for the way he kept playing around behind your back,' Damien continued. 'I wanted to take you away from him, Natalie. I wanted you so damned much…'

His lips suddenly clamped shut over the words that had been spilling from them. He made a visible effort to relax his face into a lighter expression. His mouth tilted into a rueful smile.

'Why am I talking about the past when it's the last thing I want to do? That's all over.'

'Not quite, Damien.'

She hesitated, wondering if she should simply let sleeping dogs lie. Was the compulsion to know what had happened a destructive one? Yet didn't trust only come with truth? If Damien had told her Lyn was with him…if she had told Damien she'd seen Lyn yesterday… It was what was left unsaid that preyed on the mind, providing fertile ground for doubts and misunderstandings.

'I saw Anne Smith today,' she blurted out, wanting it over quickly. 'I asked her what happened on top of the cliff. Before Ryan fell. I never believed the story about the ball, Damien.'

He closed his eyes as though wanting to block out the memory of it. 'What did she say?' His voice was completely toneless.

'She said to ask you. That only you could tell me the truth.'

He dropped her hands and walked over to the windows overlooking the ocean. He stared out to sea, his shoulders slumping for several moments, as though the secret burden he carried was too heavy to bear. Then his back stiffened and he turned around. The bleak look of desperation on his face squeezed her heart with fear.

'I lied to you about that day, Natalie. I did cover up for Brett. And for you. To save you from unnecessary pain. But it was not so much Brett's fault that Ryan died. It was mine.'

CHAPTER FIFTEEN

'NO.' THE word welled up from deeply instinctive knowledge and burst from Natalie's lips. She shook her head in absolute denial of Damien's claim of guilt. 'You wouldn't have done anything to hurt a little boy. You wouldn't have done anything to hurt Ryan. I don't believe it.'

There was an agony of desperate desire in his eyes. 'I was thinking of you. I never once considered the effect on Ryan. I wanted the whole unbearable charade to come to an end.'

'You...me...Brett...my marriage to him. You wanted it to end?'

'Yes.' It was an explosive hiss of emotion. 'Apart from your wedding night, and I couldn't believe it of him then, I never covered up for Brett's infidelities, Natalie. I wanted you to find him out. I wanted you to leave him. I wanted you to turn to me.'

'But...you were Brett's only friend.'

'He didn't love you. He didn't deserve you.' Damien smashed his fist into his other palm. 'I felt like killing him every time he talked of having had some other woman. It killed me that you seemed oblivious to it all. That if you knew of it, you tolerated it, while my own love for you had to remain secluded, hidden and unfulfilled.'

'I would never have told you, Damien. What happens within a marriage is private.'

'Private!' He made the word sound like torture. 'It was a public humiliation, a public joke. It ended up feeling like an albatross around my neck. I couldn't come to you. Without breaching trust... honour...loyalty...call it what you will...I couldn't do it. The only chance for us, Natalie, was for you to turn to me.' His eyes glittered his determination. 'So I set out to make that happen.'

'You wouldn't have meant any harm,' she defended him.

'Yes, I did. Not to Ryan. To Brett.'

'It would never have turned out that way. I couldn't turn to you. Not then.'

Natalie knew it would never have happened. To her way of thinking then, Damien had been no better than Brett. She'd despised the effect Damien had on her. She would have told herself that turning to Damien would have been akin to leaping out of the frying-pan into the fire. But Damien hadn't known that.

'I knew Brett wanted Anne Smith,' he went on remorselessly. 'All the more so because she had refused him. That didn't happen very often with Brett.'

No, Natalie thought with bitter cynicism. Brett had had the looks and the body to turn most women on. If all they'd wanted was to know what it was like with him, Brett wouldn't have left them in doubt.

'I thought a weekend in close proximity would present an irresistible challenge to him. He'd try again, and I'd make damned sure you saw it. I imagined taking you into my arms...comforting you... making you realise...' His hands lifted and fell in a contorted gesture of anguished appeal.

'But I didn't go,' Natalie said flatly, all too heart-chillingly aware of why she hadn't gone.

He shook his head as though his thoughts were too painful to dwell on. 'I was counting on it so much...so much...'

He walked over to a sofa, paused, picked up a cushion, looked down at it, plucked at its roulade edging. 'When Brett turned up at the camping site, there was only Ryan with him. You weren't the only one who was sick, Natalie. I was so sick with disappointment, I wasn't fair to Anne.'

He raised eyes that had emptied of all expression. 'I liked her as a person. She was bright, easy company. I'd dated her a few times. But that weekend I didn't give her the attention she had every right to expect. Nor could I give her what she wanted from me.'

'You didn't try to make love to her,' Natalie supplied quietly.

He tossed the cushion aside, commenced walking towards her. 'I offered only company.' His mouth twisted savagely. 'Not very good company. I paid more attention to Ryan. At least he was part of you.'

Yes, very much part of me, Natalie thought on a wave of desolation for how much she had lost when Ryan's life had been cut so short.

'I think it stung Anne's pride,' Damien went on in a weary, relentless tone. 'And there was Brett, only too ready to take up the slack. I didn't exactly throw her into Brett's arms, but I might as well have done for all the difference it made.'

'She had a choice, Damien. She knew Brett was married,' Natalie reminded him.

Damien reached out, his hands resting on her shoulders. 'Cause and effect, Natalie.'

'He had our child with him,' she said fiercely. 'Didn't she care about what my son would see and feel if she played Brett against you?'

She saw the blood drain completely from his face, leaving his skin sallow. 'It was my fault. If I'd had sex with her…if I'd invited her company…or even had Ryan with me while I adjusted a new harness…'

'What happened, Damien?'

He took a deep breath. 'It was agreed I'd make the first descent down the cliff. That suited me fine.

I didn't want to be alone with Anne, just alone by myself.'

He paused, forcing himself to recall the exact sequence of events. 'Brett and Anne were chatting by the tent when I left them. Ryan was bouncing and catching his ball. I went to my four-wheel drive. I had ropes and harnesses in the back. I fossicked around to find what I needed, taking more time than was necessary because of the bitterness in my heart.'

His fingers dug into her flesh. 'The ball did go over the cliff, Natalie. I heard Ryan calling out for Daddy to get his ball for him. I picked up my gear, slouched out from behind the Range Rover, and saw Brett and Anne. They were embracing inside the tent. Ryan saw them. He started flailing at them with his fists and crying, ''She's not my Mummy!'''

'Oh God!' Tears spurted into Natalie's eyes.

'Then Ryan hurtled out of the tent. Brett broke away from Anne to follow him. He stumbled over a tent peg. I saw that Ryan was running blindly, straight towards the cliff edge. I yelled out to him. He took no notice. He was too upset by what he'd witnessed.

'I started running, shouting. Brett picked himself up. He was closer to Ryan than I was. He ran as fast as he could, yelling and screaming at Ryan to stop. It was a mad, frantic dash. Ryan just kept going…without looking…over the edge…and Brett… Brett dived after him as though he could catch him in mid-air and somehow bring him safely back from the fall.'

Natalie flinched away, felt her path to an armchair and collapsed into it, weeping uncontrollably. Damien crouched beside her. A pile of tissues were pressed into her hand. He hugged her shoulders tightly and drew her other hand gently against his chest.

'Please…go on,' she begged, trying ineffectually to mop up the flow of tears. 'Tell me…the rest. I want to know.'

With a heavy sigh Damien withdrew his embrace and moved away. He sat on the sofa opposite her, leaning forward, forearms resting on his knees, his eyes full of sympathy and concern as he told her what she wanted to know.

'I had my mobile phone in the Range Rover. I ran back to it and called for help. I slapped Anne out of her hysteria. My mind was working in overdrive. My thoughts only for you. I told Anne what she was to say when help came. She understood. She would be the only witness. She would only have had a fragmentary glimpse of what happened. Neither she nor Brett would be implicated in Ryan's death. There would be no scandal.

'I went down the cliff on the ropes. When I reached the bottom, I worked my way around to where their bodies lay. They were together, Natalie.

Brett's arm was flung across Ryan. There was nothing anyone could do…for either of them.'

Natalie closed her eyes. Had Brett caught their son? Had he held him…held him tight? 'He did love Ryan,' she choked out, wanting it to have been that way…having the comfort of each other before the end came. 'He was…mostly…a good father, Damien.'

'If he hadn't done what he did to you…he would have been…a good man.'

Natalie tried to stem a fresh flood of tears.

'I hadn't realised,' Damien continued, 'until that moment, how much Brett loved his son. I knew he was proud of him…as he was proud of you. I didn't know he couldn't bear losing Ryan.'

Natalie shook her head. It was more than that. In many ways she had known Brett better than Damien had. She swallowed hard several times, took a deep breath. This was the time for truth. For absolute truth. No holding back. Damien was shouldering blame and guilt that had to be shared by all of them. Herself included. She would come to that.

'There was more than his love for Ryan involved in his headlong leap over the cliff, Damien. I'm sure of it. Brett couldn't have borne knowing Ryan died because of what he'd done. He had to answer to me. It would have been the end of everything he cared about. It *was* the end. I think he knew that. Maybe not in any decisive way, but intuitively.'

Damien gave her words heavy consideration, then slowly nodded. 'Perhaps, you're right. If I hadn't taken Anne, though—'

'If I had gone, or kept Ryan at home with me...' Natalie cut in purposefully.

'You were sick.'

'I wasn't sick.'

Damien frowned, his eyes uncomprehending as though he couldn't accept what she was saying.

'I pretended to be sick. Because I didn't want to go. Because I couldn't stand going...'

'Why not? You liked camping. You liked the mountains, the outdoor life.'

She flushed. 'You were going to be with us, Damien. For the whole weekend. You, living in the tent next to ours with whatever woman you took along. Because of that, Brett would want me. It always happened. The thought of you making love to another woman in the next tent. It had got to the point that I fantasised about you when he had sex with me. I hated myself for it. I couldn't bear to go. I made myself sick thinking about it. I actually threw up.'

'Why did you punish yourself like that? You had a right to say no.'

'I'm telling *you* what happened, Damien. Please listen.'

His mouth tightened, holding his feelings in as he concentrated on her words.

'Because I was physically sick, Brett wouldn't leave Ryan with me. He said I should rest and not be worried about looking after him. Besides, Ryan might catch whatever bug I had. It was better for him to go away for the weekend with his father and Uncle Damien. Because I couldn't face admitting the truth, that you were the cause of my problem, I let Ryan go...and I stayed at home.'

'It was a reasonable decision, Natalie,' Damien said in a reassuring tone.

'It was a lie. Don't you see? We all contributed to what happened. None of us foresaw the consequences of our actions, and we all have guilt to bear. But to say that you were more at fault over Ryan's death...that simply isn't true, Damien.'

He searched her eyes with urgent intensity, wanting to believe. 'After all I've told you...you don't blame me, Natalie?' he asked in a tensely strained voice.

'Wasn't it you who put the ball back in Ryan's bag?'

'It took me hours to find it.' He made a helpless little gesture with his hands. 'Ryan loved playing with balls. It was all that was left. It was something I could do. It seemed...important at the time. It was the last thing Ryan had...'

His eyes blurred with tears. 'I'm sorry, Natalie. I wanted...I didn't know how to make it up to you.

All I could do was…find a ball…and concoct a story…to lessen the blow.'

He bowed his head, shaking it in hopeless anguish. 'At the funeral, Anne wasn't sobbing because she had lost Brett. Like me, she was overwhelmed by what happened. She didn't want to be near me, any more than I wanted to be near her. The memory, the unforgettable memory of the consequences of our actions…'

'But you've been in touch since then,' Natalie said, sure in her own mind that it was no coincidence that Anne Smith had *spotted* her talent. 'You knew about my publishing contract before I told you.'

She remembered how she had been going to surprise him with what she had done by her own efforts.

'Yes, I knew,' he said heavily.

'How could you be so sure I'd go to that particular house?'

'When you asked my advice on what publishers to approach, Anne's company was head of the list. With the way we both felt, you would have got the contract regardless of what you submitted.' An ironic smile lightened the strain on his face. 'As it turned out, you are a top creative talent.'

'And you are my very good friend.' Natalie pushed herself out of the chair and went to him, falling on her knees and cupping his face in her hands, forcing him to meet her eyes. She hoped they reflected what was in her soul. 'You did your best for me, Damien. You always did. You're the best friend any woman could have. Don't you think I realise that? Appreciate it? And love you for it?'

'Natalie…' A wild hope chased the anguish away. His hands swooped to grasp her underarm and lift her with him as he surged to his feet. 'Natalie, Natalie…' It was a breath of incredulous wonderment. His arms encircled her and crushed her to him, his mouth pressing hot, urgent kisses over her hair. 'I'll do everything in my power to make you happy. Anything…'

'I want to make *you* happy, Damien.'

'You have. I am.'

'I have something to tell you.'

His mouth scorched down her neck and shoulders. 'I love you, Natalie. I love you, and only you, and always will.'

His kissing stopped. His chest heaved against her breasts. He eased his embrace to look into her eyes, anxious not to make a mistake, hopeful that he had understood correctly. 'I desire you. I long for you. I lust for you.'

'So do I, for you, Damien.'

His face lit with joy and relief. 'Everything's all right.'

Before Natalie could take another breath, he had

swung her around and was lowering her on to the sofa, naked desire blazing from his eyes.

'Damien, you must listen,' she half-protested, 'or I'll never get to tell you.'

'We'll be married...soon...'

'Of course we will.'

He was opening the buttons on her blouse, caressing the soft swell of her breasts, flicking his tongue across her nipples.

'Damien Chandler, if you don't stop that...'

'You're enjoying it,' he pleaded.

'Of course I am. But I want your full attention. I want to see your eyes.'

He brought his face up close to hers. 'Will this do?'

'My instincts were right, Damien,' she assured him, excitement dancing in her voice and manner at the prospect of the future they would share together, the family they would share together. 'When we were at Merlinmist something happened.'

'I know. I know,' he said with a touch of impatience. 'I remember vividly. But this is better, Natalie. Much better...'

'Something important, Damien.'

His eyes were quizzical, searching. 'What?'

'I intended to tell you this morning.'

'Don't drag it out like this. Tell me, tell me...'

'We're going to have a baby,' she announced on a deep sigh of satisfaction.

There was a mixture of awe and wonderment in his eyes. 'A baby!'

'Our child.'

His touch gentled, became almost reverential. 'I love you, Natalie. With all my heart.'

'I love you, too, Damien. With all my heart.'

'A baby,' he said simply, as if tasting the wonder of the word.

'You're going to be a father, Damien,' Natalie said firmly.

A look of soft tenderness spread over his face. He smiled, a smile that shone with love.

'You give me the gift of life.'

'You've given it to me.'

The smile spread into a grin before he kissed her. 'I'm going to be a daddy.'

Although born in England, **Sandra Field** has lived most of her life in Canada; she says the silence and emptiness of the north speaks to her particularly. While she enjoys travelling, and passing on her sense of a new place, she often chooses to write about the city which is now her home. Sandra says, 'I write out of my experience; I have learned that love with its joys and its pains is all-important. I hope this knowledge enriches my writing, and touches a chord in you, the reader.'

EXPECTING HIS BABY
by
Sandra Field

CHAPTER ONE

THERE was a woman in the bed.

An astonishingly beautiful woman.

Judd Harwood stood still, gazing at the sleeping figure under the white hospital bedspread. He must have the wrong room. It was a man he was looking for, not a woman. Yet instead of leaving and asking someone for better directions, Judd stayed exactly where he was, his slate-gray eyes focused on the bed's occupant. Her right shoulder and upper arm were swathed in an ice pack. Her face was very pale; the livid bruise marring the sweet curve of her jawline stood out in sharp contrast to the creamy skin. Had she been in a car accident, or fallen on the ice encrusting the city streets? Or had it been something worse? Surely she hadn't been assaulted.

His fists curled at his sides in impotent anger. Could it have been her husband? Her lover? He'd flatten the bastard if he ever got his hands on him. Flatten him and ask questions afterward. And how was that for a crazy reaction? A woman he'd never even met, knew nothing about.

He wasn't into protecting strange women. He had better things to do with his time.

His jaw a hard line, Judd continued his scrutiny. The woman's brows were delicate as wings, her cheekbones softly hollowed; he found himself longing to stroke the silken slope from the corner of her eye to the corner of her mouth. An infinitely kissable mouth, he thought, his own mouth dry. Her eyes were closed; he found himself intensely curious to know what color they were. Gray as storm clouds? The rich brown of wet earth? Her hair was

5

red, although that word in no way did justice to a tumble of curls vivid as flame.

Flame...

Blanking from his mind a surge of nightmare images, Judd gave himself a shake. He didn't have the time for this; he needed to find the fireman who'd saved Emmy. Thank him as best he could and then go back to his daughter's bedside. Emmy was sedated, the doctor had assured him of that, and wouldn't wake for hours. But Judd wasn't taking any chances.

So why was he still standing here?

Scowling, purposely not looking for the woman's name on the chart at the foot of the bed, Judd strode out of the room. A nurse was hurrying toward him, her flowered uniform a splash of color in the bare corridor. He said, "Excuse me—I'm looking for the fireman who was admitted earlier this evening...he rescued my daughter and I need to thank him. But I don't even know his name."

The nurse gave him an harassed smile. "Actually it was a woman," she said. "I don't believe—"

"A *woman?*" Judd repeated blankly.

"That's right." Her smile was a shade less friendly. "They do have women on the fire and rescue squads, you know. Room 214. Although I don't believe she's recovered consciousness yet."

Room 214 was the room he'd already been in. The room with the woman lying so still on the bed. Trying to regain some semblance of his normal self-control, Judd said abruptly, "I shouldn't have made the assumption it was a man. Thanks for your help."

"If you need to talk to her, tomorrow would be better. She won't be released before midmorning."

"Okay—thanks again."

The nurse disappeared into a room across the hall. Slowly Judd walked back into Room 214. The woman was lying exactly as she had been a few moments ago, the smooth line of the sheet rising and falling gently with her breathing. He walked closer to the bed, staring at her as though he could imprint every aspect of her appearance in his mind, teased by a strange sense that she resembled someone he knew. But who? He couldn't put a finger on it, and he prided himself on his memory. Surely he'd never seen her before; he could scarcely have forgotten her. The purity of her bone structure. The gentle jut of her wrist bones. Her long, capable fingers, curled defencelessly on the woven coverlet.

Ringless fingers. Did that mean she didn't have a husband?

Her fingernails were dirty. Well, of course they were. She was a firefighter, wasn't she?

This was the woman who'd saved his daughter's life; Judd didn't even have to close his eyes to remember the horrific scene that had greeted him when the cab from Montreal's Dorval airport had dropped him off in the driveway of his house.

Clutching his briefcase, Judd saw three fire trucks parked on the lawn, their red lights flashing into the darkness. Yellow-jacketed firefighters shouted back and forth, barking orders into two-way radios. Water hissed from coiled gray hoses. Great billows of black smoke, rising from the roof, were licked by flames that appeared and disappeared with the wicked unpredictability of vipers. For a moment Judd was stunned, his feet rooted to the ground, his heart thudding in heavy strokes that overrode all the other sounds. He'd known fear before. Of course he had. Some of the situations he persisted in subjecting himself to saw to that. But he'd never known anything as devastating as the terror that clamped itself to every nerve and muscle in his body when he pictured Emmy trapped in that heat, in the choking smoke and vicious destruction of fire.

A tall metal ladder was angled against the wall of the house, reaching toward the windows of the family wing. The wing where Emmy slept…

Judd ran forward, yelling her name. Four policemen jumped him, grabbing his arms as they fought to restrain him. A fifth went flying when Judd flung him aside. And then Judd saw a small bundled figure thrust through the window into the waiting arms of the firefighter on the ladder. He gave a hoarse shout, and as the fireman passed the bundle to another man waiting further down the ladder, the policemen finally released him.

He ran across the frozen, snow-patched lawn faster than he'd ever run in his life. As the fireman transferred Emmy to his arms, the panic in her eyes cut him like a knife, the small weight of her catching at his heartstrings.

Holding her with fierce protectiveness, he climbed into the back of the waiting ambulance. But as he did so, Judd threw a quick glance over his shoulder, in time to catch part of the roof collapsing in a shower of sparks that under any other circumstances might have been eerily beautiful. A blackened beam struck the firefighter who'd shoved Emmy through the window. The helmeted figure staggered and almost fell, and in dreadful fascination Judd watched the fireman at the top of the ladder seize a yellow sleeve, hauling the other firefighter's body over the charred sill by sheer, brute force. A cheer went up from the watchers on the ground. Then Judd turned away, shielding Emmy from the leaping flames and surreal, flickering lights…

Judd came back to the present with a jolt, licking his lips. Emmy had been pronounced out of danger from the smoke she'd inhaled. Because of her sedative-induced sleep, he'd taken this opportunity to find the firefighter to whom he owed a debt of gratitude that could never be repaid.

The woman on the bed.

She couldn't be much over five-seven or five-eight. Her features lacked the perfection of Angeline's: her nose slightly crooked, her mouth a touch too generous. Angeline was his ex-wife, mother of Emmy. An internationally known model, who wouldn't have been caught dead with dirty fingernails.

He didn't want to think about Angeline, her poise and stunning looks, her seductive body and cool, midnight-blue eyes. Not now. He'd divorced her four years ago, and had seen almost nothing of her since then.

The woman on the bed stirred a little, muttering something under her breath. Her lashes flickered. But then her breath sighed in her chest and she settled again. Somehow, in the midst of a maelstrom of smoke and flame and the night's darkness, this woman had found Emmy and carried her to the ladder, into the waiting arms of the other firefighter. To safety.

Judd walked to the foot of the bed, frowning slightly as he started reading the neatly typed words on the chart. Then the woman's name leaped out at him. Lise Charbonneau. Age twenty-eight.

His frown deepened, his eyes intent in a way some of his business associates would have recognized. Angeline still went by her own name, which was also Charbonneau. And Angeline's young cousin had been called Lise. He'd met her at the wedding, all those years ago.

It couldn't be the same person. That would be stretching coincidence too far.

But Lise at the age of thirteen or so had had flaming, unruly red hair, and cheekbones that even then gave promise of an elegance to come. She'd also had braces on her teeth and the gawkiness of a foal new to the field, and no social graces whatsoever. Her eyes, though, had been as green as spring grass, almond-shaped eyes that were already beautiful.

He searched his memory. Hadn't she been living with Angeline and Marthe, Angeline's mother, because her own parents had died tragically? And hadn't they died in a house fire?

Was that why Lise Charbonneau had become a firefighter?

Angeline's cousin responsible for saving Angeline's daughter…what a strange and unbelievable irony. Speaking of which, he'd better try to reach Angeline. He himself was always fodder for journalists; he didn't want Angeline hearing about Emmy's escape on the late-night television news.

But then the woman in the bed shifted again, moaning slightly under her breath. He stiffened to attention, going over to stand by the bed, watching her struggle toward consciousness. And to pain by the look of it, he thought grimly, reaching for the buzzer that was pinned to the pillow by her head, and with an effort restraining himself from taking a strand of her vivid hair between his fingers. Hair that could warm a man's heart. He said gently, "It's okay, I'm calling the nurse."

Her eyes flickered open, closed again, then opened more widely, focusing on him with difficulty. They were a clear, brilliant green, exquisitely shaped. Tension rippling along his nerves, Judd waited for her to speak.

The man's outline was blurred, throbbing in tandem with the throbbing in her shoulder. Lise blinked, trying to clear her vision of a haze of pain and sedatives, and this time he was more distinct. More distinct and instantly recognizable.

Judd. Judd Harwood. Standing beside her bed, gazing

at her with an intensity that made her heart lurch in her breast. He'd come for her, she thought dizzily. Finally. Her knight in shining armor, her gallant prince... How many times, as a teenager, had she fantasized just such an awakening? His big body, so broad-shouldered and narrow-hipped, his square jaw and fierce vitality: she'd known them—so she'd thought—as well as she'd known her own body. Known them and longed for them. Hopelessly. Because all those years ago Judd had been in love with Angeline.

But now it was as though all her adolescent dreams had coalesced, and she'd woken to find the first man she'd ever fallen for watching her in a way that curled heat through every limb. She'd been madly and inarticulately in love with him back then, no matter that he was married to her cousin. How could she not have loved him? To a lonely and impressionable teenager, his looks and personality had had the impact of an ax blade, splintering her innocence. Since then, of course, she'd been hugely disillusioned, all her trite little daydreams shattered on the hard rocks of adult reality.

Judd Harwood. Unfaithful husband of her beloved cousin Angeline. The man who had refused Angeline custody of her own daughter, who'd been too busy amassing his fortune to be anything other than an absentee husband and father. The jet-setter with a woman in every major city in the world.

But what, she wondered frantically, fighting to overcome the fuzziness of her thoughts, was he doing standing by her bed? And where was she anyway? Because this was no dream. The dull, thudding pain in her shoulder and the sharp needles of agony behind her eyes were all too real. So was he, of course. His thick black hair now had threads of gray over the ears, she noticed in confusion. But his eyes were still that chameleon shade between blue and gray, and his jawline was as arrogant as ever.

"Where—" she croaked.

"I've called the nurse," he said in the deep baritone that she now realized she'd never forgotten. "Just lie still, she'll be here in a minute."

"But what are you—"

The door swung open and on soft rubber heels a nurse came in the room. She went straight to the bed, smiling at Lise. "So you're awake—good. And not feeling so great by the look of you. I'll give you another shot, that'll help the pain in your shoulder." With calm efficiency, she checked Lise's pulse and temperature, asked a few questions and gave her the requisite painkiller. "It'll take a few moments to take effect," she said briskly, and glanced up at Judd. "Perhaps you could stay until she's asleep again?"

"Certainly," Judd said.

With a last smile at Lise, the nurse left the room. Judd said evenly, "You're the Lise I met years ago, aren't you? Angeline's cousin? Do you remember me? Judd Harwood."

Oh, yes, she remembered him. Lise said, "I don't want to talk to you."

She'd planned for this to come out crisply and decisively, edged with all the contempt she harbored for him. But her tongue felt like a sponge in her mouth, and her words were scarcely audible even to herself. In huge frustration, she tried again, struggling to marshal her thoughts in a brain stuffed with cotton wool. "I have nothing to say to you," she whispered, then let exhaustion flatten her to the pillow.

"Lise..." Judd bent closer, so close she could see the cleanly sculpted curve of his mouth and the small dent in his chin. A wave of panic washed over her. She turned her head away, squeezing her eyes shut. "Go away," she mumbled.

He said tightly, "I'll come back tomorrow morning. But I want you to know how grateful—oh hell, what kind of a word is that? You saved my daughter's life, Lise, at the risk of your own. I'll never be able to thank you enough."

Her eyes flew open. She gaped up at him, trying to take in what he was saying, remembering the nightmare search from room to room, the dash up the attic stairs and the child huddled at bay in the corner. "You mean the fire was at *your* house?" she gasped. He nodded. In growing agitation she said, "All I heard was that the owner was away and there was a baby-sitter and a little girl. No names."

"My daughter. Emmy."

"Angeline's daughter—she's Angeline's just as much as yours!"

"Angeline left when Emmy was three," Judd said in a hard voice.

"You refused her custody."

"She didn't want it."

"That's not what she told me."

"Look," Judd said flatly, "this is no time for an autopsy on my divorce. You saved Emmy's life. You showed enormous courage." Briefly he rested his hand over hers. "Thank you. That's all I wanted to say."

His fingers were warm, with a latent strength that seemed to race through Lise's body as flame could race along an exposed wire. "Do you really think I need your gratitude?" she cried, hating his nearness, despising herself for being so achingly aware of it. She was damned if she was going to respond to him like the lovesick adolescent she'd been; she was twenty-eight years old, she'd been around. And he was nothing to her. Nothing. She tried to pull her hand away from his, felt agony lance from her elbow to her shoulder, and gave an inarticulate yelp of pain.

Judd said tautly, "For God's sake, lie still. You're acting as though you hate me."

With faint surprise that he could be so obtuse, she said, "Why wouldn't I hate you?"

To her infinite relief, he straightened, his hand falling to his side. An emotion she couldn't possibly have defined flickered across his face. In a neutral voice he said, "You grew up with Angeline."

"I adored her," Lise announced defiantly. "She was everything I always wanted to be, and she was kind to me at a time when I badly needed it." Kind in a rather distant, amused fashion, and kind only when it didn't inconvenience Angeline; as an adult, Lise had come to see these distinctions. Nevertheless, during a period in her life when she'd been horribly lonely, her cousin had taken the trouble to teach her how to dance, and given her advice on her complexion and how to talk to boys. Had paid attention to her. Which was more than Marthe, Angeline's mother, had done.

"Adoration isn't the most clear-eyed of emotions," Judd said.

"What would you know about emotions?"

"Just what do you mean by that?"

"Figure it out, Judd," Lise said wearily. The drugs were starting to take effect, the throbbing in her shoulder lessening; her eyes felt heavy, her body full of lassitude, and all she wanted was for him to go away. Then the door swung smoothly on its hinges again, and with a flood of relief she saw Dave's familiar face.

Dave McDowell was her co-worker, almost always on the same shifts as she. She liked him enormously for his calmness under pressure, and for his rock-solid dependability. He was still wearing the navy-blue coveralls that went under their outer gear; he looked worn-out. She said warmly, "Dave...good thing you were on that ladder."

"Yeah," he said. "You were really pushing it, Lise."

"The little girl wasn't in her room. For some reason she'd slept in the attic. So it took me a while to find her."

Judd made a small sound in his throat. Emmy slept in the attic when she was lonely, she'd told him that once. And he'd been away for four days. So if she'd died in the fire because she couldn't be found, the blame could have been laid squarely on his own shoulders.

Unable to face his own thoughts, Judd turned to Dave. "My name's Judd Harwood—it's my daughter Lise rescued. If you were the man on the ladder—then I owe you a debt of thanks, too."

"Dave McDowell," Dave said with a friendly grin that lit up his brown eyes. "We make a good team, Lise and I. Except she doesn't always go by the manual."

"Rules are made to be bent," Lise muttered.

"One of these days, you'll bend them too often," Dave said with a touch of grimness.

"Dave, I weigh less than the guys and I can go places they can't. And I got her out, didn't I?"

"You scare the tar out of me sometimes, that's all."

Lise said a very pithy word under her breath. Dave raised his eyebrows and produced a rather battered bouquet of flowers from behind his back. "Picked these up on the way over. Although you'll be going home tomorrow, they say."

"Come and get me?" Lise asked.

"Sure will."

"Good," she said contentedly.

"Might even clean up your apartment for you."

Lise said with considerable dignity, "A messy room is the sign of a creative mind."

"It's the sign of someone who'd rather read mystery novels than do housework."

"Makes total sense to me." Lise grinned.

Judd shifted his position. The easy camaraderie between the two of them made him obscurely angry in a way he couldn't analyse. So Dave was familiar with Lise's apartment. Was he her lover as well as her cohort at work? And what if he was? Why should that matter to him, Judd? Other than being the woman who'd saved Emmy's life, Lise Charbonneau was nothing to him.

Yet she was beautiful in a way Angeline could never be. A beauty that was much more than skin deep, that was rooted not only in courage but in emotion. He said brusquely, "I'll be staying in the hospital overnight with my daughter. I'll drop by in the morning, Lise, to see how you are."

"Please don't," she said sharply. "You've thanked me. There's nothing more to say."

As Dave raised his brows again, Judd said implacably, "Then I'll be in touch with you later on. McDowell, thanks again—your team did a great job."

"No sweat, man."

Judd marched out of the room and down the corridor toward the elevator. He wasn't used to being given the brush-off. Hey, who was he kidding? He was never given the brush-off. Women seemed to find his looks, coupled with his money, a potent combination, so much so that he was the one used to handing out brush-offs. Politely. Diplomatically. But the message was almost always the same. Hands off.

Lise Charbonneau hated his guts. No doubt about that. Dammit, she'd been scarcely conscious and she'd found the energy to let him know she thought he was the lowest of the low. And all because of Angeline. Who in the end had dumped him as unceremoniously as if he'd been a pair of boots she was tired of wearing. Trouble is, at the time that had hurt. Hurt rather more than he was prepared to admit. During the eleven years it had lasted, he'd done his level best to hold his marriage together, and to preserve the intensity of emotion that had poleaxed him when he'd first met Angeline. But he'd failed on both counts. Hence his propensity for brush-offs whenever a woman showed any signs of getting too close, or having any ambitions toward matrimony.

Been there. Done that.

He'd have to phone Angeline first thing in the morning: assuming that she was home in the elegant chateau on the Loire that was the principal residence of her second husband, Henri. Who was, incidentally, no longer richer than Judd. Judd, however, couldn't lay claim to a string of counts and dukes in his ancestry. Far from it. If he rarely thought about Angeline, he even more rarely recalled his upbringing on the sordid tenements of Manhattan's lower east side.

The elevator seemed to take forever to arrive, but finally he was pushing open the door to Emmy's room. The little girl was lying peacefully asleep, just as he'd left her. She had her mother's dark blue eyes and heart-shaped face; but her long, straight hair was as black as his, and she'd inherited both his quickness of mind and ability to keep her own counsel. He'd loved her from the moment she'd been born. But only rarely did he know exactly what she was thinking.

As he reached over and smoothed her hair back from her face, she didn't even stir. He'd wanted to make the same gesture with Lise, although from very different motives. Motives nowhere near as pure as the love of a father for his daughter.

He hadn't seen the last of Lise. He knew that in his bones. Although if she were involved with Dave, he'd be one heck of a lot smarter to keep his distance. If he hadn't liked the first brush-off, why would he like the second any better? And he'd never tried forcing himself between a woman and her lover. Never had to, and he wasn't about to start now.

Put Lise Charbonneau out of your mind, he told himself, and focus on getting some sleep. Tomorrow he had to look after Emmy, insurance agents, the police and contractors for repairs. He didn't need the distraction of a flame-haired woman who thought he was the scum of the earth. Scowling, Judd lay down on the cot that the nurses had provided and stared up at the ceiling. But it was a long time before he fell asleep, because two images kept circling in his brain.

Emmy sleeping in the attic because she was lonely.

And the dirt under Lise's fingernails. Dirt from a fire in which she'd risked her life for Emmy's sake.

CHAPTER TWO

THREE days after the fire and her shoulder was still killing her, Lise thought irritably. She hated being off work and having so much time to think. And even more she hated feeling so helpless and ineffective. It was nearly noon, and all she'd accomplished so far today was to have a shower, make her bed and buy a few groceries. The cabbie had been kind enough to carry them upstairs to her apartment door. But she'd had to put them away, one thing at a time, because she could only use her left arm. She wasn't sleeping well, she'd watched far too much TV the last three days, she'd read until her eyes ached, and yes, she was in a foul mood.

She pulled a chair over to the counter, climbed up and reached for the package of rice. But as she lifted it in her good hand, she bumped her sore shoulder on the edge of the cupboard door. Pain lanced the whole length of her arm. With a sharp cry, she dropped the rice. It hit a can of tomatoes, the bag split and rice showered over the counter and the floor.

Lise knew a great many swearwords, working as she did with a team of men. But not one of them seemed even remotely adequate. Tears of frustration flooding her eyes, she leaned her forehead against the cupboard door. What was wrong with her? Why did she suddenly feel like crying her eyes out?

She needed a change. That was one reason. Desperately and immediately, she needed to alter her lifestyle.

It wasn't the first time she'd had this thought. But its intensity was new. New and frightening, because if she quit her job at the fire station, what else would she do? She'd worked there for nearly ten years. She didn't have a university degree, she had not one speck of artistic talent, and anything to do with the world of commerce reduced her to a blithering idiot. She couldn't even balance her checkbook, for Pete's sake.

So how could she quit her job?

With her good hand, she reached for the box of tissues on the counter; but as she tugged one free, more rice pellets rattled to the counter. The counter needed wiping. The sink was full of dirty dishes. Her whole life was a mess, Lise thought, blowing her nose and clambering down from the chair. And how she loathed self-pitying women. Maybe she'd make herself a large cherry milk shake and eat six brownies in a row. That might give her the energy to clean up the rice. If not the refrigerator.

Somewhat cheered by the thought of the brownies— she'd made them from a packaged mix, with considerable difficulty, yesterday—Lise pulled the pan out from on top of the bread bin. But as she opened the drawer for a knife, someone knocked on her door.

It was a very decisive knock. Puzzled, she walked to the door and peered through the peephole.

Judd Harwood was standing on the other side of the door.

The last person in the world she wanted visiting her.

She yanked the door open, said furiously, "No, I do not want to see you and how did you get past security?"

"Waited until someone else opened the main door," he said mildly. "You look god-awful, Lise."

"Make my day."

"Looks like someone ought to, and it might as well be me."

"Oh, I don't think so."

But as she tried to push the door shut, he neatly inserted

his foot in the gap and pried it further open. She seethed, "Judd, I'll holler blue murder if you don't go away."

He gave her a charming smile, although his eyes, she noticed, were cool and watchful. "I've got a favor to ask you," he said. "It concerns Emmy, not me, and it's important. Won't you at least hear me out?"

"Do you always use other people to gain your own ends?"

In a voice like steel, he said, "I happen to be telling the truth. Or is that a commodity you don't recognize?"

"In you, no."

"If we're going to have a no-holds-barred, drag-'em-out fight, let's at least do it in the privacy of your apartment," he said, and pushed past her to stand in the hallway.

He was six inches taller than she, and probably seventy pounds heavier. Not to mention his muscles. Lise slammed the door shut and leaned back against it. "So what's the favor and make it fast."

He stepped closer. "You've been crying."

Between gritted teeth she said, "The favor, Judd."

"What's wrong?"

"Nothing. Everything. I can't go back to work for a whole week, my right arm's useless and I'm going nuts. Do you know what I did all day yesterday? Watched reruns of *Star Wars*—for the third time. And what else would you like to know? What are you doing here anyway—slumming?"

"I told you—I have a favor to ask you."

"I've read about you. In *Fortune* and *Time* magazine. About all your fancy houses, your cars and planes, your women. The international airlines you own. All of which are euphemisms for power. Power and money. And you expect me to believe that *I* can be of use to you? Don't make me laugh."

In sudden amusement Judd said, "You don't have red

hair for nothing, do you? I didn't have time for coffee this morning—how about I put on a pot and we sit down like two civilized human beings and have a reasonable conversation.''

''I don't feel even remotely reasonable when I'm anywhere in your vicinity,'' Lise snapped, then instantly wished the words unsaid.

''Don't you? Now that's interesting,'' Judd said silkily.

She couldn't back away from him: her shoulder blades were pressed into the door as it was. ''Judd, let's get something straight. I don't like you. I don't like what you did to Angeline. So there's no room for small talk between you and me. Tell me what the favor is, I'll decide if I want to do it and then you can leave.''

''I'll leave when I'm ready.''

She tossed her head. ''Macho stuff. I get a dose of that at work, I don't need it at home.''

''Are you ever at a loss for words?''

''I can't afford to be—I work with men,'' she retorted. As, unexpectedly, he began to laugh, his sheer vitality seemed to shrink the hallway; she caught her breath between her teeth, wishing she'd gone out for coffee this morning and was anywhere but here. But Judd would have tracked her down sooner or later: that much she knew. Realizing she was conceding defeat, swearing it would be only temporary, she said grudgingly, ''Caffeinated or decaf?''

''Doesn't matter. Where's the kitchen?''

She winced. ''The living room's through there. I'll only be a minute.''

''Got a man hidden behind the stove, Lise?''

The gleam of humor in his slate-gray eyes was irresistible, and suddenly she heard herself laughing. Laughing as if she liked him, she thought in panic. ''Behind my stove is not a place any self-respecting man would want to go,'' she said, adding, ''Watch where you step,'' as she led the way into the narrow galley kitchen.

Judd stopped in the doorway. ''Well,'' he said, looking around. ''If Dave cleaned up your apartment the other day, he's a better firefighter than a Molly Maid.''

''Dave doesn't live here!''

''Is he your lover?''

''What gives you the right to ask a personal question like that?''

He hesitated perceptibly. ''I'm not sure. *Are* you and Dave lovers?''

Not for anything was she going to expose the relationship between her and Dave to Judd Harwood's knife-blade gaze. ''No comment,'' she said stonily.

''I see…in that case, I take my coffee black,'' Judd said. ''With honey if you have any. Did you throw the rice at the wall?''

She rolled her eyes. ''I was trying to put away the groceries, banged my shoulder on the cupboard and dropped the rice. The bag burst. As you see.''

''Rice is a symbol of fertility,'' Judd said lightly. ''Isn't that why they throw it at weddings?''

''Did they throw it at yours?''

His lashes flickered. ''No. Angeline was into gold-leaf confetti. Nothing as ordinary as rice.'' Angeline had never wanted to have a baby; her figure had been more important to her than her husband's longing for children. Emmy's conception had been an accident, plain and simple.

For a moment Lise would have sworn there'd been genuine pain underlying Judd's voice. But the next moment his eyes were guarded, impenetrable as pewter. She'd imagined it. Of course she had. Judd Harwood hurt because of something she'd said? What a joke.

He said casually, ''Where do you keep your vacuum

cleaner? I'd better get rid of this mess before you slip on it and break your neck.''

He owned the largest and most luxurious airlines in the world; she couldn't pick up a daily paper and not know that. And he was about to vacuum her kitchen floor? Something so ordinary—to use his own word—had never figured among her romantic fantasies all those years ago. As a teenager, she'd been more apt to picture him maddened by desire, carrying her in his strong arms away from Marthe, from the ugly brick house in Outremont, and the boredom of homework and appointments with the orthodontist.

"The vacuum's in the hall cupboard," Lise said edgily. "I'll wipe all the rice that's on the counters onto the floor."

"You do that."

As he left the room, she stared after him. Her whole nervous system was on high alert; any remnants of self-pity had fled the minute Judd had pushed his way into her apartment. But she could handle him. She wasn't an impressionable and innocent teenager anymore; she'd been around the block a few times and learned a thing or two. No, she was more than a match for Judd Harwood. Scowling, Lise fished a cloth from among the dishes piled in the sink and started pushing the rice grains onto the floor. Which could do with a darn good scrubbing.

When Judd came back in, he'd shed his leather bomber jacket and was rolling up the sleeves of a blue cotton shirt. His jeans were faded with wear, fitting his hips snugly. Her gaze skewed away. She said rapidly, "I still can't use my right arm—I feel such a klutz."

"No permanent damage, though?" he asked; she would have sworn his concern was real.

"Nope. Just a Technicolor shoulder," she said, and watched his gaze drop.

She was wearing a T-shirt that had shrunk in the drier; it was turquoise with orange hummingbirds flitting across her breasts. The bruise on her jaw was a putrid shade of yellow. How to impress the man of your dreams, Lise thought dryly, and said, "I'll get out of the way while you vacuum. This kitchen's never been big enough for two."

Reaching for the plug, Judd remarked, "Perhaps that's why you haven't married?"

Cordially she responded, "Why couldn't you be faithful to Angeline?"

"I was."

She snorted. "You'll have to do under the cupboards...you wouldn't think one bag of rice could make such a mess."

"Changing the subject, Lise?"

"You're quick," she said with a saucy grin.

"You're so goddamned beautiful," he said with sudden violence.

He couldn't mean it; flattery must be his standard practice when he was anywhere near a woman. Nevertheless, Lise flushed to the roots of her hair. "*Me?* I'm a mess."

"*Thank you, Judd.* That's considered a more appropriate response."

"Maybe in the circles you move in. But I don't want your compliments, Judd. They're as useless as your wedding vows."

He straightened to his full height. "While we were married, I was never unfaithful to Angeline."

"Tell it to someone who cares."

"I could make you care," he said softly.

Her breath caught in her throat. "I don't think so."

"Are you daring me, Lise?"

"No, Judd. I'm telling you I'm out-of-bounds as far as you're concerned. Off-limits. Uninterested."

"We'll see," he said with that same dangerous softness.

"You'd better move—this kitchen, as you so rightly remarked, isn't big enough for the two of us."

Something in his steady gaze caused her to back up. With as much dignity as she could muster, Lise retreated to the bathroom, where she dragged a brush through her tumbled curls and pulled on a loose sweatshirt over her T-shirt. How to stop feeling sorry for yourself, she thought, poking out her tongue at her reflection. Invite a cougar into your apartment. A starving, highly predatory cougar.

Uneasily she gazed in the mirror. Her cheeks were still flushed and her eyes were shining. Stop it, she told herself. He's not a knight in shining armor come to rescue you. His breastplate's tarnished and he abused his vows. Just you remember that.

Unfortunately he was still the most vibrantly masculine man she'd ever laid eyes on. That hadn't changed. Sexy didn't begin to describe him. It went deeper than that to a confidence that was bone-deep, an unconscious aura of power as much a part of him as his thick black hair and deep-set, changeable eyes.

Why did it have to be *his* daughter she'd rescued? She didn't need Judd in her life. He frightened her, she who could force her way through choking smoke and the crackle of flame.

The vacuum cleaner had been turned off. Steeling herself, Lise went back to the kitchen, said politely, "Thank you," and reached for the coffee beans, which were in the container marked Flour. But she couldn't unscrew the lid with one hand.

Judd said, "Here, let me," and took it from her. In utter fascination she watched the play of muscles in his wrist as his lean fingers undid the jar. "Where's the grinder?" he asked.

This was all so domesticated, she thought wildly. As

though they were married. "In the cupboard by the sink. Ignore the muddle."

As he opened the cupboard, two cookie sheets clattered to the floor. "You live as dangerously at home as you do at work," Judd said, and fished out the grinder.

She blurted, "What's the favor, Judd?"

"Coffee first."

With bad grace Lise hauled out the pot, shoved in a filter and located mugs, cream and sugar. "You sure like getting your own way."

"It's how you get to the top—knowing what you want and going after it."

"Judd Harwood's Philosophy of Life?"

Standing very close to her, yet not touching her, Judd said, "You've got a problem with that?"

"What happens to the people you climb over on the way up?"

"You see me as a real monster, don't you?" He grabbed the pot, poured water in it and plugged it in. "The favor's this. Emmy's having nightmares. About the fire. She wakes up screaming that someone in a mask is coming after her. I thought if she could meet you, it might help."

Lise said slowly, "I was wearing an oxygen mask, because of the smoke. And our clothes are very bulky. So I must have looked pretty scary."

"Would you come to the house, Lise?" Judd raked his fingers through his hair. "I know it's asking a lot—using your spare time for something related to work. I just can't stand hearing her scream like that in the middle of the night."

His voice was rough with emotion. And if he was faking that, she was a monkey's uncle. Knowing she had no choice, knowing simultaneously that she was taking a huge risk, far bigger than when she'd blundered her way to the attic, Lise said, "Yes, I'll come."

"You *will?*"

"Did you think I wouldn't?"

"I wondered."

"*I'm* not a monster, Judd. When do you want me to come—today?"

"The sooner the better. She gets home from school around three-thirty."

"Then I'll arrive at four."

"That's astonishingly generous of you."

His smile filled her with a mixture of feelings she couldn't possibly have analyzed. She shifted uncomfortably. "No, it's not. She's a child, Judd, and I know about—well, never mind."

"Your parents died in a fire, didn't they?"

A muscle twitched in her jaw. "I've said I'll come. Don't push your luck."

"I'll send a car for you."

"I'll get a cab."

"Is independence your middle name?"

"I'll take that as a compliment," she said mockingly, and reached up in the cupboard for a couple of mugs. But at the same time Judd stepped closer. Her hand brushed his arm, the contact shivering through her. Then, with one finger, he traced her cheekbone to her hairline, tugging gently on a loose red curl, his every movement etched into her skin. "You're an enigma to me, you know that?" he said huskily.

He was near enough that she could see the small dark flecks in his irises; his closeness seemed to penetrate all her defences, leaving her exposed and vulnerable in a way she hated. She tried to pull back, but somehow his other arm was around her waist, warm and heavy against her hip. Her heart was hammering in her rib cage, a staccato rhythm that further disoriented her. He drew her closer, his gaze pinioning her. Every nerve in her body screamed at her to run. Resting one hand on his chest, Lise tried to push back; but the heat of his body seeped through his cotton shirt, burning her fingers. Heat, the tautness of muscle and bone, and the hard pounding of his heart...she fought for control, for common sense and caution, and all the while was losing herself in the deep pools of his eyes. Then Judd lowered his head and with a thrill of mingled terror and joy Lise knew he was going to kiss her.

She tried once more to extricate herself, pushing back against his encircling arm. "Judd, don't," she gasped. "Please—don't."

His answer was to find her mouth with his own, closing off her words with his lips. And at the first touch Lise was lost, for fantasy had fused with reality, and reality was the passionate warmth of a man's mouth sealed to her own, seeking her response, demanding it. Her good arm slid up his chest, her fingers burying themselves in the silky dark hair at his nape. Her body swayed into his, soft and pliant. She parted her lips to the urgency of his tongue, welcoming its invasion; he pulled her against his chest as his kiss deepened. Raw hunger blossomed within her, hunger such as she'd never known before. It did away with constraint, made nonsense of caution. Blind with need, she dug her fingers into his scalp and felt the hardness of his erection against her belly.

The shock rippled through her. She heard him groan her name in between a storm of brief, fierce kisses on her lips, her cheeks, her closed eyelids. As though he were exploring her, she thought dimly, as a mariner would explore the inlets, coves and shores of a newly discovered land. Her breasts were soft to his chest, and the turmoil of desire that pervaded her whole body was like a conflagration. She didn't want to fight it. She wanted to go with it, follow into whatever dangers the flames might lead her.

Break all the rules. As Dave so often accused her of doing.

Like a dash of cold water, the image of Dave's pleasant face thrust itself between her and Judd. She'd sometimes wondered if Dave was falling in love with her; certainly he was her best friend, a man she'd worked with and knew through and through, as only those who work in constant danger can know one another. But Judd…Judd was her enemy. What was she thinking of to kiss him this way, so wantonly? So cheaply?

With a whimper of pure distress, Lise shoved hard against Judd's chest. Like a knife wound, agony ripped its way along her right arm to her shoulder. She cried out with pain, turning her face away from him, involuntary tears filling her eyes.

"Lise—what's the matter?"

"Let go of me," she said raggedly. "Just let go!"

"For God's sake, don't cry," he said hoarsely.

"Judd, let me go!"

As he released her, she sagged against the edge of the counter, her breath sobbing in her throat, and said the first thing that came into her head. "You didn't have to kiss me like that—I'd already agreed to go and see Emmy."

"You think I kissed you as a kind of insurance policy?" he snarled. "Is that what you think?"

"What else am I supposed to think?"

"I kissed you because I wanted to! Because you're utterly beautiful and you've got a temper like a wildcat and you're courageous and generous. Because I craved to taste your mouth and touch your skin. To tangle my fingers in your hair."

Lise's cheeks flared scarlet. Judd was telling the truth, she thought faintly. Every word he'd just said was the simple truth. Or the not so simple truth. "You—you can't do that," she stammered. "You're the man who was married to my cousin. I don't like you, and we live in totally different environments—we're worlds apart in every way that matters. Yes, I'll come and see Emmy this afternoon. But that's it. No more contact. Ever.''

"Do you respond to Dave the way you just responded to me?''

"That's none of your business!''

"Come clean, Lise.''

"It's lust, Judd, between you and me—that's all. Nothing we're going to act on and how do you think I feel kissing a man I despise? Lousy, that's how.''

"You don't even know me!''

"I know Angeline.''

"Impasse,'' Judd said softly.

"So why don't we skip the coffee?'' She ran her fingers through her hair. "I'm sure not in the mood for small talk.''

"What happened between you and me just then is rarer than you might—''

"Ask the expert,'' she said nastily.

"Don't, Lise,'' he said in a raw voice. "We don't need to trade cheap shots. Both of us deserve better than that.''

"In your opinion.''

His jaw tightened. "You're not going to listen to reason, are you? Your mind's made up that I'm the villain of the piece and Angeline— '' he gave a harsh laugh "—why, Angeline's the blond-haired angel. Grow up, Lise. No marriage breaks up with all the fault on one side. Especially when a child's involved.''

"Why wouldn't you give Angeline custody?'' Lise demanded. "And don't tell me it's because she didn't want it.''

"What else am I supposed to tell you? It happens to be true.''

She gave an impatient sigh. "And why were you away when the fire started? It was a business trip, wasn't it?"

For once she'd knocked Judd off balance. He stared at her blankly. "You could say so."

She pounced. "You were away with a woman, weren't you? Why else would you be hedging?"

"I was not!"

"You know what I hate about this?" Lise flared. "You're lying to me, Judd. About Angeline. About the women in your life. And yet you expect me to fall into your arms as though none of that matters." Gripping the edge of the counter so hard her knuckles were white, she said, "I wish you'd go. I've had enough of this. More than enough."

"It's not over, Lise," he said with menacing quietness. "Don't kid yourself on that score."

"There's nothing to be over—because there's nothing between us!"

"You're dead wrong. I'll see myself out."

He pivoted and a moment later the door closed behind him. Lise stood very still. Her knees were trembling as though she'd been running uphill for half an hour; her heartbeat sounded very loud in the sudden silence. One kiss, she thought numbly. How could one kiss turn her life upside down?

When Dave kissed her, she never felt anything remotely like the fierce hunger that had enveloped her just now and that had made nonsense of all her rules. Dave's kisses were as pleasant as the man himself. Which might be one reason why she and Dave had never gone to bed together.

She'd go to Judd's house this afternoon, do her best to allay Emmy's fears and then she'd leave. And that would be that. If Emmy was there, Judd could hardly kiss her again.

But if he did, what would she do?

CHAPTER THREE

PROMPTLY at four o'clock the cab turned into Judd's driveway. The ornate iron gates were open, leading into stands of mature birch, oak and evergreens, where the snow lay in soft drifts: a small forest in the midst of the city. Then Lise was dropped off in front of the house. Except it wasn't a house. It was a mansion.

Right out of her league.

The night of the fire she hadn't taken time for anything other than working out where the bedrooms were in the family wing. Now she stood for a few moments, gazing upward. Despite the trampled grass, and the scaffolding against the damaged wing, it was a beautiful house, U-shaped, the lower story built of gray stone, the upper shingled in sage-green cedar. Rhododendrons and azaleas were clustered against the stonework; immaculate snow lay over an expanse of lawn bordered by tall pines. A tree house nestled in the branches of a maple, while a small pond had been cleared for skating. For Emmy, thought Lise, admiring the way the late afternoon sun gleamed orange and gold on the windows.

It was a very welcoming house.

It didn't fit what she knew of Judd Harwood.

She carried her bag of gear across the driveway, climbed the front steps and rang the doorbell. Almost immediately, Judd opened the door. "Please come in," he said formally. "I told Emmy you'd be here soon."

He was wearing dark trousers with a teal-blue sweater. No man should look that good, Lise thought. It simply wasn't fair. His features were too strongly carved to be

33

considered handsome; it was the underlying energy, his sheer masculinity that was so overpowering. She said with a careful lack of warmth, "Hello, Judd, nice to see you," and walked past him into the house.

The foyer with its expanse of oak flooring was painted sunshine-yellow, a graceful spiral staircase drawing her eye upward. An eclectic array of modern paintings intrigued her instantly with their strong colors and sense of design. By the tall windows, the delicate branches of a fig tree overhung clay pots of amaryllis in brilliant bloom.

Color. Warmth. Welcome. The only jarring note was, elusively, the smell of smoke. Confused and disarmed, Lise blurted, "But it's beautiful."

"What were you expecting? Medieval armor and poisoned arrows?"

Patches of red on her cheeks, she looked him full in the eye. "Where's Emmy?"

"In the guest wing—we've had to seal off the family wing. So the playroom's makeshift, and a lot of her favorite toys couldn't be rescued." His mouth tightened. "She was clutching her favorite bear when you found her...she won't let it out of her sight even though it stinks of smoke and I'm sure acts as a constant reminder."

"Plush," Lise said. "She told me his name while I was carrying her out of the attic."

For a moment Judd's eyes were those of a man in torment. "The fire chief figures it was a fault in the wiring. The housekeeper and her husband raised the alarm—they live in a cottage just behind the house, they had family visiting them that night. The baby-sitter had a headache, she'd taken so many painkillers she was out like a light on the couch. If it hadn't been for you, Lise..."

Lise couldn't stand the look on his face; with an actual physical effort, she kept her hands by her side when all she wanted to do was smooth the lines of strain from around his mouth. "If it hadn't been me, it would have been Dave or one of the other firefighters," she said non-committally. "Why don't you take me to the playroom?"

"Yeah...Maryann, the housekeeper, is up there with Emmy." He shoved his hands into his pockets. "What's in the bag?"

"You'll see."

"Here, let me take your coat."

As he reached out for her sheepskin jacket, she quickly slid out of it, not wanting him to touch her. He said, "So you haven't forgotten."

She didn't pretend to misunderstand him. "There'll be no repeat."

"Not here. Not now."

"Nowhere. Ever."

He raised one brow. "Are you daring me, by any chance?"

"Emmy, Judd."

"I didn't get where I am today without taking a risk or two—you might want to remember that."

She said amiably, "Oh, I take risks, too. But I choose my risks. Show some discrimination."

"Whereas I go after every available female?"

"Plus a few that aren't. Me, for instance."

"Lise," Judd said flatly, "are you involved with Dave?"

She could lie, tell him that she and Dave were a number. And if she did, she had the feeling Judd would leave her strictly alone. But she'd never been any good at lying, and she'd waited too long. "There's no easy answer to that question. Yes. No. Neither one cuts it."

"I don't think you are," Judd drawled. "Just as well, considering the way you kissed me."

"And how many women are you involved with, Judd?"

"Platonically, several. But I don't have a lover, if that's what you mean. Haven't had for some time."

His eyes were fastened on her face; he must have been aware of her quickened breathing. "Do you expect me to believe that?"

"Yes," he said in a hard voice, "as a matter of fact, I do."

"Then you're clean out of luck."

"The media can make a hotbed of romance out of a handshake, it's how they earn their keep—you might want to remember that."

She said coolly, "No smoke without a fire."

He had the audacity to laugh. "I shouldn't argue with the expert—but there's no fire without some basic chemistry. Until you came along, I'd been doing just fine without either one."

Into her mind flashed an image she'd never been able to forget: Judd and Angeline in the back garden in Outremont. Locked in each other's arms, kissing in a way that had shattered her adolescent naiveté. "You and Angeline had chemistry."

"Initially, yes."

"So it doesn't last."

"Not if there's too little else to support it."

"Not if one of the partners transfers it elsewhere," she flashed. "Even if I am arguing with the expert."

"You listen to me for a minute! I'm a very rich man—money equals power in our society, and power's an aphrodisiac. So yes, there are women after me. All the time. But, like you, I prefer to exercise choice. And what's easily available isn't always what's desired."

"I'm not playing some sort of hard-to-get game!"

"I never thought you were." Briefly Judd touched her cheek, removing his hand before she could back off. "I have the feeling you're just being yourself. And you have no idea how refreshing that is, after the circles I move in.''

''Who else would I be but myself?'' she said with some asperity.

''When we're talking my kind of money, you'd be surprised what hoops people will jump through.'' Restlessly he moved his shoulders. ''Let's go find Emmy—I'll carry your bag.''

She trailed up the stairs behind him, wondering if she'd ever had such a disturbing or inconclusive conversation. Had it been a drawing of battle lines? A stating of two mutually incompatible points of view? Or of Judd's intention to pursue her regardless of her wishes?

Did she want the answer?

The stairs opened into another generous hallway with an exquisite Persian carpet in faded shades of red and blue. The two paintings, unless she was mistaken, were a Matisse and a Modigliani. She should be wearing something by Chanel or Dior, Lise thought with wry humor. Not khaki pants, a tangerine sweater and loafers, with her hair pulled back in a ponytail. Then Judd opened a paneled door. ''Emmy?'' he called. ''Lise is here.'' And Lise followed him into the room.

It was a charming room, painted eggshell blue, with a child's four-poster bed canopied in white muslin. Lise's feet sank into the carpet. ''Hello, Emmy,'' she said.

Emmy was dressed in denim overalls, her straight dark hair shining in the light. Her blue eyes—Angeline's eyes, Lise thought with a twist of her heart—were fastened on the bear in her arms. Plush. Who still reeked of the smoke of her nightmares. ''Hello,'' Emmy said, and didn't look up.

Lise hadn't rehearsed any course of action, trusting she'd know what to do when she got there. She watched Judd drop her bag on the carpet and walked over to Emmy, hunkering down beside her. "Your dad says you're having nightmares about the fire."

"Mmm."

Still no eye contact. "I expect I looked very scary," Lise said matter-of-factly. "So I brought my uniform with me, so you can see what it's all for. Why I have to dress up in all that stuff."

Trying not to favor her sore arm too obviously, she pulled out her long waterproof pants with their silver braces, and the boots with the strips of fluorescent tape on them, and began talking about them in a quiet, uninflected voice. She moved to the jacket, the straps for the oxygen tank, and her helmet with its protective shield, trying them all on as she went; and was steadily aware that Emmy was listening, even though the child was giving nothing away. Then, finally, she took out her mask, and saw Emmy's dark lashes flicker. "See, these are the head straps, they're adjustable. And this black coil connects with the oxygen tank I carry on my back. Feel it, you can make it longer and shorter. Sort of like a Slinky toy, did you ever have one of those?"

Tentatively Emmy reached out her hand, poking at the coil. "It changes the way I look," Lise said, and held it up, putting her face behind it. "But it's still me. Nobody scary. Nobody who needs to be in a nightmare." Lowering the mask, she put all the reassurance she possibly could into her smile.

"It's too big for me," Emmy said.

"Yes, it is. It might fit Plush, though."

Emmy blinked. "Do you think he wants to wear it? Isn't he scared of it, too?"

"Why don't we try it on and see?"

With some reluctance, the little girl passed over her bear. Carefully Lise fastened the mask to his face, tightening the straps around his caramel colored fur. "There," she said. "He doesn't seem to mind it, does he? In fact, he looks rather dashing, don't you think?"

"Maryann wants to put Plush in the washing machine with lots of soap so he won't smell of smoke," Emmy said in a rush. "But I don't want her to. I keep him around all the time. That's why he was in the attic with me."

Emmy had given Lise the perfect opportunity to satisfy her curiosity. "Were you in the attic because you were running away from the fire?" she asked with a careful lack of emphasis.

For the first time, Emmy looked right at her. "Oh, no. When my dad's away and I'm lonesome, I sleep in the attic."

And does that happen often?

Fortunately Lise hadn't asked the question: merely thought it. But she was aware of a steady burn of anger that Judd could so cavalierly leave his daughter alone while he went off on business trips. Or so-called business trips, the ones where he was with a woman. How *could* he?

"Well," she said easily, "I'm really glad it was me who found you and Plush. You were both very brave to keep each other company. He's earned a pot or two of honey for that, I'd say—if he's anything like Pooh Bear."

As Emmy gave a small chuckle, Lise's lips curved in response. "A little something at eleven," Emmy said shyly.

To her dismay, Lise wanted very badly to hug Emmy; and knew it would be the wrong move. Too soon. Too much. She said gently, "Would you like to take Plush's mask off?"

Her small fingers very nimble, Emmy loosened the clasps and eased the mask away from the bear. "He likes it better without it," she said.

Lise laughed. "So do I. It has its uses, but it's not what

you'd call comfortable.'' With no ceremony, she started shoving all her gear back in the bag. ''All these clothes make me as fat as Pooh the time he got stuck in Rabbit's front door.''

If she'd hoped for another of those sweet smiles from Emmy, Lise was disappointed. The child was clutching Plush to her chest, and in some very real way had retreated from her. Had she, Lise, reached Emmy? Helped in any way that would be lasting?

A tap came at the door, and a plump elderly woman in a flowered housedress came in the door carrying a tray of tea and cookies. Judd introduced Lise to Maryann, the housekeeper, who gave her a disconcertingly keen look before leaving the tray and closing the door behind her. Emmy drank a glass of milk and ate an oatmeal cookie, answering Lise's artless questions with unfailing politeness and no warmth whatsoever. In the course of her job, Lise often visited schools, and rather prided herself on her rapport with children. But whatever her gifts in that direction, they weren't working today, she thought unhappily, wondering why it should matter so much that a small, blue-eyed girl should rebuff her.

It was a relief when Judd got up and said casually, ''I'm going to carry Lise's gear downstairs, Emmy, and drive her home. Maryann's in the kitchen and I'll be back in a few minutes. Say goodbye.''

''Goodbye,'' Emmy said, looking at Lise's shoes rather than her face. ''Thank you for coming.''

''You're welcome,'' Lise said, infusing her voice with genuine warmth. ''It was nice to meet you, Emmy.''

Emmy, pointedly, said nothing. Lise trudged downstairs behind Judd. Standing in the gracious foyer, she asked, ''Do you think I did any good?''

Judd said ruefully, ''I very rarely know what my daughter's thinking, and yes, I would suspect you did. You handled it beautifully, Lise, thanks so much…and now I'll drive you home.''

Lise didn't want Judd within fifty feet of her apartment. Not after the last time. ''I have a couple of errands to run,'' she said, ''I'd rather get a cab. And I'm sure Emmy needs you more than I do. So she won't get lonesome again.''

''Do you think I'm not blaming myself?'' Judd said harshly. ''Give me a break.''

''Angeline always complained about how much you were away.''

His lips tightened. ''I'm sure she did.''

''Is there a phone nearby? For the cab?''

''You're in an almighty rush to be out of here.''

She was; she was terrified he might touch her again, and the alchemy of his body transform her into a woman she scarcely knew. Then Judd took her by the arm, and Lise's whole body tensed. He said tautly, ''I have a proposal…and hear me out before you say anything. Emmy's out of school for the next few days, it's March break. I want to get her away from the house and the smell of smoke and all the repairs, so we're going to Dominica—I have a property there. I want you to come with us.''

''Me?'' Lise squawked. ''Are you nuts?''

''I'm both sober and in my right mind,'' Judd said curtly. ''For one thing, I'd like you to be around in case the nightmares persist. Secondly, it's a small way I can thank you for saving her life. And thirdly, you're on sick leave and very obviously at a loose end. I could even add a fourth incentive. It's March in Montreal—wouldn't anyone rather be on a beach in the West Indies?''

Lise had never been south. Never lazed on a tropical beach or swum in a sea the color of turquoise. For a moment sheer longing to do something so irresponsible, so remote from her normal life, caught her in its grip. Palm trees. Papayas and mangoes. A holiday. A real holiday away from emergencies and sirens and the tragedies that inevitably went with the job. Away from weeping women, charred ruins, smashed cars on an icy highway. Away from the three or four men at the station who would never accept her as someone who could do the job as well as they, no matter how hard she tried. She was so tired of it all. Ten years' tired.

A holiday with Judd.

How could she even be contemplating such a move? She was the one who was nuts. Trying to tug free, Lise said in a raw voice, "I can't, it's a ridiculous idea."

"Give me one good reason why you can't go."

For a horrible moment Lise couldn't think of one. "Emmy doesn't want me around," she blurted.

"She'd get over it."

"I'd be using you."

"You let me worry about that."

"Judd, I can't go! I've never in my life gone away with a man who's a stranger and I'm not going to start now."

"Come on, we met years ago, I'm not exactly a stranger."

She stared up at him. He was smiling at her, a smile of such calculated charm that all her alarm bells went off. Judd was obviously expecting her to capitulate. In bed and out? she wondered, and heard herself say, "Anyway, there's Dave."

"There's also the chemistry, Lise. Between you and me. The kind that starts conflagrations."

Willing her knees not to tremble, Lise glared up at him. "Let's have some plain talk here, Judd Harwood. I'll spell it out for you. You're quite a guy. Tall, dark and handsome nowhere near describes you. You're sexy, rich and powerful, your smile's pure dynamite and your body would drive any woman from sixteen to sixty stark-raving mad. Why wouldn't I respond to you? I'd have to be dead in my grave not to. But it doesn't mean a darn thing—I don't even like you, for Pete's sake. So please don't feel flattered that I just about fell into your arms, it's nothing to—''

Judd said flatly, ''Great snow job, and I don't believe a word of it.''

''That's your ego talking!''

''Dammit, Lise,'' he exploded, ''there's something about you that's different. I don't normally ask a woman I've spent less than three hours with to go away with me and my daughter. Especially my daughter. You can trust me on that one.''

''Whether I trust a single word you say is completely irrelevant. I'm not going to Dominica with you. I'm not going to the local grocery store with you. Now will you please call me a cab?''

Judd stood very still, looking down at her. Her eyes were as brilliant as emeralds in sunlight, and her face was passionate with conviction. She wasn't playing hard to get, he knew that in his bones. But she was wrong. Dead wrong.

What *was* Dave to her? And what had Angeline told her over the years?

He couldn't answer either question. All he could do was add two more. When was the last time a woman had said no to him? Or had turned down an all-expenses trip to a tropical paradise?

Never.

He didn't like it one bit. So what was this all about? His bruised ego, as Lise had suggested?

He was damned if this was just a question of hurt pride. It had to be about more than that.

About more than the ache in his groin and his passionate hunger to possess her? His thoughts stopped short. He said tightly, ''I'll call a cab. If Emmy has more nightmares, will you come back?''

"If you're in Dominica, I won't be able to, will I?" Lise said, tossing her head.

The light through the tall windows caught in her hair, an alchemy of gold and copper. His body hardened involuntarily and with an impatient exclamation Judd turned away, taking his cell phone out of his pocket and dialing the nearest cab station. Four minutes, he was promised. So he had four minutes to persuade a stubborn, red-haired woman to change her mind. Casually he turned back to face her. "You're right," he said, "it was a crazy idea, I allowed my concern for Emmy to override my common sense. Sorry about that. Anyway, you must have been south before, lots of times."

"No. How long before the taxi comes?"

"A couple of minutes. Come off it, Lise, you must have been to Bermuda or the Bahamas. Or at least to Florida."

"The furthest south I've been is Boston and who do you think would take me on a romantic tryst to the tropics? The fire chief?"

Why not Dave? "You don't need me telling you you're a beautiful woman. So don't pretend there haven't been men in your life," Judd said tersely.

"Sure there have been. They stick around until the first time I get called out on emergency and I'm gone for six hours. Or until my first string of night shifts when I come home exhausted at 6:00 a.m. and have to sleep all day so I won't be a basket case the next night. Or until they get jealous of me spending all my working hours with men. Be honest, Judd—you wouldn't like it any better than the rest of them."

Her hours of work didn't bother Judd in the slightest; he could put in some pretty horrific hours himself. It was the danger she was exposed to that made the blood run cold in his veins. But he wasn't about to tell her that.

"Dave knows the score," he said, "he works shifts as well. So why haven't you gone south with Dave?"

"He's never asked me," Lise said airily. "Oh, there's the cab. Bye, Judd."

He picked up her bag of gear and followed her outdoors. "We haven't seen the last of each other."

She gave him a dazzling smile as she opened the door of the taxi. "Have a great time in Dominica."

He reached in front of her and deposited the bag on the back seat. When she stooped to follow it, he pulled her into his arms, twisting her around and kissing her hard on the mouth. Before he could lose control, he stepped back, letting his arms fall to his sides. "See you," he said.

Her nostrils flared; her cheeks were bright patches of color. "Over my dead body," she snapped, clambered into the back seat with none of her usual grace and slammed the door. The cab disappeared into the trees round the curve of the driveway.

Ordinarily Judd's next move would be to send an extravagant spray of orchids. Or a bottle of Dom Pérignon along with a big box of the world's most expensive chocolates. Or all three. Somehow he didn't think any of the above would cut much ice with Lise.

So what was he going to do? Let a female firefighter defeat him? Cut his losses and forget he'd ever met her?

He'd seen another side of her upstairs in Emmy's bedroom; allied to a volatile mixture of courage and passion, he could now add sensitivity, warmth and humor. She'd even made Emmy smile. Perhaps, he thought painfully, Emmy needed Lise as much or more than he did.

Need her? He, Judd Harwood, needing a woman? All he needed was Lise's body. He'd better not forget that. If he could only slake his hunger for her, make love to her the night through, he'd be able to put her behind him and forget about her, just as he always had with every other woman but Angeline.

He'd vowed after Angeline left that he'd never fall in love again, and he'd meant every word of it.

The woman wasn't born who could change his mind on that score.

CHAPTER FOUR

LISE leaned her head back on the seat of the taxi. She'd been exaggerating when she'd told Judd she had errands to do. She didn't, not really. She had precisely nothing to do. That was the trouble. She rubbed at her lips with the back of her hand, trying to erase the fierce pressure of his mouth on hers, remembering all too clearly how her heart had leaped in her breast and how every cell in her body had urged her to respond.

Dominica? With Judd? She'd be better off leaping from the top floor of a burning building.

She'd given the cabbie the address of her apartment. So what was she going to do? Go home and scrub the kitchen floor with her one good arm? Watch *Star Wars* for the fourth time?

She could go and see Marthe.

Lise sat up a little straighter. Marthe had been Judd's mother-in-law. Yes, she'd visit Marthe.

It had been many years since a grieving, terrified seven-year-old girl had gone to live with her Tante Marthe and cousin Angeline in the big brick house in Outremont. Not once in those years had Marthe hugged Lise or spontaneously kissed her with warmth and caring; or, for that matter, comforted the nightmares that had racked Lise's sleep after the fire that had killed her parents.

No wonder she'd been unable to refuse Judd's request to try to cure Emmy of her nightmares. What choice had she had?

For as long as Lise could remember, all Marthe's love had been wrapped up in her exquisitely beautiful daughter,

47

Angeline; finally, when the hurt had threatened to over-whelm her, Lise had worked out that there was no love left over for a stray niece. Yet, out of a sense of duty, Lise still dropped in to visit her aunt, who lived with a succession of maids and housekeepers in the same ugly mansion in a French area of the city.

This vibrant mix of cultures, French and English, was one of the things Lise enjoyed most about Montreal, a city built on an island in the wide St Lawrence River; in her leisure time she loved its bistros and brasseries, the liveliness of its music and its joie de vivre. And it was home to her now; she'd lived here for twenty-one of her twenty-eight years.

Half an hour later, having left her gear at her apartment, Lise was ringing the doorbell of Marthe's house. The maid led Lise to a formal parlor at the back of the house, where Marthe was sitting in a pale wash of sunlight writing a letter. She was wearing a black wool skirt with an impeccable blue twinset, as pale a blue as her eyes; her pearls were perfectly matched, her gray hair rigidly curled. "Hello, *Tante,*" Lise said pleasantly. "Is this a good time for a visit?"

Marthe offered a powdered cheek to be kissed and ostentatiously folded the letter so Lise couldn't read it. "Of course," she said. "As you know, the hours are long for me."

Resolutely refusing to feel guilty, Lise said cheerfully, "Even though it's cold out, the sun is lovely. Are you writing to Angeline?"

"I haven't heard from her for nearly two weeks," Marthe said fretfully, "and I get no satisfaction when I call the château, she's always out or unavailable. Mind you, her social life is very important, she mixes with the very best people, as you know. Last week she was on a Mediterranean cruise with the Count and Countess of…"

Marthe was launched; Lise settled in to listen and ask the occasional question. Angeline was now in her mid-thirties and did very little modeling, preferring to devote herself to the jet-set crowd. It must be—Lise did a quick calculation—four years since Angeline had spared time on one of her rushed Montreal visits to get in touch with Lise by telephone; there hadn't been the opportunity for a visit. It had been around the period when the custody of Emmy had been settled; she could recall the conversation as clearly as if it were yesterday.

"Emmy will be with Judd," Angeline had said, a break in her beautifully modulated voice.

"Not with you?" Lise asked, appalled.

"Only for the occasional holiday."

"But, Angeline, isn't a child's place with her mother?"

"Judd will be good to her, I'm sure."

Angeline was crying, Lise was certain of it. "I can't believe he'd take her from you," she burst out.

"I have to believe it will be for the best," Angeline whispered.

"The man's heartless! Heartless and horrible."

"I don't want to fight him—there'd be so much publicity, and Emmy would be harmed by that."

"You're so generous," Lise exclaimed. "Poor little Emmy."

"Please, Lise, let's talk about something else," Angeline said, her voice quivering. "Have you seen the latest Donna Karan collection? I'm ordering one of everything—absolutely fabulous use of line and color."

"You're also very brave," Lise said forthrightly. "And yes, I did see an article in a magazine about her collection, rave reviews everywhere…"

With a jerk she came back to the present, to Marthe saying crossly, "Really, Lise, have you been listening to a word I've said?"

"I was thinking about Angeline," Lise said truthfully. "About how brave she was when Emmy went to Judd's custody."

"Judd!" Marthe spat. "He manipulated every one of his legal connections, and used to the hilt the fact that Angeline was moving to France. As if that would have made any difference to a three-year-old."

"I've met Emmy…she has Angeline's eyes," Lise said. "As you probably know, there was a fire three days ago at Judd's house—I was part of the crew."

Marthe clutched the arm of her chair with her arthritic, diamond-encrusted fingers. "Judd Harwood ruined my daughter's life. Once a month the child comes here for Sunday lunch, and that's all the contact I'm allowed."

One more strike against Judd, that he would keep his daughter from her grandmother as well as her mother. "Do you find Emmy shy?" Lise asked diplomatically.

"The child barely says a word. He's poisoned her against me, I know he has."

"How long since Angeline's seen her?"

"She finds it terribly painful to see her," Marthe replied. "Angeline was always so sensitive. As sensitive as she's beautiful." She gave Lise's casual attire and flaming curls a disparaging look. "It's unfortunate you didn't inherit the same looks, Lise. Of course my sister was no beauty."

Inwardly Lise winced; disparaging comparisons between her and her cousin had always been one of Marthe's themes. How could red hair and green eyes compare with Angeline's svelte blond elegance? She said lightly, "Well, we can't all be world-famous models, *Tante*."

"I'd hoped to go to France for Easter. But Angeline's put that visit off, something to do with Henri's schedule."

Marthe's mouth was a discontented line. "Perhaps she'll come this way instead," Lise suggested.

"She hasn't mentioned that as a possibility. But then she's so busy…three weeks ago she went to Monaco for a wedding, I have pictures here from one of the society magazines.''

Marthe was an avid collector of clippings; obediently Lise admired the gathering of glossy aristocrats in their designer outfits. Angeline, as always, looked radiant; she was on the arm of an Italian newspaper magnate. "Henri was busy with the vineyard,'' Marthe sniffed. "Naturally Angeline never lacks for escorts—something Judd willfully misconstrued as infidelity.'' Viciously she dug her nails into the brocade arm of her chair. "As if Angeline would break her vows. And as if he were innocent in that respect. You have no idea what my poor daughter suffered from that man.''

Judd no doubt kissed every woman as though there was no tomorrow, Lise thought painfully. Today he'd tried to tell her she was special; but the words meant nothing. His entire history mitigated against any such possibility. She said in a neutral voice, "He's very attractive.''

"Angeline was so young when she met him. Young and impressionable. If I'd known then what I know now, I would never have allowed the match to happen.''

Lise rather doubted this; Marthe had always given her daughter everything she wanted, and all those years ago there had been no doubt that Angeline wanted Judd. At thirteen, Lise had been quite acute enough to know that.

Luckily the maid entered the room with a silver tea tray, preventing Lise from following her train of thought; the conversation limped along, and half an hour later, Lise stood up to go. Marthe presented the same cool cheek, and with a feeling of strong relief, Lise started to walk home.

She needed the exercise; even more, she needed to exorcise Marthe's chronic discontent. But everything she'd learned today had only confirmed what she already knew:

Judd had treated his wife disgracefully. There wasn't a worry in the world that she herself would fall for him. Not again.

Her foot skidded on a patch of ice. Judd wasn't all bad, though. She would swear he loved Emmy. Unless he was a consummate actor, his pain and helplessness in the face of the little girl's nightmares had been all too real.

Stop thinking about him, Lise scolded herself. You'll never see him again and that's the way it should be. So get on with your life, and figure out what you're going to do next. Quit your job? Work in a bookstore? Take a veterinary assistant's course? Or spend all your savings to lie on a beach in the Caribbean and feel the sun on your face?

No way. She couldn't afford to do that.

When Lise finally reached her own street, the first thing she saw was Dave's battered Honda parked outside her apartment block. As she hurried into the lobby, he was pushing her buzzer. "Hi," she said warmly, pleased to see him; he was so uncomplicated, so straightforward after Judd.

He grinned at her; although she did notice with faint unease that he looked unusually tense. "I was just visiting my aunt," she added, "and decided to walk home."

"Want to go to the bistro for a bite?"

"Love to."

But when they were seated across from each other, twining the cheese from onion soup around their spoons, Lise said abruptly, "What's up? You don't seem yourself."

"I'm not. There's something I want to ask you."

His brown eyes looked at her without guile; but his fingers were clamped around his soup spoon as though it were an ax he might use to break down a door. "Go ahead," she said slowly.

"We've dated quite a bit, Lise. Gone to movies and

house parties, had meals together.'' He gazed at his whole wheat roll as if he wasn't quite sure what it was. ''I've kissed you good night. Sometimes we hold hands. But that's it. Something has always stopped me—''

''Dave, I—''

''No, let me finish.'' He looked up. ''You're off for the next few days and I've got five days' vacation I have to take before the end of March. Let's go away together, Lise. To a cabin in the Laurentians. To a fancy hotel in Quebec City. It doesn't really matter where. I just want to spend time with you.'' He covered her hand with his. ''I want to go to bed with you.''

Her lashes dropped to hide her eyes. Twice in one day, she thought in dismay, and wished with all her heart that Dave hadn't chosen tonight, of all nights, to break the silence of years. She gazed down at his hand. She could feel its weight, its warmth, of course she could. But she felt no desire to press it to her cheek, to trace the lines in his palm with her tongue. To hold it and never let go. If it had been Judd's hand...in a confused rush, she muttered, ''That's sweet of you. But—''

''I'm doing this all wrong,'' Dave announced. He suddenly stood up, came around to her side of the table and pulled her to her feet. Then he kissed her very thoroughly and with obvious enjoyment.

Lise stood still in his embrace, discovering within herself a strong urge to weep. Because she felt nothing. Absolutely nothing. Then Dave released her and stepped back. Someone gave a wolf whistle from one of the other tables. Ignoring it, Dave urged, ''Say yes, Lise. Please say yes.''

''I can't, Dave,'' she whispered. ''I just can't.''

''Why not? We can go away together, see what happens. No pressure, just spend some time with each other.''

She had to end this. ''I'm not in love with you,'' she

said desperately. "Not the least bit. So I can't go away with you, it would be wrong for both of us—I could never give you what you want."

She could feel the stillness in his body; his fingers were clamped around hers with something of the strength with which he'd hauled her through the burning window at Judd's house. Lise added with a weak smile, "Your soup's getting cold."

"You really mean it, don't you?" As she nodded unhappily, Dave demanded, "Is there someone else?"

"No!" How could she possibly tell him what happened to her when she came within ten feet of a man she despised? "I'm really sorry," she muttered. "But I know I'm right. You're my friend, Dave. And that's all I want."

Dave dropped his hands to his sides, sat down and automatically started to eat again. Lise sat down as well. Her shoulder was aching and she felt as though the day had gone on entirely too long. But she couldn't walk out on Dave; he deserved better than that. Valiantly she tried to talk about work and the snowstorm that was predicted, and when the waiter finally brought the bill, she could have cried with relief. Dave then drove her home. Pulling up outside her building, he said stiffly, "I'd rather we didn't date for a while. If it's all the same to you."

"So we won't be friends anymore?"

"Someday. Just not right now."

"I'm thinking of quitting the job anyway."

She hadn't meant to tell Dave that. He said incredulously, "*Quit?* What for? What else would you do?"

"I'm tired. I've done this job for ten years and I've had enough. I need a break. A rest."

"Good thing the rest of us don't feel that way."

She said more strongly, "Don't lay guilt trips on me, Dave, please. Look, I've got to go. Take care of yourself, won't you? And I'm truly sorry."

Before he could answer, Lise got out of his car and hurried indoors. By the time she'd opened the inner security door, Dave had driven away. She ran up the stairs to her floor, unlocked her apartment door, closed it behind her and sagged against it. She'd hurt Dave. A lot, by the look of his face. What was the matter with her? She couldn't respond to a good man who was dependable and brave; yet a man who manipulated those closest to him as though they were pieces on a chessboard had awoken her body to passion and hunger.

There was no sense in it. No sense whatsoever.

Lise woke the next morning to a leaden sky and a forecast for snow and freezing rain. In the cool morning light one fact seemed inescapable: she'd probably lost Dave's friendship last night. Which hurt. A lot.

One more reason to quit her job, she decided. The only bright spot in the day was that her shoulder felt better; nor was it quite so luridly hued. She'd phone a couple of friends to see if they were free for lunch; and then she'd go shopping. When the going gets tough, the tough go shopping: a motto Lise had always rather approved of. It beat taking aspirin.

After her shower, Lise pulled on her robe, which was full-length, made of fuchsia-colored fleece, and clashed with her hair. Fuchsia made a statement, she thought, grinning at herself in the mirror. Although maybe not a fashion statement. At least, not one Angeline would approve of.

Her hair, still damp, stood out in a cloud around her head. She'd buy a paper while she was out, and check the job market; she'd also phone the technology institute that ran the course to become a vet's assistant. What she wouldn't do was sit around bemoaning the loss of Dave…or think about Judd winging south with Emmy. No future in that.

Lise was cutting into a honeydew melon for breakfast when the doorbell rang. The knife slipped, slicing her index finger rather than the melon. She mouthed a very pungent word under her breath. Surely it wasn't Dave, hoping she'd changed her mind. Wrapping a wad of tissues around her hand, she went to the door. But her finger was bleeding rather profusely; trying to tighten the tissue, which was already splotched with red, she undid the latch and said, "Dave, I—oh. It's you."

"Yeah," said Judd, "it's me. What have you done to your finger?"

"It's only a cut."

In two seconds he was in the door, had deposited a suitcase on the floor, and was wrapping a pristine white handkerchief around her finger. Lise tried to pull free. "You'll ruin your handkerchief—don't make such a fuss!"

"Head for the bathroom," Judd ordered. "My turn to rescue you."

"I don't need rescuing," she retorted through gritted teeth. "And what are you doing here anyway?"

He said with a sudden, charming grin, "Oh, hadn't you guessed? I'm kidnapping you. Or, to be more accurate, Emmy and I are kidnapping you. She's waiting downstairs in the limo—we're on our way to the airport."

"Rich people don't do the kidnapping—they get kidnapped," Lise said peevishly, and allowed herself to be pulled in the direction of the bathroom, where in short order Judd taped her finger. He did it in a very businesslike manner; Lise concentrated her thoughts on ten-foot snowbanks and the Antarctic ice cap.

"There," he said. Then, taking his time, he surveyed her from head to foot. "You sure like bright colors."

She grimaced. "As a kid, I always inherited Angeline's

clothes. Pastels that looked fabulous on her and made me look like a sick puppy.''

With sudden violence Judd thrust his hands into the soft, tangled mass of her curls. ''We always come back to Angeline, don't we?'' he muttered. ''I'll tell you one thing—you're as different from her as fuchsia is from pale pink.'' Then he bent his head to kiss her, his tongue laving her lips, demanding entrance.

Lise stood as rigid as a post; and this time she thought about Angeline, and about Emmy sleeping in the attic because she was lonely for her father. Suddenly, with all her strength, she pushed away from Judd, wrenching her head free. How dare he take her for granted? Assume that she was panting to be kissed by him? ''Go to Dominica, Judd Harwood,'' she seethed. ''Or go to hell. I don't care where you go as long as you're out of this apartment in two seconds flat!''

''Go get dressed, Lise,'' he countered, and to her fury she saw that he was laughing at her. ''Anything'll do. Bring sunglasses.''

''You don't get it, do you? You just don't get it. I'm not going to Dominica with you!''

''You've got to. Emmy's expecting you.''

''Emmy doesn't care one way or the other what I do.''

''I asked her if she wanted you to come.''

''And what did she say?''

Judd hesitated, remembering the actual words of that conversation with unfortunate accuracy. ''Would you like Lise to go away with us, Emmy?'' he'd asked.

''If you want her to.''

''I'm asking about you. What you want.''

Emmy said elliptically, ''Her hair's really pretty.''

''It is, isn't it? She works hard at her job, Emmy, I'm sure she could do with a holiday.''

''She's nicer than Eleanor.''

Judd winced. He'd dated Eleanor, daughter of an earl, just long enough to discover she had ice water in her veins and disliked small children. "I think Lise liked you," he ventured, and received in return one of Emmy's silent, inscrutable looks.

He came back to the present; Lise was gazing at him just as steadily. He had no more idea what Lise was thinking than he'd had with Emmy, he thought in exasperation. He'd built a multimillion-dollar business from the ground up and he couldn't think what to say to a woman he barely knew? He opened his mouth and heard himself say, "Emmy wasn't what you'd call enthusiastic."

Lise said dryly, "For once, you're being honest."

"You deserve honesty," Judd said slowly, and knew he'd said something very profound. What the devil was going on? He didn't like subterfuge, but never before with a woman had he had this burning urge to avoid even the smallest of deceits. Lise looked a little disconcerted, he noticed. Good. If he was off balance, it wouldn't hurt for her to be, too.

"I'm not going," she said evenly, crossing her arms over her breasts. "Emmy won't be disappointed, and I'm sure you'll manage to find someone else."

"I don't want someone else. I want you."

"No way."

Judd held on to his temper. Taking her by the hand, he walked down the hallway toward the front door, where he undid the gleaming leather suitcase he'd brought with him. "I went shopping yesterday," he said. "For you."

"You mean you bought me clothes?" Lise demanded, her green eyes full of hostility.

"Yeah. Figured your wardrobe probably wasn't loaded with stuff suited for the tropics."

"How did you know what size?"

"I've held you in my arms, Lise."

She blushed scarlet, in interesting contrast to both her robe and her hair. Ignoring her flaming cheeks with a disdain he had to admire, she gave her head a defiant toss. "You're going to be busy when you get back from Dominica," she said. "Returning everything."

"Beachwear, a couple of nightgowns, shorts, tops and an outfit for dinner," he said equably. "But why would I bother returning them? I'll just keep them for the next woman who comes along. Right?"

"So you were planning on buying me?" Lise flashed. "Stick a few fancy clothes in a suitcase and she'll follow me anywhere? Panting like a puppy dog?"

"No," he said tightly. "That wasn't the plan. I can't buy you, Lise—you think I haven't figured that out yet?"

"I don't want your money. Or your clothes."

She was telling the truth, he thought in a great surge of exhilaration. It was a long time since he'd been wanted for himself. Not for his money, his possessions, or the power he wielded. He said the obvious. "You want me, though."

"Maybe I do. It's called lust. So what?"

"So come to Dominica with me and Emmy. Separate bedrooms, a private beach and a swimming pool, and no responsibilities."

"I can't, Judd," Lise said in sudden anguish. "That's not the way I operate. I'd be using you—don't you see?"

She meant every word she was saying and she wasn't playing hard to get; he'd stake his whole fleet of jets on that. Putting all the force of his personality behind his words, Judd said, "You saved Emmy's life, Lise. You might be forgetting that. I'm not. Three days in the sun— not much recompense for something that's beyond price."

Her eyes dropped before the blazing intensity of his to the suitcase open at his feet. Then she said in a strangled voice, "What's underneath that yellow thing?"

That yellow thing was a very expensive coverup for a

miniscule bikini. Judd knelt, pushing it aside to reveal a jade-green silk dress with cap sleeves, a plunging neckline and a long flare of skirt. "Quite by chance I saw it in the window of a boutique near Westmount Square. It seemed to belong to you—Lise, what's wrong?"

Her hands were clasped in front of her; tears glimmered in her eyes. Swiftly Judd stood up, taking her by the shoulders. "Don't you like it? It's just that I could picture you—"

Her words tumbled over one another. "I saw it, too. Last week. Before I met you. I was shopping one day, just wandering, and I saw it in the window and it was so beautiful and I knew I'd look wonderful in it, that it was made for me. I also knew I couldn't possibly afford it, and where would I wear it anyway? To the annual firefighters' dinner? To the drugstore? It was from another woman's life. Not mine." She shivered. "I—it scares me, Judd. That you saw it and bought it because you knew somehow that it belonged to me."

"Lise," Judd said harshly, "go put on jeans and a shirt. You're coming with us, and I swear I won't as much as lay a finger on you the whole time we're there. And when you get home, you can keep the dress—it's yours."

A tear slowly trickled down her cheek. She said raggedly, "I never cry. I can't afford to, too many awful things happen in my job and four or five of the guys would give their eyeteeth to see me behave like a typical female."

Judd ached to take her in his arms and kept his hands rigidly at his sides. "A few days away from your job," he said quietly, "that's all I'm giving you. That and a dress that'll make your eyes look like a tropical sea."

She scrubbed at her cheeks with the back of her hand. "I'll go and get ready," she muttered. "I won't be long."

With none of her usual grace, she scurried from the room. Judd watched her go. He'd said he wouldn't touch her; he had no idea how he was going to stick to that vow. But he'd have to keep his hands off her even if it killed him. Because he'd promised. Stooping to close the suitcase, he carefully tucked the dress away. He owed it a huge debt of gratitude; Lise had capitulated because of it.

He'd done some difficult things in his life. But he had the feeling that nothing would measure up to the challenge of staying out of Lise Charbonneau's bed.

CHAPTER FIVE

IT WAS evening. Judd was indoors putting Emmy to bed. Lise was sitting by herself on the tiled patio that overlooked the ocean, where the sun had set in barbaric splendor. The first stars were piercing a sky soft as velvet; the doves had fallen silent, and the brilliant magenta hues of the bougainvillea that clambered over the trellises had been swallowed by darkness. How long since she'd relaxed so completely in a setting so utterly beautiful? So luxurious?

Never.

She'd stepped outside her ordinary life the minute she'd climbed into Judd's limo outside her apartment. The uniformed chauffeur. The sleek private jet on the tarmac at Dorval, bearing the elegant logo of one of Judd's international airlines. And then, hours later, the arrival at the villa here on Dominica's east coast, the forested grounds opening to reveal a sprawling bungalow artfully constructed of native materials, its interior painted in tranquil pastels and open to the ocean breeze. Flowers everywhere, hibiscus and orchids and scarlet anthurium. Delicious meals that she, Lise, neither had to prepare nor clean up. She felt as though she were living in a dream, as though none of this was real.

Judd, so far, had been a perfect companion. Unobtrusively he'd made sure she had everything she needed, and he hadn't as much as laid one finger on her. He was keeping his promise.

A faint breeze stirred the palm trees, whose fronds clashed gently together like taffeta skirts. Lise stretched out a little more comfortably on the teak recliner, feeling the silk of her loose cream trousers slide against her thighs; her shirt was also silk, in a subtle shade of primrose yellow. Clothes Judd had chosen and paid for.

She should go to bed before he came back. Just in case his promise was an empty one and he planned to seduce her in this paradisiacal setting. Her lashes drooped to her cheek. She could trust him. Surely. It would be small thanks for saving Emmy's life were he to make love to her against her will.

Too sleepy to worry, too tired to remember how she'd fallen into his arms as easily as ripe mangoes fell from the trees on his estate, Lise closed her eyes. The soft gossip of the waves gentled any fears she might have had. Her breathing settled into a slower, deeper rhythm.

Ten minutes later Judd walked back out on the patio. It led from the spacious open-air dining room, which was edged with banks of purple and white orchids, toward the pool and the beach, so that house and sea were linked in a way that pleased him. Then he stopped short.

Lise had fallen asleep.

The golden light from the dining room angled across her face. Her hair glowed like a banked fire; her breasts rose and fell with her breathing. There were blue shadows under her closed lids, he noticed with a catch at his heart. Or at least he supposed it was his heart. How would he know? Other than Angeline, he'd never allowed the women in his life to affect him emotionally. No time to. No need to. No desire to.

His thoughts marched on. Today he'd gotten what he wanted: Lise here in his beloved Dominican retreat. For four nights. Yet in her apartment when he was trying to persuade her to come, he'd promised he wouldn't seduce her.

You're a goddamn fool. Why else did you invite her here?

Why else indeed? Gratitude, of course. But even that, deep though it went, seemed a pale force compared to his aching need to possess Lise. To make her his own in the most primitive way possible.

Lust. That's all it was. It was a long time since he'd been with a woman; and he certainly wasn't in love with her.

He'd fallen in love once, at the age of twenty-three, with Angeline. He could remember as if it were yesterday his first sight of her. He'd come out of the office tower in Manhattan where he'd been negotiating the purchase of four Boeing 737s, negotiations where he'd put his entire financial future on the line; as a result, adrenaline was racing through his veins. He'd crossed the street, glancing at the small crowd that had gathered on the sidewalk to watch a photo shoot, and then he'd seen her: an exquisite creature with a swath of straight blond hair and eyes of a midnight-blue. She was modeling a flared mink coat; diamonds blazed at her lobes and around her throat. Their eyes had met and he'd known instantly that he was going to marry her. That he wouldn't rest until he had.

Eventually they had married. But they hadn't lived happily ever after. Far from it.

Never again.

Lise stirred in her sleep. Her neck was crooked at an awkward angle; asleep, she looked both younger and more vulnerable. Less likely to bite his head off, he thought wryly. Yet wasn't her spirit one of the many things that drew her to him? Maybe tomorrow he'd see that Emmy had her supper early, and ask Lise to wear the green dress for dinner.

And then what? Leave her at the door of her room without as much as—his own words—laying a finger on her?

What had possessed him to make that promise, so easily spoken, so impossible to achieve? He was no saint, that he knew.

But for tonight, he'd better keep the promise.

He stooped and gathered Lise in his arms. She mumbled something under her breath. Then, in a way that made his heart thud in his chest, she curled into his body with a small sigh of repletion. The warmth of her cheek seared through his shirt; her fragrance drifted to his nostrils, hinting of a tangled garden filled with light-dappled flowers. And hummingbirds, he thought, remembering her T-shirt the day he'd cleaned up the spilled rice, the way it had hugged the curves of her breasts.

His face set, Judd stood up. Holding Lise in his arms, he marched across the patio and through the dining room. The bedrooms were angled to catch the trade winds; his was next to Lise's. As he pushed open the door to her room with his knee, inadvertently her elbow bumped the door frame. Her eyes jerked open, startled as a young bird's. He said quickly, "It's okay, you fell asleep and I was just—"

Her gaze had flown to the shadowed bedroom with its big bed heaped with soft pillows. She cried, "Judd, you promised!"

Swiftly he crossed the room and dumped her on the bed. "And I'm keeping that promise," he said through gritted teeth. "Don't you believe one word I say?"

Lise lurched to her feet, shoving her hands into her pockets. She'd been dreaming about Judd, the heat of his skin suffusing the dream, entwining her in its magic. And now here he was, his big body looming over hers to the soft whisper of the winds in the palm trees. Belatedly, she noticed something else: he didn't look the slightest bit interested in seducing her; he was far too angry for that.

Trying desperately to gather her wits, Lise said stiffly, "I'm sorry, I jumped to conclusions."

"You sure did."

"I've apologized, Judd."

"Next time, try giving me the benefit of the doubt."

"There won't be a next time."

Judd's breath hissed between his teeth. "Damn right there won't," he said, turned on his heel and marched across the room, shutting the door behind him with exaggerated care. Lise stood very still. She wanted to scream and yell. She wanted to pound the pillows until feathers flew all over the room. She wanted Judd in her bed.

Slowly she sank down on the mattress, her eyes wide in the darkness. The dream, she thought numbly. She was simply trying to transpose a dream into reality. Or else her judgment and coolheadedness were being destroyed by the total sense of unreality that had taken hold of her in the limo and stayed with her ever since she'd arrived in this gorgeous retreat.

Of course she wasn't going to make love to Judd. She'd made some mistakes in her life, but that would outdo them all. Big time.

Judd had made a promise to her. Now she was making one to herself. Don't make the smallest move to encourage him. Treat him like a piece of furniture if that's what it takes. But stay out of his bed and don't let him in yours.

Her fists were clenched in her pockets; she made a valiant effort to relax them. She'd be all right. Of course she would. If she could handle a whole fire station full of men, she could handle Judd Harwood. On which resolve Lise stripped to her underwear, pulled the sheets to her chin and eventually fell asleep.

At the breakfast table, which was shaded by vines hung with big, lemon-yellow blossoms, Emmy made it clear she wanted to spend the morning on the beach. "Sure," Judd said, adding easily, "bring your sunscreen, Lise, and wear a hat."

"Oh, I think I'll hang around on the patio and read."

He raised one brow. But all he said was, "The room across from my bedroom is a library—help yourself."

So Lise was settled in the same recliner when Judd and Emmy left for the beach. Judd in a pair of navy trunks took Lise's breath away; she dragged her eyes from the breadth of his tanned back, the taper of his waist, his long, tautly muscled legs. It wasn't fair, she thought wildly, burying her face in her book. No man should look that good.

But she was keeping her promise.

Unfortunately Emmy plunked herself down on the sand well within view of Lise. Which meant Lise had to watch the long curve of Judd's spine as he knelt beside Emmy building a sand castle; and then watch him cavorting in the waves with his daughter. She could have joined them. She didn't. But she did very soon throw her book down on the tiles with an exclamation of disgust, and go indoors to change into her bikini. At least she could work off some energy in the pool.

The bikini, chosen for her by Judd, comprised two scraps of yellow-flowered fabric that left very little to the imagination. Lise hauled her hair back with a ribbon, marched back outdoors and dived into the long, rectangular pool, which glittered turquoise in the sun. She began with a breaststroke that favored her sore arm, gradually working up to an overarm crawl as her muscles loosened in the warm, buoyant water. The exercise calmed her. After all, she could be back in Montreal, clinging to the fire truck as it careered through the icy streets. Anything was better than that. She darn well wasn't going to ruin this holiday just because of Judd Harwood. Or Judd Harwood's body.

Somersaulting at the near end of the pool, she pushed off, arrowing through the water with her eyes open. Then Emmy's body suddenly cannonballed into the pool in a swirl of bubbles. With a strong thrust of her left arm, Lise burst upward to the surface. Judd was in the pool, too, his slate-blue eyes laughing at her. "We're playing tag," he said. "You're it, Lise."

"I'm getting out now," she sputtered.

"Catch me if you can," Emmy yelled.

Emmy was laughing, too; she looked very different from the little girl huddled in terror in the far corner of an attic. Oh God, thought Lise, get me out of here, and swam toward the child as fast as she could. But at the last minute Emmy dove deep and suddenly Judd was beside Lise. "Bet you can't catch me," he teased.

Play it safe. Remember your promise.

Go for broke.

Lise lunged for him, but he twisted away from her, splashing water in her face. With a vengeful cry she went after him, slicing through the water, angling so she headed him toward one corner of the pool. At the last minute she dove and touched him on the knee before streaking to the very bottom of the pool. Then he was swimming alongside her, his body wavering in the rippled light. Swiftly he stroked closer and kissed her hard on the mouth; her eyes still wide-open, she watched him rise to the surface.

Badly out of breath, Lise pushed off from the bottom, gulping in mouthfuls of air when she reached the surface. In a flurry of spray she set off in pursuit of Emmy. Even under eight feet of water, she'd loved being kissed by Judd. Technically, of course, he still hadn't broken his promise. He'd only touched her with his lips. Not with his fingers.

Twenty minutes later all three of them climbed out of

the pool. Lise said breathlessly, "That was fun—you're a good swimmer, Emmy."

Emmy gave Lise one of her level looks. "Dad taught me," she replied and reached for her towel.

It wasn't so much what Emmy said, Lise thought ruefully, but how she said it: as though she were closing a door in your face. Judd said casually, "Here, have a towel."

Water was trickling down his chest, his body hair slick to his skin. The curve of his rib cage, the hollow at the base of his throat, his narrow hips: he entranced her, Lise thought helplessly, grabbed for the towel and buried her face in it. Stay away from him. Ignore him. Pretend he's a chair by the side of the pool.

What a laugh.

Sally, who ran the kitchen, had put glasses of guava juice and a plate of roti and sliced pineapple on the teak table that was shaded by a huge beach umbrella near the pool house; further shade was cast by tulip trees and palms. Lise hauled the yellow coverup over her head and sat down, discovering that she was ravenous and that her shoulder felt not too bad at all. Judd told a couple of very amusing stories about flights he'd monitored in the early days of his airline company; not to be outdone, Lise described some of the trees she'd climbed to rescue cats who hadn't wanted rescuing. And all the while she was aware of Judd watching her, of his eyes on her shoulders, her breasts, her thighs. He was very discreet; Emmy, she was sure, had no inkling of what he was doing. But she, Lise, knew. She felt as though he were undressing her. As though his eyes were stroking her as tangibly as his long, lean fingers would explore her flesh.

He wasn't laying a finger on her. Yet she felt seduced.

She ate the last crumb of roti on her plate and finished

her juice. Then she said brightly, "I'm going to have a nap. See you both later."

"Sleep well," Judd said blandly.

Lise hurried across the tiles in what was unquestionably a retreat. She showered in her luxuriously appointed bathroom, dried her hair, then lay down on the bed, wearing one of the two nightgowns Judd had chosen. Silk, again, sensual as a caress. Certain she was too keyed up to sleep, Lise closed her eyes; and opened them to the low slant of sunlight through the louvered windows.

She'd slept for nearly five hours. Quickly she got up, dressing in the same pants and top she'd worn last night; they covered her more completely than any of the other garments Judd had chosen. Then she ventured out into the hallway. Emmy and Judd were sitting on the patio, playing checkers, and for a moment she observed them from the shadows. There was an ease between them, she thought painfully. A connection that was very real. Judd, in other words, was a good father.

This didn't fit Angeline's description of him as an absentee father who had snatched his daughter away from her mother from motives of revenge and control. Or had Angeline simply implied all that, and Lise herself had filled in the gaps?

He couldn't fake being a good father. Certainly not with a child as astute as Emmy. Lise backed further into the shadows, then fled toward the library with its polished rosewood shelving, where she curled up in a deliciously comfortable bamboo chair and did her best to concentrate on the words on the page. She felt both lonely—or was excluded a more accurate word?—and frightened. She didn't like either emotion.

Half an hour later, Judd came looking for her. Dressed in cotton shorts and a T-shirt, his hair ruffled, he stationed himself in the doorway. "What's up, Lise?" he said roughly. "What—or who—are you hiding from?"

"I'm not hiding! I'm reading."

"Dinner's ready."

"Fine. I'll be right along."

"Don't wait for me, in other words," he said with dangerous quietness.

"I need to brush my hair, put on some lipstick."

"You don't need either one—you're one hundred percent gorgeous just as you are."

Lise stood up, smiling in spite of herself. "You can stroke my ego anytime you like."

"Don't you *know* how beautiful you are?"

"Angeline's beautiful. I'm average."

Judd ran his fingers through his hair. "Who told you that?"

"Marthe. Over and over again, while I was growing up."

Judd said a very rude word under his breath. "Do something for me, will you? Repeat five times a day, *I'm a beautiful woman. Judd says so.* Got it?"

"But I'm not sophisticated! Or elegant."

"You're real," he said.

Lise swallowed hard. He meant it. Temporarily speechless, her throat tight, she heard him add, "There's something else. You slept for five hours this afternoon—you're exhausted, aren't you?"

"I'm not used to the heat."

He gave her a scathing look. "Give me a break. You're worn-out, you think I can't see that? So I've got a proposition for you. We'll talk about it this evening after Emmy's in bed."

"No proposition you can mention could possibly interest me and you sure are good at giving orders."

"I didn't get where I am by letting people walk all over me. So don't try it."

Her temper rising, Lise said, "I'll do what I damn well please."

"You're pushing your luck, sweetheart."

"Don't call me that!"

"I don't mean it literally—trust me."

She didn't know which was worse, his high-handedness or his sarcasm. In a voice smooth as cream, she said, "You did mention dinner, didn't you?"

"I pity the guys who have to share the fire truck with you," Judd said pithily.

Brushing the petals of the bronze lilies in a bowl on the table, an involuntary smile curving her mouth, Lise said, "Fire truck—what fire truck? It all seems a million miles away."

"Good," said Judd. "Then I've achieved something at least."

Lise bit her lip. "I'm really grateful to be here, Judd, please don't misunderstand me. And yes, I'm tired. But it's more than that. I don't want to get involved with you—even assuming you were willing, which I doubt. My life and yours are miles apart, and that's the way they've got to stay. So if I'm keeping a certain distance between us, I'm acting out of self-preservation, that's all."

He stepped nearer. "You speak your mind, don't you?"

"Saves trouble in the long run."

"You sure are different from any other woman I've ever met. And yes, I'm including Angeline," Judd said with suppressed violence.

He was standing so close she could see the dark curl of his lashes, and the curved line of his lower lip, so cleanly sculpted, so infinitely desirable. She wanted to run her fingertip along it. As her heart rate quickened, Judd grated, "I have no idea why I made that ridiculous promise."

"I made one, too. If it's any help," she said with a faint grin. "To keep my hands off you."

Twin devils danced in his eyes. "Did you indeed? But by mutual agreement promises can be broken."

"No, they can't! We're totally wrong for each other and I've never indulged in casual sex."

"Casual wasn't exactly what I had in mind," Judd responded. "And now, since Sally the cook is almost as quick-tempered as you, we'd better head for the dining room."

That was something else she'd noticed in the last twenty-four hours: the mutual respect between Judd and his employees. "You're very good with your staff," she said reluctantly.

"I'm not an ogre!"

Just the sexiest man I've ever laid eyes on. But fortunately Lise hadn't said that. Walking around him, she headed for the dining room.

After dinner Judd put Emmy to bed; then he and Lise played chess out on the patio. At five minutes after midnight, he said, lightly, "Checkmate."

"Ouch," said Lise, "I should have blocked your bishop two moves ago."

"You play well."

"Stephan taught me—one of my buddies on the night shift. It's a good way to stay awake." She gave him a limpid smile. "As I'm not on the night shift now, I'm going to bed. Good night."

As she pushed back her chair, he got up. "You notice I haven't mentioned my proposition," he said lazily. "I've decided to save it for later."

"Good for you," she responded amiably. "Saves us having another fight...I'm all for that."

"There's more than one way to avert a fight." His hands at his sides, Judd leaned forward and kissed her full on the mouth, a leisurely kiss of devastating intimacy. His tongue traced her lips; then he moved to her cheekbones, her closed lids, the long line of her throat. From a long way away Lise heard him murmur her name.

She felt boneless, weightless, ravaged by hunger, yet fed as she'd never been fed before. Nor had he laid a finger upon her. Frantically Lise drew back, her eyes like dark pools under the tropic sky. "No, Judd, please..."

"Just kissing you good night."

Her nipples were thrusting against her silk shirt; her whole body felt on fire. "Don't play games with me," she begged. "I'm not in your league, don't you see?"

"I kissed you because I wanted to. And you stayed because you wanted to. Admit it, Lise."

His eyes seemed to drill their way through her skull. "Wanted?" she cried. "I had no choice!"

With a whimper of pure distress, she whirled and ran for her room. She shut the door and jammed a fragile rattan chair under the handle, a ruse that couldn't possibly keep Judd out were he determined to enter, but which made her feel minimally better. One kiss and she was a basket case, she thought despairingly. Never in her life had she responded to a man the way she did with Judd.

She now understood why she'd never gone to bed with Dave. But years ago, when she was new at the job, she'd fallen in love with a firefighter from another district in Montreal, and had had a short-lived affair with him. The sex hadn't been great, even to someone of her very limited experience; and the ending of the affair, when he'd discovered that her address in Outremont didn't mean that she had old family money, could have been farcical if it hadn't been both humiliating and hurtful.

In the years that followed, the men she occasionally dated always got discouraged, sooner or later, by her dedication to a demanding and dangerous job with irregular hours. That was fine by her; her affair had destroyed something in her, a quality of trust that wasn't easily reestablished.

It was still fine by her, she thought fiercely. Meeting Judd hadn't changed anything. On which not entirely truthful conclusion, Lise managed to get to sleep.

The next day Lise, Judd and Emmy took off for the day, buying some lovely Carib baskets in Roseau, Dominica's charming capital, then walking to Trafalgar Falls, where they swam in the pool at its foot. They were home in time for dinner; Lise went to bed early. No chess game. No kisses under a velvet sky. No proposition. Whatever that meant.

Their final day, they hiked into the national park in the northern sector of the island. Lise loved the rain forest, so entangled, so deeply green, so shadowed by the huge buttressed chataignier trees. It smelled damp and fecund, and the small brightly colored birds that flickered through its branches entranced her.

Judd carried Emmy on his shoulders a lot of the way; Emmy, Lise knew, had not had a single nightmare since they'd arrived on the island. If Angeline had been wrong about Judd's capabilities as a father, had she also misled Lise about other facets of his life?

This was a new thought for Lise. She'd learned something else as well: that Judd could keep a promise. He had indeed not laid a finger on her the last two days. In fact, he'd withdrawn today in a way she could scarcely pinpoint yet knew to be real. She should have been relieved. She wasn't. Rather, his casual manner toward her made her intensely irritable. Perhaps he'd decided she wasn't worth the trouble. After all, the world must be full of women who'd fall into bed with him at the slightest encouragement.

One thing was clear, though: Judd had made her a promise and he'd kept it.

For whatever the reason.

When they got back to the villa, Emmy was packed off to bed with supper on a tray. Although she'd been nothing but polite to Lise the last three days, a few times Lise had caught the little girl simply staring at her, as though trying to fathom her; yet Lise felt no closer to her than she had when they'd set out. What had Judd told Emmy about the custody battle? Maybe he'd implied that Angeline didn't want her own daughter; which would explain Emmy's hesitancy to trust another woman. Or maybe, Lise thought more cynically, there'd been so many women in Judd's life that Emmy no longer bothered.

Her last dinner on the island. Tomorrow they were flying back to Montreal, to winter and normality, to her next shift at the fire station. Her bruises had faded beneath her carefully acquired tan; she was fit enough to go back to work. A prospect that gave her very little joy.

She opened her closet door. The jade-green dress was hanging there; she had yet to wear it. Smoothing the fabric with her fingers, she laid the dress on the bed, then spent the better part of five minutes staring at it in much the same way that Emmy had stared at her. Judd buying this dress had brought Lise to his villa. So was she going to leave without wearing it? Was she going to opt for the safe cream trousers and yellow shirt once again?

Was she a woman or a mouse?

Lise rummaged in her own suitcase for her prettiest underwear and her gold sandals. Then she made up her face with care, painted her toenails and fastened gold hoops to her earlobes. Finally she eased her body into the jade silk, linking its gold chain link belt around her waist.

The mirror showed her a stranger, a lissome creature with a cloud of red curls, whose eyes reflected the glorious hue of a garment that clung at hip and waist and breast. She looked sensual. Voluptuous. Available. Oh, no, thought Lise, I can't wear this.

A tap came at her door. "Dinner is served, missie."

It was Sally's assistant, who came from Roseau. "I'll be right there, Melanie," Lise called, closing her eyes in panic. How could Judd construe her appearance as anything other than the most blatant of invitations? Yet intuitively he'd chosen for her an outfit she'd longed—hopelessly—to possess.

Dammit, she was going to wear it. Even if walking into the dining room would require more courage than facing a three-alarm blaze. Squaring her shoulders, Lise left her room.

CHAPTER SIX

JUDD was gazing out at the darkened beach over the ledge of orchids in the dining room; because there was a local festival in town that evening, Sally and her assistant had the rest of the night off, and dinner had been served buffet-style on the vast mahogany sideboard. Emmy was already asleep. Perfect timing for seduction, he thought savagely. A seduction that wasn't going to happen. All he had to do was keep that goddamned promise for one more night and then he'd be home free.

Out of sight, out of mind? Would that work where Lise was concerned? He wasn't so sure. But it was worth a try.

What other option did he have?

A whisper of footsteps crossed the tiled floor. Alerted to Lise's presence, Judd turned around; his smile of welcome froze to his lips. For the space of five seconds he was struck dumb. Then he walked around the corner of the table, stopping only a few inches away from her and letting his gaze wander over her from head to foot. Her bare, rounded arms and creamy throat. The jut of her breasts and gentle indentation of her waist, clasped in gold. The smooth swell of her hips. Only when his eyes came back to her face did he realize that she was panic-stricken, the pulse fluttering at the base of her throat, and her spine rigid. Her expression that of a woman who knows she should be anywhere but where she was.

Clearing his throat, he said huskily, "To tell you you're beautiful is meaningless. Yet what else can I tell you? I— hell, Lise, I don't know what to say."

To his horror he saw that tears were glittering in her

eyes. Her temper he rather relished; her tears pierced all his defences. Because she'd told him she never cried? Craving to put his arms around her from the simple need to comfort her, knowing that if he did so he would have broken his promise, Judd stood still, his arms taut at his sides. He'd made that promise with very little thought for the consequences and as a means of getting Lise here to his villa: a manipulative promise, he thought stringently. But somehow over the last few days it had come to mean something. He had to keep it. For her sake and for his. And what the devil that meant, he didn't know. Didn't even want to know.

Lise was watching him, her face as unreadable as Emmy's. Then she drew a deep breath and reached out, taking his right hand in hers and very deliberately bringing it to rest on her shoulder. She said unsteadily, "All four fingers on me. How about that?"

His heart was pounding in his chest like a drum. Lise was releasing him from his promise...what else could her gesture mean? Judd said hoarsely, "Lise, I—are you sure?"

"No. Maybe. Oh God, I don't know."

As always, her honesty knocked him off balance. Angeline, so he'd come to understand, had never lied to him wittingly; she'd simply adjusted the truth to suit her needs in the moment. At first, very much in love, he'd made allowances for this. Later, as the months and years passed, he'd lost the ability to trust her; and had come to realize that trust was the essential foundation for love.

He said clumsily, "You always tell the truth, Lise, don't you? You blurt it out. You throw it in my face. Or you simply say it. Because that's how you live your life."

She didn't pretend to misunderstand him. "Not much room for lies when you're searching for a child who's lost in smoke and flames."

He flinched. Then, in a voice he scarcely recognized as his own, he asked the obvious. "Why did you put my hand on your shoulder?"

"Why did I wear this dress?"

"Two unanswerable questions?"

"You kept your promise—don't think I didn't notice. That's got something to do with it."

"Yeah…that crazy promise came to mean something. Something important."

Briefly she looked terrified out of her wits; he could feel her shrinking from him beneath his fingertips. "I could always plead temporary insanity," she faltered. "Maybe that's the only reason that makes any sense."

With a muffled groan Judd took her in his arms, and was instantly and achingly aware of the slenderness of her waist and the warmth of her hips, of the way her breasts brushed his shirtfront. He wanted with all the impulsions of his sexuality to make love to her as she'd never been made love to before. To ravish her, delight her, give her the most intense pleasure he was capable of. Don't, Judd, he thought ferociously. Don't go there! She's starting to trust you because you've kept a promise. Don't blow it. Not now. She deserves better than that.

Pulling back, he said roughly, "Lise, we'd better eat."

He felt her sudden stillness; she was staring at his shirt as if she'd never seen a row of buttons before. With careful politeness, she said, "Yes. You're right. Of course."

"If we don't," he said, "you know what's going to happen?"

This time a shiver ran through her. "Yes," she said in a low voice.

The emotion Judd felt now was undoubtedly tenderness. For him a totally new emotion, one that not even Angeline in those early days—and nights—had called up. There'd always been something detached about Angeline, a portion of herself kept firmly to herself; only later had he wondered if that had been part of her fascination for him: that he could never quite reach her core, no matter how hard he tried.

Run, he thought. Run for your life, buddy. Because if you make love to this red-haired woman, you'll never be the same again. You know that. And maybe she knows it, too. You don't want that kind of involvement. You swore off it years ago.

He moved away from her so that her hand fell to her side and said with a lightness that sounded almost genuine, "Sally will have my hide if we don't make at least an inroad into the food she's prepared. You haven't seen Sally on the warpath—not much puts the fear of God in me, but she sure does."

"Do I scare you, Judd?" Lise asked.

Of all the questions she could have asked, she'd chosen the one that was the most impossible to answer. He'd given enough away already by keeping that stupid promise. That's all you're getting, Lise Charbonneau, Judd thought. No more involvement. No, ma'am. Definitely not part of my game plan. He said coolly, "Other than Sally, I don't let women scare me."

Her lashes flickered. Then she lifted her chin; her courage stabbed him to the heart. "I get the message," she said. "So what's for dinner? And did Emmy go to sleep all right? She hasn't had any nightmares at all, has she? It was a good idea to bring her here, it's easy to see how much she loves the place. Not that I'm surprised, it's so beautiful."

Lise wasn't normally a chatty woman; her ability to be comfortable with silence was something else he'd noticed about her. He'd noticed a lot, Judd thought grimly, and said, "Cold pumpkin soup. A conch salad, plantain, curried shrimp, Creole pork chops...want me to go on?"

"Sounds wonderful," Lise said, with a smile that didn't quite reach her eyes.

The next hour Judd would long remember as one of the most excruciating in his life. He and Lise were painstakingly polite to each other, each talked at length about totally impersonal subjects, and they ate as though appeasing Sally were all that mattered. But finally they'd finished the sliced mangoes cooked in a ginger syrup, and had drained delicate china demitasses of coffee. Lise said with an artificial yawn, "I think I'll say good night, Judd, we have a long day ahead of us tomorrow."

"Sleep well," he said with just the right touch of detachment, and watched her leave the room. A few moments later he heard the decisive click of her bedroom door. Only then did he let his breath out in a long sigh.

You're a fool, Judd Harwood. You had your chance and you blew it. You could have bedded her. Gotten her out of your system.

A little voice sneered in his head, You figure one night with Lise would cure whatever's wrong with you? Now that really does make you a fool.

Come off it. She's just a woman. And I'm not in love with her, nowhere near.

You want me to list all her attributes? Starting with courage and ending with passion?

Oh, shut up, Judd thought irritably, and got up from the table. He carried the uneaten food back to the kitchen, storing it in the refrigerator; he blew out the candles; he checked on Emmy, who was sprawled across her bed fast asleep. There was no sound from Lise's room. Cursing himself, Judd went to his own room, had a shower that he tapered off to cold, with no noticeable effect, and pulled on the briefs that were all he wore to bed. Then he gathered a stack of articles he'd been meaning to read for the last two weeks, and tried to concentrate.

Angeline had never slept in this bed. She'd wanted the trendy islands where the jet set gathered, where there were casinos and nightclubs. Not peaceful Dominica with its dark sands and sleepy little capital. The only woman he'd ever brought here was Lise.

He wasn't going to think about Lise. Tomorrow he'd drop her off at her apartment and that would be that. Luckily Emmy had kept her guard up; he didn't need that further complication. His jaw tight, Judd picked up a pen and started jotting down notes.

Two hours later, he'd managed to whip up a half-decent level of concentration on an article about rising jet fuel costs. His brow furrowed, he quickly numbered the main points of the argument. Then a sudden, bitten-off cry of terror ripped the peaceful night air; his pen skidded on the page and he raised his head, like an animal sensing danger.

Emmy. Another nightmare.

Not bothering to pull on any clothes, Judd was out of bed in one quick movement and was running down the hallway. But as he flung open his daughter's door, he saw that Emmy was peacefully asleep, her arm thrown over Plush.

It hadn't been Emmy who'd screamed. So it must have been Lise.

He didn't bother tapping on Lise's door. Shoving it open, hearing it swing shut behind him, Judd said urgently, "Lise—what's wrong?"

Her voice quavered across the room. "S-something landed on the b-bed."

As he switched on the light, the biggest lizard he'd ever seen scurried across the bedclothes to the floor and vanished under the bed. With a gasp of horror, Lise cowered against the head of the bed. Judd sat down on the bed and started to laugh.

Shuddering, she sputtered, "It ran across my f-face and

woke me up—shut up, Judd, it's not the slightest bit funny!''

He laughed all the harder. ''You can enter burning buildings and deal with car wrecks, and a lizard makes you scream? Oh Lise, I've found your feet of clay.''

''You try it! Claws clinging to your cheeks and it's so damn dark you can't see your fingers in front of your face—Judd, will you please stop laughing?''

She was sitting up straight now, the covers around her waist, her hair a wild tangle around her furious face. He said, ''They get in through the louvers. If it's any comfort, the lizard was probably much more scared than you.''

''It's no comfort whatsoever.''

And suddenly Judd became aware that he was sitting on Lise's bed clad in nothing but a pair of briefs; and even more aware of the creamy rise and fall of her breasts in her silk nightgown. When he'd purchased it, he'd pictured it clinging to her body in all the right places. It clung all right, he thought, his mouth dry; and did what he'd been craving to do ever since he'd first seen Lise lying semiconscious in a hospital bed in Montreal. Leaning forward, he took her by the shoulders, his fingers clasping her warm skin with acute pleasure. Then he kissed her upturned face, exposing all his fierce hunger for her. It was a kiss that seemed to go on forever. A kiss, he thought dimly, that she was more than returning.

Her arms were around his neck; her breasts were pressed to his bare chest. In passionate gratitude he felt her open to the thrust of his tongue, her own tongue playing with his with an eroticism that made his head swim. Lise wanted him. Wanted him as badly as he wanted her.

Had he ever doubted that?

Judd buried his hands in the silky mass of her hair, his lips sweeping the curve of her cheekbones; as he did so, the fragrance of her skin filled his nostrils. He pushed

down the thin straps of her gown, kissing her collarbone
and the gentle hollow of her throat. Then he found the firm
rise of her breast; his heart thudding against his rib cage,
Judd cupped its weight, teasing her nipple to hardness. Lise
moaned his name, her palms splayed against his chest, her
fingers playing with his body hair in a way that inflamed
him. He kissed her again, straining her to him, knowing
there was nowhere on earth he would rather be than in
Lise's bed. With Lise.

Her gown fell to her waist. He dropped his head to the
sweet valley between her breasts, kissing first one ivory
curve of flesh, then the other, feeling her fingers in his
hair, tracing the hard lines of his skull. Raw need overcoming all caution, he pushed back the covers, twisting to
lie down and drawing her down beside him. "Take off
your gown, Lise—I want you naked."

With only a trace of shyness, she pulled the blue silk
over her head and threw it to one side. Judd pushed up on
one elbow, drinking in the soft arc of her waist and swell
of hip, the darker tangle of hair at the juncture of her
thighs, the slender length of each leg all the way to the
arch of her instep. He was not a man normally at a loss
for words. "Lise, you're exquisite," he said huskily.

She said, scarlet-cheeked, "No fair, Judd—you're still
dressed. Sort of."

He was also fully aroused, as she must be aware. He
yanked off his briefs, tossing them to the floor. "Come
here," he said; and then for the space of several minutes
said nothing else. His intent silence was broken only by
Lise's small gasps of delight, gasps that turned to broken
cries as he found the wet pink petals of flesh between her
thighs, teasing them open, stroking them with nothing but
an impassioned desire to bring her as much pleasure as he
could.

She threw back her head, writhing beneath his touch,

whimpering his name over and over again; as the tension gathered in her body, she held onto him with all her strength, her green eyes drowning in sensation. Then suddenly she was overwhelmed by the inexorable rhythms of release, her cries echoing in his ears as he held her close. The frantic hammering of her heart was as his own. Feeling as though he held the whole world in his arms, Judd murmured, "Lise…Lise, you're so incredibly beautiful."

Her face was pushed into his shoulder. "I—I never knew it could be so sudden. So powerful."

"And it's not over yet," he said, running his hand down the long curve of her back and drawing her closer to his erection. "We've only just begun."

She looked up, her irises shining like emeralds, laughter sparking their depths. "So I see," she said, and gave a sudden thrust of her hips toward him.

He gasped with pleasure. Then he felt her fingers encircle him, stroking the taut length of his penis. As his face convulsed, he muttered, "Keep that up and you're in trouble."

"Another promise?" she said hopefully.

"Yeah, it's a promise," he growled. "And I'm going to keep it. Kiss me, Lise."

She offered her lips with a generosity that touched him to the core. Then, infinitely seductive, she moved down his body, tasting his skin, laving his nipples with her tongue, and tracing the hard angle of one hipbone. "I love your body," she whispered, taking him in her hands again and caressing him until Judd wondered if he could die of pleasure.

Before he could lose control, he lifted her to straddle him. She slid over him, enclosing him in wetness and heat. In intimacy, he thought, pulling strands of her vivid hair to lie over the tilt of her breasts, and watching the play of expressions on her face. She was hiding nothing, he knew that. And would not have wanted it otherwise.

She rode him with fierce concentration, her knees braced on either side of his body, her breasts gently bouncing. He took her by the waist, loving the smoothness of her skin and her agility, aware through every nerve ending of the primitive building of impulsions older than time.

He wanted her closer, her face so near that he could see every change of expression. Holding her so that he stayed locked within her, Judd pulled her down, rolling over so that she was on her back and he covering her body with his own. He could lose himself in the green depths of her eyes, he thought. Lose himself and find himself? Find a man he scarcely knew? He said impetuously, "Hold me, Lise. Move with me."

"Oh, Judd..." she whispered, her irises deep pools of tenderness as she brushed her breasts against his body hair, back and forth with a delicious sensuality that spiked his hunger for her until it was all-consuming.

He thrust deep inside her, aware with every fiber of his being of her involuntary response. "Tell me you want me," he demanded. "Tell me, Lise."

She locked her arms around his waist and kissed him with passionate intensity, nibbling at his lips as she whispered, "I want you more than I can say. I want—oh, Judd, now. Please, now."

He was more than ready. Seized by his body's primitive rhythms, yet never so swept up that he lost sight of her face drowned in rapture, Judd cried out her name, again and again. Then, to his infinite gratification, he sensed her own pulsations, echoing his own: and heard her cries mingle with his. Fused, drained, at one with her with a completion that was unlike any union he'd ever known, Judd emptied within her. And wondered if he would ever be entirely separate from her again.

His forehead fell to her shoulder. His throat heaving, his heart trying to force its way out of his chest, he clung to her as if he were the one who was drowning. She said softly, "Judd, are you all right?"

And how was he supposed to answer that, when a love-making he hadn't planned had taken him to a place he'd never been before? "Complicated question," he muttered. "You sure know how to ask 'em."

"Yes or no will do," she murmured.

Alerted by something in her voice, Judd looked up. "My turn. Are you okay?"

"I feel—" Lise hesitated, then added in a rush, "I feel almost as though I was a virgin, someone who'd never made love before…I guess there aren't any words, Judd." With one hand, she smoothed the hair back from his sweat-damp forehead; and with a sudden tightness in his chest, he saw that her fingers were trembling.

He took her hand in his, kissing the backs of her knuckles. "Let's not try for words, then."

He drew her down to his shoulder, and closed his eyes; slowly the tumult in his body subsided and he became aware of himself again as a separate entity. As a man who definitely didn't want to try for words. After all, didn't that suit him right down to the ground? He didn't want to say things in the heat of the moment that he'd then be required to live up to. Women always took what you said to the bank. He didn't want commitment. Ever again. Freedom was the name of the game. Independence. It was the way he'd lived his life ever since his divorce, and just because a woman with hair like flame and a body that ravished all his senses had burst into his life didn't mean he had to change anything.

All the more reason not to change.

Burying his face in her throat, Judd said, "You're one heck of a woman, Lise Charbonneau."

There was the smallest of pauses before she said pertly, "Why, thank you. You're quite the guy yourself."

"I'm going to set up a one-man society for the preservation of lizards."

As he'd hoped, this made her laugh. "Yuk," she said.

He wrapped his arms around her and discovered something else: that he still wanted her. That there were a myriad ways of making love to her he hadn't tried yet, and even the thought of them turned him on. Get her out of his system? Who was he kidding? Maybe the lizard hadn't done him a favor after all, Judd thought grimly. If he'd had any smarts, he'd have stuck to his promise.

"What are you thinking?" Lise whispered.

Her face was clouded with uncertainty in a way that hurt Judd deep inside. To hell with caution, he thought. Right now her happiness was more important than a few niggling doubts. And why should he be so afraid of commitment? The word hadn't even been mentioned between him and Lise. Besides, hadn't he always taken what he wanted? "Can't you tell what I'm thinking?" he asked, easing a little closer to her. "Although I'm not sure my thought processes have much to do with it. Are you interested in a repeat?"

Her chuckle was full of mischief. "I suspect I could be persuaded."

"Good," said Judd, and set about to do just that, using all his skills of imagination and empathy.

The thing he hadn't quite counted on was how Lise met him more than halfway, with a generosity and abandon that aroused him to a fever pitch. Images of her spilled through his brain: the fullness of her breasts, swollen from his kisses; the tightness of her thighs, wrapped around him; the long curve of her spine, the wonderment in her emerald eyes as he caressed every inch of her body, committing it to memory in spite of his own best intentions. She was

his, all his and only his, was his last thought before she
tumbled into the abyss of release, pulling him with her
every step of the way.

Overwhelmed by the sheer physicality of sensation,
aware of being flooded by an uncomfortable blend of tenderness, protectiveness and terror, Judd held her close, and
with a distant part of his brain wondered how he was going
to say goodbye to her tomorrow. Goodbye? More like
hello, he thought with another of those surges of fear. How
often did a man and woman mate with such total involvement? Such a blissful satiation of needs and desires?

He had to get of here.

But Lise's head was resting on his chest, her hair tumbling over his rib cage in glorious abandon. Against his
belly he could feel the racing of her heart; her breath
wafted his skin. So what was he going to do? Tell her he
was leaving right now because he was frightened out of
his wits? He was a grown man, for God's sake. Men
weren't supposed to be scared of women. Anyway, it took
a lot to scare him.

Judd lay still and imperceptibly felt her breathing slip
into the rhythms of sleep. So the choice was made: he had
to stay. For now.

Was he going to say goodbye tomorrow? Is that what
he wanted? If he were smart, that's what he'd do. He
wasn't into commitment. Whereas Lise, he suspected, was
the kind of woman to play for keeps.

Deadlock.

Did he want to hurt her? Surely not. Or was it already
too late? So should he hurt her now, rather than later?

How was he going to drop her off at her apartment door
and go home to his celibate life as if last night had never
happened? This was the payoff for breaking promises,
Judd thought caustically. And suddenly remembered his
proposition, the one he hadn't yet broached to her. In the-

ory, it was for Emmy's benefit. But in practice, it would certainly affect him.

With aching clarity he remembered something else: how ardently and trustingly Lise had opened to him, offering him unstintingly all the gifts of her body. Was he going to throw them back in her face? He gave an impatient sigh. He was known throughout the business world for making momentous decisions with the rapidity of gunfire; yet when it came to Lise, he felt immobilized by doubts and second thoughts and then still more doubts.

Keep your proposition to yourself, Judd Harwood. Goodbye is just a two-syllable word.

CHAPTER SEVEN

LISE woke to the soft cooing of doves in the jacaranda trees outside her room. Automatically she reached for Judd; but found only tangled sheets and a pillow. Her eyes flew open. She was alone, she thought in confusion. Alone and naked in her own bed.

Her skin smelled of his, her body suffused with a delicious languor; she hadn't dreamed their lovemaking. It had been real, wondrously and heart-wrenchingly real.

Where was he?

Emmy. Of course he couldn't stay in bed with Lise and risk his daughter finding them there together. But couldn't he have woken her before he left? Held her close and kissed her before leaving her alone?

Her nightgown was still lying on the floor, startlingly blue against the pale tile; and a hundred memories flooded Lise's mind. She'd had to travel all the way to a small tropical island to learn how powerful and utterly beautiful the act of love could be. And it had taken Judd to teach her.

As if a lizard's claws had scraped her face, Lise was suddenly visited by a paralyzing insight. Why wouldn't Judd be more than competent in bed? He was experienced. He'd had wealthy and sophisticated lovers who traveled in the same world as he. She, Lise, must have seemed impossibly naïve and inept.

What had Angeline said to her once in the back garden in Outremont, on one of her rare visits home after her marriage? "Of course, women throw themselves at him all the time. You can't really blame him for taking what's offered—he's only human, after all.''

At the time, Lise had concluded Angeline was being far too forgiving. Now she felt a blush of shame rush from her chin to her forehead. Last night she, Lise, had offered herself to Judd. He'd had the grace and the forbearance to refuse. But later, in her bed, he'd taken advantage of what she'd so freely made available. And who, indeed, could blame him?

Last night she'd become one in a string of women. She'd cheapened herself in her own eyes, let alone in his. How could she have done that? If she hadn't kissed him so fervently when he'd sat on her bed, if she hadn't fallen into his arms with the ease of a wave curling onto the beach, he'd have left her alone. Kept his promise.

She couldn't stand her own thoughts. Lise jumped out of bed, tossed her nightgown under the pillow and hurried into the bathroom, where she turned on the hot water full force in the shower, and scrubbed herself vigorously with lilac-scented soap to remove every trace of Judd from her skin.

But how was she going to erase him from her memory? Her senses? How to forget the feel of him, the huskiness in his voice when he'd told her how beautiful she was, the laughter and passion and delight he'd brought to her bed?

She would forget him. Eventually. She had to.

Dressing quickly in a bright cotton skirt and peasant blouse that she hadn't worn yet, Lise opened her door and stepped out into the sunlit hallway. If she hesitated, she was lost. Fixing a smile to her lips, she walked into the dining room. "Good morning, Judd...where's Emmy?" she said casually. "Oh good, more papaya. And aren't those fresh croissants?" Her back to him, she poured herself a cup of coffee.

"Emmy's on the beach with Sally and her husband," Judd said. "How did you sleep?"

He sounded so damn sure of himself. So cool, so detached. As if he'd never been within ten feet of her bed. Lise turned around, her face set. "When did you leave my room?"

"Around five. I didn't know what time Emmy might wake."

"We should never have—"

"We did, Lise," he said with menacing softness. "The question is, what do we do now?"

"You take me home. We say goodbye."

"Just like that?"

"What else do you suggest?"

He hesitated fractionally. Then he said in a clipped voice, "A few days ago I mentioned a proposition I had for you."

"You put it into action last night," she said nastily.

"Don't, Lise. Don't cheapen what happened between us."

She put down her fork. "So what did happen, Judd?"

"We made love. Twice." His jaw hardened. "For me it was an unforgettable experience."

"Just like all your other unforgettable experiences."

His eyes flashed as though sunlight had glanced across a knife blade; instinctively she shrank from him. "You're determined to think the worst of me."

"And the worst of myself," she said bitterly.

"Are you saying you regret what happened?"

"Of course!"

"I don't believe you! I was with you, I held you and kissed you and heard you cry out my name—you were being most truly yourself with me. How can you possibly regret that?"

"It was a one-night stand," she cried. "I've never done that before—and I never will again."

Restlessly Judd moved his shoulders. She wasn't telling him anything he didn't already know: that she was a woman of principle. Okay, Judd. Decision time. If you keep your mouth shut, last night stays as a one-night stand, and you don't try to see her again. Ever. Or else you can take a gamble. A huge gamble, because it involves Emmy.

He needed his head read.

Emmy needs Lise.

The three short words replayed themselves in his mind; and Judd knew them for the truth. Not giving himself time to retreat from them, he said flatly, "Why don't you hear me out? About this proposition, I mean." He took a deep breath, feeling his tension level move up another notch. "I'd like you to take a position in my house as Emmy's companion. You'd get her off to school in the mornings, be with her when she comes home, stay with her when I'm away or if she's sick. Your weekends would be free whenever I'm home. But obviously I'd expect you to quit your job at the fire station." He then mentioned a rate of pay that made Lise blink.

She said the first thing that came into her head. "Do you always try to buy people?"

"I'm talking about hiring you. Not buying you."

"And where would I sleep?"

He said with careful restraint, "Once the repairs are finished, you'd have your own suite of rooms off the main wing."

"And in the meantime?"

"We'd all be in the guest wing."

So angry she no longer cared what she said, Lise fumed, "So for an amount of money that, as you must know, is a fortune to me but peanuts to you, you'd be getting a mistress and a nanny all in one? You'll forgive me, I'm sure, if I refuse.''

He stood up, his hands jammed in his pockets. ''You persist in distorting everything I say. You're the one who made a play for me before dinner last night—or are you conveniently forgetting that? And if you didn't enjoy yourself in bed with me, you should quit being a firefighter and become an actress, you'd make a fortune. Listen to reason for a minute. If you lived in my house, you and Emmy could get to know each other better. You wouldn't be so tired. Nor would you be putting your life at risk every day the way you do now.''

Oh, wouldn't I? she thought crazily. Shows what you know, Judd Harwood.

She could have told him she was desperate to quit her job; had been for weeks. She didn't. ''The answer's no,'' she said in a stony voice.

''I am not hiring you as my mistress, as you so charmingly put it.''

''You're not hiring me for anything!''

''You've got to be the most stubborn and contrary woman on the face of this earth,'' Judd grated. ''You'd be good for Emmy, Lise, I know you would.''

''Emmy doesn't even like me.''

''She would. Given time.''

Lise said furiously, ''I'm not going to be the one who salves your conscience so you can travel to all the trendy resorts and society parties and neglect your own child.''

''Is that another direct quote from my ex-wife? Seems to me both of you conveniently manage to forget that I have a job, which requires a fair bit of travel. And which happens, of course, to have paid for this trip.''

Her lips set mutinously. ''So after last night, how much do I owe you?''

He took her by the shoulders, his jaw a tight line. ''A

remark like that is what cheapens you. Not anything you did in bed with me last night, Lise.''

He was right. Of course. Her body slumping in his hold, Lise said with the kind of honesty that only desperation brings, ''Judd, I was a fool to come here. And even more of a fool to wear that dress last night. I'm sorry I made a play for you, I wasn't thinking with anything other than my hormones. The best thing we can do is go our separate ways tomorrow and forget that last night ever happened. Please.''

''Hormones,'' he repeated in an unreadable voice.

''Well, of course. What else could it be? We don't even like each other—we're certainly not in love with each other. So we can't possibly jeopardize Emmy's peace of mind, her security, for something that's no more than lust.'' Then, from the corner of her eye, Lise caught movement. With patent relief she added, ''Thank goodness—here comes Emmy with Sally.''

For a moment Judd's fingers increased their pressure; her head jerked up. ''We're not through with each other—no matter what you say.''

Of their own volition, Lise's eyes fell to his mouth, and instantly she was tortured by memories of how Judd had kissed her last night with such passion and inventiveness. Don't go there, she thought frantically. Not now. ''There are some people you can't control, Judd. And I'm one of them.'' She pulled free of him. ''I'm going to pack. See you later.''

He made no move to stop her; his whole face had closed against her. Lise hurried down the hall and into her bedroom, shutting the door with careful restraint. Then she stared dry-eyed at the room in which she'd found such bliss. The wide bed with its exquisite painting of a blue heron over the headboard. The collection of jade carvings on the recessed shelf against the far wall. A serenely beautiful room she was deliberately leaving, to go back to her real life.

Moving like a robot, she began folding the garments in the closet into her two suitcases, separating those Judd had bought her from the rest. Her brain, belatedly, had begun to work. Why had Judd invited her to become Emmy's companion? He loved Emmy. Why would he risk his beloved daughter growing fond of a woman who was nothing but an employee?

Maybe this time Angeline was right: that Judd always treated people like chessmen on a board, disposable objects to be moved according to his own design and for his own ends. So that he won, Lise thought unhappily. Because winning was the name of his game.

His reasons didn't matter. She'd said no and she'd meant it. Nothing could be more impossible than for her to live in the same house with Judd, no matter how big a house or how often he was away. She couldn't bear to do that. It would destroy her.

Ten hours later the limo drew up outside Lise's apartment block. A messy mixture of snow and ice pellets was falling from a gray sky. The snowbanks edging the streets were dirty, while the pedestrians looked hunched and grumpy. Lise said in a voice that sounded totally artificial, ''Emmy, it was lovely being with you. I hope it won't be too hard going back to school. Judd, I—''

''I'll walk you to the door.''

''There's no need for—''

The look he gave her would have stopped a fire truck in its tracks. Lise got out of the limo and as he reached in the trunk for the cases, said sharply, ''I only want my own.''

''Do you have to argue about everything? You're keeping the clothes I bought you and that's the end of it.''

The raw cold seemed to have penetrated her very bones. Shivering, Lise said, "This is the end of it, you're right," and prayed he hadn't heard the pain underlying her words. She tramped through the snow to the front door and held it open for him. Then she said, "I can carry the cases, Judd."

He put them down on the floor. His eyes were an impenetrable gray. As cold as the sky, she thought, and said clumsily, "Your villa, the pool, the rain forest—it was all so beautiful...thank you."

As if the words were forced from him, he said, "When you go back to work, for God's sake don't go taking risks."

"I saved Emmy by taking risks."

A muscle twitched in his jaw. "If you change your mind about the job I offered you, call me. Goodbye, Lise."

"Goodbye," she whispered, and watched him walk away from her, out the door, across the sidewalk and into the limo. Which smoothly accelerated into the traffic.

He was gone. He hadn't kissed her, and he'd made no mention of another meeting. He'd gotten the message. Finally.

She took the elevator to her floor. Her apartment looked cramped and untidy. Lise turned up the heat and started to unpack, her own suitcase first, then the one Judd had given her. But when she came to the jade-green dress, her hands stilled. For the space of a few glorious hours, she'd become the kind of woman who could wear such vividly hued and provocatively designed silk. She'd discovered that woman in Judd's arms, clasped to his naked body. But now she had to go back to being herself. Blue jeans. A firefighter's rubber boots.

If Judd hadn't bought that dress, she wouldn't have gone to Dominica. She wouldn't now be paralyzed by a pain that served only to remind her of those dreadful days after her parents died in the fire, when she'd lost everything known and familiar and taken for granted.

If she hadn't gone away with Judd, she'd still have known who she was.

March merged into April. Winter clung to the city, burying the crocuses and early daffodils in layers of snow and freezing rain. Highway accidents abounded; a rash of false fire alarms had every firefighter in the city on edge. Not that Lise wasn't on edge to start with.

The first week she was home she scarcely slept, and when she did, her dreams were haunted by images of Judd. Erotic images, that woke her to an empty bed and a body aching with need. Terrifying images, where he was trapped in a burning jet and she couldn't rescue him. From these she woke drenched in sweat, her heart racing in her breast.

How could he, in so short a time, have affected her so strongly? More pragmatically, how was she to endure the long night hours alone in her apartment? Her only choice seemed to be turning off her body altogether. Driving herself so hard at work that she was tired enough to sleep when she got home.

Forgetting that she had a body. Let alone any sexuality.

The second week was a nightmare. Three people died in a suspected arson. Dave broke his arm in a warehouse fire; Stephan inhaled smoke and ended up in intensive care.

Lise's last shift that week was on Thursday. She got off at six, changed into street clothes and, instead of going home, hurried down the street to the nearest pub. She needed warmth and people and noise. She needed a glass of red wine along with a hot meat pie and French fries smothered in gravy. Too bad about cholesterol. Simple comfort was more important.

She was going to quit her job. The decision had, somehow, coalesced this week. So she needed to strategize how best to do it, and also how to pay for the vet's assistant course she was almost sure would be her next move.

Lise found a table in a secluded corner, placed her order and let the first mouthful of wine slide down her throat. Then she uncapped her pen, took out her notebook and began totting up her finances, frowning prodigiously. If only she hadn't blown so much money on her trip to Paris and Provence last summer; it had made a huge dent in her savings. Money she could now have used.

"May I join you?"

Lise would have known that voice anywhere. As her heart gave a treacherous leap of mingled panic and joy, she looked up. "Hello, Judd."

He looked impossibly handsome in dark cords, a leather bomber jacket and a deep blue sweater, his black hair disarrayed by the wind. He flung his jacket over the back of the chair and sat down; the waitress, Lise noticed sardonically, came to their table immediately. After Judd had ordered a beer with fish and chips, he leaned forward, his eyes running over her face. "You look god-awful," he said succinctly.

"How did you know I'd be here?"

"I followed you from work."

"Really?" she snapped. "And why did you do that?"

"Figured it was time I tried buying you again," he said with a feral grin.

She took a big gulp of wine. "I don't come cheap."

"You said a mouthful there," Judd said acerbically.

"You're a born manipulator."

"I just work on the facts."

"You work on other people's weaknesses."

Judd raised his brows. "You're admitting to having some?"

Oh, yes, Lise thought, I have weaknesses: one of them's

sitting right across from me. And dammit all, for the first time in two weeks, I feel alive.

The waitress deposited Judd's beer in front of him. He raised his glass. *"Salut."*

She said levelly, "Are you reoffering me the job as Emmy's companion?"

"At double the salary," he remarked.

Lise played with her glass, watching light dance fiery-red in the swirling wine. How clever of Judd to wait until her resistance was at its lowest ebb, when she was overwhelmed by the horrifying images of the last few shifts. Her resources drained, her tiredness bone-deep.

She had to leave her job, before she cracked under the strain. Or—perhaps worse—withdrew all her humanity and stopped caring.

Her gaze shifted to her notebook, the numbers mocking her with their inadequacy. If she went to work for Judd, in four months she could save enough for the vet's assistant course. And she could hand in her notice at the fire station; she was only required to give two weeks. She'd more than proved she could hold her own in a male-dominated world; she'd be finished with a job that was pushing her to the limits of her endurance.

Feeling her heart racket around in her rib cage, she said slowly, "I won't commit to any longer than four months."

Had she been watching Judd, she would have seen triumph flare in his eyes, and as quickly be extinguished. He leaned forward. "Why only four months?"

"Because that's long enough to save the money I need for a course I want to take."

"What kind of course?" Judd rapped. After she'd briefly described it, he added, "You've got this all thought out."

"I've wanted to quit the station for at least six months."

"You never told me that."

"No, Judd, I never told you that."

"What else aren't you telling me, Lise?"

"That's for you to find out," she said, and smiled at the waitress. The meat pie smelled delicious; for the first time in days she had an appetite. She could leave her job. Start afresh. She gave Judd a brilliant smile and picked up her fork.

He said evenly, "I'm not sure I'll ever understand you."

"You're hiring me as Emmy's companion, not yours. So you don't have to."

"When can you start?"

"In a couple of weeks."

"What about your apartment?"

"At the salary you're paying me, I can afford to keep it—I'll need it in four months' time."

"And what if Emmy has gotten fond of you by then?"

The smile died from Lise's lips. "You should have thought of that before you offered me the job." She hesitated. "Let's be frank here, Judd. We're using each other—you won't have to worry about Emmy being lonely when you're away, and I'll save the better part of twelve thousand dollars. This arrangement, in other words, is to our mutual advantage. And I'll be sure to tell Emmy right from the start that it's only temporary."

"You've covered all the angles but one."

She knew immediately what he meant. As color mounted in her cheeks, she announced, "There'll be no repeat of what happened in Dominica—you'll have to agree to that before I'll even think of moving in."

"You'd have to agree to it, too, Lise. You were, after all, the instigator."

"I wish I'd never seen that dress!"

"Eat your French fries," Judd said, "you've lost weight."

"Whereas you look in the pink of health."

"I knew I was going to see you again. I just wasn't sure when," he said blandly. "Were you pining for me, Lise?"

"Get off my case."

He laughed. "Your hair's just as red and your temper hasn't suffered. What kind of dreams have *you* been having?"

Lise choked on a chip, hastily gulped some wine and strove for a semblance of dignity. "Nightmares," she said, "with you as the main character."

He suddenly sobered. "Emmy had one last night. Which is yet one more reason I followed you here."

"I don't think I'm the person to help her with those."

"I believe you are," he said with finality, and with equal finality changed the subject. "Do you come here often?" She nodded. "Alone?"

"Not always."

"How's Dave?" Judd asked, his eyes watchful on her face.

She shivered. "He broke his arm on Monday in that warehouse fire…he could very easily have been killed."

Judd said with sudden violence, "Will you please take care of yourself the next two weeks?"

She looked at him in puzzlement. "You sound very vehement."

"It's an entirely accurate reflection of how I feel," Judd said, squeezing lemon on his fish with vicious strength.

"You're not in *love* with me, Judd?"

"Let me tell you something. I fell in love with Angeline when I was twenty-three—you were there, you must have seen how I felt about her. I worshiped the ground she walked on. But our marriage didn't work out. The long-term effect was to immunize me against ever falling in love again. Been there, done that, got the T-shirt. Once was enough, in other words."

"Do you still love her?" Lise blurted.

"What would be the point?"

Which, thought Lise, wasn't really an answer at all. And who could blame him if he did? At the height of her modeling career, Angeline had been voted one of the ten most beautiful women in the world.

"To get back to the dangers of your job," Judd said tautly. "I don't have to be in love to hate the thought of you falling six stories through a burning building."

Her emotions in a turmoil—because hadn't Judd as much as admitted he was still in love with his ex-wife, a woman he had treated very badly?—Lise said, "I'm always careful. I don't want to end up a statistic in the annual report."

"When's your last shift?"

She pulled her daybook out of her backpack, flipping through the pages. "Two weeks from today. I get off at eight."

"I'll pick you up first thing Friday morning. That'll give you time to get settled before Emmy's off school for the weekend."

Two weeks from tomorrow. "You know something?" Lise said faintly. "I'm certifiably insane to have agreed to this. You and I are adults, presumably we can look after ourselves. But Emmy—I don't want to hurt Emmy." She leaned forward, her face passionate with sincerity. "Get someone else to look after her, Judd. Someone who'll stay and give her the security she needs. Not me."

In a voice like steel, Judd said, "It's too late to back out—you've agreed to come."

Her chips were cold and soggy, and the congealed gravy turned her stomach. Lise pushed her plate away. There was one more question she should have asked. What if she herself grew fond of Emmy? What then?

But she hadn't thought to ask it, and it was too late now.

She'd let a man's implacable will move her around the board as if she had no will of her own. A pawn to his king.

Checkmate, indeed.

CHAPTER EIGHT

"FINISHED with your dinner, ma'am?"

The waitress was standing by their table. "Yes, thanks," Lise stumbled. "No dessert, just coffee."

"Same here," Judd said. As the young woman hurried off, he added harshly, "You look like your best friend just died."

"I'm frightened," she whispered. "And I don't scare easy."

Judd's fingers tightened round his knife. Then he put it down, reached over and covered her hand with his own, saying forcefully, "Lise, it'll be all right. You'll see."

His palm was warm, his fingers lean and strong. As heat raced along Lise's arm into her body, desire pounced on her, predator to prey; desire was always lying in wait for her when she was anywhere in Judd's vicinity. "I can't live in your house!" she cried. "I just can't—we're mad to even consider it."

"Cream and sugar, ma'am?"

Her cup of coffee had been plunked in front of her, brown liquid slopping into the saucer. "Yes," said Lise. "Please."

The waitress then presented Judd with the bill. "You two have a nice evening," she said.

Waiting until she was out of earshot, Judd said coldly, "You hate the ground I walk on, don't you?"

Did she? Was it that simple? "It doesn't matter how I feel about you," Lise responded with equal coldness. "Emmy is my only concern for the next four months.

Emmy, not you." She added in open challenge, "Will she be seeing her mother in that four months?"

"Angeline can see her anytime she chooses."

"That's not an answer."

"It's all the answer you're getting."

The coffee tasted like dishwater and Lise was suddenly exhausted. She opened her wallet and threw a bill on the table. "I'll see you in two weeks."

"Eight-thirty Friday morning. I've got meetings at ten."

Rap music battering her eardrums, the fetid air making her dizzy, Lise stood up and pulled on her jacket. "I may emigrate to Mongolia," she announced. "Do you think the yaks would like my dress?"

"Anything with an ounce of red blood in it would like your dress," Judd said. "I happen to own Air Mongolia—you can let me know what the service is like."

"The only way I can afford to fly to Mongolia is as a stowaway," she said pithily. "Goodbye, Judd."

"See you, Lise," he said with a grin that both infuriated and entranced her.

She strode out of the pub and into the crisp evening air. Exhausted she might be. Ready to go home she wasn't. Impulsively she decided to visit Marthe and tell her about the new job. It beat going back to the dishes in the sink. Or sitting on the chesterfield, along with a pile of unfolded laundry, thinking about Judd. Pulling on her mitts, Lise set off at a brisk pace down the sidewalk.

She was near the bus stop when a man's voice hailed her. Dave was across the street, waving at her. She dodged through the traffic, disproportionately pleased to see him. "Hi," she said, glancing at his cast. "How's the arm?"

"I've been shifted to admin for the next month," he said. "You know how I love filling in forms. Got time for a coffee?"

Five minutes later they were seated in the local coffee

bar, which played jazz rather than rap and served drinkable coffee into the bargain. They chatted a few minutes, then Lise said abruptly, "Dave, I don't want you hearing this from someone else—I'm handing in my notice tomorrow."

He put down his mug so sharply that coffee slopped on the table. "You're quitting."

"I'm burned-out. No pun intended."

"You could join me in the office for a while. Simple."

"I can't—I need a change, Dave. A complete change. I'm sick of disasters and tragedies and night shifts. So I'm going to take a course to be a vet's assistant." She took a deep breath. "In the meantime, I've been offered a job as sort of a live-in nanny. That way I can save some money."

"Sort of a nanny?" Dave said quizzically.

"Remember the little girl in the attic, three weeks ago? It's with her."

"The one whose father I met in the hospital." Dave gave her an inimical look. "I didn't know you'd kept in touch with him."

"I knew him years ago—he's my cousin's ex-husband."

"You want to watch out. He looked like the kind of guy who takes what he wants and too bad about the consequences."

"I can look after myself," Lise said; and wondered how true that was.

"He didn't like the way you and I were kidding around."

"Dave, it's a job, that's all. A job." If she said that often enough, would she start to believe it?

"I'll miss you," Dave said. "I just wish—"

Distressed, Lise said, "I'm so sorry, Dave—but I know I'm not the one for you. Once I'm not around, maybe you'll find someone else, you're such a good man and—"

"So why aren't you interested?"

Because a man with hair black as the night and eyes gray-blue as the sea has taught me about passion…she couldn't possibly say that. "It's just the way it is," she said helplessly. "I—won't you wish me well? And I'd really like to keep in touch."

He said soberly, "Take care of yourself, that's all."

He was the second man to tell her that this evening. A few minutes later she said goodbye to him on the sidewalk and ran for her bus. She was burning bridges right and left, she realized with a frisson along her spine. She'd tell her aunt tonight, and tomorrow she'd hand in her notice. It really would be too late then to change her mind.

Her aunt was home, and offered the usual cool cheek to be kissed. Lise was given a very small glass of sherry. After they'd discussed the weather, Lise said with rather overdone nonchalance, "Oh, by the way, *Tante,* I'm leaving my job at the fire station in a couple of weeks. As an interim position, I'm going to be a companion for your granddaughter, Emmy. I thought you might be pleased to hear that."

"You mean that man hired you?"

"Emmy's father? Yes."

"Lise, don't be ridiculous—you must stay away from him! He'll ruin your life the way he did Angeline's."

"I'm not planning on marrying him, *Tante.*"

"He doesn't marry his women anymore," Marthe said bitterly. "Just discards them when he's done."

Lise said with assumed calm, "Then I'll be a good influence for Emmy."

"You're not listening to me! Let me show you something," Marthe said, spots of color in her withered cheeks. She fumbled among the magazines on an antique cherrywood table, pulling out a plastic folder and passing it to Lise. "This will change your mind."

Nervousness fluttering in her chest, Lise opened the folder. Her aunt had cut photos from society magazines and glued them into a makeshift scrapbook; each picture had Judd in it. Judd with a woman, always a beautiful woman in designer clothes, elegant and aristocratic. Almost never the same woman, Lise noticed with a sinking heart. Quickly she flipped through the pages. The pictures were undated, nor were their sources given. But why should that matter? The message was clear. Judd got around. Judd changed women as easily as he changed his clothes. What else did she need to know?

The last photo was of a striking brunette in a Valentino gown at the opening of the opera in Milan; Judd was smiling down at her, his tuxedo emphasizing his arrogant masculinity. So this is what jealousy is like, Lise thought miserably. A knife being twisted in her heart.

Marthe said sharply, "You're in love with him."

Lise's head jerked up. "I'm not!"

"He won't pay someone like you any attention. You're not beautiful like Angeline, and you don't have money. Nothing to recommend you."

It was the message of Lise's childhood; yet it still had the power to wound. However—and this Marthe must never know—Judd had paid attention to her. For one night on a tropical island, he'd made love to her as if she were the only woman in the world.

She wasn't. And how that hurt.

Drawing on all her fortitude, Lise closed the folder and replaced it on the table. "As you say, I'll be quite safe— I'm not his type at all. And I do believe I'll be good for Emmy." Rather proud of herself, she added with a trace of mischief, "And aren't you glad I won't be wearing firefighter's boots anymore?"

Marthe said fractiously, "You make a joke out of everything. When I talk to Angeline, I'll tell her how stupidly you're behaving.''

. ''How is Angeline?''

''She's very unhappy. Her husband, so she believes, is having an affair…I want her to come home, but she insists her place is with him.'' Marthe sighed. ''She's very loyal.''

Lise had had enough. ''I must go, *Tante*. I'll let you know how I get on with Emmy. Perhaps I can bring her for a visit one day.''

''He won't let you,'' Marthe said venomously. ''He's never forgiven me for being Angeline's mother. He's evil, Lise. Evil through and through.''

Evil? The man who had made love to her with such passion and generosity? Every cell in Lise's body repudiated such a judgment. Quickly she kissed her aunt goodbye and escaped from the overstuffed room. Her heart sore, she started walking home, the images of Judd and all his elegant companions dancing in front of her eyes. Did he bring women like that home to his big stone house? How would she bear it?

But as Lise marched along, swinging her arms to keep warm, a small voice of reason asserted itself. Her aunt had never been known for kindness; and had doted on Angeline with obsessive single-mindedness for as long as Lise could remember. To make a scrapbook like that, to call Judd evil—surely those weren't the acts of a rational woman.

What was the truth about Judd and Angeline's marriage? About Emmy's custody? Would she ever find out?

Two weeks later, at eight o'clock on Thursday night, Lise started to pack for her move to Judd's. Today had been her final day at the fire station; last Saturday the crew had taken her out for dinner, and she had been touched to realize how deeply she'd carved her niche in that over-whelmingly masculine world.

She'd neither seen nor heard from Judd in the interim. He'd be picking her up in the morning to take her to his home for the next four months. Four months. It sounded like forever. But she'd applied for the veterinary course, and the interviews had gone well; so that was something to look forward to.

If she were honest, she was dreading the next four months.

Snow was whirling outside the window in eddies as pale as ghosts. Maybe the blizzard would go on all weekend, she thought hopefully, and she could stay right where she was. She folded two shirts and placed them in her case, adding jeans and a couple of turtlenecks. Rummaging in the bathroom cabinet, she added shampoo and conditioner. Then she knocked a box off the shelf: her tampons. She'd need those, she thought casually, and started stuffing them in a corner of her case.

Her hands suddenly stilled. Ice encased her heart as her brain frantically started making calculations. How long since she'd taken this box out of the cabinet? Since she'd had a period? She was overdue. Two weeks overdue.

She counted backward on her fingers. Sixteen days overdue.

She was never late. She could set a calendar by her cycle, she was so regular.

No. Oh God, no. She couldn't be pregnant. She couldn't be.

She and Judd had used no protection. When he'd burst into her room the night the lizard had run across her face, he'd been wearing nothing but his briefs. And it hadn't exactly been a planned seduction. Anything but.

She was pregnant.

With a whimper of distress, Lise buried her face in her

hands, her shoulders bowed. Could it be true? Was she really pregnant? Or had all the stresses of the past few weeks conspired to knock her off schedule? Hadn't she, purposely, tried to shut her body down ever since she'd left Dominica, in an effort to cope with her desperate longing for Judd?

There was a drugstore five blocks away where she could get a pregnancy test. But she'd already heard on the radio that most businesses had closed early due to the storm. Nor would she have time in the morning before Judd picked her up.

How was she going to face him with this nightmare hanging over her head?

She wasn't pregnant. Of course she wasn't. For once in her life her timing was off. And with good reason. Judd's lovemaking had turned her into a different woman, one she'd never known existed. Why wouldn't this be reflected in her body's rhythms?

But the ice had spread from her heart to the rest of her body, all the way to her fingertips. She'd taken her pleasure. And now she was paying for it.

If she truly were pregnant, she couldn't possibly stay at Judd's for four months: he'd find out. How could she have been so reckless as to make love with him, and so stupid to ignore something as rudimentary as birth control?

Because she'd fallen in love with him? All over again as an adult?

Oh, no, Lise thought grimly, I'm not going that route. There's no way I'd fall in love with a man I neither like nor respect. Not an option.

I'm not thirteen. I'm twenty-eight.

Automatically she shoved a pile of socks and underwear into her suitcase; and added the box of tampons. Because she'd be needing them. Of course she would. In fact, now that she'd realized the problem, she wouldn't be surprised if she got back on track overnight.

Somewhat cheered by this conclusion, Lise folded some skirts, trousers and a couple of dresses. Then she took down the photo of her parents from the bookshelves, rubbing the dust from the gold frame. Her mother's thin, intelligent face, her father's infectious grin: she bit her lip, knowing that at some deep level she still missed them. They'd been wrenched from her so traumatically and so finally amidst the smoke and flames that dreadful February night…and hadn't she, the last ten years, been making reparation over and over again by plunging herself into that same world of fire and tragedy?

Involuntarily her hands gripped the picture frame more tightly. If she were pregnant, she was carrying their grandchild. Extending her parents' bloodline into the future. Briefly, warmth curled soft arms around her, enclosing her in a joy as tender as it was fragile. She must take care of herself. For her unborn child's sake.

But then Lise's mind made the next leap. She was also bearing Judd Harwood's child. Fruit of his body, son or daughter of his name. Just as much his as Emmy was.

He'd want the child for himself—wouldn't he? He hadn't allowed Angeline custody of Emmy. Why would he allow her, Lise, to keep this second child?

One more pawn on his chessboard.

She wouldn't let him take her child. She couldn't.

Lise suddenly became aware she'd bitten her lip until it bled. What was she thinking of? She didn't even know for sure she was pregnant, and she was already worrying herself sick over what Judd might do. Tomorrow morning she'd ask him to stop by the drugstore on their way to his house. She had to know, one way or the other.

Quickly Lise finished packing. Then she spent three hours wielding a dustcloth and the vacuum cleaner, until the apartment had never looked better and she felt tired enough to sleep.

She did sleep. But when she got up to the beep of the alarm the next morning, she soon realized that she was now seventeen days late. No miracles in the night. Only a stretching of her nerves to the breaking point.

She dressed in a denim skirt with a purple silk shirt she'd bought on sale. After pulling her hair back with a leather barrette, Lise made up her face with care, using more blusher than usual, and a bright lipstick. Lastly she pulled on her tall boots and hunter-green wool coat, also bought on sale. Pirouetting in front of the mirror, she decided she looked just fine. Businesslike. Carefree. In control.

What she didn't see was the deep uncertainty in her green eyes, or the tension along her jawline. But when she opened the door to Judd five minutes later, his gaze flew to her face. "You look like you're going to your own funeral," he rapped.

His slate-gray eyes seemed to see right through her, stripping her of everything but confusion and terror. Deliberately she counterattacked. "You don't look so good yourself."

"Don't I? That's because I wasn't taking it for granted you'd be here. You did mention Mongolia."

"Is winning that important to you?"

"I wonder if you'll ever quit thinking the worst of me?"

"I decided in Dominica that you were a good father," Lise blurted, then paled involuntarily. What if she were to make him a father for the second time? What then?

"Lise, what the hell's the matter?"

He was gripping her by the shoulders of her coat, his face only inches from hers; she wanted to kiss him so badly that she could feel the warm, sure pressure of his lips against her own. Pulling back, Lise said jaggedly,

"I've committed myself to the next four months in your house—what else could be the matter?"

His expletive made her wince. "Let's go," he said harshly. "The streets are a mess, and I don't want to be late for my meeting. Is this all you're bringing?"

He picked up the two larger cases, while Lise took her overnight bag. With a feeling of fatality, she locked the door of her apartment behind her, and went down in the elevator with Judd. He was driving a sleek navy-blue Cherokee with leather upholstery; he piled the cases in the back, and Lise climbed in. As they pulled away from the curb, she said, "I couldn't get to the drugstore last night. Would you mind stopping at the nearest one—it'll only take me a minute."

He nodded curtly. She looked out the window, trying to think of something to say and failing miserably. Judd parked in the lot to one side of the mall and pocketed his keys, reaching for the handle on his door. Lise faltered, "There's no reason for you to come—I won't be long."

"Emmy needs a new toothbrush."

"I'll pick one up for her."

He gave her a sharp look. "You planning on running away?"

"I've had two weeks to do that."

"Then let's go," he ordered. "My time's limited."

Lise trailed into the drugstore, bought an assortment of things she didn't need, and paid for them. She didn't even look in the relevant section; what was the use? On Monday, as soon as Emmy was in school, she'd get a bus downtown. Which meant she had to live with suspense for three more days.

It seemed like a life sentence.

She sat in silence as they drove to Judd's house, which, as before, took her breath away with its elegant proportions, the stone a soft gray against the snow, smoke drifting from one of the many chimneys. As he pushed open the oak front door, Judd said, "The repairs should be finished in the next two to three weeks, and then you can move into your own suite of rooms."

However, Lise's bedroom and private bathroom in the guest wing were spacious and attractive; they were also next door to Emmy's room, on the far side of which Judd was sleeping. Too close, thought Lise, and heard him say, "The staff all know you're here and will help out in any way they can. Emmy's home for lunch and then again at three. I expect to be out all day and most of the evening."

So for today, at least, she didn't have to endure Judd's company. He rasped, "Do you have to look so relieved?"

"I don't know why you're angry," she cried. "You've got what you wanted—I'm here to look after Emmy and you can stay out all night if that's what turns you on."

"I'll tell you what turns me on," Judd said, and planted a kiss full on her mouth. A brief kiss, fired by a mixture of anger and desire that made the blood rocket through Lise's veins. Hunger flowered in its wake; she swayed toward him, and in a distant part of her brain knew she would do it all over again: fall into his arms and into his bed without a thought for the consequences.

What kind of woman did that make her?

A very foolish woman.

"Don't ever deny that you want me, Lise. It's written all over you."

His voice was hard, without a trace of emotion; and suddenly she knew what was wrong. "But you don't want me anymore—not really," she said in a voice she scarcely recognized as her own. "What's free for the taking, you despise—you told me that once."

"I also told you I wasn't bringing you here as a resident mistress. And I meant it."

She cried, "Then why am I here?"

"Money. Isn't that what you said? Twelve thousand dollars."

He was right. She said tonelessly, "You'll be late for your meeting."

"Lise, I—" He broke off. "You'll do just fine. Emmy may take a while to come around, but I know she will sooner or later. Just make yourself at home."

He turned on his heel and was gone. Her knees feeling like wet cardboard, Lise sat down hard on the bed. If Judd didn't want her, why had he kissed her? Simply to assert his mastery? And if he did want her, then why was he so insistent that she wasn't here as his mistress?

None of it made any sense.

Eventually she got up and started to unpack, and gradually grew calmer. Her feet sank into the Chinese carpet that overlaid the wall-to-wall cream pile. The furniture was of waxed pine, the Roman shades and bedspread a soothing pattern of pinks and greens, which was reiterated in two big vases of freshly cut, pink-streaked peonies. Her bathroom was the ultimate in luxury with its gold fittings and deep Jacuzzi.

When she went downstairs, Lise met Maryann the housekeeper again, along with the maids and the groundskeeper. Friendly without being obsequious, they all contrived to make her feel very welcome. Then Emmy arrived home for lunch. The little girl left her snowsuit and boots in the back porch, looking up at Lise through her long dark lashes. "Dad said you're going to live here for four months."

"That's right. Then I'm taking a course so I can help vets with sick dogs and cats," Lise said matter-of-factly.

"I want a dog. But Dad says I'm not quite big enough yet."

"What kind of dog?"

The subject of dogs, cats and horses saw them through

lunch, which they ate in a delightful alcove off the kitchen, overlooking an enclosed orchard. Again the child baffled Lise with her combination of good manners and reserve. Surely it was self-protective. But why?

After school, the two of them played in the snow, Lise helping Emmy build a rotund snowman with a carrot nose and eyes made out of rocks. Emmy had color in her cheeks when they went in, and ate her supper with gusto. Lise helped her in the bath, then read to her from an assortment of books. As Emmy's eyes drooped shut, Lise said softly, "Sleep well, Emmy. I'm just next door if you need me."

"When will Dad be home?"

"Later this evening, he said."

"G'night," Emmy murmured, cuddling her cheek into Plush's body in a way that made Lise want to cry. Blinking, she turned off the light and left Emmy alone, going to her own room and turning on the bathwater. There was a very real risk that she could grow more than fond of Emmy. How to guard against that, she had no idea. She did know something, though. She was going to stay in her own rooms for the rest of the evening, and not risk seeing Judd again.

She was still seventeen days late.

CHAPTER NINE

THE next morning when Lise went downstairs for breakfast, Emmy and Judd were already seated in the alcove, Judd drinking coffee, Emmy devouring oatmeal. Judd was dressed in an immaculate business suit with a figured silk tie. He glanced up as Lise came into the room. "Good morning," he said with crushing formality. "I was just telling Emmy there's been a mix-up in Singapore and I've got to go there right away. I should be back by midweek."

Masking a surge of relief that made her feel lightheaded, Lise tried to look as cool and collected as he. She could go to the drugstore Monday when Emmy was in school, and she'd have a couple of days to contemplate the results before she had to face Judd again. "I hope it's not a real emergency," she said.

"Nothing that can't be fixed," he answered dismissively. "By the way, a new Walt Disney movie opened last week, Emmy was wondering if you'd take her."

Lise smiled at the little girl with real warmth. "Of course, I'd love to."

Judd took a sheaf of bills from his wallet. "Here's an advance on your first paycheck," he said coldly. "And this is expense money for things like movies. I don't expect any accounting of it."

She was his employee, that was the message. One among many, Lise thought with painful accuracy, and took the money, stuffing it into her pocket. "Thank you," she said stiffly.

"I'll let Maryann know when I'll be back. I always call

121

Emmy just before her bedtime when I'm away, so if you could make sure she's available for that.''

"Of course." Helping herself from the bowl of fruit salad on the side table, Lise clamped down on her temper: she might hate taking orders from Judd, but she had accepted the job, after all. And wasn't this one more piece of evidence that Judd was a good father?

"We get our report cards on Tuesday," Emmy said. "I'm pretty sure I got all *A*'s."

"We might have to go to McDonald's to celebrate," Judd said with a grin that didn't include Lise.

Lise sliced a flaky croissant in two and slathered it with homemade apricot jam, endeavoring to look on the bright side. She didn't have a trace of morning sickness and her appetite was great; so maybe, just maybe, she wasn't pregnant. Monday. She'd know Monday. Not much longer to wait.

Once Judd had left, Lise purposely kept Emmy busy; and was rewarded with the first sense that the barrier between Emmy and her might be lowering. Emmy wanted to talk about the movie afterward, something Lise always liked to do; when Judd phoned, at seven-thirty on the nose, Lise heard Emmy mention her own name several times.

Judd didn't ask to speak to her. For which, Lise told herself fiercely, she was glad. What did she have to say to him? That in thirty-six hours she'd know if she were pregnant by him?

Actually it was closer to thirty-eight hours. And the pregnancy test came up positive. Lise sat down hard on the bed in her own apartment. She was carrying Judd's child. She was going to be a mother. Amidst a turmoil of emotion she was aware of a shaft of pure, unquenchable joy.

She clutched it to her. Later she'd worry about the enormous difficulties of her situation: the unforeseeable and undeniable consequences of an unplanned, ill-judged pregnancy. But for now she was happy. Quickly she picked up the phone and made an appointment with her family doctor for the following week. Then she drove back to Judd's. Of all the complications that surrounded her like a thicket of thorns, only one thing was clear. She wasn't going to tell him. Not yet.

Not ever?

On Wednesday night, Lise went to bed early. Judd was expected home some time that night; she wasn't yet ready to face him. The happiness that had enfolded her in the apartment on Monday had gone underground, leaving her racked by foreboding and nameless fears. Judd saw too much. He was far too intelligent to deceive for long. What was she going to *do?*

The changes in her body would take place inevitably and according to their own schedule: nothing she could do about that. The only plan she'd formulated was to stay with Emmy for two months rather than four, save every penny she could, and then move somewhere like Halifax, where she could live more cheaply and take the same veterinary course. Already she'd handed in her notice for her apartment; she couldn't afford to keep it.

Needing comfort, she put on her oldest flannelette nightgown and made herself some hot chocolate before bed. She fell asleep around eleven, a restless sleep in which images of disaster flickered in and out of her mind. When she found herself sitting bolt upright, her heart racing, she thought it was her own dream that had woken her. Then she heard a thin cry of distress from the room next to hers. She was out of bed and into Emmy's room in a flash, gathering the little girl in her arms. "It's all right, Emmy, I'm here," she said. "You're safe, I won't let anything happen to you."

Clutching Lise in her thin arms, Emmy burst into tears. Lise rocked her back and forth, murmuring words of comfort. "Do you want to tell me about it?"

Emmy spilled out a confused story about a huge bonfire and dancers with masks who kept pushing her nearer and nearer the flames. Her heart aching, Lise did her best to defuse the dream's terror; and was rewarded when Emmy snuffled, "I'm glad you're here. Sometimes I m-miss having a mother."

"I'm glad I'm here, too," Lise said; and felt guilt flood her that she would be leaving even sooner than Emmy was expecting. Emmy needed stability; which was just what Lise couldn't give her.

A few moments later, Emmy's body sagged in Lise's arms; she'd fallen asleep. Very carefully Lise lowered her to the bed, tucking the covers around her and making sure Plush was snuggled close. The little girl's fall of dark hair on the pillow, the soft puffs of her breathing, filled Lise with the same tenderness she'd felt earlier toward her unborn child.

If she grew to love Emmy, she'd be in even deeper trouble.

She padded toward the door, wrapped in her own thoughts, and walked right into the man who was standing half-hidden by the door. With a tiny shriek of alarm, she pushed against his chest with her palms. "Judd—you scared me!"

He pulled her away from Emmy's doorway until they were out of earshot. Then he said roughly, "Did she have another nightmare?"

His arms were still around her; he was wearing trousers and a shirt unbuttoned to the waist. The feel of his skin, warm, hair-roughened, lanced Lise with an agony of desire. Taking refuge in anger, she said, "Emmy still misses her mother."

"I heard that."

The one question whose answer she couldn't understand burst from Lise's lips. "How *could* you have denied Angeline custody?"

He said in a voice as cutting as a honed blade, "Let's get something straight, once and for all. I'm sick to death of being the villain in this divorce. Angeline's second husband, who can trace his ancestors back to the fourteenth century, didn't want another man's daughter in his fancy château. Especially a man who haled from the worst tenements in Manhattan. So Angeline very prettily decided Emmy would be better off in a familiar environment with me."

"That's not—"

"Angeline had an affair two years before that. In New York. She's not clever enough to hide her tracks, so I found out. She didn't really understand why I was so upset. You need to know something about your cousin—what she wants in the moment, she takes. Like a kid on a hot day stealing a carton of ice cream, not realizing it'll melt and make a big mess before she can eat it all. Angeline's not a bad person. She just doesn't understand that there are consequences to her actions. That people can get hurt in the process."

"But—"

"We patched that one up. More or less. But then along came Henri, rich, aristocratic and available. Angeline doesn't like conflict. So she wrote me a note, left me to do the explaining to Emmy, and took the Concorde to Paris. End of story. I divorced her. It was only later, when I took Emmy to visit Marthe, that I realized that Angeline, no doubt with the best of intentions, was delicately suggesting to all and sundry that I'd been less than ethical in my dealings with her." He moved his shoulders restlessly.

"I could have sued her, I suppose, for defamation of character. I chose not to. For Emmy's sake."

His voice had the undeniable ring of truth. But hadn't Angeline's also had that same ring, in those scattered conversations over the years? Although now that Lise looked back, Angeline had never said outright that Judd had taken custody; it had all been insinuated, more in sorrow than in anger. So was Judd right? Was Angeline greedy like a child, with a child's lack of empathy for those she wounded?

Had Lise's worship of her cousin blinded her to Angeline's very real faults, while emphasizing her virtues? Lise said crisply, "The last time I saw Marthe, she showed me a scrapbook full of photos of you with different women. Dozens of photos."

"You never give up, do you?" Judd said unpleasantly. "Everywhere I go, women flock around me—dollar signs in their eyes. I'm not saying I haven't had affairs since the divorce, that wouldn't be true. But I've already told you that the whole time Angeline and I were married, I was faithful to her."

Wondering which of all those women he'd had affairs with, knowing she'd hate them on sight, Lise took a steadying breath. "I didn't know you grew up in poverty."

"I'm not ashamed of it. But I don't go around advertising it, either."

"Are your parents still alive?"

He said in a clipped voice, "I never knew my father, he was gone long before I was born. My mother died when I was five. Of undernourishment and overwork."

In deep distress Lise whispered, "But you were younger than Emmy."

"Don't go feeling sorry for me."

She said quietly, "Where did you live after that?"

"Orphanage. Could have been better, could have been

worse. I always knew I'd be out of there as fast as I could, and that I wouldn't be back...I don't know why I'm telling you this, I never talk about it.'' His clasp tightened on her shoulders, and in the semidarkness his eyes were like shards of slate. ''Do you believe me, Lise—that I was faithful to Angeline?''

Lise hesitated a fraction too long. He said with ugly emphasis, ''You're going to have to choose. You can believe Angeline. Or you can believe me. One or the other. And until you do, I'm going back to that promise I made before we went to Dominica—and this time, don't try changing my mind. Because it won't work.''

''You're arrogant enough to assume I'd want to change your mind.''

''Yeah,'' he drawled, ''I am.''

''You know something? I learned a great many swear-words driving in the fire truck the last ten years, not one of which would do justice to the way I feel right now.''

He let go of her and stepped back. ''Then maybe you'd better go back to bed.''

She was pregnant by this man? Halifax, here I come, thought Lise, and said sweetly, ''I do hope you sleep well.''

''You might want to buy a new nightgown with some of the money I'm paying you.''

Anger and amusement teetered in the balance; despite herself, amusement won. Lise said, ''No way—I've had this since I was seventeen.''

He surveyed her from the ruffles at her throat to the rather frayed frill around her ankles. ''Very sexy,'' he said.

''I'm attached to it.'' Lise wrinkled her nose charmingly. ''Sort of like Emmy and Plush.''

''You look about seventeen in it.''

''No kidding? Then I'd better hang on to it.''

"Unfortunately it's not acting as a deterrent. I still want to kiss you senseless."

"You can't. You promised," Lise said breathlessly.

"Go to bed, Lise. Now. Alone. And that's an order."

It wasn't the moment to remember how she'd writhed in his arms in the velvety darkness of a Caribbean night. Almost tripping over the hem, Lise hurried to her room, fell into bed and pulled the covers over her head. She was in bed and she was definitely alone; although every fiber of her being ached for Judd to be here with her.

For that to happen, she had to choose which one to believe. Judd, the man she'd made love with. Or Angeline, the cousin she'd adored.

On Sunday Judd, Emmy and Lise went tobogganing on the slopes of Mont-Royal, with its panoramic view of skyscrapers and the sweep of the St. Lawrence River. Lise, without being too obvious about it, took only the safe runs, leaving Emmy and Judd to go over the jumps and capsize several times. Emmy's cheeks were pink from cold and happiness; Judd looked so young and vital that Lise had to avert her eyes. She was trying very hard to repress the knowledge of her pregnancy, afraid that if she didn't, Judd would take one look at her and discern her secret. But the unfeigned pleasure he was taking in his daughter's company hurt something deep inside her. She couldn't seriously be contemplating moving to Halifax and never telling Judd he was the father of two children, rather than one?

When they got back to the house, they headed for the back door with all their wet gear and Emmy started lobbing snowballs indiscriminately at her father and Lise. Lise retaliated, ducked to avoid a big gob of snow flung by Judd, tripped and fell backward into a deep, fluffy snowbank. Icy crystals trickled across her cheeks and down her neck. Emmy tumbled on top of her, thrusting more snow down her collar.

Laughing so hard she couldn't stop, Lise gurgled, "That's cold—stop, Emmy! I'll read you six stories before you go to bed, I promise—"

Emmy picked up one last mittful of snow and let it fall over Lise's flushed cheeks. "You're really pretty," she said spontaneously. "I'm glad you live with us, I like you a lot."

The laughter died from Lise's face. She said unevenly, "Thanks, Emmy. I like you, too. Very much."

"That's good," Emmy said. "Dad, can we have hot chocolate when we go in?"

"I think that could be arranged," Judd drawled, and pulled Lise to her feet, keeping hold of her hands so that for the space of a few seconds she was standing close to him. "I agree with you, Emmy—Lise is very pretty."

His eyes were lingering on her mouth; she could almost taste the heat of his lips on hers. In a strangled voice, Lise muttered, "There's cold water running down my back and I want three oatmeal cookies with my hot chocolate."

"A woman of immoderate appetites," said Judd, and released her.

"You got it," she said, and scurried for the back porch, the image of his sculpted mouth shivering along her nerves. As she pushed open the door and stepped inside, the heat hit her like a blow. Her vision blurred. The row of coats hanging on hooks swooped and dived like a flock of great birds, while the floor rushed up to meet her. From an immense distance Lise felt someone grab her before she could hit the gray ceramic tiles.

Her limbs were as useless as spaghetti. Blackness shot with all the colors of the rainbow swirled through her brain. Then she was on the floor, her head shoved between her knees. The colors were swallowed by a red haze.

Dimly wondering if she was going to be sick, Lise heard Emmy's frightened whisper, "Dad, is she okay?"

"Sure," Judd said calmly. "It was just the heat, Emmy. You know Maryann, she likes to keep the place as hot as Dominica."

As Emmy gave a weak giggle, Lise raised her head. "S-sorry," she mumbled. "I don't know what came over me."

"Your face is white, just like the snow," Emmy announced.

Little wonder, thought Lise dazedly; she felt drained and utterly exhausted. She never fainted. Never. Then in a spurt of pure terror she realized the cause must be her pregnancy. Of course. She didn't have morning sickness, but she couldn't hope to escape all the symptoms. She said more strongly, pushing against the floor, "I feel better now, I'm sorry I—"

Judd said forcibly, "Don't be in such an all-fired hurry."

His arms were around her shoulders and she could smell, elusively, the masculine scent of his skin, so achingly familiar, so longed for and so out of reach. Her eyes skidded from the concern in his face. She said clumsily, "I'm fine, Judd, it was just the heat and—"

With genuine interest, Emmy said, "Did you used to faint when you went to fires? Because they're really hot."

Lise gaped at her in horror. Emmy had put her finger on it: Why would an ex-firefighter faint because of a little heat? Say something, Lise, she thought. Anything at all. Because you can't risk Judd guessing why you fainted. "We're already wearing all that gear I showed you," she stumbled. "So we're hot to start with."

Judd interposed, "Why don't you go and ask Maryann to rustle up the hot chocolate, Emmy? I'll take Lise into the den."

Emmy pulled off her boots, hung up her snowsuit and ran for the kitchen. Judd knelt in front of Lise and eased her boots from her feet. Snow had melted in his hair; his lashes were very dark against his cheek. Just as, involuntarily, her hand reached out to brush a strand of hair back from his forehead, he looked up. His eyes burned into hers as though he'd stripped her naked; as though every secret she'd ever harbored must be known to him. Then his mouth plummeted to hers, and another kind of heat surged through her body. With a moan of delight, Lise kissed him back, withholding nothing.

For moments that felt like forever to Lise, their lips clung together, his big body crouched over her. From behind them, Emmy said, "That's what people do when they're going to get married. My friend Charlene told me."

Judd's mouth wrenched itself from Lise's. He surged to his feet and for the first time in their acquaintance Lise saw that he was at a loss for words. Emmy added, her heart-shaped face alive with interest, "Is that why Lise came to live here? Because you're going to get married?"

"No!" Judd raked his fingers through his disordered hair. "Of course not. She's here to look after you, Emmy. That's all."

"Then why were you—"

"There are some things you won't understand until you're older," he said repressively. "Did you ask Maryann about the hot chocolate?"

"She thought you might want coffee instead. That's why I came back."

"You go and tell her hot chocolate's fine, Emmy."

Emmy headed for the kitchen, her mouth a mutinous line. Judd said irritably, "She's quite intelligent enough to know she's been given the brush-off. I was a fool to even touch you. It won't happen again. Believe me."

Lise did. Bereft, aroused, furious, frightened...what

other emotions were left for her to feel? She pushed herself to her feet, staggering a little, and faltered, ''This evening I'll remind her that I'm only here temporarily.''

''You do that.''

''I don't understand why you're so angry—you're the one who kissed me!''

''You think I don't know that?'' he exploded. ''You just have to look at me with those big green eyes and I act with as much common sense as a teenager. And about as much restraint.''

''And how you hate it,'' she whispered.

''That's as good a word as any for the way I feel right now.''

''So why don't you fire me before we get into any worse trouble? Emmy already likes me...oh God, Judd, I should never have come here.''

''You know what?'' he snarled. ''I've built up an international fleet of airlines, made a fortune into the bargain, and everything I've ever learned flies out the window when I'm anywhere near you. Explain that to me, will you?''

''Basic chemistry. Your words.''

His expletive made her wince. He said flatly, ''I'm going to the kitchen before Emmy comes looking for us again. One last thing, Lise—what happened just now, it's not going to happen again. Do you hear me?''

''You're repeating yourself,'' she retorted, and hauled down the zipper on her parka. ''You loathe being out of control, Judd Harwood, that's your problem.''

''I also loathe being psychoanalyzed!''

''Especially when it's a mere woman who's gotten to you,'' she added recklessly, hauling off her toque and shaking out her hair.

Judd took a step closer to her, tipping up her chin with one finger. ''There's something you ought to know about me—I pick up challenges that other men run from. So don't push me too far.''

Her eyes dropped from the threat in his, as instinctively she stepped backward. But her voice, she was proud to notice, sounded quite sure of itself. ''Hadn't you better find Emmy?''

''Remember what I've just said. For your own sake.''

He strode down the hall toward the kitchen. Although adrenaline was charging through her veins, Lise's knees still felt as shaky as a day-old kitten's. For a woman known to keep her cool in emergencies, she wasn't doing very well.

But at least Judd wasn't suspicious about her dizziness.

He hated being around her. The last thing he needed to know was that she was carrying his child.

A couple of days later Lise, Emmy and Judd were eating lunch together in the solarium. Another symptom of pregnancy seemed to be an overriding lethargy; Lise felt tired and dull-witted, and was glad to let Emmy carry the bulk of the conversation. At the end of the meal, Judd said curtly, ''Once Emmy's gone back to school, Lise, would you come to my office for a minute?''

''Of course,'' she said coolly.

When she tapped on his door, he got up from his desk, his expression inscrutable. ''Are you coming down with the flu? You don't look your best.''

Her lashes flickered. ''I'm fine,'' she replied. ''That wasn't why you wanted to see me, surely?''

''I'll be out of town from Thursday until the following Tuesday,'' Judd rapped. ''I've left the details of my trip in this envelope, you'll only need to open it if I'm delayed.''

''You're away a lot,'' Lise said, giving him an unfriendly stare.

"I moved to Montreal with the mistaken idea that it would be nice for Emmy to stay in touch with her grandmother," Judd said tersely. "By the time it became obvious that was a lost cause, Emmy had settled in here and made friends. So I stayed. But the upshot is I have to travel a lot."

"Be honest, Judd. You value money more than people. Business comes first—Angeline used to complain about that."

"Once her career took off, Angeline did photo shoots all over the world," Judd snapped. "Although I'm damned if I know why I'm justifying what I do to you."

"No wonder Emmy gets lonesome."

"She doesn't have to be lonesome now that you're here."

"You're her father. Her ultimate security."

"You're determined to pick a fight, aren't you?" he accused. "I told you to choose between Angeline's version of our marriage and mine. I can see that you've decided to believe my ex-wife. Good for you. Just don't go poisoning Emmy's mind against me, will you?"

Lise's head snapped up. "You think I'd do *that?*"

"How do I know?" Scowling, he added, "Take tomorrow off—I want to tell Emmy my plans and spend some extra time with her."

A day away from Judd sounded like heaven. Because being with him was sheer hell.

Hell? Lise thought in faint dismay. That was a strong word. She really did need a day off. A day away from Judd Harwood, his daughter and his business trips.

Maybe he was going to see a woman. Why else would he leave the details of his trip in a sealed envelope?

She'd start cleaning out her apartment tomorrow, she

thought fiercely. It was a job she was dreading. But it would keep her mind off Judd. And his women.

Or one particular woman. The one he'd be with the next few days. How she detested the thought of him in another woman's arms!

CHAPTER TEN

JUDD left on Thursday, with the briefest of goodbyes to Lise. On Friday afternoon, while Emmy was in school, Lise went to her family doctor and was told that she was indeed pregnant. She took the pamphlets he offered about nutrition and health care, evaded his tactful questions and drove back to Judd's.

Emmy brought three friends home from school, which kept Lise satisfactorily busy. But once Emmy was in bed, Lise went to her room. Too restless to read, she flicked on the TV, watched a sitcom during which she didn't laugh once, and then switched to the news channel. Posturing politicians, terrorist bombings, demonstrations...then a dusty airstrip surrounded by listless trees. One of the two planes involved in a Red Cross relief airlift into the Sudan had crashed; the camera zoomed in to show a group of people standing by the second plane, and suddenly her attention sharpened.

She'd know that man anywhere, the tall, black-haired man dressed in a scruffy khaki shirt and bush pants. Judd. Judd in Africa delivering food and medical supplies to refugees, when he was supposed to be on a business trip. With a woman.

It couldn't be Judd. But it was. The announcer's voice said that there'd been no fatalities, and the next clip began. Lise ran from her room, went to Judd's study and ripped open the white envelope. In it, neatly typed, was his itinerary from Montreal all the way to the Sudan, with a list of phone numbers where he could be contacted at all times.

He wasn't away on business. He wasn't making more

money. He certainly wasn't with one of the elegant women in Marthe's photos. Instead he was working for the Red Cross under circumstances both dangerous and difficult. Remembering how she'd accused him of being mercenary, Lise cringed with shame.

Once again he'd taken her by surprise. And Angeline's assessment of his character was beginning to seem more and more unlikely...ruthless businessmen motivated entirely by greed didn't risk their lives flying aid planes for refugees. Lise suddenly found herself sitting down hard in Judd's leather-backed chair. The other plane had crashed. There was a very real risk in what he was doing.

If something happened to him, she couldn't bear it.

Hunched over, her arms wrapped tightly around her belly, Lise sat very still. Judd was right. She did have to choose between his version of events and Angeline's. She couldn't have it both ways. Against her lifelong loyalty to her beautiful cousin with her casual kindnesses, she had to balance a man who had made love to her with passionate intensity, who adored his small daughter and who was willing to risk his life for the sake of people far less fortunate than he.

Trust, she thought. Which one do I trust?

Surely you learned something about a man when you made love with him? Judd's total attention, his care of her, his eliciting from her of a passion she hadn't known herself capable of—didn't all that add up to a man who gave as well as received? His face had been as naked to her as his body, she thought humbly. He, too, had been shaken by the sheer intensity of their mating. Hadn't he called it unforgettable?

Ever since he'd told her about his background, she'd carried an image in her mind of a little boy with a shock of black hair consigned to an orphanage in one of the world's biggest cities. Bereft of family. Brought up by strangers. That had to have marked him, to have shaped the man he'd become.

Whereas Angeline had grown up with a mother who doted on her, unable to refuse her anything. To Marthe, her daughter's external beauty mirrored equal beauties of soul. But was that true? Indulgence of every wish perhaps wasn't the best thing for a young girl. Neither was uncritical worship. Who could blame Angeline if she'd grown up with a child's greediness for pleasure and love? Marthe had to bear some of the blame for that. Furthermore, how could Angeline have learned about responsibility if Marthe had always shielded her daughter from the consequences of her actions?

These were new thoughts for Lise. Long overdue thoughts, she decided, and got up from the chair. She should go back to her room, just in case Emmy woke.

For a moment she looked around her. The desk was antique walnut, the carpet delicately faded Tibetan wool. Over the desk hung an oil painting of the desert: ochre sand, gray-green sage, a huge bowl of blue sky. Space, she thought. A landscape that challenged. A dangerous landscape. Judd had grown up in a hostile environment, he knew what it was like to fight for his life.

These, too, were new thoughts. Am I falling in love with him? Is that what's happening? Don't, Lise, don't. He doesn't love you. He's sworn he'll never fall in love again.

With anyone. Including you.

As tears shimmered in her eyes, Lise fought them back. She couldn't have Judd now any more than all those years ago. He was out of reach, as impossible to attain as it would be for her to purchase his house on a firefighter's salary. But she was carrying his child, and for that she was passionately grateful. Never mind about the difficulties, the sacrifices that would be called for. She would be the mother of Judd's child. If she couldn't have Judd, that was the next best thing.

Lise went back to bed and fell asleep; and the weekend, despite a constant undertow of worry about Judd's safety, was oddly peaceful and fulfilling. While she was still subject to occasional dizziness, there was color back in her cheeks from all the time she and Emmy were spending outdoors. Deliberately she chose to ignore that the bond was imperceptibly deepening between her and Judd's daughter. There was nothing she could do to prevent it, and both of them were enjoying it.

Judd was due back Tuesday afternoon; on Monday night Lise put on her old nightgown, took a bundle of magazines to bed and switched off her light about eleven. She'd see Judd again tomorrow, she thought, curling up under the covers; and was aware of a confused mingling of panic and happiness. Conjuring up the image of his face, she hugged it to her and eventually drifted into a deep sleep.

Lise lay still under the covers, her eyes wide-open. Was it a noise that had woken her? Or a deep intuition of another person where there should only have been herself and Emmy? Every nerve on edge, she heard the soft fall of footsteps in the hallway. Her heart gave a great lurch. How could an intruder have gotten past the security system? And what should she do?

There was a phone in Judd's room. She'd sneak in there and dial 911. Moving with extreme care, she sat up and eased her legs free of the covers. The digital clock by her bedside said 3:18 a.m.

Lise edged across the thick carpet toward the door, which she always left ajar, the better to hear Emmy. On the way, she picked up the smooth marble carving of a dolphin that stood on the lacquered table; it was reassuringly heavy in her grip. Cautiously she peered around the door.

The hall was empty. She had to pass Emmy's room to get to Judd's. Clutching the statue in her right hand, her heart thrumming in her chest so loudly she was sure the intruder must hear it, she crept along the cool oak flooring. The boards had been laid impeccably; not one of them creaked. Emmy's door, too, was ajar; silent as a ghost, Lise slid past it and glided toward Judd's bedroom.

It was empty. In one swift glance Lise took in the taupe linen that covered the walls, the cream linen on the big bed. Two huge Schefflera plants flanked French doors that led out onto a terrace. The room's single painting was an abstract, a shimmer of greens and blues. Swiftly she reached for the phone.

"What the hell—"

Lise whirled, raising the statue in front of her defensively. Then her arm fell to her side. "Judd," she quavered, "I—I thought you were a thief."

To her horror, a wave of faintness washed over her. Her knees buckled. She sank down on the bed, her breathing shallow in her throat, fighting back the red mist in her brain.

Judd flipped on a light switch. Then he knelt beside her, gently detaching her fingers from the statue. "Your hands are like ice," he said. "Lise, what the devil are you doing in my room?"

She flushed scarlet. "I heard something—it woke me. So I was going to call 911."

Judd said the obvious. "I got home early...what's the statue for?"

"To bash you on the head, of course."

"You're brave as a lion, you know that?"

He was still caressing her cold fingers; she stared at his

hands in fascination. ''I was scared out of my wits,'' she confessed.

Raising her eyes, she looked full at him. He was still wearing an outfit much like the one she'd seen on TV; dark circles shadowed his eyes, and a long scrape ran from one wrist almost to his elbow. ''Judd,'' she said, ''I saw you on the TV news. In Sudan.''

He swore under his breath, his jaw tight. ''I was too busy arguing with the airport officials to even notice the media until it was too late. But I didn't figure it'd go international.''

Again she stared absorbedly at his hands, feeling warmth creep back into her own. ''Why didn't you tell me the truth? About your destination, I mean.''

''I don't tell anyone I do that stuff.'' He paused, then added tautly, ''I was in Venezuela doing airlifts the time of the fire. You can guess how I felt about that. But this time I knew Emmy would be safe with you. I trust you with her, Lise. Totally.''

Moved to tears, Lise faltered, ''The day you left, I accused you of being greedy and mercenary...I'm so sorry.''

''You couldn't have known.''

She looked up, gazing straight into his eyes. ''You're a good man,'' she said unsteadily.

''I'm no angel, Lise. One reason I do it is for the risk, the adrenaline, the need to push my limits—nothing very saintly about that.''

''You do it. That's what's important.''

He shifted uncomfortably, releasing her hands. ''I shouldn't be anywhere near you—I stink. No showers, and I was in too much of a hurry to get home to bother changing.''

The words spoke themselves. ''We could shower together,'' she said; and waited with bated breath for his response.

He stood up, pulling her to her feet. "You're wearing your sexy nightgown," he said, his features inscrutable. "Difficult for me to resist you in that."

"You see," she went on, as if he hadn't spoken, "I believe you. Not Angeline. I figured that out on Friday, the night I saw you on TV…I'm only sorry it took me so long."

"You're so generous," Judd said roughly. "You take my breath away."

With a radiant smile, Lise pulled his head down and kissed him full on the mouth. His stubble of beard rasped her chin; his response, instant and intense, soared through her body. Wasn't this why she'd taken the job as companion to Emmy? So she could be with Judd?

"Shower," he growled against her lips, nibbling them with erotic urgency. "I think I'll burn these clothes."

Sweeping her into his arms, he strode across the room to the bathroom, where a raised ceramic platform with a sunken Jacuzzi overlooked a small enclosed garden of pines and hemlocks. The shower was paneled in polished granite, with massage water jets at different levels; as Judd put her down and began stripping off his clothes, Lise stood still, almost faint with desire. When he was naked, he came over to her, easing her gown over her head, his gaze drinking in the gentle curves of her body. In quick distress, she said, "How did you scrape your arm? And you've got bruises all down your ribs."

He said awkwardly, "Getting one of the crew out of the crashed plane—we were afraid of fire, so we weren't being overly careful. Let's not talk about it, Lise, not now." He reached over to turn on the water and said with a boyish grin, "Last one in's a chicken."

As the jets pummeled her flesh, enveloping her in steam, Lise twisted her hair on top of her head. Judd advanced on her, the bar of soap in his hand, and suddenly she was laughing in exhilaration at the sheer joy of being with him again. She splashed him, her green eyes gleaming with mischief. He grabbed for her, running his hands down her body, then trapping her against the smooth tile and kissing her until she was breathless, boneless with longing. The pelt of dark hair on his chest was slick to his wet skin; water trickled from the concavity of his ribs to his navel. "You're so beautiful," she breathed.

His face intent, he cupped the weight of her breasts in his palms, stroking them to their tightened tips; and all the while he watched the play of expression on her face. In sudden impatience, he said, "I want you in my bed. Now."

"There's nowhere I'd rather be."

Swathing her in a towel, wrapping one around his hips, Judd led the way back into his room. Very gently he rubbed the water from her skin; then he began raining kisses on her lips, her throat and the silken slopes of her breasts. Smoothing her hips with long, rhythmic strokes, he drew them closer to his body, pressing her into his erection until she gasped with pleasure. They fell on the bed in a tangle of limbs. Judd's quickened breathing and heavily pounding heart echoed in her ears; she was encompassed by him, forgetful of anything in the world but him. She was where she belonged.

Then Judd reared up on one elbow. "Last time I didn't even think of protection. Not until the next day. Should I use something, Lise? Or are you--"

She stared at him blankly. She was pregnant. She didn't need protection. And now was the perfect time to tell him. She said faintly, "No, you don't need to use anything."

"I thought you were probably on the pill," he said with a crooked grin. "Should have asked, I know—but it all happened so fast in Dominica, I forgot all the normal rules."

The rules he used with other women, she thought sickly. Had they all been as willing as she? Falling into his bed like a ripe apple from a tree? Judd said urgently, "What's wrong? Why are you looking at me like that? Protection's an obvious issue, I'd have thought—I've never liked the idea of bringing an unwanted child into the world."

What of the child in her womb? Would he regard that as unwanted? Of course he would. Because Judd wasn't into commitment: he'd made that clear to her days ago. He'd been married once, and once was enough.

Then one more dimension of her dilemma tumbled into Lise's brain. If Judd were to find out she were pregnant, he'd probably insist on marrying her, to legitimize his child; she knew him well enough for that. So she'd have forced him into an unwanted marriage, a marriage he'd resent. As he would resent her, who was its pretext.

She couldn't—wouldn't—do that. Not for anything.

With the swiftness of panic, Lise twisted free of him, stumbling to her feet by the side of the bed. Crossing her arms over her breast, horribly aware of her nudity, she faltered, "I can't make love to you. I mustn't."

In a single lithe movement Judd rolled over and stood beside her, his body looming over hers. "What's going on, Lise?"

"We shouldn't be doing this. There's no future in it for either of us, we both know that. I'm sorry—I shouldn't have led you on the way I did, it was wrong of me."

"We're both adults. What happens between us in bed— it's unique and we'd be fools to pass it up."

"And that's where we're different," she said in sudden bitterness. "I'm a typical woman, the kind you read about in magazine articles—I can't have an affair with you just because the sex is great. Making love has to mean more than that! We're not in love, Judd—and you made it very clear you never want to fall in love again. So I'm pulling out now. Before I get hurt.''

He frowned. ''Are you saying you're falling in love with me?''

''No! I'm saying I don't want to risk that happening.'' In a low voice, she added, ''I'm not cool and sophisticated like all those other women you date. I could get hurt by you. And I'm not going to let that happen. That's what I'm getting at.''

In a sudden angry movement, Judd ripped the spread from the bed. ''Here, put this around you.''

She hugged the softly woven cloth to her body, grateful for its warmth, glad she was no longer naked. Knowing she'd never have a better opportunity, she added in a rush, ''I think I should leave before four months. It's not fair to Emmy for me to hang around.''

''You need the money.''

''I'll get another job—I can always do the course a year later.'' She'd have to anyway, because of the baby. But she couldn't tell him that.

''Stay,'' Judd said with sudden urgency, clasping her by the shoulders, all the force of his willpower in his words. ''Give us the chance to get to know each other better. Who knows—both of us might change.''

Briefly Lise was suffused with a hope as fragrant as rose petals. Or was it joy at the mere thought that Judd might change, might be open to more than just a passing affair?

Might fall in love with her? Might *want* to marry her?

But then her heart clenched with pain, hope crushed like a withered leaf. She couldn't stay, for the obvious reason that before long her pregnancy would reveal itself and become a weapon over Judd, a means to secure a hasty commitment that afterward he would regret. ''No,'' she said in a stony voice. ''I can't stay.''

His fingers dug into her shoulders with cruel strength.

''Then I'd suggest you start looking for another job right away,'' he said with icy precision. ''Because you're right, Emmy's feelings are involved—she's starting to get fond of you. She doesn't need a second mother figure leaving her in the lurch.''

Lise flinched. ''You seem to be forgetting that you're the one who offered me this job.''

''I haven't forgotten—it was one of the stupidest decisions I've ever made. Like I said, common sense goes out the window as far as you're concerned.''

Once again he was looking at her as though he hated her. He certainly didn't look as though he had the remotest interest in making love to her anymore. Hugging her dignity as well as the bedspread, wondering if she could make it to the door without tripping and falling flat on her face, Lise said, ''I'll do my best to be gone within the week.''

''Fine,'' said Judd; and released her so suddenly she staggered.

Lise looped the spread to her knees and scuttled back to her own room. Closing the door, she collapsed on the bed. Her body ached with unfulfilled need and her soul felt bruised and battered. She'd been exiled. Exiled from Judd and from Emmy. Shut out from the possibility of happiness, all because her own body had betrayed her. What a cruel irony that the intimacy she'd shared with Judd was now banishing her from any hope of deeper intimacy.

Tomorrow she'd start looking into a move to Halifax. She couldn't stay in Montreal, the risk was too great of meeting Judd when her pregnancy was more advanced. Or after the baby was born. Either prospect made her shudder in terror.

But even worse would be a forced and loveless marriage. Anything was better than that.

CHAPTER ELEVEN

LISE was ready to leave the house at nine the next morning. She'd woken with a sore heart and a plan of action. She'd go to her apartment and do some more cleaning in the morning, then in the afternoon she'd get on the Internet at the library and start researching her move east. She'd feel better when she'd taken some action, she told herself stoutly, running down the stairs in her jeans and an old red sweater, pulling on her ski jacket as she went. The sooner she left here the better. For everyone.

By driving herself hard all morning, she got her bedroom and the bathroom stripped to the essentials; she was back at Judd's by quarter to twelve, in lots of time for Emmy. She was pulling off her jacket in the foyer when the doorbell rang. It was too early for Judd, who'd said he'd bring Emmy home from school for lunch. Swiftly Lise pulled the door open.

"Angeline!" she exclaimed, her face blank with shock.

"You should never wear red," Angeline said. "Didn't I teach you anything all those years ago?"

Horribly conscious that her hair was a mess and the red sweater none too clean because she'd been lugging bags of garbage to the basement of her apartment building, Lise said lamely, "Won't you come in?"

Angeline waved to the limousine parked in the driveway, then sauntered into the hallway, putting down the big package she was carrying. She was dressed in a sheared mink coat, dyed sapphire-blue; her cream wool pants and cashmere sweater were complemented by gleaming alligator boots. Her hair was an artful tumble of curls to her

147

shoulders. She said calmly, as if she turned up on the door-step every other day, "Where's Judd? Not away, I hope."

"No. He should be here very shortly. With Emmy."

"My darling little Emmy...how is she?"

"Fine," Lise said baldly.

"And what are you doing here?" Angeline asked, wan-dering over to examine a Steuben bowl filled with tulips.

"I work here. As a companion to Emmy."

Angeline swung around, her pale blue eyes openly spec-ulative. "Judd hired you?" Lise nodded. "How very odd," Angeline said. "I suppose he was grateful after the fire."

"I suppose he was," Lise said evenly. "I'm going to ask the same question—why are you here, Angeline? A surprise visit all the way from the Loire?"

"That's really none of your business."

Lise flushed; and to her relief heard a car pull up out-side. The front door opened and Emmy burst through. She saw Lise first; shucking off her boots, she cried, "Guess what? The picture I drew last week of us tobogganing won a prize at the art show."

She flung her arms around Lise and hugged her. Lise's arms went around the little girl in a reflex response: a response she liked very much. Then she looked up and saw that Judd was watching them; and shivered from the open hostility in his gaze. He didn't want Emmy showing her such open affection, because he knew Lise was leaving as soon as she could. Then Judd's eyes swiveled sideways. He said in blank shock, "Angeline—what are you doing here?"

Emmy stiffened in Lise's embrace. She, too, looked over at the beautiful woman standing beside the tulips, a woman very much at her ease, who looked as though she owned the palatial foyer rather than being an uninvited guest. "I

thought it was time I came to see my little daughter,"
Angeline said. "How are you, *ma chérie?*"

Emmy stood up straight, one hand clutching the hem of
Lise's sweater. "I'm fine."

"Aren't you going to give *me* a hug?" Angeline asked
with a winsome smile.

Obediently Emmy walked across the polished oak and
stood as rigid as a doll while Angeline folded her in her
arms. "I've brought you a present," Angeline said, indi-
cating the package. "All the way from Paris."

"That's nice," said Emmy.

"Aren't you going to open it?"

Emmy undid the box, pulling out a very large, fluffy
brown bear. "I already have a bear."

"That dreadful old thing you had four years ago?"
Angeline shuddered delicately. "Time you threw it away,
ma petite. This one's new and much bigger."

"But I love Plush."

For a moment Angeline looked less than doting. "You
inherited your father's stubbornness, I see. This is a very
expensive bear, Emmy, from the most exclusive toy shop
in Paris."

Emmy said woodenly, "Thank you very much."

Smoothly Judd interrupted. "You might as well join us
for lunch, Angeline. Emmy doesn't have long before she
goes back to school. Lise, why don't you lead the way?"

So Lise, her hips swinging in her slim-fitting jeans,
headed for the glass-enclosed solarium, where copper
bowls of hyacinths and daffodils spilled glorious shades of
azure and gold, filling the air with fragrance. Angeline was
like a hyacinth, she thought: complex, extravagant and effortlessly beautiful. Had she really come to see Emmy? Or
was her real aim Emmy's father?

As if he'd read her mind, Judd said, "I'm sure you had
motives other than Emmy for coming this far, Angeline."

"They'll keep until later, darling."

Inwardly Lise winced. Judd said in an expressionless voice, "You never were any good at keeping secrets—and now is as good a time as any to tell me why you're here."

Angeline pouted her full lips. "You always could get anything out of me," she said gaily. "Old friends of Henri's live near here—Paul and Marie Gagnon...he's a retired bank president. They're having a gala concert in their home tomorrow night, some famous pianist or other. I'm invited, and I managed to get you on the list, too. I know it's very last minute, but you remember how I always loved spontaneity." Her smile, intimate and dazzling, hinted at other shared memories.

"The Gagnons—don't they have a son who used to be based in New York? Will he be there, Angeline?"

Angeline's laugh was brittle. "How would I know?"

With a touch of grimness, Judd added, "And where's Henri?"

"Doing something terribly important to the vineyard. But of course he'd never stop me from coming."

Judd said bluntly, "Get an invitation for Lise, and I'll go with you."

Angeline frowned, small lines marring her perfect forehead. "For Lise? Why?"

"She saved our daughter's life—or are you forgetting that? It's the least you can do."

Lise had been quiet long enough. If Judd thought she was going to tag along to some fancy party as an unwanted third, he could think again. "I don't want to go," she said with finality.

Judd's slate-gray eyes clashed with hers. "But I want you to," he said. "And I'm your employer—you'll go, Lise. It's an order."

She could quit. On the spot. "I have nothing to wear and no time to shop."

"Tomorrow morning. At Gautier's."

Gautier's was world famous for its designer label garments. "No," said Lise. "I can't afford Gautier's, even on the salary you're paying me. And I will not allow you to buy my clothes." Once had been more than enough.

"We'll leave at nine-thirty," Judd said.

He was treating her like a child. Or was he punishing her for leaving his employ? For refusing to make love to him? Her cheeks flushed with temper, Lise opened her mouth for a scathing retort, then noticed Emmy listening to this interchange with wide-held eyes. She clamped her lips shut. But Angeline had no such scruples. "Darling, Lise would be out of her depth...much kinder to leave her home with Emmy."

"The three of us go. Or you can go on your own," Judd said in a tone that brooked no argument.

Angeline's pout wasn't quite so decorative this time. "But who will stay with Emmy? Surely you wouldn't leave her here alone? Again."

"Maryann and her husband will stay with Emmy. And the Gagnons live only a few blocks from here...although your concern is very touching, Angeline."

Angeline had never been attuned to sarcasm. "Of course I'm concerned," she cooed. "Emmy's mine as much as yours."

Emmy chewed on her sandwich and said nothing, although Lise could see the child was picking up far more than the words that were being exchanged. Lise said, "If I'm as much out of my depth as you think I'll be, Angeline, I can always leave early."

"You'll leave when we're all ready to leave," Judd announced, his gray eyes inimical.

Lise glared at him and pointedly addressed herself to her croissant, which was smothered in avocado and shrimp and deserved more of her attention than it had been getting. Judd knew she wouldn't start an argument when Emmy was present. But Emmy wouldn't always be around; and she'd never liked dictators.

Angeline said sweetly, "You and I must have dinner at *Chez LaBelle*, Judd—for old times' sake. That was my favorite place, remember?"

He said impassively, "It went out of business six months ago. We'll have dinner here tomorrow evening."

"I may not be able to get an invitation for Lise," Angeline said with a touch of sharpness, "it's very late for that."

"Just mention my name," Judd said, "it'll work wonders. I've known Paul for years."

Lise chewed on a pickled onion. Judd wasn't acting like a man in love with his estranged wife; if he were, Lise was the last person he'd want tagging along to the gala. Or was he giving out the message he wasn't about to fall into Angeline's arms the moment she turned up?

What ordinary woman could compete with Angeline?

Judd started describing some of Emmy's accomplishments at school, drawing his daughter into the conversation; and eventually the meal was over. Emmy and Lise went upstairs to find some gym gear, Emmy staying behind to clean her teeth. Lise went back downstairs, her footsteps silent on the thick carpet. As she came around the corner she saw Angeline and Judd silhouetted against the tall windows that overlooked the driveway. Judd's back was to her. They were standing very close together, Angeline talking animatedly, Judd's attention focused on his beautiful ex-wife. Then Angeline pulled his head down and kissed him, her tapered fingers caressing the silky black hair at his nape.

Just so had she, Lise, caressed him. For a split second she was frozen to the spot. Then she backed up with frantic speed, her heart thrumming in her breast, her fingers ice-cold on the banister. She'd thought she'd known what jealousy meant the day Marthe had shown her the photos; but she'd known nothing. The pain that filled her body now was unlike anything she'd ever experienced. Unbearable. Unmendable.

Then Emmy came charging down the hall, her gym bag in one hand. "I'm going to be late—is Dad ready to take me back to school?"

With a valiant effort at normality, Lise said, "Give him a shout, I just need to go to my room for a minute."

She was being a coward. But she couldn't face Judd after what she'd seen. Hidden by the curve of the stairwell, she heard Emmy call out, and Judd's deep voice answer. Then Angeline purred, "I'd love to come and see your school, Emmy."

"All right," said Emmy with something less than enthusiasm.

The front door closed. Silence fell. Lise leaned against the nearest wall, hugging her arms to her body, wishing she'd never come to this big stone mansion that was owned by a man with a heart of stone. Last night Judd had wanted to make love to her, Lise. Today he was kissing his ex-wife.

If she had any sense, she'd run from here right now and never come back. But she couldn't do that to Emmy. If Judd had been telling the truth, Angeline had left her daughter without saying goodbye. She, Lise, couldn't do the same thing. It would be too cruel.

She was trapped.

Sharp at nine-thirty the following morning Lise presented herself at the front door. She was wearing her best wool skirt, of hunter-green, with leather boots and a matching hip-length green coat. Her chin was well up; her eyes openly unfriendly.

Judd said sardonically, "Good morning to you, too."

"Let's not pretend I'm doing this for fun, Judd. And don't push me, I can quit anytime."

"But you won't. Because of Emmy."

"Do you always use your opponent's weakest point as leverage?" she said bitterly.

"I do what it takes."

"Then let's go dress me up like some kind of mannequin. Who'll be on display tonight as one of Judd Harwood's two women."

"Is that how you see it?" he rapped.

"How else am I to see it?" Her temper got the better of her. "I saw you yesterday, kissing Angeline."

"She threw herself at me. That's what you saw."

"You weren't exactly struggling."

"You didn't hang around long enough."

"Why would I? To check out if your technique's the same with her as with me?"

His breath hissed between his teeth. "Watch it, Lise. Or I might be tempted to demonstrate my technique."

"Don't you dare!"

His answer was to clamp his arms around her, pull her toward him and kiss her hard on the mouth. Like a flash fire, Lise's anger flared into desire, hot, compelling and unquenchable. Then Judd as suddenly thrust her away. His chest heaving, he snarled, "I told you not to push me too far and that kiss had nothing to do with technique."

"No—it was about power! About winning. Because you can't bear to lose. Especially to a woman."

The morning sun pouring through the tall windows glinted in her hair and shot sparks from her brilliant eyes. Judd took a long, shuddering breath. "Maybe," he said harshly, "it was about feelings."

She wasn't going to go there; not with Judd. "Maybe it was about ownership."

His eyes narrowed. "Catch-22. If I don't kiss you, it's because I'm after Angeline. If I do, it's because I'm some kind of Don Juan. You've got it wrong about me winning all the time—with you, I can't."

The bitterness in his voice shocked Lise. If she weren't pregnant by him, might she have softened, asked him what he meant? But all her intuition screamed that if Judd knew she were pregnant, he would insist on marrying her: because it was his child she was carrying. His. Ownership indeed. She said in a toneless voice, "We'd better go. I want to be back for Emmy at lunchtime."

"Right. Emmy. She's your only concern, isn't she?"

"You're paying me to look after her."

"Do you love Emmy, Lise?"

Her jaw dropped. She remembered the fervor with which Emmy had hugged her this morning, the delicacy of the child's bones, her searching eyes and quick-witted grin. "I won't let myself—I can't afford to."

"Because you're hell-bent on vanishing from her life."

And what was she to say to that? *If you saw me in six months, you'd understand why?* Lise bit her lip and heard Judd say forcefully, "Lise, tell me what's bothering you."

"Nothing's bothering me, other than you. Judd, let's go."

"You've got to be the most infuriating woman I've ever met! Bar none."

"It's the red hair," she said flippantly. "Too bad it doesn't come out of a bottle. What color dress are you going to buy me this time?"

Briefly he reached out to stroke her vivid curls. "Naked is how I prefer you."

A fierce blush scorched her cheeks. With an indecipherable exclamation, Lise pushed open the door and saw the limo waiting for them, the chauffeur at the wheel. All the way downtown she sat in her own corner, staring out the window. At Gautier's it came as no surprise that she and Judd were ushered into a thickly carpeted private room with two women to serve them. Lise disappeared into the changing room, was supplied with an uplift bra, and was eased into the first dress. It was black and frighteningly elegant.

Feeling awkward and unsure of herself, she marched out to the paneled, gilt-edged mirrors and Judd's discerning eyes. He shook his head. "Not you, Lise."

It wasn't. He was right. She almost had to be poured into the next dress, which was silver lamé with a price tag that made her blanch. Before Judd could say anything, she announced, "Marilyn Monroe I'm not. I don't want this one."

"You'd stop traffic," he said, and winked at her.

A reluctant grin quirked her mouth. "Even if I can't sit down."

Back in the changing room, Lise riffled through the rack of dresses, beginning to enter into the spirit of the search; neither black nor white became her, she hated pastels, and anything red, orange or pink made her hair look like a five-alarm fire. So that dispensed with a fair number of the gowns. Then her hand stilled. The fabric was shot silk, dark green with an iridescence of sapphire; the bodice tight, the skirt paneled over a pencil-slim underskirt. She said, "I'd like to try this one."

The saleswoman said, "Madame has good taste."

Which probably meant she'd picked the most expensive dress on the rack. It was eased over her head. It fit perfectly, Lise knew that right away, and slipped her feet into the high-heeled sandals the salon had provided. Her head held high, she walked out of the changing room.

Judd got to his feet, his face intent. "That's it," he said. "Perfect."

In silence Lise looked at her reflection, almost the reflection of a stranger: a tall, flame-haired woman whose ivory shoulders supported narrow straps, and whose cleavage was a soft valley cupped by the stiff, dark silk. The floating panels subtly emphasized the slit in the underskirt; she looked elegant, sexy and very feminine. She'd never worn a dress one-tenth as beautiful. And never would again. Especially in the next few months.

"You'll need shoes to match," Judd said; and within five minutes Lise had selected sandals whose narrow straps made even her feet look sexy. Gossamer-thin stockings were added, and toning makeup. Then Judd obtained a swatch of the fabric and asked for everything to be delivered. Once Lise was in her street clothes again, he took her by the arm. "Vaison's next," he said.

Vaison's was the local equivalent of Tiffanys in New York. Lise said in alarm, "Whatever for?"

"The finishing touch," he said with a wolfish grin.

"Whatever you buy, I'm not going to keep," she said, hands on her hips.

"You haven't seen it yet. So how do you know? And I'm certainly not going to return it the next day— so you might be stuck with it."

"You drive me crazy—you know that?"

"It's entirely mutual," Judd replied.

She looked at him through her lashes. "Wow—finally we have something in common."

"Oh, we have more than that in common," he said, his gaze skimming her body. "Here we are."

In Vaison's the level of personal attention Judd received was again an eye-opener for Lise. He showed the swatch of fabric, made a quick sketch of the neckline of her dress, and said, "A pendant, I think. Something simple. Emeralds and sapphires, perhaps?"

"I believe we have just the thing, *monsieur*."

The pendant brought from the vault was a single faceted

emerald flanked by two sapphires, the stones inset in gold and hung from a delicate gold chain. Lise, beyond speech, again looked at herself in the mirror and knew intuitively that it was the perfect jewelery for her gown. Emerald earrings were produced; as the salesman retreated to the vault again, she hissed, "Judd, you can't do this! What am I going to do—wear them when I'm grooming a dog? Or cleaning out cages? You mustn't! You've spent far too much money already."

"The dress needs jewelery," he said inflexibly. "You can sell them afterward. It'll help pay for your course."

"You can't give them to me! I won't let you."

"The women who come here generally don't argue with the men who—Lise, what's wrong?"

She was near tears. "This is a travesty," she said incoherently. "I really hate it, Judd."

"Travesty of what?" he demanded.

"Of what gift giving should be. Two people who care for each other choosing something the other will like. It's not one-sided. It's nothing to do with money and power. Don't you *see?*"

"Don't you like the pendant?"

"I love it. But that's not the point." As the salesman approached, she muttered, "Never mind. I knew you wouldn't understand," and stood by mutely as the jewels were wrapped and paid for. After Judd again requested delivery, he and Lise went outside. "I made a hair appointment for you at Gautier's, two-thirty," he said. "They'll give you a manicure as well."

People jostled her on the sidewalk; the sky was a heavy gray, the air milder and thick with rain to come. Lise felt very tired. She said, "I've had enough of this. More than enough. I'm going to walk home, I need to be alone for a while. But I'll be there for Emmy at lunchtime."

"Lise," Judd said deliberately, "about the pendant.

Seeing you at home with Emmy, whose life you saved, is gift enough for me. Watching the two of you play in the snow or share a joke together...nothing you could buy me can equal that. And emeralds are nothing in comparison.''

She gazed at him in silence. She wanted to bawl her head off, she wanted to scream and yell and stamp her feet; as if she were three years old, not twenty-eight. ''I—I'll see you this evening,'' she muttered.

''I want you to know something else. It's very clear to me—it always has been—that you're not one bit interested in my money.'' He gave her a crooked grin. ''I like that. Very much.''

The wind ruffled his black hair; his smile made her heart melt. The words tumbled out before she could stop them. ''The way we were in bed—that had absolutely nothing to do with money.''

''I may be like a bull in a china shop where you're concerned, but I did understand that much.''

''I can't imagine why I said that. This is a crazy conversation.''

''Maybe it's a real conversation.''

As she made an indecipherable sound, Judd rested his hands on the shoulders of her jacket. ''The pendant—I want you to keep it, Lise. Three stones, an emerald and two sapphires. Think of Emmy and you and me—there might so easily have been no emerald.''

But you and I—we're not a couple. We're not a matched pair of sapphires. ''Oh,'' she said.

''Will you keep it? It's important to me that you do.''

Her green eyes were full of confusion. ''I—I guess so.''

He kissed her swiftly on both cheeks. ''Good. Off you go, or you'll be late for lunch, and I'll miss my conference call.''

He turned, walking back in the direction of the parked limo. Lise set off the other way. Just when she had Judd all figured out, he said something that threw her, that made her see him in a different light. As a result of which, she'd just accepted a hugely expensive gift from a man who didn't know she was carrying his child. She was purposely deceiving him, and simultaneously accepting jewels of a beauty and extravagance beyond her imagining.

Jewels and gratitude, she thought with painful honesty. That was all Judd was offering her. Along with a healthy dose of lust.

He wasn't offering love. Or commitment.

CHAPTER TWELVE

AT EIGHT o'clock that evening Lise was dressed and ready for the gala. She and Emmy had shared supper on a tray in Lise's room, and Emmy was now curled up on Lise's bed along with Plush; the bear Angeline had given her was conspicuous by its absence. As Lise put the finishing touches to her makeup, Emmy said with undoubted sincerity, "You look like a fairy princess."

The one who gets the prince? But the prince didn't want her. Or, at least, only in his bed.

Maybe, just maybe, this dress would change his mind?

The thought had come from nowhere. I don't want Judd, Lise thought in panic. I don't love him. Of course I don't.

Or do I? Would I give a hundred pendants to have him hold me in his arms and tell me he loves me?

She dragged her attention to the mirror. Her hair was piled high on her head, exposing the creamy length of her throat; the dress fit her like a glove, its shimmer of dark greens and blues subtly emphasizing the deep green of her eyes. The pendant glittered above her cleavage, while the earrings sparkled and shone. She looked poised and very elegant.

The poise was fake.

But the dress was real. Could it, perhaps, make Judd look at her with new eyes? Eyes that went deeper than her body?

The body that was carrying his child. She didn't want her baby to be fatherless; she herself had loved her father deeply, and had missed his steadfast presence for years.

So was that it? She wanted Judd simply so her child would have a father?

With her usual incurable honesty, Lise knew she was evading the truth. She wanted Judd for himself. Body and soul. She wanted his ardor, his tenderness, his laughter and intensity. For herself. As well as for her child. So was that love?

Emmy said with a pleasurable shiver, "You look like you've just seen a ghost."

Lise's gaze jerked back to the little girl on the bed. "I— I was daydreaming."

"I bet my dad will think you look like a princess, too."

"Your mother will outshine me, Emmy."

"But you're nicer," Emmy said naively.

Lise fought down a smile. "Thank you for putting the pendant on for me," she said; she'd found the clasp too intricate to manage on her own.

"It's jazzy. Dad must like you a lot to give it to you."

Lise said gently, "He's grateful to me, Emmy, that's all. You mustn't build castles in the air."

Which is precisely what she herself had been doing.

Tomorrow, she thought. Tomorrow she must somehow break the news to Emmy that she'd be leaving very soon. That she was moving away and severing any connection between the two of them. She dreaded it. But it had to be done, and done with all the sensitivity and care she could muster.

"I'd better go down," Lise said, "it's time to leave."

Emmy bounced off the bed and tucked her hand in Lise's. "I'll come, too."

To feel Emmy's warm fingers curled around her own was the most bittersweet of sensations. She loved Emmy. No question of that. It was going to hurt horribly to say goodbye to her. Pushing these thoughts aside, Lise smiled down at the little girl. "Thanks for all your help."

So when Lise descended the circular staircase to the foyer, where an austerely designed Belgian chandelier cast pools of golden light, she had Emmy's moral support to give her courage. Judd and Angeline were standing at the foot of the stairs waiting for her. Judd looked startlingly handsome in a tuxedo and pleated white shirt; as for Angeline, her silver gown made her look like a real princess: the one who did get the prince, Lise thought with a wrench at her heartstrings.

Judd said spontaneously, "You look magnificent, Lise."

His smile was so high voltage that Lise felt her fragile composure tremble. "Thank you...how are you, Angeline?"

Angeline was staring at Lise as if she'd never seen her before; when she noticed the pendant, she looked like a schoolgirl who's just found out someone else has beaten her to first prize. "I presume Judd chose your dress," she said with the nearest thing to malice she was capable of. "He always did have good taste."

"Actually I picked it out on my own," Lise replied.

Angeline produced the moue made famous on many a billboard. "We're getting my mother on the way to the Gagnons', she's coming, too. She was wrong when she said you'd never be beautiful like me."

It was impossible to dislike Angeline, Lise thought ruefully; although the prospect of Judd and Marthe in the same car made her shudder. "That's very generous of you," she said, and meant it.

Angeline glanced over at her daughter. "I'd love a hug, *petite*—although don't muss my dress."

Emmy complied dutifully. Then she said, "You look cool, Dad."

Judd picked her up and swung her high over his head. "Thanks, sweetheart. You'll be fine with Maryann, she's going to stay in the guest wing all night."

"She said I could watch TV until nine-thirty."

"Just go easy on the chocolate-coated popcorn."

I wish I was staying home and watching TV, Lise thought. And fifteen minutes later when Marthe, in ice-blue satin, joined them in the limo, wished it even more sincerely. Marthe was frigidly polite to Judd, overly solic-itous with her daughter and, after one affronted look that took in the designer gown and the jewels, ignored Lise completely.

That was fine with Lise. There were enough potential pitfalls in the evening ahead without adding Marthe's acid tongue. Nevertheless, she couldn't suppress a quiver of anticipation when they drew up outside the Gagnons' huge—and, in her opinion, hugely ugly—medieval-style castle. Pillars, archways, buttresses and turrets, it had them all. As for the inside, she swiftly gained an impression of a decorator-perfect and soulless house, with none of the individuality of Judd's eclectic collection of cherished ob-jects.

The Gagnons, however, were gray-haired, rotund and friendly; their only son, Roland, who was visiting from New York, was blond and sleekly handsome. He kissed Angeline, whom he obviously knew, on both cheeks, gave Judd a look of cool assessment that rather puzzled Lise and shook Lise's hand with enthusiasm. "Delighted to meet you," he said, his boyish grin laden with charm. And just before the concert began in an anteroom to the elegant ballroom, he slipped into the seat next to Lise. She'd man-aged—rather successfully, she thought—to lose Judd and Angeline in the crush; and Roland's company was cer-tainly preferable to Marthe's.

"Didn't think I'd ever get to stop shaking hands," he whispered. "Once this is done, the dancing begins. Real music."

"You don't like classical music?"

"It's okay if you're over sixty-five. The Viennese waltz crowd will be in the ballroom after this concert's over. But the real action—disco and hip-hop—will be in the great room at the back of the house. I want to dance with you, Lise."

"Thank you," she said limpidly. "How do you know Angeline?"

"Oh, I met her a couple of years before she left for France," he said vaguely. "What's with you and Judd?"

"He's my employer." As Roland gave her a knowing look, Lise added more sharply than she'd intended, "I look after his daughter."

"Okay, okay...oops, here comes the piano player. I'd better shut up, Mum can't stand it when I talk through her kind of music. What's the difference, I say, cover one kind of noise with another." He grinned. "Makes her very cranky."

Roland might be a lightweight, thought Lise, but at least he was keeping her mind off the way Angeline had been commandeering Judd's attention all evening. She inspected her gilt-embossed program, settling down to enjoy herself as best she could. The pianist was world-class and the music did calm her; but afterward Judd tracked her down, insisting she accompany him, Angeline and Marthe to the ballroom, where an orchestra was tuning its instruments and white-jacketed waiters were passing champagne and delicious hors d'oeuvres. Roland vanished, having promised to rescue her in half an hour. With grim determination, Marthe engaged Lise in conversation.

So it was Angeline Judd led onto the dance floor first. They made a strikingly handsome couple, Lise thought with a painful twist of her heart; despite her own beautiful dress and her jewels, Judd had been nothing but punctiliously polite to her. Wishing she was sitting on her perch

at the back of the fire truck, where at least she'd know
who she was, she said, ''Angeline looks lovely, Marthe.''

Marthe said in a staccato voice, ''She's left the count.
She's coming home to stay. She and Judd will remarry.
For Emmy's sake.''

Some champagne slopped from Lise's glass onto the
skirt of her dress. Her lashes flew down to hide her eyes.
Of course. Why hadn't she guessed there was a motive
behind Angeline's sudden appearance? And that it would
be tied in with Emmy?

Angeline and Judd a couple again. Angeline, Judd and
Emmy a family.

Her fingers trembling, Lise scrubbed at the damp stain
on her dress. In a totally artificial voice, she said, ''Look
what I've done, how silly of me. Please excuse me,
Marthe, I'll try toweling it dry in the ladies' room.''

She pushed back her chair. The myriad lights from the
crystal chandeliers blurred in her vision; frantically she
held back tears that if they once started might never stop.
Asking one of the waiters for directions, she fled the ballroom.

The washroom was adorned with vases of red roses in
front of gold-framed mirrors. Perhaps she could hide in
here for the rest of the evening, Lise thought crazily. At
least Judd couldn't come after her.

He wasn't going to come after her. He was going to
remarry Angeline, Emmy's mother. Thank God she, Lise,
had had the sense to keep her pregnancy to herself. But
what would it be like giving birth to Judd's child and
knowing that Judd was forever lost to her?

Other women came and went, chattering and laughing.
Eventually Lise got up, repaired her lipstick and headed
for the great room where strobe lights flashed and the
heavy beat of the bass throbbed through her body. As she
edged further into the room, Roland waved at her. ''Been

looking everywhere for you,'' he said. ''Even braved the ballroom, how about that? Let's dance.''

Anything was better than the numb despair that had her in its grip. So Lise began to dance, her limbs feeling heavy and awkward. The noise level was too loud for conversation; the pulsing lights both hid and revealed her.

When the band stopped for a break, Roland led her toward the buffet table, which was laden with an array of food that at any other time would have taken her breath away. She was picking at some tiger shrimp when she saw, across the width of the room, Judd's broad shoulders. She ducked behind another couple, but it was too late: he'd seen her. She could run, once more, for the washroom. But a stubborn kind of pride kept Lise where she was.

He strode up to her; in the intermittent light, she saw that he was in a towering rage. He rasped, ''Where the hell have you been?''

''Dancing. With Roland.'' Who, she noticed, was applying himself to his braised scallops as if Judd didn't exist.

''It's time you danced with me.''

''I don't think so, Judd. You may have clothed me. But you don't own me.''

His breath hissed between his teeth. ''I've danced with Angeline twice. I've danced with her mother, which was an interesting experience. I've danced with Roland's mother and two of his sisters. And now I'm going to dance with you.''

''I don't want to dance with you!''

He took her by the arm, his fingers digging into her bare flesh. ''We'll discuss this somewhere else.''

Briefly Lise contemplated staging a full-blown scene. It was tempting; it might even make her feel better. But the Gagnons had welcomed her with genuine hospitality, and Roland had been kind to her in his own way; they deserved better of her than that. "Let go of me," she said. "I'll come of my own free will or not at all."

Unwilling admiration flickered over Judd's face. "You've got spirit, I'll give you that," he said, and slid his hands with lingering sensuality down her arms to her wrists. Lightly clasping the fingers of one hand, he raised them to his lips, and kissed them one by one.

Lise stood rooted to the spot, fury and desire exploding in her veins. She snatched her hand back, said to Roland, "I'll be back. Very soon," and marched across the dance floor. But before she could reach the far side of the room, the percussionist struck three heavy chords, and the band picked up the beat. She pivoted to face Judd. "You wanted to dance. Then dance."

The beat echoed the racing of her heart. She threw herself into the music, moving her body with overt sensuality and no caution whatsoever. Pouring her turmoil of emotion into the music, she danced as she'd never danced before, her eyes glittering, her hips gyrating, her cheeks flushed from far more than exertion. The whole length of the song, Judd's eyes never left her, as in pagan invitation she flaunted herself in front of him. The song ended in a flourish from the electric guitars. Judd whirled her into the circle of his embrace and kissed her full on the mouth.

Lise melted into him, kissed him back and from a long way away heard a chorus of wolf whistles. Abruptly Judd pushed her away. "We've got an audience," he drawled. "Too bad."

He looked thoroughly in control of himself and of the situation. Whereas Lise felt as limp as a rag doll. In a cracked voice she said, "Are you happy? You've had your dance. Now you can go back to Angeline."

"What if I don't want to?"

"I think you do...I know you do. Regardless, let me spell something out." She took a deep breath, only wanting this to be over. "I'm not another option, Judd. I never have been and never will be."

In a voice like ice, Judd said, "Are you telling me the truth, Lise? Think about it very carefully before you answer."

He'd given her her chance; and she had no choice, she had to take it. Because she was pregnant with his child. "Yes, it's the truth," she said steadily. "I'll tell Emmy tomorrow that I'm leaving, and I'll be gone right after that."

"Fine," Judd said, turned on his heel and threaded his way toward the entrance.

Lise watched him go, standing as though turned to stone in the middle of the dance floor. Judd wouldn't be back, not this time. He'd go straight to Angeline. Who'd welcome him with open arms.

She'd done it. And what a place, Lise thought wildly, to realize your heart's broken.

The next song started. Once again she ran for the ladies' room, this time searching her evening bag and discovering she had more than enough money to get a cab back to Judd's house. That's what she'd do. And in the morning she'd tell Emmy she was leaving right away. A clean break. A new start.

She could do it. She was known for her courage, wasn't she?

She'd rather face a burning warehouse full of explosives than either Emmy or Judd. And that really was the truth.

Fifteen minutes passed. Feeling ten years older, Lise pushed herself to her feet. Twelve hours from now she'd be back in her apartment; and a week from now, with any luck, she'd be on her way to Halifax.

She could do it. Because she had to.

Her face pale, she walked back into laughter, music and the buzz of conversation. The Gagnons should be pleased;

the party was a success. All she had to do was find a phone and she'd be out of here.

"Hey," said Roland, "you looking for me?"

"Roland, will you call me a cab?" she asked with the directness of desperation. "I—I've got a headache. But I don't want Judd to know I'm leaving."

"Oh," Roland said easily, "that's no problem. He and Angeline just left. They took off in a taxi. For Angeline's hotel, I think that's what she said."

For a horrifying moment, the room dipped and swayed. I won't faint, Lise thought with fierce concentration. I won't. Holding onto the one thing she knew, she repeated, "A cab, Roland? Please?"

"Sure—you don't look so great. But you won't mind if I stay here?"

Roland, she was almost sure, would have another pretty girl in tow before half an hour was up; while she herself craved to be alone. "Of course not."

Calling on all her good manners, Lise made her farewells to her host and hostess, and allowed Roland to escort her under an umbrella to the taxi. It was raining, the wind blowing gusts of drops across the wide driveway. She scrambled into the cab and Roland slammed the door shut. Lise gave Judd's address and sank back against the seat. Too distraught to think, she blanked from her mind any thought of what Judd was doing now. Judd and Angeline.

She'd have lots of time for that. And how could she blame Judd? She'd given him the brush-off loud and clear. That he'd run so quickly to Angeline was nothing to do with her and everything to do with his proposed remarriage.

Minutes later she was running upstairs in Judd's house, holding her skirts up so as not to trip. Maryann was already in bed; Emmy was fast asleep, three books and Plush spread over the covers. Lise stood in the doorway, feeling yet another crack open in her heart. How could she so quickly have come to love Emmy?

This was the last night she'd ever stand here like this, listening to Emmy's breathing, a little girl whose life she had saved and who had thereby utterly changed her own life.

Quickly Lise went into her own room. The jeans and shirt she'd been wearing earlier in the day were still flung on the bed. Ordinary clothes. The kind that she'd be wearing from now on. Impulsively she kicked off her elegant sandals and reached for the zipper on her gown, frantic to be rid of it and all it stood for; and a couple of minutes later, wearing her jeans and shirt, was yanking the pins from her hair, brushing it until it stood in a cloud from her face. The emerald earrings she flung on the bureau; but once again the clasp on the pendant defeated her.

Scarcely thinking, Lise pulled on her rain jacket and rubber boots and dropped the front door key in her pocket. She'd go for a walk. She couldn't stand to go tamely to bed, where she'd be alone with feelings and thoughts she wasn't sure she could face. She'd always loved storms. And a little rain wouldn't hurt her. The last thing she picked up was the flashlight that was stored in the drawer in her bedside table.

The wind howling along the driveway buffeted her so hard she had to lean into it, while rain drove its cold pellets into her face. Lise didn't care. Now that she was finally alone, she was free to weep, for tears would mingle with the rain trickling down her cheeks; but the desolation in her heart was too profound for that. At some deep level she felt betrayed.

Judd had made love to her; and now was making love with Angeline. How *could* he?

Head down, eyes almost shut, she ploughed along. She had no idea what she was going to do when she reached the main road. Turn around and go meekly to bed? Walk the deserted streets until she was exhausted? She'd decide when she got there, she thought, and was almost glad to feel the pull in her muscles from the exercise.

Her flashlight made a small puddle of light on the wet black tar. Lise switched it off, letting her eyes adjust to the darkness; she was easily able to discern the edge of the driveway. Branches rattled in the wind, which thrashed the boughs of the tall pines and hemlocks. If she closed her eyes, she could almost imagine she was beside the ocean, listening to the hiss of waves, the crash of surf against the rocks…

Light suddenly shone against her closed lids, brilliant and unforgiving. Her eyes flew open. A car was hurtling toward her up the driveway, the headlights throwing long gold beams through the wet trees. Then the driver sighted her and in a scream of brakes the car ground to a halt scarcely ten feet away from her. It was the limo. Lise stood still, feeling as though her heart had leaped into her throat. The driver's door opened and Judd lunged out.

Judd. The last person in the world she wanted to see.

CHAPTER THIRTEEN

GLANCING from side to side like a cornered animal, Lise took to the trees. But her hands were too cold to turn the flashlight on, and once she left the circle of light thrown by the car, she was in utter darkness. Her boot caught in a root. She almost fell, saving herself by grabbing at the nearest trunk. The baby. She had to think of the baby. She couldn't risk losing it by running through the woods in the middle of the night.

With a sob of frustration, Lise turned around and waited for Judd to catch up with her. His flashlight wavered through the undergrowth. Twigs cracked underfoot. He stopped only a foot from her and shone the light full in her face. "You little idiot—I could have killed you! What in heaven's name are you doing out on a night like this without even a flashlight?"

Lise said with icy calm, "I have a flashlight. And you're the last person I was expecting to see. Where's Angeline? In the car waiting for you? So you can go to bed with her?"

He dropped his flashlight to the ground and took Lise by the shoulders. "What the devil's Angeline got to do with this? Don't you understand? I came as near to running you over as I ever—"

In the dim glow of light, Lise saw that he was white about the mouth; and somehow this was the spark that ignited her rage. "If you expect me to apologize, you're going to wait a long time," she seethed. "And you're not stupid, Judd, you know as well as I do that Angeline's got everything to do with this. But do you know what's so

173

awful? That I had to come back here at all. That I can't leave tonight because tomorrow morning I have to tell Emmy I'm going—I won't let someone else tell her, I couldn't stand to have that on my conscience. I can't even risk running away in the woods! I'm trapped. And I never wanted to see you again. Never, do you hear?''

She seemed to have run out of words. Her nails were digging into the bark of the tree trunk, rather like Judd's fingers were digging through her jacket. He said in an odd voice, ''Why can't you risk running through the woods? You're not scared of the dark or the storm—or you wouldn't be out in the first place.''

She was sick to death of deception. And she had nothing left to lose. Lise said flatly, ''Because I'm pregnant.''

''What?''

''You heard. I'm pregnant. By you.''

The wet plume of a hemlock brushed Judd's shoulder. He didn't even notice. After a silence that seemed to last forever, he said in voice Lise had never heard before, ''You weren't on the pill in Dominica.''

''Why would I be? There wasn't a man in my life. Dave was just a friend.''

''So when we nearly made love here, you were already pregnant. No need for protection.''

''That's right,'' Lise said, and with a distant part of her brain realized how relieved she was to have the truth in the open. ''I should have told you then. But I was afraid to.''

''The day you fainted—that was why.''

''Yes.'' In a rush she went on, ''You don't have to worry, I won't make any claim on you. Or on your money. I've given up my apartment and I'm going to move to the East Coast. Next week if I can swing it. Emmy will never know, and as for you and Angeline, you can both forget all about me.''

She couldn't have disguised the bitterness she felt. With none of his usual economy of movement, Judd bent and picked up the flashlight, shining it in her face again. She stared back, hostility masking any other emotion; and was glad she hadn't wept. He didn't deserve her tears.

A sudden gust ripped through the trees, driving rain straight at her. Instinctively Lise ducked. Swiftly Judd pulled her closer, shoving the light in his pocket as he sheltered her with his big body. He was wearing a raincoat over his tuxedo; to her nostrils drifted the scent of his cologne.

It was the final straw. Filled with a chaos of rage, longing and pain, Lise beat on his chest with her fists. "Let go! How dare you even touch me? I hate you, Judd Harwood—I hate you!"

A shudder ran through his body. He pushed her away, his eyes like dark pits in his face. "We're going to the house and have this out, Lise. Now."

"I'm not getting into the limo with Angeline!"

"For God's sake," he exploded, "Angeline's back in her hotel. Nowhere near here. Are you going under your own steam or do I have to pick you up and carry you?"

"I can still walk," she flared. "I'm pregnant—not breakable." Only her heart was broken, she thought wretchedly, and realized that deep down she must have cherished a fantasy of telling Judd she was pregnant and of having him enfold her in his arms and promise to love her forever.

Just like in the fairy tales.

Judd swung the flashlight to show their path, and led the way out of the trees. When he opened the passenger door, he must have seen how Lise's gaze flickered to the back of the empty limo before she climbed in. He said savagely, "You don't believe one word I say, do you?"

"Why should I?"

He slammed the door and moments later climbed in beside her, putting his foot on the accelerator so they raced up the driveway. The wipers swished away the curtain of rain; the house looked dark and ominous, a black bulk against the sky. Lise huddled in her seat. She felt cold and very tired. Yet one piece of information kept circling her exhausted mind. Angeline was back at her hotel.

What did that mean? And was it true?

Judd pulled to a halt by the front door. She climbed out before he could come around to open her door, and headed up the steps. Judd unlocked the door. The warmth brushed her cheeks as tangibly as a caress, and she began to shiver.

Judd said roughly, "You're soaked. Come on upstairs and I'll start a bath for you."

She had to know. "Why did you leave the Gagnons' party with Angeline?"

"We're not going to have that discussion while you're dripping on the carpet like a drowned rat."

"Are you going to marry her?"

With an impatient exclamation, Judd pushed her in the direction of the stairs. "What in hell would I do that for?"

"For Emmy's sake. Of course."

"I am not now or ever going to remarry Angeline. Once was enough, thank you. And you can take that to the bank." He took Lise by the elbow, hurrying her up the stairs. "I wouldn't marry her for my sake or for Emmy's sake. Emmy loves *you,* Lise—her mother's a stranger to her. Now where do you keep that disgraceful old nightgown you've had for seventeen years? It looks like this is the night to wear it."

He wasn't going to marry Angeline. "Is that the truth, Judd?" Lise whispered.

He stopped dead at the top of the stairs; she felt the force of his willpower like a blast of sheer energy. "Lise, I may have lied to you by omission, but never by commission. Yes, it's the truth. I'm no longer in love with Angeline, and I have no desire whatsoever to marry her.''

"Oh," said Lise, and discovered she was shivering again.

Judd suddenly swept her up into his arms. "I was in control until I met you," he said in a raw voice. "I had women figured out, and my life was just the way I wanted it. Straight track all the way to the horizon, all signals go. Then I meet up with a female firefighter with hair like flame and a temper to match, and I'm off the rails. Explain that to me, will you?"

She couldn't. She was too busy fighting the temptation to bury her face in his wet raincoat and sob her heart out. But she wasn't going to do that.

Not yet.

In short order Judd put her down beside her bed and marched into the bathroom to fill the Jacuzzi. He came back to find her standing exactly where he'd left her. He said levelly, "I've turned the heat up in the bathroom. Where's your nightgown?"

"Second drawer down."

He pulled it out and threw it on the bed. Then he walked over to Lise and drew down the zipper of her jacket, a small gesture that woke in her an agony of memories. She flinched away from him. His hand froze partway down. He said, "You do hate me, don't you? You can't even stand to have me near you."

How was she to answer that? As her lashes fell, hiding her eyes, she told the literal truth. "I don't know anything anymore."

"Go have your bath," Judd said. "Once you're warmed up, you should get some sleep."

His voice was devoid of emotion. All her movements like those of a robot, Lise yanked down her zipper, passed him her soaked jacket and walked past him to the bathroom, picking up her nightgown on the way. Closing the door, she stripped off the rest of her clothes and got in the tub.

The hot water laved her skin; she sank down in it, turned on the jets and floated boneless as a doll. Gradually she began to feel warmer. And with warmth came emotion, and with emotion the awakening of a desperate need for truth.

She had to know what had happened tonight. Judd no longer loved Angeline and didn't want to marry her. That, however, wasn't the same as saying he'd fallen in love with Lise. Yet she'd disrupted his life, thrown it off the rails. Whatever that meant.

Was he worth fighting for?

Wasn't that the real question? Nothing to do with Angeline, and in a very real way nothing to do with the baby in her womb. It was a question for her, Lise. For her and for Judd. Because, of course, she loved Judd. Through and through, with all her heart. Had done for weeks.

Dazedly Lise watched the ripples and bubbles in the hot water, and discovered that she was smiling with pure joy. Why had it taken her so long to admit that simple, earth-shattering truth? Hadn't it been her hidden love that had impelled her to tell him she was pregnant? To stop deceiving him about something that was of utter significance to both of them? No matter what happened.

Swiftly she leaned forward and turned off the taps. Then she climbed out onto the bath mat, pulled a towel from the rack and wrapped it around her. The pendant Judd had given her was nestled between her breasts. One emerald and two sapphires, the colors of leaves and of water: the colors of life. Still smiling, Lise pulled the door open.

The bedroom was empty.

For a moment she stood transfixed, feeling terror pluck at her composure. Was she being an utter fool to think

Judd wanted anything more of her than he'd already had?
That he might, given time, come to love her not as the
mother of his child, but as herself?

There was only one way to find out.

On bare feet she tiptoed down the hallway. His bedroom
door was shut. Biting her lip, she very slowly turned the
handle and eased the door open, all in total silence.

Judd was sitting on the edge of his bed, his back to her,
his head buried in his hands. He'd stripped to his black
trousers; the line of his spine was a long curve of defeat,
all his arrogance and pride gone.

She couldn't bear to see him like that.

Lise slipped through the doorway and just as softly
closed it behind her. As the latch clicked, Judd's head
jerked up. He looked over his shoulder, saw her standing
there and pushed himself to his feet. "Lise," he said
hoarsely, "what are you doing here?"

"I had to come," she gulped. "I need to know what
happened tonight with Angeline. I need to know how you
feel about me carrying your child—please, Judd, won't
you tell me?"

His jaw was tight and there were dark shadows under
his eyes. Lise found she was holding her breath, her pulse
racketing in her chest. The rest of her life depended on
what happened next, she was under no illusion about that.
Praying desperately that he wouldn't shut her out, she
waited for him to speak.

He crossed the room. "You're still wet."

"I—I guess I am," she said lamely.

"And you're still wearing the pendant."

"I can't undo the catch, it's too small. But I—"

He said, "Angeline came running up to me after I left
you on the dance floor at the Gagnons. There'd been an
emergency with Emmy, she'd fallen down the stairs and
was crying for me. I wasn't about to question one more

emergency, not after the fire. Angeline had a cab all lined up—so off we went, top speed, Angeline filling me in with all the details…until I happened to look out the window of the cab and see we were going in the wrong direction. Well, you can probably guess the rest. No emergency. No fall down the stairs. Angeline had decided to take me to her hotel and seduce me. Step one in the remarriage campaign."

"That's where Roland told me you'd gone," Lise said. "To her hotel. Together."

"So that's why you ran off into the woods—"

"Wouldn't you?"

"Roland is the lover Angeline had in New York while she and I were still married. No doubt, for old times' sake, she asked him to pass along that message to you." His voice gravelly with anger, Judd said, "I'm sorry, Lise. How could you possibly have known what was really going on?"

Remembering the way Roland had been so cool with Judd, Lise said, "It seems very obvious about Roland—now that I do know."

"Let me finish with Angeline. The count's dumped her, to put it crudely. An indiscretion on her part. Unfortunately, Henri wasn't amused, and chose not to forgive his wife for having an affair with one of his best friends. So Angeline, who's used to living in the lap of luxury, decides I'm not such a bad deal after all, and comes hightailing back to Montreal with marriage on her mind. All for Emmy's sake, you understand." He ran his fingers through his hair. "I took her to her hotel in the cab, went right back to the Gagnons to look for you, discovered you'd left and raced back here in the limo. End of story."

"Marthe told me Angeline had done the leaving and was planning to remarry you."

"Poor Lise. Everyone telling you everything but the truth."

"You really don't want Angeline?"

"I do not. It's you I want, Lise."

She swallowed. "The way you wanted me in Dominica?"

Briefly he rested his finger where the pulse beat at the base of her throat. He said huskily, "I'll never stop wanting you that way."

But that's not enough. Lise said carefully, "So you're still not into commitment. Let alone marriage."

"You're pregnant. Of course we'll get married."

"No, Judd—I won't marry you just because I'm pregnant. The child and I both deserve better than that."

"The child deserves a father."

"Any child deserves a father. But if the parents don't love each other, the marriage is flawed from the start. I can't do that, Judd, I just can't."

"You don't love me," he said in an unreadable voice. "That's what you're saying."

She tilted her chin. "You don't love me. So why should it matter to you how I feel?"

"I told you I've lied by omission," Judd said with sudden violence. "I had no intention of showing you in Dominica what our lovemaking meant to me. How deeply it affected me, body and soul. I wasn't into commitment—you're right. So why would I say that your beauty and generosity had knocked me sideways, had made me re-examine the way I've been living the last four years? That I was starting to want you in all the ways a man wants a woman? In his bed every night, waking up beside him in the morning...I wasn't going to tell you that, Lise, because it scared the hell out of me."

"If we got married just because of the baby," Lise said deliberately, "how long before you started to resent me?

Underpaid Firefighter Traps Millionaire Into Marriage Of Convenience. It's classic. And I won't do it.''

"It's my child, too. We're both responsible.''

He sounded so reasonable, so cold-blooded. She said raggedly, "I'll move away as soon as I can. I promise I won't make any—''

"Lise, hold on, I'm doing this all wrong.'' Judd took her in his arms, his eyes running over the gentle slopes of her shoulders to where the pendant sparkled in the valley between her breasts. "Why did you come here like this? Half-naked and so beautiful I can hardly think straight?''

She tried to pull the towel higher. "It was stupid of me, I didn't stop to think.''

He stayed her hand. "When you came around that door, I was sitting on the edge of the bed convinced I'd lost you. Forever. That the woman I want to spend the rest of my life with hated my guts.''

"But—''

"Yes, I was scared in Dominica, you'd turned my life upside down and I've always been into control. Lise, don't you see? I'm trying to tell you I love you. I was in love with you in Dominica, I probably fell in love with you when I first saw you lying in that hospital bed. I love you and I want to marry you. But if—''

"Not just because of the baby?'' she blurted.

"I want to marry you for yourself. But how can I ask you to do that when you told me out in the woods that you hate me?''

"You love me,'' she repeated blankly.

"All I'm asking is that you stick around,'' he said with repressed violence. "Stay here with me and Emmy. Because I can't stand the thought of you moving away. Of us being separated by half a continent.''

"I won't move away. Why would I do that?'' Lise's

smile broke through, as radiant as sunrise. "You see, I love you, too."

His hands tightened around her waist. "Would you mind repeating that?"

She laughed out loud. "I love you, Judd Harwood. Love you, love you, love you…is that enough repetitions?"

He said in a dazed voice, "I don't think I can have too many. You're sure, Lise?"

"As sure as I'm standing here wrapped in a very damp towel. Judd, dear Judd, I love you with all my heart."

He pulled her closer. Then he lowered his head, kissing her as though there was no tomorrow. As though, Lise thought exultantly, he held paradise in his arms. She looped her hands around his neck, feeling the heat of his skin burn into hers, glorying in the thrust of his tongue and fierce pressure of his mouth.

Judd raised his head long enough to mutter, "The towel's slipping."

"So it is," she said demurely.

Laughter sparked his eyes. "What are you going to do about it?"

"How about nothing? Letting nature take its course?"

"Lise," he said with sudden urgency, "you will marry me?"

"Yes. Oh, yes, Judd. It would make me happier than I've ever imagined I could be."

"Thank God," Judd said. "It's more than I deserve. I was so insistent that I never wanted to commit myself to anyone other than Emmy that I refused to see what was right under my nose. You. Stubborn. Hot-tempered. Fiery and passionate."

She chuckled. "Not half as stubborn as you."

"Stop interrupting," he said, kissing the tip of her nose. "I not only shut you out. I was also hell-bent on denying

I'd fallen in love with you. I'm sorry, sweetheart. Truly sorry.''

His lips were now wandering down her cheek to her throat. She said shakily, ''You're forgiven.''

''Did I also say you're astonishingly generous?''

He'd found the curve of her breast; the towel was now around her hips and her whole body was one ache of desire. ''I don't think you mentioned that,'' she whispered, dropping kisses on his thick black hair. ''I'm so happy, I'm almost scared to believe this is all true. I'm not going to wake up, am I?''

He straightened, drawing her closer. ''The only place you're going to wake up is in my arms. In my bed. Lise, I swear I'll always be here for you. That I love you with all the strength in my body and the power of my soul.''

Touched to the core, Lise said softly, ''That's the most beautiful thing anyone's ever said to me. Oh, Judd, I do love you.''

He said, ''Let's go to bed. Now. Because sometimes words just aren't enough.'' Then his smile broke through. ''Besides, I want to see you wearing nothing but an emerald and two sapphires.''

''You think I'll look okay like that?''

''I know you will,'' he said, and set out to convince he was right.

Not that she took much convincing.

EPILOGUE

THE next morning the alarm clock woke Lise with a jump. As she reached over to flip the switch, she realized first that she was stark naked and secondly that she was in Judd's bed. He said lazily, "Good morning…how did you sleep?"

"Very little," she said, blushing. "Thanks to you."

"I aim to please."

"Oh," she said, "you do, you do."

"I'd better get up. Just in case Emmy comes looking for me. Good thing we set the alarm." He slid a hand down her hip. "Still love me?"

"More than ever. If that's possible."

"Perhaps," he said, his slate-gray eyes very serious, "love just keeps on growing."

"We could hang around each other and find out."

"What a good idea." His fingers circled her belly suggestively. "There's nothing I'd like better than to spend the morning in bed with you. But duty, in the form of my daughter, calls." He hesitated. "She'll be our daughter, Lise. Because Angeline's heading back to Europe—all her contacts are there. How do you feel about being Emmy's stepmother?"

"I love her already," Lise said simply.

"Let's tell her at breakfast that you're planning on staying. Forever."

Because she felt almost languid with happiness, it was half an hour before Lise slipped into her seat at the breakfast table. Judd and Emmy were already there. Emmy said cheerfully, "Did you have a nice time last night?"

185

For a moment all Lise could think of was the hours she'd spent in Judd's arms making love. Then she remembered the gala and her long green dress. "Oh, yes, it was lovely," she gabbled. "How about you? Was the popcorn good?"

"Fabulous." A faint shadow of anxiety crossed Emmy's face. "My friend Charlene phoned this morning. She forgot to tell me yesterday that our school concert's in three weeks. You'll still be here, won't you, Lise? Will you come to it?"

Lise smiled at her. "Yes, I'll be here. And I'd love to come to the concert." She glanced over at Judd, feeling absurdly shy. "Actually, we have something to tell you, Emmy."

Judd reached across the table and took Lise's hand in his. "How would you feel about Lise and me getting married, Emmy? That way Lise would always be here."

Emmy's big blue eyes went from her father to Lise. "Married?" she squeaked. "For real?"

"Definitely for real," Judd said. "For real and forever."

"That's a great idea! You wait til I tell Charlene."

Lise had tears in her eyes. "I'm so glad you're happy."

Emmy shoved back her chair and ran around the table to hug Lise; her long black hair smelled sweetly of shampoo. "Course I am. You're fun and real and brave."

It was an interesting endorsement, thought Lise, smiling through her tears. "I also make very good chocolate maple fudge—did I ever tell you that?"

"Yummy." Then Emmy pulled back, gazing speculatively from Lise to her father. "I've got a question. D'you think sometime you could make me a baby brother or sister? Charlene has one of each and they're kind of cute."

"I'm sure we could manage that," Judd said with a straight face. "Would you mind if it was fairly soon?"

"Oh, no." Emmy gave Lise a kiss flavored with pancake syrup, and hugged her father. "I've got such a lot to tell all the kids at school," she crowed. "Oh, I'm so excited. Can I be a bridesmaid?"

"Sure," said Judd. "We'd better pick a date. How about two weeks from Saturday, Lise?"

"Fine," Lise said breathlessly.

"Maybe some of the fire trucks could come," Emmy said, her head to one side. "Like in a parade."

"A quiet wedding," Judd said firmly.

"I bet if I have a brother or sister it'll have red hair," Emmy added artlessly.

And indeed when Matthew Judd Harwood was born seven and a half months later, he had unwinking slate-blue eyes and a thick fuzz of bright red hair.

Carol Marinelli is a nurse who loves writing. Or is she a writer who loves nursing? The truth is Carol's having trouble deciding at the moment, but writing definitely seems to be taking precedence! She's also happily married to an eternally patient husband (an essential accessory when panic hits around chapter six) and is a mother to three fabulously boisterous children. Add a would-be tennis player, an eternal romantic and a devout daydreamer to that list and that pretty much sums Carol up. Oh, she's also terrible at housework!

Watch out for Carol Marinelli's latest emotionally exhilarating title:
ONE NIGHT IN EMERGENCY
On sale *this month*, in Medical Romance™!

Carol Marinelli also writes for
Modern Romance™

DR CARLISLE'S CHILD
by
Carol Marinelli

For Mario.
With love and gratitude for all your support.

CHAPTER ONE

ALL eyes were on Lucinda Chambers as she walked onto the paediatric cardiac unit at Melbourne Central Women's and Children's Hospital, and she knew it. Pushing her shoulders back, she assumed what she hoped was a confident poise and, reminding herself to breathe, she made her way over to the group of white coats huddled around the nurses' station.

'Ah, Miss Chambers.' Professor Hays held out his hand and Lucinda accepted his handshake firmly. 'I trust you had a pleasant flight.' Without waiting for her reply, he turned and addressed his loyal followers. 'As you know, Miss Chambers joins us today from Queensland, bringing with her a wealth of knowledge and talent from which we can all benefit. As you know, until Mr Felix returns from overseas Miss Chambers will be the only consultant on my team so I am, of course, counting on you all to give her every assistance.' He paused for a moment as the group murmured their agreement.

Lucinda smiled back at the faces, some curious, others indifferent and a couple downright hostile. Her appointment as Consultant Paediatric Cardiothoracic Surgeon had caused more than a few raised eyebrows. At thirty-four she was considered young for such a senior position and a woman to boot. Cardiothoracic surgery was still predominantly male-dominated, even in these so-called liberated times. For a woman to make it in this field took more than just talent with a scalpel.

But, then, Lucinda had it all—good-looking by any stan-

5

dards, with long thick hair, an exquisite shade of chestnut, flawless creamy skin and a curvaceous, supple body that belied the never-ending take-aways, hospital canteen food and diet Coke that she survived on.

More relevantly, she also happened to be the daughter of two of Queensland's most prominent cosmetic surgeons who were ambitious in the extreme where their daughter was concerned. Her mother, despite being possibly the least maternal woman ever to give birth, had been almost pathological in her desire for her daughter's success, planning her education and career almost from the moment of conception.

Though confident she had got the job on her own merits, Lucinda acknowledged that her breeding hadn't been a hindrance. The fact that there were a couple of noses out of joint amongst her new colleagues came as no particular surprise.

'Well, enough of the introductions for now. We'll get started on the ward round, but there will be a small luncheon in the function room at noon so we can welcome Miss Chambers properly. I hope to see you all there.'

As the charge nurse wheeled a large trolley containing the patients' files and X-rays, the group followed. Professor Hays was leading, of course, with the charge nurse to his left and slightly behind. Lucinda assumed her position just to his right and slightly back, with the rest of the procession bringing up the rear in order of merit. It was old-school and had probably been abandoned years ago on most other wards, but Professor Hays was a stickler for formality.

'A small speech would go down well at lunchtime,' he said in low tones to Lucinda. 'To introduce yourself. Just a few words, very informal, nothing to worry about.'

'I'd be glad to,' Lucinda replied confidently as her stomach turned 360 degrees. The thought of facing that adverse group did nothing to inspire her. The charge nurse turned and gave her an almost imperceptible wink and Lucinda winked back. Looking at her name badge, she saw that her name was Ann Benton. Her face, apart from Professor Hays's, had been the only friendly one she had seen so far. For the first time that day Lucinda's smile was genuine.

'First we have young Billy Carlisle.' Ann introduced the young boy sitting cross-legged on his bed, clutching a large unfriendly-looking robot.

'Mr Hughes, perhaps you'd like to brief Miss Chambers and the students on Billy's condition?'

Pete cleared his throat and spoke in the low tones, which enabled the staff to hear but not the patient.

'Billy Carlisle, five years old. Born by emergency C-section at thirty-five weeks gestation due to premature labour with malpresentation and foetal distress. At birth a heart murmur was noticed and subsequent testing showed a large ventricular septal defect.'

Lucinda glanced over to the bed at the young boy trying to get his mother's attention as she filed her nails. Her heart skipped a beat. He was easily the cutest child she had ever seen. Raven curls framed his pale face, his lips were full and tinged with blue yet Lucinda just knew that once he had the surgery to correct the cardiac defect he'd been born with they would be a dark red. His eyes were a vivid green. Glancing up, he caught her staring and gave her a cheeky smile.

For a second she froze, about to look away in her usual fashion, but for some reason she couldn't explain Lucinda found herself smiling back.

Pete Hughes continued with his speech and Lucinda tore her eyes away from the young boy and forced herself to concentrate.

'We were initially hoping to avoid surgery but his condition has started to deteriorate due to development of an associated atrial septal defect. As you can see, he's cyanosed and is having trouble keeping up with his peers. Billy also suffers from chronic asthma, which currently is proving difficult to control and is exacerbating his cardiac problems. He's scheduled for Theatre on Wednesday.'

The entourage moved closer around Billy's bedside, and a couple of students stood with their stethoscopes poised as Billy resignedly undid his pyjama top and let them listen to his chest.

'Good morning, Gemma.' Professor Hays greeted the child's mother in a surprisingly familiar fashion.

'Is it?' she barked rudely. 'Seb was supposed to be here an hour ago. I've got an appointment in the City at ten.'

'Seb's still in Theatre. I know Casualty had a couple of urgent cases this morning—he shouldn't be too much longer,' Professor Hays answered soothingly. So that was why he was being so familiar. Her husband must be a doctor here. Professor Hays turned to Lucinda.

'Young Billy's father is Sebastian Carlisle, one of our consultant anaesthetists,' he explained to Lucinda. 'An excellent anaesthetist—I know you'll enjoy working with him,' he said in a booming voice, then added in quieter tones, 'He talks to his patients while they're under, mind. I've never quite worked him out.'

'Well, I've got some forms I need him to sign before I go. Can't somebody page him?' Gemma asked petulantly.

'And for a second I thought she was here for her son,' Ann muttered darkly into Lucinda's ear, then, smiling brightly, she turned to the agitated woman. 'No worries, Gemma, I'll have someone do that now,' she said, nodding to the ward clerk as she spoke. 'Was there anything you wanted to ask Professor Hays about Billy?'

Gemma frowned slightly. 'Seb deals with all the medical side of things.'

Ann ruffled Billy's hair. 'I'll be back to you later, sport. You can choose this morning's video.'

His eyes widened. 'Can I? Then I want—'

'*Robot Savers*!' said Ann, Professor Hays, Pete Hughes, a couple of other doctors and all the nursing staff in unison. The only one who didn't join in the fun was his mother, who looked pointedly at her watch.

'How did we guess?' Ann laughed. Lucinda had no idea what they were talking about but she again found herself smiling at the cheeky little scamp who had everyone wrapped around his finger. Everyone that was, except his mother.

Gemma stood up. 'About time,' she said pointedly as the ward doors opened and a doctor dressed in theatre greens entered. Lucinda felt her stomach muscles tighten. There could be no doubt it was Billy's father. He had the same vivid green eyes and the same raven curls, but with just a sprinkling of silver which gave him a certain air of distinction. His height and build increased his air of authority. Standing well over six feet, even in his baggy theatre gear one couldn't help but notice his athletic physique. Now, Sebastian Carlisle was most definitely her type, but married, Lucinda reminded herself. Wasn't it always the way? All the decent men, it seemed, were already spoken for.

Sebastian Carlisle pointedly ignored his wife's acid remarks as he made his way to his son's bedside, his haughty face softening as he kissed Billy.

'I was on my way over when you paged me.' He nodded politely to the professor. 'Is everything all right?'

'No, everything is not all right,' Gemma rudely interrupted Professor Hays's assurances. 'I have an appointment at ten and you know I needed to talk to you this morning.'

Sebastian seemed unfazed by the argumentative tones of his wife.

'And you know that I'm a doctor. I can't just walk out halfway through an operation. Anyway, I'm here now.'

The staff had started to move on to the next bed but Lucinda noted that Billy's respiration rate was increasing and he was starting to use his accessory muscles. 'Ann, when did Billy last have a nebuliser?'

'An hour ago.'

Gently Lucinda sat the young boy forward and, lifting his pyjama top, listened to his chest.

'He's a bit tight. Give him another 2.5 mg of Ventolin.' She checked his drug chart. 'He's got a PRN order.' Lucinda turned to Jack Wells, the junior intern. 'Have a listen to his chest later on, he might need his medication reviewed again.'

Jack nodded, blushing when she addressed him, and hastily scribbled Lucinda's orders into the notebook he was carrying as they moved on to the next bed.

'Good morning, Bianca, and how are we feeling?' Professor Hays's cheerful, booming greeting seemed a ridiculous contrast to the young painfully thin girl lying exhausted against her mountain of pillows. Yet somehow the frail teenager summoned up the strength to remove her oxygen mask and give the professor a thumbs-up sign.

'Good,' she gasped. 'And you, Prof?'

He laughed heartily. 'Oh, you know me—in a rush as always.'

Bianca said something but the words were inaudible as she coughed and struggled for breath. Ann, however, used to the young girl, leant over the bed and translated for the benefit of the entourage. 'What time's tee-off?'

Everyone laughed, yet Lucinda knew it was tinged with sadness and that the fragile form on the bed, laughing and joking with the professor like a school pal in the playground, was more than just a patient to the staff here.

Professor Hays turned his back on Bianca and spoke in low tones to Lucinda, but before he even started to talk she had guessed the diagnosis.

'Bianca Moore, thirteen years old, end-stage cystic fibrosis. She's on the waiting list for a double lung and heart transplant. She's held her own for a long time, but in the last fortnight her condition has started to deteriorate rapidly.'

Ann put up the latest chest x-rays. The group gathered round and studied the films as Professor Hays went into greater detail about Bianca's condition. Lucinda listened as she flicked through Bianca's blood results.

'Her potassium's high,' she stated.

'We're aware of that and it's being corrected. She's been given Resonium,' Pete Hughes answered smartly, his casual voice belying the menacing look in his eyes. Lucinda could almost taste the animosity. Professor Hays said nothing, but Lucinda could feel his scrutiny and knew only too well he was assessing how she dealt with her new status.

'Which is the right treatment, of course,' Lucinda answered calmly. 'But her potassium isn't just slightly raised—it's dangerously high. Shouldn't she be on a cardiac monitor?'

Pete Hughes threw her a look of utter contempt but his voice conveyed the same friendly tones. 'I think she's on enough monitors, don't you? I spoke with Bianca and she got very distressed. She likes to get up and have a shower. She's on all the right treatment—it should be resolved by this evening.'

Lucinda understood his judgement, far more than he realised. The child had been through enough. A cardiac monitor curtailed the few privileges that Bianca had left, like a morning shower. Yet she also knew he was letting his involvement with the patient cloud his judgement. They weren't here to make friends. They were here to save lives, and if Bianca was going to be upset by a cardiac monitor then so be it. Better that than have a child who had already been through so much die from something as preventable as a cardiac arrhythmia caused by a raised potassium level that they were aware of.

'I'd like Bianca on a cardiac monitor, please.' She turned to Ann, who nodded and wrote the order on a pad.

'Now, if that's possible.'

Ann smiled warmly. 'No worries.' Turning to a junior colleague Ann relayed her message and in seconds a cardiac monitor appeared by the grumbling Bianca's bedside.

'It will probably come off tonight,' Lucinda said firmly, knowing a day was a lifetime to this child.

Ann sat her up and deftly placed the red dots that would hold the monitors' leads onto Bianca's chest. The upright motion allowed an increase in the air entry into her damaged lungs, giving more clarity to her feeble voice.

'What's your name?' she demanded. Lucinda kept her feet firmly planted on the floor and her shoulders back.

'Miss Chambers.' She heard the unanimous intake of breath from her colleagues at her obvious distancing from the patient. The only person who didn't seem offended was Bianca.

'You're not very friendly, are you?' she stated matter-of-factly.

Lucinda approached her bedside and leant over, her face inches away from Bianca, beckoning her as if to share a secret. 'I might not be very friendly,' she whispered into her ear just loudly enough for everyone to hear, 'but I'm a great doctor.' Pleasingly, her words seemed to appease Bianca and the young girl gave Lucinda a weak thumbs-up sign, a gesture that at this stage Lucinda didn't know how much she would come to cherish.

Her reputation as hard had obviously followed her from Queensland, but it didn't concern Lucinda. She had learned long ago that in her line of work emotions and cardiothoracic surgery simply didn't mix. She had lost count of the times she had cried into her pillow at night over a young life lost, until finally the only way for her to cope had been to erect the barriers and retain a cool distance.

The round took ages. Once they had finished with the cardiac unit they made their way along the hospital corridor, losing Jack Wells *en route* when he was paged to return there and Pete Hughes who was urgently needed in Casualty.

Somewhat depleted, they arrived on NICU, the neonatal intensive care unit, to see pre- and post-operative patients. Here, more than anywhere, lives hung precariously in the balance, the lives of tiny babies whose conditions were monitored second by second by the dedicated and highly skilled nursing staff, who knew that even the smallest variance could indicate imminent disaster for their fragile charges. Lucinda looked into the incubators at the little scraps fighting for survival against all the odds. The constant beeping and monitor alarms in the unit was something Lucinda had grown used to by now, but for new parents the whole experience was terrifying.

Sue Washington met them and introduced herself as the charge nurse.

'I'm sorry, Andrew's busy, so you'll have to put up with me taking you around.'

Professor Hays motioned his acceptance and the round commenced.

'Andrew Doran is the neonatologist here,' Sue explained.

'You'll meet him in a few moments—he's actually with one of your patients, a micro-prem.'

'How many weeks' gestation?' Lucinda asked.

'Twenty-four weeks,'

Lucinda's grimace didn't go unnoticed. 'And the fact she's one of ours doesn't sound too promising?' Lucinda ventured.

Sue gave her a knowing a look. 'Exactly. Kimberley Stewart was born with nearly every problem in the book, and what she wasn't born with she's collected along the way. She went back to Theatre last night with necrotising enterocolitis. I can safely say that at the moment her cardiac defect is the least of her problems, so you can hazard a guess at how sick she is.'

Jack Wells, somewhat breathless, appeared, notebook poised, his face even redder than before. 'Sorry, sir, I got held up with Billy Carlisle.'

Professor Hays frowned. 'How's his chest?'

'Fine now but I had to give him a further neb. His asthma worsens every time his mother leaves and now Gemma is demanding that he be moved to a side ward. That's the last thing he needs but try telling it to that awful woman.'

'That's enough, Dr Wells,' Professor Hays said sharply. 'You don't know all the circumstances.'

Jack Wells's face was practically purple now, and Lucinda could tell he was angry.

'I know enough to know that she leaves Billy on his own too much already, without him being moved to a side ward. Something needs to be said.'

Lucinda had only met Jack that morning but she could tell his outburst was out of character. Professor Hays seemed to realise this, too, and ignored his junior's insubordination, addressing him this time in a kinder tone.

'I know you're concerned—we all are. Sister Benton has

tried to have a word with Gemma. It's very awkward, with Seb being a doctor here.' Professor Hays then addressed Lucinda. 'Gemma and Seb are divorced,' he explained. 'Mrs Carlisle apparently feels very uncomfortable in the hospital. She assumes that we're all on Seb's side and gets easily upset, which, of course, translates to Billy. It's not doing his asthma any good.'

Lucinda frowned. She really couldn't care less about the Carlisles' marital disputes, but when it affected her patient that was another matter.

'Perhaps I could have a word with them?' Lucinda offered. 'Billy needs to have his parents around at the moment. If I talk to both of them together, lay it on the line so to speak, Mrs Carlisle can hardly accuse me of favouritism.'

'But you'll be working closely with Seb. It's hardly a great start to your working relationship,' Professor Hays pointed out.

Lucinda considered this but only for a moment.

'From all accounts, Sebastian Carlisle is a fine doctor, and shall continue to be whether he likes me or not. I can understand that it's hard for you all to say anything about this, given that you know him personally, but I'm here to treat patients, not to win a personality competition. If Billy's asthma is suffering because of his parents, it needs to be addressed.'

Professor Hays nodded. 'Very well. You're right, of course.' He turned to Jack. 'Are they both still here?'

Jack nodded. 'Gemma's seen the side ward is empty and is demanding that Billy be moved now.'

Professor Hays scratched his bald head. 'Maybe it would be for the best if you did speak to them. I'll finish up here with Jack.'

On the ward an exasperated Ann met Lucinda.

'I'm going to have to move him,' she said angrily. 'I've tried telling Gemma that Billy should be out on the main ward, mixing with the other children. The last thing he needs is to be feeling sorry for himself in a side ward, but she just won't listen to reason. Anyway, I like to keep a side ward free for the really sick ones.'

Lucinda tried to be objective as she scanned Billy's notes. 'She's probably exhausted. She's more than likely worn out from sleeping by Billy's bed, and Seb being stuck in Theatre was probably the last straw.'

Ann scoffed at this. 'Worn out? She only arrived five minutes before the ward round and she only popped in for half an hour yesterday. Poor Seb's run ragged, juggling a theatre list and trying to be both mum and dad.'

'Well, that's his problem and Billy's reaction to it is mine. Don't worry, Ann, I'll speak to them now.'

Lucinda made her way over to the bedside. 'Could I have a word with you both, please, in Sister Benton's office?' She smiled at Billy. 'We won't be long.' She made her way to the office and sat at the desk as the Carlisles entered. Lucinda didn't waste any time with small talk.

'I understand that you want Billy to be moved to a side ward. Can I ask why?'

'I'm happy for him to stay on the main ward,' Seb said evenly. 'It's Gemma that wants him to be moved.'

'Of course you're happy for him to be on the main ward. It's all right for you—everyone loves Seb,' Gemma snapped, and then turned her angry stare on Lucinda. 'I'm the one who has to put up with the hostility from the nurses just because Seb has custody of Billy. I know what they're all saying behind my back. "There's the woman who walked out on her husband and child." They all hate me.'

'I'm sure that's not the case,' Lucinda said calmly, but Gemma was insistent.

'Oh, I'm telling you that's exactly the case. How would you like it, day in day out, stuck here like a sitting duck for all the snide comments, with everyone judging you. You don't know what it's like, having a child with a hole in the heart—' Her voice was rising and Lucinda cut short her protests.

'You're right, I don't know what it's like to have a sick child and, to be honest, I'm not sure how I'd cope. However, the fact of the matter is Billy's asthma is worsening and he needs a parent to stay with him at the moment as much as possible.'

'Its pure attention-seeking.' Gemma said dismissively, as Seb rolled his eyes at her ridiculous comment.

Lucinda's voice remained calm but she felt the hackles of irritation rising.

'Mrs Carlisle, I can assure you Billy's asthma is far more serious than attention-seeking behaviour. There may be a link with you going, but that's related to his anxiety, and anxiety is increasing the frequency and severity of his attacks. Now, personally I feel that the last thing Billy needs is to be moved to a side ward. He's a bright little boy and he knows those wards are used for the really ill children. He's already spent too much of his young life in hospital and, no doubt, he's somewhat anxious about the surgery. The last thing he needs is to feel further isolated. Children need company, even if it's just to have someone in the next bed to grumble to about the lunchtime shepherd's pie.'

Gemma started to protest but Lucinda put her hand up to halt the woman and continued authoritatively, 'However, if by moving him it means that you feel more comfortable and are prepared to stay around a lot more, well, then, I agree that would be a valid reason for him to be moved to a side ward.'

Gemma opened her mouth to speak but Lucinda still hadn't finished.

'At the moment I understand that you're still on call?' She looked at Seb who nodded at her question.

'Which means that you can't guarantee being around all the time.'

'I'm off roster when he has his operation,' Seb said. 'I'll be able to stay then.'

Lucinda nodded curtly, trying to ignore the unsettling effect his deep voice was having on her.

'Well, Mrs Carlisle, think about it. Whatever you decide, though, I'll have a word with the nursing staff. I would hope that you're mistaken, but if there's any truth to your feelings of hostility from the staff it needs to be addressed. You've got enough on your plate at the moment without it being added to unnecessarily.'

Gemma looked at her, surprised, as if the last thing she'd expected had been someone to come down on her side. 'I'm not imagining it.'

'Then I'll speak to them.'

'Thank you,' she said, somewhat appeased.

'But I would still like you to think about what I've said. I really think Billy will do better out on the main ward, but I'll leave the decision to you.'

'I'll think about it,' she grudgingly agreed, and then turned to Seb. 'I'm going to pop down to the canteen for a coffee. I'll let you know what I decide.'

Seb gave her a tight smile. 'Sure, Gemma.'

'Thanks for that,' he said once Gemma had gone, turning those gorgeous green eyes on Lucinda. 'Ten minutes ago she was all set to move the bed in there herself. Now at least she's thinking about it.'

'I wasn't aware, until Gemma mentioned it, that you have full custody of Billy. It must be hard.'

Seb gave a thin smile but he wasn't giving anything away. 'It can be, but the good times far outweigh the bad.' He quickly changed the subject. 'Gemma does have a point, though. As much as I think we've got the best nursing staff in the world here, they are noticeably cool towards her. Not only is she saddled with the reputation of walking out on her family, she's also been thrown into my environment and, fair or not, the staff tend to come down on my side. Unfortunately everyone has an opinion on the subject.'

Lucinda thought about this. She was also somewhat surprised by Seb's ability to be fair to his ex-wife, who even with the best will in the world was not the most likeable of people.

'Well, they'll have to learn to keep it to themselves,' she said firmly. 'They're here to look after not just Billy but the whole family. Gemma deserves the same respect as you.'

'I agree.'

Lucinda softened a little. He really did seem to be trying hard in these very difficult circumstances. 'Can't you take some annual leave, stay with Billy a bit more?' she said in kinder voice.

Seb shook his head. 'I'm already in the red with my annual leave. I asked to go on compassionate leave, but half the anaesthetic department has come down with flu so they can't let me go till the operation and even then it will only be for a couple of weeks. We had a necrotising enterocolitis and a ruptured appendix last night while the on-call had an emergency thoracotomy. What am I supposed to do then? You can see for yourself how keen Gemma is to stay.'

Lucinda pondered for a moment but they both knew there was no easy solution.

'I'm sorry if I came on a bit strong, but something had to be said.'

Seb waved his hand. 'You really don't have to apologise. You were quite right to say something. I'd have done exactly the same. Hopefully Gemma will take heed.'

He smiled and for a moment his face had the same cheeky look as his son's, but the effect was somewhat more disturbing.

'Well, Miss Chambers, I'm sorry we had to meet in these circumstances, but I've heard a lot of good things about you and I'm looking forward to working with you.' He held out his hand and Lucinda shook it, noticing the firmness of his grip. 'Now, if you'll excuse me, I'd better get back to Billy.'

'Of course.'

As Seb left the room Ann entered.

'How did it go?'

Lucinda shrugged. 'I'm not sure if Gemma will change her mind but Dr Carlisle seemed very amicable.'

'I could think of a few words other than "amicable" to describe him. He's gorgeous, isn't he?' she said saucily.

Lucinda didn't respond. Ann, happy-go-lucky, middle-aged and with a wedding ring on her finger, could make comments like that and get away with it. For Lucinda, however, that type of talk could only lead to gossip and innuendo.

'Gemma did say she felt some hostility coming from the nursing staff.' Lucinda watched as Ann puffed up, on the defensive, but Lucinda carried on talking. 'And I can understand why. You're obviously all fond of Seb but, Ann, it has to stop. Gemma is Billy's mother, and the staff have to forget that his father is Seb. Now, I don't know all the circumstances of the break-up, but I can also be pretty sure that the rest of the staff don't know them either, and certainly not from Gemma's viewpoint. I think it might be prudent for you to have a word, Ann, just to be sure.'

Ann gave a grudging nod. 'You're probably right. I'll speak to them now. We're all a bit guilty, I guess. It's hard to be objective...'

'Well, you'll all just have to try harder, for Billy's sake,' Lucinda retorted, and Ann nodded sheepishly.

'Fair point.'

'I'd better be going. I was supposed to be in Admin half an hour ago. Let me know if there's any more problems with the Carlisles'.

Making her way out of the ward, she noticed Seb and Billy playing happily with a board game. Billy was laughing, with no hint of breathlessness now, as Seb lounged on the bed beside him. Ann was right. Sebastian Carlisle *was* gorgeous, that was undeniable. But he also had a five-year-old son and a wife from hell—or rather an ex-wife, she corrected herself, trying to ignore the sense of relief that thought gave her.

CHAPTER TWO

BY THE time Lucinda had been photographed for her security pass and had filled in a mountain of forms, the morning had disappeared and any hope of preparing a speech for her welcoming luncheon were gone.

In view of her seniority, the catering department had prepared a sumptuous array of finger food with not a single polystyrene cup or paper plate in sight. However, like Lucinda, for most of the senior staff attending, the lunch was a formality and not a pleasure. Professor Hays was the one exception. His glowing speech and obvious delight at having her on board made Lucinda inwardly cringe, but she smiled and shook his hand as he welcomed her onto the platform to address her new colleagues.

The polite but somewhat forced applause did nothing to quell her nerves; neither did the openly hostile look Pete Hughes was throwing her. Andrew Doran looked at his watch, wanting to get back to his babies. Seb, now dressed in a suit, fiddled with his tie, no doubt anxious to return to his son's bedside.

'I know we're all busy people so I'll make this brief.' Her voice was clear and steady, and she stood straight, her white coat discarded for the luncheon.

She wore a cream cashmere dress that clung becomingly to her curvaceous figure; her dark hair, thick and glossy, rippled over her shoulders. Lucinda, in fact, looked like a woman who had spent hours getting ready for this moment. In truth, that morning she had jumped under the shower and spent a mere five minutes blow-drying her long hair and about half that again to add just a touch of eyeliner and lipstick. Her complexion was so clear there was no need for foundation or blusher. Lucinda's looks entirely spoke for themselves.

Her clothes were ludicrously expensive and well tailored, but even that was with reason. With her impossible schedule, she had little or no time for clothes-shopping, so twice a year she set aside a day for what she considered a tiresome necessity, not a luxury, and purchased a select few pieces that would last and look smart. Not one person in the room could have guessed at her apprehension.

'Firstly, I'd like to thank Professor Hays for his words of welcome and for giving me the opportunity to work with him in such a prestigious hospital. I have no doubt I shall learn a lot.

'While I'm proud to be here, I think it's very important to remember that were it not for other people's misfortunes there would be no Melbourne Central, and hence no need for us. So on that note I'll thank you all for coming to welcome me on board and let you get back to the people that really matter—the patients.'

'Hear, hear,' somebody quipped as everyone started clapping, and this time the applause was genuine. Several people came up and shook her hand as she left the platform and congratulated her.

'Nice speech, direct and to the point, like this morning.'

Lucinda swung around at the deep, familiar voice. Seb's green eyes were smiling at her now and Lucinda reluctantly recalled Ann's words.

'That's me,' she said lightly, then added, 'How's Billy?'

'He's settled now, and still out on the main ward, thanks to you. It's their rest time so I thought I'd come and welcome the new consultant as we got off to a rather bad start this morning.'

Lucinda smiled. 'It must be hard, having your son as a patient in the same hospital you work at.'

'Absolutely. Every emergency page I hear sends me into a cold sweat in case it might be Billy, and while it's nice that I can pop down and see him between patients, it's rather embarrassing to have all your dirty washing aired in public.'

Lucinda waited for him to elaborate but he'd obviously said all he was going to on the subject. She stood there uncomfortably, desperately trying to think of something to say. Despite her excellence at public speaking and confidence when discussing medical matters, once on a more social level Lucinda invariably found herself feeling awkward.

After a moment's silence it was Seb who spoke again. 'Pete Hughes looks as if he's at a funeral,' he observed.

'I think he'd like it to be mine.'

Seb gave her a wry smile. 'All's fair in love and promotion. He'll get over it.'

Lucinda's eyes widened. 'So that's his problem? I wish Professor Hays had warned me. I had no idea he was in the running.'

Seb shrugged dismissively. 'He never was. Pete just liked to think he stood a chance. He likes to party a bit too hard for the prof's liking. Much as Professor Hays might look a bit dotty at times, he knows exactly what goes on. Pete's going to need to do a lot more spadework before he wins him over. Anyway, enough about work. How are you settling in Melbourne? Have you found somewhere to live yet?'

She knew he was probably just being polite, but under his steady gaze Lucinda couldn't help but feel that Seb's interest was genuine and she found herself answering back in a softer, less businesslike tone.

'I only arrived on Saturday morning, but I'm starting to find my way around. I found somewhere to live before I came, thank goodness. Admin finally gave me my roster this morning—it wouldn't have left much time for house-hunting.'

'Tell me about it,' he groaned. 'So where are you living?'

'At Southbank, the new apartment complex.'

Seb let out a low whistle. 'They look pretty plush, I saw the advertisements for them. They'd be handy for work, too.'

Lucinda nodded. 'Five minutes away. How about you?'

'Nothing so flash, or near, I'm afraid. I'm more the "renovator's delight" type, not that I ever seem to find the time to renovate. Mind you, that can have its advantages when you've got children. Billy may be past the scribbling-on-walls stage, but footballs hurtling through the air and remote-control cars crashing into the plasterwork aren't the best recipe for a luxury home—not that you'd know about that sort of thing,' he added.

Lucinda laughed. 'Actually, I do know what you mean. I've got a godson in Sydney—'

'Miss Chambers, sorry to interrupt.' Professor Hays smiled broadly, looking anything but sorry, and Lucinda's sentence was left unfinished. Seb gave her a slightly questioning look but there was no chance to complete the conversation as the professor had other plans.

'Its nearly time to head over to NICU. Mr Doran wants us there to discuss one of the infants,' Professor Hays explained to Seb. 'Fabulous speech, don't you think? It doesn't do any harm to be reminded who we're here for. I think Miss Chambers is going to be a real asset, don't you agree, Dr Carlisle?'

Seb nodded in agreement and, turning back to Lucinda,

for a second his gaze flickered downwards, his eyes travelling briefly over her body. Lucinda felt her heart rate quicken.

'Absolutely,' Seb replied, his voice deep and rich. 'A real asset.' Replacing his empty glass on the table, he excused himself and left. For a split second Lucinda had the craziest notion to run after him. To tap on his shoulder and explain that what she'd been trying to say had been that she'd moved into her friend's house whilst she'd been on a placement and had seen at first hand the destruction a toddler could cause. That she wasn't so shallow as to think a godson in any way gave her an insight into parenthood. But, of course, she didn't. What would be the point? she reasoned. Sebastian Carlisle had, after all, only been there today to be polite. He'd probably forgotten their conversation as soon as he'd walked out of the door. So why couldn't she just forget it? Lucinda wondered as she joined the professor and walked along the corridor towards NICU, for all the world appearing to listen intently as Professor Hays spoke. Why couldn't she?

Walking along Southbank, the delicious fragrant aroma of the Suriyan Indian Restaurant was just too good to ignore.

'Lovely to see you again, Doctor. You took the job, I gather?'

Lucinda smiled at the greeting, touched Vijay had remembered her.

'Your delectable butter chicken was a very favourable deciding factor. I think we'll be seeing a lot of each other. I'll have it to go tonight, though.' Her friendly remark wasn't untrue. Southbank, set along Melbourne's Yarra River, with its multitude of shops, restaurants and food court all open until late into the night, meant that she would never have to worry about cooking. Not that she didn't enjoy it but the ridiculous hours she worked hardly left enough time for shopping, let alone preparing meals. This cultural melting pot set in such beautiful surroundings offered her a different choice every night, but Indian food was definitely a favourite.

Vijay handed her a card. 'You ring me before you leave the hospital and I'll have your order waiting, no worries. If you're on call, my son will come and deliver to you,' he said in his Indian accent, peppered with Australianisms. 'I know how hard you doctors work. You see my son?' Vijay pointed to a strapping teenager setting up the restaurant tables. 'He was no bigger than this...' Holding up his hands, Vijay showed such an impossibly tiny gap between them that Lucinda knew, unless his son was a medical marvel that even she hadn't heard about, Vijay was exaggerating, but she didn't spoil the story, enjoying the light-hearted banter. 'But when you see him now, such a fine young boy... Your hospital makes many miracles.'

'Do you want a garlic naan?' he added more as an afterthought.

Lucinda shook her head. 'Not very fair on the patients. What was that lovely bread I had last time, with fruit and nuts?'

'Ah, my sweet mincemeat naan. Very good choice, Doctor. And how about some beautiful saffron rice to go with your chicken?'

How could she refuse?

Minutes later Lucinda nodded briefly to the doorman as he pressed the lift button for her. Letting herself into her twentieth-floor apartment, Lucinda set the white plastic bag containing her dinner onto the gleaming benchtop. The cleaner had obviously been in as the morning's breakfast dishes and discarded clothes were all back in their various cupboards, making the place look more like a sterile hotel room than ever.

Her mother had organised the apartment for her through a real-estate contact, and while it was sumptuous, with glittering bay and city views shimmering through the full-length windows, it didn't do much for Lucinda.

Kicking off her cream suede shoes, she wiggled her toes luxuriously in the thick white carpet. White everything really, she noted, except for the black granite benchtops and stainless-steel appliances. Yes, it was luxurious, but hardly homely. There was nothing remotely personal about it. Still, she could set about finding somewhere more to her taste in a few months when she had the job under control.

Checking the answering machine, Lucinda couldn't help but feel a stab of disappointment that her parents hadn't rung to see how her first day had gone. Then she checked herself. What did she expect? Instead, there were a couple of boring messages, one from her new bank, the other from the caretaker of the apartment block warning her of a fire-alarm check. She toyed with the idea of ringing her parents, but what was the point? They were probably out at some restaurant.

Instead, she put the foil cartons into the cooker, set it on low and then ran a deep bath. Slipping into the water, she closed her eyes, resting her head back as she reflected on her first day as a consultant. It had taken a lot to get here, so why now, she wondered, when she was at the top, or at least very near, didn't she feel happier? Why wasn't she lying in the bath in this marble bathroom with a self-satisfied grin and a glow of achievement?

Because there was no one to share it with. Lucinda tried to ignore the thought and pulled out the plug, wrapping herself in a huge bathrobe, but that inner voice wouldn't go away. Because for all your talk and bravado, you're not that hard and you do care.

Listlessly she served up her dinner and, carrying the plate

over to the sofa, took in the gorgeous sunset. The whole of Melbourne lay before her, the bay shimmering gold. It was a view made for sharing.

For a second Lucinda felt so lonely it hurt. She had never had a problem attracting the opposite sex, and was never short of offers for dates. But her relationships, if you could call them that, never seemed to get anywhere. Men didn't like playing second fiddle to her career and the gloss soon wore off for her, too. Maybe she set her sights too high? But what was wrong with that? She wanted to get it right the first time. Imagine ending up like Sebastian and Gemma Carlisle? What a mess. Casting her mind back, she remembered the way Seb had looked at her at the luncheon.

'A real asset,' he'd said, but it was the *way* he'd said it. Lucinda felt her stomach tighten just at the memory of his voice. Sebastian Carlisle was gorgeous, disturbingly so, but completely out of bounds, of course. Lucinda didn't have a hard-and-fast rule about not mixing business with pleasure, but on the whole avoided it. Who needed the complication? Anyway, on Wednesday she would be operating with Professor Hays on his *son*. The word was a sobering thought.

Covered by the green sterile theatre drapes and with a multitude of wires, tubes and monitors attached to his body, the small form lying on the operating table was unrecognisable as Billy. But there was an increased air of tension in the theatre that morning as all of the staff worked alongside and knew Sebastian Carlisle well. The fact it was Seb's son lying there didn't mean Billy would get better treatment—all the young patients were afforded the best possible care. But it did mean that each staff member had a personal stake in this operation for they had all heard about

Billy and his setbacks and achievements relayed in Seb's deep drawl over the past five years.

For Lucinda, however, the emotions that ran through her when the boy was prepared with a Betadine solution and a large occlusive dressing placed over the site of incision to reduce his chances of infection came as a total surprise. Her air of tension had nothing to do with the fact his father was an anaesthetist at the hospital. This morning it was all to do with Billy.

When she had popped into the ward that morning for the pre-op round he had again given her the benefit of that cheeky smile and she'd felt her hardened heart melt slightly. She'd smiled back at him and, more amazingly, had stopped to listen when Billy had turned his robot on for her benefit, watching as the metallic figure had clunked around his bedside table. Gemma had been nowhere to be seen, but Seb had been there, smiling appreciatively at her for taking the time to indulge Billy.

'Thanks for that.' He'd come up to her as she'd left the ward. 'He might seem all right but he's pretty nervous.'

'You, too?'

Seb had nodded. 'I know technically it's a pretty straight-forward operation, but that's the medical side of me trying to rationalise things. At the end of the day it keeps coming back to me that it's my son's heart that's being operated on.'

'We'll take good care of him,' she'd said in her most confident voice as she'd stridden off towards the theatres. It was what she said to all the parents but for some reason this time it hadn't seemed enough, and she had been left wishing she could have somehow comforted him more.

But like the rest of the theatre staff, Lucinda put her emotions to one side as the operation commenced and Professor Hays made his incision. Billy's temperature was brought down to reduce his body's demand for oxygen and he was placed onto heart bypass. Professor Hays was indeed a skilled operator and Lucinda's talent complemented his skills. Neither was the type for small talk or background music. They worked in quiet harmony, with only the occasional exchange of words.

Their attention was completely focused on the small damaged heart until finally, with her back aching, Lucinda sat up on her stool and Professor Hays instructed the perfusionist that Billy was ready to be weaned off the bypass machine. The tension in the room increased again but lifted as the small heart filled with blood and started pumping.

'Good work, everybody. Miss Chambers, I'll leave you to close Master Carlisle and I'll go and speak to his parents, let them know how well it went.'

Lucinda stayed with Billy in the recovery room, writing out the post-operative instructions and ordering the multitude of drugs Billy would be needing, as well as the intravenous fluids orders. For the next twenty-four hours he would be in Intensive Care on a respirator to allow him to rest and to enable the staff to concentrate on his heart. But, all being well, he would then be moved off the intensive care unit and back onto his old ward, but in the four-bedded high-dependency section.

A nurse escorted Seb, Gemma and a woman Lucinda didn't recognise to the gurney where Billy lay. Lucinda stepped away slightly, allowing them nearer. Only Gemma held back.

'Mummy and Daddy are here and Aunty Isabella. Professor Hays said you've been a very brave boy. We're all so proud.' Seb's words were gentle and comforting but Lucinda could hear the break in his voice, could see the tension in his shoulders as he leant over the trolley, his strong brown hands gently caressing his son's face.

'It went very well.' Lucinda said gently to Gemma,

knowing Professor Hays would have said the same thing but realising it was all they would want to hear. 'He's heavily sedated but talk to him, hold his hand.'

Seb turned to his ex-wife. 'Come on, Gemma, hold his hand let him know we're all here for him.' His voice held no malice, just a hint of pleading. Gemma stepped forward and hesitantly picked up one of Billy's pale hands.

'Mummy's here, Billy.' But it was Seb who spoke. Gemma just stood there, frozen. 'Talk to him Gemma, please,' Seb said gruffly.

Gemma replaced Billy's hand on the starched blanket. 'I have to make a phone call. I'll be down in the canteen.'

'Gemma, please,' Seb pleaded, but it fell on deaf ears. Gemma hurriedly left the recovery area.

'Just let her go,' Isabella said wearily.

'Sometimes all the equipment can be a bit intimidating,' the theatre nurse ventured, but Seb said nothing and Lucinda was sure she could see a glint of tears in his vivid eyes as he gently stroked his son's hair. Lucinda carried on writing up the charts, relaying her instructions to the theatre nurse as she wrote them. The nurse would in turn pass on her orders to the intensive care staff.

The porters arrived to wheel the gurney over to Intensive Care.

'We'll get him over now, Dr Carlisle,'

Seb nodded. 'Isabella, will you go and tell Gemma they're moving him? I want to stay around.'

Isabella gave Billy a quick kiss and made her way out of the recovery area as the staff checked and rechecked the oxygen and equipment on the trolley to ensure they were prepared for any eventuality on the short journey across to the unit.

'I'll come and let you know when they're ready for you to see him, Seb,' the theatre nurse said kindly but firmly.

Seb nodded resignedly and Lucinda knew that he wanted more than anything to go with his son, but though he had been allowed into the out-of-bounds theatre recovery area it was better that they settled Billy away from Seb. He wasn't a doctor here, but the child's father.

As the trolley moved off Seb made his way over to the small annexe off the recovery area.

Lucinda watched as he walked off, his face etched with anxiety and his usual air of confidence gone. She had given him the usual spiel on the ward, and it had left her feeling empty. It was time for something more.

Sometimes words did help, but then there were times when knowing when to say nothing helped more. As Lucinda made her way into the annexe she knew it should be Gemma here, that Billy's parents should be comforting and leaning on each other through this terrible angst-filled time. But for some reason Gemma was instead sitting in the canteen, making her calls, leaving Seb to battle with a myriad emotions in that small sterile room.

Lucinda knew there was nothing she could say to help so instead she went and sat quietly beside him. It was a moment or two before Seb acknowledged she was there and when he finally spoke his voice was thick with emotion.

'He's been through so much, poor kid. It's bad enough with all the operations and his asthma, but his mum and dad breaking up as well and now Gemma can't even bear to hold his hand. It's like she doesn't want to even be in the same room with him.' His voice broke. 'How much can one little guy take?' Seb took a couple of deep breaths and sat up straight, embarrassed at betraying so much feeling. 'I'm sorry. You don't need to hear all this,' he said in a gruff voice.

But Lucinda shook her head. 'Please, don't apologise. I know it's awful for all of you.'

Seb continued tentatively as if he had to justify his words. 'It was just so awful to see him like that. More than anyone, I knew what to expect but it was still a shock. The prof told me it went well, told me a bit too much detail really.' He winced. 'There's some things you really don't need to know.'

'I understand,' she said, but the words came out wrong and she almost heard her mother's affected tones in her voice.

Seb turned and gave her a cynical look. 'Ah, yes,' he said dryly. 'After all, you've got a godson.'

Lucinda stiffened. She knew he was hurting but at least she was here, at least she was trying. She stood up smartly. 'I'd better get back.' Her crisp demeanour returned and she made no attempt now to hide it, but Seb was contrite for his sarcastic words and he stood up as well, his hand reaching out and touching her arm as she turned to go.

'That was completely uncalled for. I know you're trying to help.'

Lucinda said nothing. Acutely aware of the warm strength of his hand on her bare arm, she found herself unable to tear her eyes away from his steady gaze. It was Seb who finally broke the spell.

'Thank you,' he said simply. 'Thank you for being here.'

Lucinda nodded. For a moment she was speechless, bewildered by the turbulent thoughts he so easily evoked. Finally she found her voice. 'I really do have to go now.'

They left the annexe together. Seb returned to Billy and Lucinda made her way to the sink where she started the long and tedious process of scrubbing for the next operation. But for both there was a gentle disquiet, a lingering feeling that something special had happened in those few moments. Something good and strong, a tiny foundation from which to build.

CHAPTER THREE

'WE ARE honoured.' Ann Benton looked up from her desk and gave Lucinda a tired smile as she entered the nurse unit manager's office. 'A registrar and a consultant on the ward on a Saturday evening. Is one of my patients sick that I don't know about?'

Lucinda shook her head. 'I hope not! One of the premmies on NICU went into atrial fibrillation. She's kept us all on our toes this afternoon,' Lucinda explained. Little Kimberley's heart had been beating too rapidly and causing a lot of concern. Lucinda had been called in for an emergency consultation and after a multitude of tests and drugs the baby's arrhythmia was starting to settle. 'Who else is here, then?'

'Pete Hughes. He's going out with one of my nurses. We're short tonight and Ellen offered to stay till seven, so Pete's hanging around, otherwise we wouldn't see him for dust.'

Lucinda raised her eyebrows but didn't comment. 'How are my patients—any concerns?' she asked instead.

'You mean, how's Billy? You really have got a soft spot for him, and here was me expecting an ice queen. You're as soft as butter, Miss Chambers.' Ann had an ability to say exactly what everyone was thinking and somehow manage not to cause offence. Lucinda knew all about her own reputation and it was in some way a relief to be able to let down her guard with this likeable, knowledgeable woman.

'Billy's fine. We've taken him out of high dependency this morning and he's back on the general ward now. He'll probably be going home on Monday or Tuesday, but then that's up to you, of course. He's already watched his favourite video three times.'

Lucinda gave a small chuckle. 'So he's definitely turned the corner. Has his mum been in?'

Ann gave a knowing look. 'Yes, she's making the occasional appearance—dressed to the nines with not a hair out of place, unlike most of the other mums in this place who hardly manage to pull on a pair of leggings and a T-shirt and run a comb through their hair. Mrs Carlisle certainly doesn't let her son's illness curtail her. Hard to understand, isn't it?' she said glumly. 'He's so cute you just can't imagine her not wanting to be with him.'

'Ours is not to reason why,' Lucinda said matter-of-factly, although privately she agreed with every word.

'I know, I just worry for Seb. You were right to say something about the way the staff were treating Gemma. I try not to let my feelings for Seb show but, well, we've been friends for years, and it's hard seeing him go through the mill. Not that Seb ever complains. As close as we are, I never really know what he's thinking. He keeps his emotions pretty much under lock and key.'

After Lucinda's reprimand Ann had addressed the ward staff, making things easier not only for the Carlisles but for the nursing staff, too. Ann had apologised to Lucinda for letting things get so out of hand but Lucinda had only been grateful the problem had been so easily sorted. From this unsteady beginning a firm friendship was being forged.

'Seb seems to be coping. I mean, I spoke to him after the operation and he was pretty upset, but any parent would be.'

Ann gave her a surprised look. 'Seb was upset? In front of you?'

Lucinda nodded. 'But it's only to be expected. Billy had just had major heart surgery. You seem shocked—why?'

Ann gave a small shrug. 'Like I said, I've known Seb a long time, and I've never seen him with his guard down.'

Lucinda thought for moment. 'Professor Hays apparently went into rather a lot of detail about the procedure. Maybe it was that.'

'Maybe,' Ann replied, but she didn't sound convinced. 'I'm just glad someone was there with him when he was upset.' She gave Lucinda a smile. 'He doesn't deserve to be alone.'

Under Ann's beady eyes Lucinda felt the beginnings of a blush, and she hastily changed the subject—the last thing she needed was Ann to realise she had a crush on Sebastian Carlisle. What would that do to her reputation? 'Any other concerns on the ward?'

Ann gave a worried frown. 'I'm a bit concerned about Bianca Moore. I know she's not strictly your patient until she has her transplant.' Ann automatically touched the wooden desk. 'And let it be soon, please, God. But I can't get hold of the intern. Her parents brought her in a burger and chips and normally she'd wolf it down, but she hasn't touched it, though there's nothing I can put my finger on. For all I go on about Pete Hughes, he's been good enough to look over her notes—that's what he's doing now.'

At that moment Pete walked in. Dressed casually in jeans and a white T-shirt, he still looked immaculate.

'Evening, Lucinda. How's Kimberley?' His comment was professional but the trace of bitterness in his voice didn't go unnoticed by either woman.

'She's had some more Lasix and we've digitalised her. She's not too good, though. How's Bianca?'

Pete placed the file on the desk in front of Ann. 'I've

had a look and she seems fine. Maybe she just wasn't hungry.'

'Thanks for looking anyway.' Ann gave a small shrug but Lucinda could tell she was still worried.

A pretty young nurse knocked on the office door. 'I've handed over my patients to Sister Spencer—they all seem fine. Billy Carlisle is just having another nebuliser.'

'Is his mum there?' Ann asked.

'No, she just left, but his dad's with him. He's going to stay the night again in the doctors' on-call room next door once Billy's asleep. He said to call him any time Billy wakes up.' She smiled at Pete. 'Are you done?'

Pete nodded. 'See you, ladies—hopefully not till Monday,' he added half-jokingly. Lucinda gave a rueful smile. Weekends on call, even as a consultant, were rarely if ever that quiet.

'Was that Kimberley Stewart you were talking about?' Ann asked, pouring two coffees.

Lucinda nodded. 'Do you know the family?'

'No, it's just my nosy nature. She's the micro-prem on NICU, isn't she?' As Lucinda nodded Ann pulled a worried face. 'Any chance she'll make it, I mean realistically?'

Lucinda took a sip of her coffee before she answered. Kimberley and her family had been causing a great deal of anxiety and it was actually nice to be able to talk about it with Ann. 'If she doesn't it won't be for the want of trying, but realistically, no, I don't think there's much hope.'

Ann didn't say anything and Lucinda found herself continuing. 'It's such a shame. Her mother has idiopathic infertility.'

'In English, please,' Ann said. 'I'm on a cardiac ward, remember?'

'There's no reason that can be found as to why she can't get pregnant,' Lucinda explained. 'Apparently they've been trying for years. This pregnancy was after their sixth and final attempt at IVF.'

'Final?' Ann questioned. 'Why?'

'They can't afford to do it any more, either emotionally or financially. Their marriage is under a terrible strain. I went to the team meeting about them, and from what Sue Washington was saying they're hardly talking. Janine, the mother, is completely wrapped up in Kimberley. Mark, the father, has to head back to work on Monday. It's not the ideal situation but Kimberley's seven weeks old now.'

'And the bills don't stop coming in just because you've got a sick child,' Ann added.

'Exactly. The nurses were just telling me it's their wedding anniversary today. Ten years, can you imagine? I don't seem to be able to manage ten weeks in my relationships.'

Ann laughed. 'You just haven't met the right man yet. Tod and I have been together twenty-five years now and I couldn't imagine it any other way.' She thought for a moment 'It's a shame they can't go out for their anniversary, get away from the hospital for a while.'

Lucinda nodded. 'It's a shame all round. Anyway, there's not much I can do about it. I'm a doctor, not a marriage guidance councillor. Who am I to offer advice?' She stood up to go. 'Thanks for the coffee. Do you want me to have a look at Bianca for you before I go? I can tell you're still not happy.'

Ann gave a relieved smile. 'Please. I don't want to go worrying her. She knows more about her condition than us, but I'm sure she's not right.'

Lucinda made her way down the darkened ward. By seven-thirty the lights were down and the children were being settled. There was strange background music coming over the intercom with the sound of running water and birds chirping. Ann had been given some CDs to try out that supposedly relaxed children. Lucinda wondered if she'd be burning incense next!

Seb hadn't made it to the on-call room and lay sound asleep next to Billy, his long legs dangling uncomfortably from the small bed. Billy was held firmly in the crook of his father's muscular arm with his head resting on Seb's broad chest. They looked the picture of contentment. It was hard to believe, seeing them lying there so peacefully, the problems they had both faced.

'You still awake?' Lucinda stood at the side of Bianca's bed. The young girl gave her a suspicious look.

'What are you doing here?'

'Just checking on my patients.'

'Why? You're a consultant. Shouldn't you be at some fancy ball on a Saturday night?'

Lucinda gave a small laugh. 'You make it sound very glamorous. I'm new. I like to make sure of things myself— I'll go home later.' Lucinda looked at the take-away cartons. 'Didn't fancy your burger, huh?'

Bianca shook her head. 'No, but I'm starving now. I could murder a pizza. I might ring out for one.' She leant over to her drawer. 'Mum didn't leave any money.' Bianca lay back dejectedly on the pillows.

Children this ill were invariably and understandably spoilt by the staff. If their day could be made easier with a new video game or something nice to eat, the ward funds covered it, and Lucinda had no doubt that this case would be no exception.

'I'm sure we can stretch to a pizza. Do you want me to ask Ann to order you one?'

Bianca shook her head. 'I can ring myself. I've got my own phone,' she said importantly. 'But the nurses are all busy and all the other kids are asleep. I'm the oldest on the ward except for Toby and he's too sick. It's no fun eating pizza on your own.'

Whether it was some sixth sense of Ann's that she heeded or not, for some reason Lucinda didn't ignore Bianca's hidden plea.

'I guess I haven't eaten yet. All right, then, you ring for a pizza and I'll stay for a slice—on one condition, though.'

'Name it,' Bianca wheezed.

'You let me take some blood and have a quick listen to your chest.'

Bianca rang for the food while Lucinda collected the various pieces of equipment she would need to take Bianca's blood. Wheeling the stainless-steel trolley to the bedside, she smiled as Bianca grudgingly offered her arm.

'I'm going to listen to your chest first.'

Bianca sat forward and matter-of-factly lifted her gown. Her chest sounded as bad as ever but not worse, as far as Lucinda could tell.

'I'll do the blood now. What did you order?' she asked by way of distraction as she swabbed the area and slipped the needle in.

'Supreme, but with no anchovies. How much are you taking?' Bianca yelped. 'I'll have none left the way you lot carry on.'

'I haven't finished yet.' Lucinda transferred the blood from the syringe into the various tubes and bottles she had selected. 'I'm going to do some blood gases as well.'

'What tests are you doing?'

'The usual—a full blood examination to check for any anaemia or signs of infection, U and Es to check for any electrolyte imbalance, and also some blood cultures.'

'They normally only take them when I've got a temperature,' Bianca said knowingly.

Lucinda nodded as she took the arterial blood gases from

the young girl's wrist. 'That's right, there's supposed to be more chance of isolating bugs when the temperature's high and the infection is particularly active, but sometimes an infection still shows up when the temperature's normal and you're least expecting it. Now, you press on that for a few minutes while I get rid of these.'

Lucinda popped the blood gases into a bag of ice and wrote the pathology slips in her extravagant scrawl. Having labelled all the bloods, she placed them in the pathology bags and made her way back to Ann's office.

'I've taken some bloods,' she said to Ann. 'They'll need to go straight down as I've taken blood gases.'

'I'll ring for a porter. What do you think?' Ann asked.

Lucinda retrieved the slips from the bags and wrote 'Urgent' on each order. Shaking her head, she looked up at Ann. 'That you're not happy and that's good enough for me. Everything seems all right on examination, but she is a bit pale and she does seem...' Pausing, Lucinda tried to think of the right words 'A bit clingy perhaps. She's apyrexial and she's on just about every antibiotic we've got in the pharmacy. Still, it's worth doing some blood cultures just in case she's brewing something.' Lucinda hesitated a moment. 'Bianca's ordered a pizza. I said I'd stay for a slice,' she said rather too casually as she made her way out of the office.

'As soft as butter,' Ann called after Lucinda. 'As soft as butter.'

Half an hour later Lucinda pulled the curtains and settled into a seat at Bianca's bedside.

Bianca handed her a slice of pizza, her pale face beaming. 'There you go, Miss Chambers.'

Lucinda felt a stab of pity as she watched Bianca swallow a handful of the enzyme capsules cystic fibrosis patients needed to take before eating in order to help their bodies digest food.

'You can call me Lucinda as we're sharing a pizza,' Lucinda said. 'But tomorrow morning its back to Miss Chambers,' she added sternly as Bianca smiled happily, not remotely bothered by her tone.

'You're very pretty,' Bianca said suddenly.

'Thank you.'

'I wish I was pretty.'

'But you are.' Lucinda said truthfully. 'You're gorgeous.'

'I'm too thin and spotty, and these disgusting braces. Yuk.' She made a face.

'I know how you feel, I had braces at your age but they'll come off soon and it will be more than worth it. Being cooped up in here doesn't help, and once you get the transplant you'll fill out and the spots will go before you know it. You really are going to be very beautiful.'

'If I get the chance,' she said poignantly, and she turned her face to the television screen.

Lucinda had finished her slice of pizza but absentmindedly she picked up another as she became engrossed in the film Bianca had turned on. The speaker lay on Bianca's pillow, forcing Lucinda to strain to catch all of the words, but it didn't mar her enjoyment—after all, it was one of Lucinda's all-time favourites. They watched in amicable silence, until the young boy on the screen movingly asked his widowed father things to remember about his dead mother. Lucinda turned and saw silent tears pouring down Bianca's face.

'Why don't you turn it over?' she suggested.

Bianca shook her head. 'No, I'm enjoying it, believe it or not.' She gave a loud sniff. 'I'm not afraid of dying for myself. It's just Mum and Dad and my brother, Lewis. I

feel so sorry for them. I know how sad they'll be. I just
wonder how they'll manage.'

Lucinda sat very still. There were times in medicine for
platitudes and optimism in the face of the worst odds. But
there was also a time when the possibility of death, however unwelcome, however vehemently opposed, needed to
be faced. Just because they were talking about it, it didn't
mean they were accepting or giving in. Bianca simply
needed to talk.

'They'd be sad, of course,' Lucinda said after a while.
''Devastated, no doubt, but in time things would get better.
They'd have wonderful memories, and go on loving you
and talking about you. They'd be all right. Have you spoken to them about it?'

'I've tried, but they just get so upset. I want to tell them
I'm not scared and how much I love them, but they just
change the subject.'

'It's hard for them, Bianca, but they know how much
you love them. Sometimes that's the one thing that doesn't
need to be said.'

'Am I going to die?' The question, though half-expected,
still tore through Lucinda.

'Bianca, I can't say no. I want to but I can't, the same
way I can't make that sort of guarantee to any of my patients. But I can promise that I'll do my very best to make
sure you don't, and you have to promise to keep fighting.'

'I lie here at night and I wish more than anything for
new lungs and heart, and then I feel awful because it means
I'm wishing someone dead.'

Lucinda shook her head fiercely. 'No, you're not. You're
wishing you could live and that's entirely different. And,
anyway, wishing doesn't make a scrap of difference.
Terrible things happen, accidents happen. You lying here,
wishing for a new heart and lungs, doesn't change fate. It

would happen anyway. You mustn't feel guilty for wishing you were well.'

Bianca coughed. 'Not well exactly. I'd still have CF, but at least I'd have a clean slate to start with. A new set of lungs for this horrid disease to ruin.'

Lucinda gave her a smile. 'Maybe it won't. There's a lot of progress being made with the treatment of CF but you don't need me to tell you that.' She pointed to the pile of books by the bed. 'I'd better watch my back if you decide to take up medicine. It might be me having to call you Miss Moore.'

Lucinda stood up 'Now, I'm off home. You get some sleep after the film finishes.' She made her way to the curtain, but Bianca called her back.

'Lucinda, is there a happy ending?'

'You'll just have to wait and see,' Lucinda said matter-of-factly, but, seeing Bianca lean back on the pillows, her face softened. 'Of course there's a happy ending,' Lucinda said gently, wishing silently that her words didn't just apply to the film.

Popping her head into the office to say goodnight, she saw Ann tapping away on the computer.

'Are you still here?' Lucinda asked.

'I could say the same for you. I'm just looking to see if any of Bianca's bloods are back. Then I've just got to check the drugs and hopefully then I can get home. Here we are,' she added as the results popped up on the screen. Lucinda looked over her shoulder.

'Nothing out of the ordinary yet for Bianca. I'm off, then. Goodnight.'

Tired now, Lucinda took the lift down one floor and made her way to NICU to check on Kimberley, promising herself a lie-in next morning if her pager didn't go off.

The all-too-familiar sound of the overhead display system crackling into action stopped her in her tracks. As a consultant she wasn't on the cardiac arrest or medical emergency teams, but the hospital had an overhead visual display board that gave information as to where any such emergency was located. The protocol was such that all doctors in the vicinity were to proceed to the area to enable a rapid response. Even before the numbers flickered onto the screen Lucinda just knew what to expect. '000 1 PCUG.' Which translated to 'cardiac arrest, 1st floor, Paediatric Cardiac Unit, General Ward.'

The lifts were out of bounds during any hospital emergency, so Lucinda ran to the stairwell beside the lift, taking the stairs two or three at a time. Coming out onto the corridor, she only just avoided colliding with Seb as he burst out of the spare on-call room. One look at his stricken face told her exactly what he was thinking, and she longed to comfort him.

'I just left the ward,' she said somewhat breathlessly as she ran along with him. 'Billy was fine.' But she knew Seb wouldn't be reassured until he saw his son for himself.

Running onto the ward, they found that ordered chaos reigned. Curtains had been pulled around all the children's beds, leaving only Bianca's exposed. The headrest was off and a nurse was inflating Bianca's lungs with an ambu-bag as Ann knelt astride the young girl, massaging her chest. Another nurse was pulling up drugs and a third was attaching electrodes to Bianca's chest.

'What's the story?' Seb said sharply, instantly taking charge as he took over Bianca's airway, suctioning her deftly. 'Stop the compressions,' he ordered as he expertly inserted a tube down her throat and inflated the cuff, thus securing her airway.

'She's in asystole.' Lucinda said as she checked the monitor.

'I checked her and she seemed fine. I went back less than a minute later to say goodnight and found her like this,' said Ann, resuming the cardiac massage. 'Thank God I went back.'

With Seb in control of Bianca's airway, Lucinda was free to concentrate on her heart. 'So she hasn't been down long?' Lucinda said as she inserted various drugs into Bianca's intravenous line. 'Keep up the massage for a minute, Ann—give these drugs a chance to work.' Ann pumped away as the cardiac arrest team arrived, but they didn't take over as the team already working on Bianca was far more senior. Instead, they assisted, all working together to save this precious young life.

'OK, stop,' Lucinda ordered. Every eye was on the monitor. A rhythm was picked up. 'Sinus bradycardia,' Lucinda said. 'Give me some more adrenaline.' A syringe containing the cardiac stimulant was immediately passed to her.

'Adrenaline 1 in 10,000—3 mls,' Lucinda stated as she gave the drug. It was duly charted, along with the time given, by a nurse. Bianca's heart rate picked up. 'Normal sinus rhythm,' Lucinda said with a note of triumph as she looked around the bedside. 'Well done, everyone.'

'She's fighting the tube,' Seb said. 'I'm going to sedate her and we'll get her over to Intensive Care stat. It's all right, little lady.' Seb spoke tenderly into Bianca's ear. 'You're going to be OK now.' The sedative drugs took effect and Seb, Lucinda and the arrest team wheeled Bianca to the PICU as the other staff set about tidying and replacing the equipment on the resuscitation trolley and settling the other children, who had been awoken by the commotion.

The cardiothoracic physician arrived shortly after they got to PICU and Lucinda handed over to him.

'Poor kid,' he said when she'd finished. 'And her poor

parents, too. Ann just rang to say they're on the way. I'm not looking forward to talking to them.'

Seb had walked over to join them and Lucinda suddenly found herself momentarily tongue-tied.

'Not the nicest part of the job, I guess, but someone has to do it,' Lucinda said crisply, and then inwardly kicked herself. It had been an emotional night and in an attempt to maintain her composure she had again come across as clinical and uncaring.

The look that passed between the two men didn't go unnoticed by Lucinda.

'I'm just going to check on Ann,' Seb said, breaking the uncomfortable silence. '*She'll* be pretty upset by what's happened.'

Lucinda heard the inference and in an attempt to redeem herself offered her assistance. 'I'll come along, too.'

Seb merely shrugged and didn't say a word as they walked across to the ward. Only when they got to the doors did he speak. 'Just go easy on her, Lucinda. They're more than just patients to Ann.'

'Fancy another coffee?' Ann offered, her voice heavy.

Lucinda nodded her acceptance and took a seat. Over and over the evening's events Ann went, picking Lucinda's brains, desperately searching for a reason for Bianca's sudden crash, but Lucinda simply couldn't come up with an answer. Finally it was Seb who put the night's events into perspective.

'Who knows why, Ann? It isn't always clear-cut. Maybe the blood cultures will show up a massive infection, maybe it was a mucous plug, perhaps her little body had simply had enough.'

'Maybe she was just unlucky,' Ann said, and Lucinda saw the sparkle of tears in her eyes.

'She was bloody lucky if you ask me,' said Seb in a firm voice.

Lucinda and Ann turned to him questioningly.

'I'd hardly call her lucky.' Ann said sharply.

'Oh, I don't know. If she was going to arrest anyway, what are the chances of having a cardiothoracic and an anaesthetic consultant ten seconds away, along with a charge nurse with a hunch who hovered around all night instead of going home? I tell you this much—if ever my number's up I wouldn't mind having such a crack team in the vicinity.' Ann gave a small smile and Lucinda knew Seb had made her feel better—herself, too, for that matter—but Seb wasn't done cheering Ann up yet.

'You know Ann's nickname, don't you?' he asked Lucinda.

''Don't, Seb,' Ann begged, but he wasn't going to be deflected.

'The Resuscitator!'

Lucinda let out a throaty laugh. 'I've been called worse.'

Ann joined in the laughter, visibly better for the light-hearted banter that might have seemed callous to some, given the previous tragic events, but when you dealt with life-and-death situations regularly black humour was almost mandatory to save you from going under. Ann picked up her bag. 'I'm off. I'd better find out what my feral teenage sons are getting up to without Mum on a balmy Saturday night. If you think Billy's causing you sleepless nights now, Seb, just wait until he hits puberty—the fun really begins then. My boys will turn me grey.'

Ann bustled off.

'She's great, isn't she?' Lucinda stated.

'Golden. I asked her to change her annual leave when Billy's op was brought forward so she'd be on duty while he was a patient, and she did. Nothing against the other staff, of course, but Ann really is one in a million.' He stood up and flicked the venetian blinds. Lucinda watched his strong profile illuminated by the ward lights as he gazed out at his sleeping son, and she felt the familiar knot of tension in her stomach that occurred when Seb was around. 'I feel so guilty,' he said out of the blue.

'Why?' Lucinda demanded.

'All the time I was running to the ward I was just praying that it wasn't Billy.'

'Of course you were. Billy's your son.' Lucinda recalled the conversation she'd so recently had with Bianca and felt her throat tighten. 'Just because you were wishing it wasn't Billy, it doesn't mean you wanted it to be Bianca.'

Seb turned and gave her a thin smile. 'I need some air. One week exclusively breathing the hospital's air-conditioning is sending me crazy. Will you join me?'

They took the lift and then the stairwell up to the roof. The air seemed to hum with tension and Lucinda wondered if she was imagining things. Could this beautiful man possibly be feeling the same way about her? Had he felt that instant attraction, too? Surely not, she reasoned. He had his mind on other things at the moment and evidently he thought she was as hard as nails. But as he took her arm and led her across the roof she was acutely aware of his touch, and Lucinda was positive his hand lingered a moment as they came to stand on the roof's edge.

Her legs felt somewhat unsteady, and it had nothing to do with vertigo, Lucinda acknowledged as she leant against the wall and looked out over the City. The view was almost identical to the one from her apartment. Flinders Street Station was lit up like a fairground, the arts centre like a miniature Eiffel Tower. It was stunning and so much better shared.

'Times like this I almost wish I smoked.' Seb said, his voice carrying in the night air.

'No, you don't.'

For an age Seb stood quite still, drinking in the view. Finally he spoke. 'Billy will be home next week, and the week after that I'm expected back at work.'

'You and Gemma will manage,' she said with more conviction than she felt.

He turned and faced her then and Lucinda saw the pain in his features.

'Gemma's leaving to live in New South Wales, a job offer she "simply couldn't refuse" came up.'

Lucinda gasped. 'Does Billy know?'

'Yep, we've known for a couple of weeks. It hit him pretty hard. She'd made her mind up before we knew that Billy's operation was going to be moved forward. It's all too far gone for her to put it off and, anyway, I think that now Billy knows it's going to happen it might just be better to get it over and done with so we can all start to move on. It's been pretty tough for a while on all of us.'

'Seb, that's awful. I don't know what to say,' she said truthfully.

'Not so awful. I got Billy out of it. I'd go through the whole thing ten times over for that——all I want is for Billy to be happy.'

'But how will you cope?' She voiced his fears for him.

'I don't know,' he said heavily. 'I just don't know. Since we divorced, Gemma's hardly been around but any help is better than none. My sister Isabella is coming down for a month when I have to go back to work, and she's bringing her kids. She lives in Ballarat, though. I can't keep relying on her—she's got a life, too. I'm going to have to do a lot of thinking. There's going to have to be some changes. Anyway,' he said, 'that's enough about me. What about

you, Miss Chambers? You look like a woman who knows
where she's heading. So what's it to be—professor, chief
of staff? What is it you want out of life?'

Lucinda hesitated. Seb had been so open, so honest that
she wanted to tell him her dream, but how could she when
it was something she hardly dared admit even to herself?
How could she tell him that a part-time GP juggling too
many children's packed lunches sounded good from here?
He would never understand. 'We'll see,' Lucinda said non-
committally. 'Consultant will do for now.' She shivered
suddenly. 'It's windy up here. I'm cold.'

'That can be fixed.' Seb's voice was deep and she was
sure she could hear an invitation in his words, but Lucinda
wavered, filled with uncertainty. The temptation to slip into
his arms, to be warmed and comforted, was overwhelming;
but what if she was wrong? What if she had misread the
signs? If he moved just an inch, gave some further indication as to what he was implying, she would have gone
to him without hesitation. But instead she stood there, staring at him for the longest time, until it was Seb who
dragged his eyes away.

'We'd better go back down' he said eventually. 'Billy
might wake up.'

Lucinda managed a smile. 'You go,' she said quietly. 'I
might stay up here a while, take in the view.'

'Later,' he murmured, and then he was gone.

Lucinda hugged her arms to her chest, colder now without him near. Careful, she warned herself, tread carefully.
Sebastian Carlisle would be very easy to fall in love with
but he came as a package—Seb and Billy. It was a serious
consideration, one that could only lead to complications,
and Billy was simply too precious to even consider hurting.

CHAPTER FOUR

CONCENTRATING on her stroke as she cut through the empty pool, Lucinda found a temporary escape from the jumbled emotions that had kept her awake for most of the night. After ten laps she climbed out of the water, making her way to the poolside shower. The icy cold jets were refreshing and invigorating. For a moment she contemplated using the gym equipment—after all, the endless take-aways had to catch up sooner or later. Instead she dried herself and dressed casually in khaki shorts and a linen blouse, tying her damp hair back with a scrunchie.

Southbank was setting up for the day, and a few revellers were stretching out Saturday night, buoyed up by their casino winnings, and were singing as they walked along the riverside. Lucinda bought the Sunday papers and settled herself at a cane table shielded from the early morning sun by a large umbrella. She ordered a café latte and as she had done ten lengths of the pool succumbed to the waiter's suggestion of warm croissants with butter and honey.

Melbourne was awakening. Joggers and power-walkers strutted their stuff along the riverbank, effortlessly avoiding the pavement artists who were touching up their work. The huge turrets that flanked the casino were shooting flames half-hourly in an impressive performance that seemed to go unnoticed by the regulars, but to the uninitiated like Lucinda it was breathtaking. Bianca would love it here.

In that instant Lucinda acknowledged the real reason for her insomnia. The time she had spent with Seb last night had been pleasantly unsettling to say the least, but it hadn't kept her awake. If anything, she had longed to go to sleep just to relive those moments again. No, the real reason she had tossed and turned had been a little girl who had been given only the smallest shot at life. Lucinda felt the sting of tears in her eyes and grappled in her bag for her sunglasses. Why couldn't they just stay nameless? Instead, it was Bianca, Billy, Kimberley and countless other children who had come before them. She remembered the name of every child that had died in her care, and it hurt. It really hurt. Reaching for her mobile, she started to dial the hospital's number then decided against it. Bianca deserved a bit more than a phone call so instead Lucinda settled her bill and made her way across the bridge to the hospital.

Instead of going straight to Paediatric Intensive Care she made her way to the cardiac ward, with the excuse that she was checking on all her patients. But deep down the thought of entering PICU and not seeing Bianca there was too upsetting. The news, if bad, would be gentler coming from Ann.

She didn't need an excuse. Ann knew why she was there as soon as she saw her.

'Couldn't sleep, huh?'

'How is she?'

Ann gave a small shrug. 'Still alive, but only just. She had a massive MI in the early hours. Thirteen years old and she's had a heart attack.'

'Why wasn't I called? She could have—'

Ann shook her head. 'They're treating her conservatively or you'd have been paged long ago. She's not a candidate for surgery—she just wouldn't survive. What she needs is a transplant. She's been moved to the top of the list, so maybe a match will come in soon. Don't go too far this weekend—hopefully we'll be needing you. You've got your pager?'

Lucinda lifted her blouse slightly and showed the pager, used only for transplants, strapped firmly to her belt. 'Glued to me. I'd better go over to PICU and have a look at her.'

Ann nodded. 'Her parents want to talk to you.'

'To me? Do they want to go through the transplant procedure?'

Ann shook her head. 'No, it's a bit more personal than that. I told them how you'd watched a film with her last night. I guess they just need to hear how she was.'

'I'm not exactly dressed properly,' Lucinda said somewhat formally, in a vain attempt to delay the inevitable.

'I'm sure that's the least of their concerns,' Ann said. 'It would mean a lot to them if you had a quick word.

Lucinda nodded her assent, and turned to go.

As she made her way out of the ward an angry little bundle dressed in pyjamas and a dressing-gown rushed past her, just about sending her flying.

'Whoa, there.' She grabbed hold of the dressing-gown and turned the little boy around.

'Where are you off to in such a hurry, Billy? You shouldn't be running on the ward, you know.'

He gave her an indignant look.

'I was going to the toilet, but there isn't any paper,' he said accusingly, as if it was her fault.

'Well, I'm sure the cleaners will be here soon, or the nurses will be out on handover in a while.'

'But I need to go *now*,' he said simply.

Lucinda looked around. Not a domestic in sight, and the only nurse left on the ward was giving some intravenous drugs to a patient. Lucinda picked up a box of tissues from the nurses' station. 'Here,' she said. 'Use these.'

Billy looked at her as if she'd gone completely mad.

'I can't use these. Ann said we weren't to waste tissues.'

'I think she was referring to the paper aeroplanes you

were all making with them the other day. I'm sure she won't mind.'

But Billy wasn't going to be deflected.

'I need some toilet paper.'

His little face worked up as if he might start crying and Lucinda sensed the urgency in his demand.

'OK,' she said with a sigh. 'You go on to the toilet and I'll bring you some.'

'You won't forget?'

'Cross my heart.' He hurried off and Lucinda spent the next five minutes trying to locate the store cupboard. Finally she found it and, rummaging around, she gave a little laugh. This was ridiculous. She was a consultant, taking orders from a five-year-old. Still, when you had to go…

Finally she found the paper and made her way back to the toilets in time to find Billy at the sink, washing his hands.

'Here you are.'

'I found some,' he said. 'On the window-ledge. But thanks.' He took the roll and placed it under his dressing-gown.

'What are you doing?'

'I'm going to keep it in my locker—they're always running out here.' He turned and stared directly at Lucinda. 'Is Bianca dead?' he asked completely out of the blue.

Lucinda hesitated, somewhat taken back by the directness of his question. 'No, she's been moved to the intensive care ward.'

'That's what Ann said, but I thought she was just trying not to upset me. Is it her heart?'

Lucinda nodded. 'Sort of.'

'Well, if it's her heart, why can't you fix it? You fixed mine.'

'It's a bit more complicated than that, but I am going to

try. I'm going to talk to her parents now.' Billy finished drying his hands.

'Bye, then.' He gave her the benefit of his cheeky grin and ambled back to his bed, carefully depositing the precious paper in his locker first.

Lucinda shook her head and smiled. Really, he was just too cute.

She put on a theatre gown and washed her hands before she entered the PICU. The next half-hour was spent with the registrar, going over Bianca's results. From the workstation she could see Bianca, her thin body covered by a sheet, attached to the monitors she so fiercely hated. Her terrified parents and brother were sitting rigid at her side, willing her to hold on, to fight to stay alive. It was indeed a heartbreaking scene but Lucinda pushed aside all emotion and concentrated on the task in hand. Bianca needed her medical skills, no more, or so she thought. When her discussion with the registrar concluded and they both resignedly agreed that all they could do was continue the current treatment and wait for Bianca's ship to come in, she asked the charge nurse to bring Bianca's parents to the interview room. Outside the door Lucinda took a few deep breaths before she knocked and entered. The sorrow in the faces that greeted her was familiar.

'Mr and Mrs Moore, I'm Miss Chambers. You asked to speak with me?'

'Oh, Doctor, thank you for coming in to see Bianca this morning.'

Lucinda gave a small nod. 'I've been talking with Mr Hill, the PICU registrar, and for now all we can do is wait and hope for a suitable donor.'

'Sister Benton said you spent some time with Bianca last night before she…' Mrs Moore struggled to speak. 'Before she was taken so ill. We wanted to thank you. It would have meant so much to Bianca. She thinks a lot of you—you're her favourite.'

'Me?' Lucinda said surprised. 'But I've only been in the hospital a week. Surely she would have had others…'

Mrs Moore gave a small laugh through her tears. 'You know what teenagers are like. Bianca thought you were so "cool". She was raving on and on about you. When Sister Benton called and broke the news she said that you'd shared a pizza and watched a film with her. It probably didn't mean much to you—I understand that—but for Bianca, well, she doesn't have much of a life. Last night would have been very special to her. She really admires you.'

Lucinda's eyes misted over and she hastily looked down at the notes in front of her. It was a trick she often used. The writing might as well have been in Chinese but it gave her something to do, something other than looking into Mr and Mrs Moore's tortured eyes. After a moment she looked up at the strained faces, desperate to hear something—anything—about their daughter.

She faltered for a moment unsure of how much of their conversation to reveal, unsure if she could do this and still remain in control, but deep down she knew Bianca's words weren't hers to keep. They had been meant for Bianca's family.

'Bianca spoke about you all last night.' She smiled gently at Lewis, a ten-year-old who should have been out at the beach or on his skateboard, not sitting in an intensive care interview room, trying to comfort his parents. 'How much she loved you, how much you loved her. Bianca also told me that she wasn't scared of dying. Her main concern was how you'd all cope if it happened.'

The sob that escaped from Mr Moore's lips tore through Lucinda. Instinctively he reached for his wife and son, wrapping his arms around them as they sobbed together. Lucinda sat quietly for a couple of moments until they were ready to continue.

'What did you say when Bianca said that?' Mr Moore asked, choking on his tears.

'That you'd be all right, you'd lean on each other and go on loving her wherever she was, and in time the hurt would ease and you'd be left with wonderful memories. I also told her that we had no intention of letting her die, though, and that she had to go on fighting, which she is.'

'Thank you.' He could barely get the words out and Lucinda knew it was time to leave them, to let them comfort each other. 'If you want to talk again just have the PICU staff page me.'

As she made her way along the highly polished corridor, her trainers barely making a sound, Lucinda knew she had done the right thing. Despite the Moores' tears, she had brought comfort to that family, and letting her guard down last night had meant she had got closer to Bianca. Yet surprisingly it hadn't made today any worse. It had actually made it a bit more bearable.

'Sorry, I wasn't looking where I was going.'

'Me neither.' Janine Stewart's red-rimmed eyes met hers as Lucinda bumped into her.

'How's Kimberley?'

'Stable, whatever that means. It's the only word we want to hear at the moment. Whoever said that having a premature baby was like riding on a roller-coaster wasn't wrong.'

'It must be very difficult,' she agreed, knowing how futile her words sounded.

Janine didn't seem to mind. She ran a hand through her untidy hair. 'I'd like to think that this time next year I'll be up to my elbows in nappies and Vegemite toast soldiers, but the dream's starting to fade a bit.'

Lucinda simply didn't know what to say. For the millionth time she berated herself for her inability to vocalise her feelings. The bleeping of her pager came almost as a relief. 'Sorry,' she said apologetically. 'I'll see you on the unit later when I come to check on Kimberley.'

Walking into the canteen, Lucinda picked up the phone to dial the switchboard. Through the glass window she could see Janine slowly making her way back along the corridor, back to her cotside vigil, and not for the first time Lucinda wished she could have said something to help.

The page turned out to be Switchboard merely doing a routine check. Replacing the receiver, she turned and saw Seb eyeing the lunchtime blackboard without much enthusiasm.

Casually she made her way over to him. 'Anything catch your eye?'

He turned and smiled. 'Now it does. You're far more tempting than anything in here.'

Lucinda gave a low laugh. 'I don't think I should let that go to my head. Beef stew and soggy cauliflower are hardly much competition.'

'On the contrary, I happen to be a big fan of the beef stew, and soggy cauliflower is a particular favourite of mine, but I'm thinking of having a splurge and ringing out for dinner tonight.' He paused for a moment. 'Do you fancy sharing a curry with me? We could use the on-call room.'

Lucinda was caught completely off guard. Desperate to accept, but not wanting to appear to eager, she forced herself to pause for a moment before answering. 'That would be great,' she answered casually. 'I'm actually going to be in my office tonight, doing some paperwork.'

Seb smiled. 'I've an even better idea, then. Why don't I

get it sent up to your office if you're going to be in there anyway? At least we'll have some privacy.'

'Sure,' she replied as nonchalantly as she could with her heart in her mouth.

'Great.' He gave her the benefit of his smile. 'I'll look forward to some real food and adult conversation tonight. Billy's hunger for *Robot Savers* hasn't diminished one iota and the rest of the children have got me changing videos, fetching drinks, playing board games and cutting out shapes. It's exhausting. I'll be glad to come back to work for a rest. About eight, then,' he added as he started to go, then changed his mind. 'There is one condition, though,'

Lucinda gave him a quizzical look. 'And what's that?'

'That we talk about you for once. Even I'm getting sick of hearing about me.'

As Lucinda made her way up to NICU her heart was hammering wildly and she scolded herself for overreacting. He had only asked her to share a curry after all; it was no big deal. Pushing the button for the lift, she finally gave in. Who was she kidding? It *was* a huge deal—a night on her own with Sebastian Carlisle!

'How's Kimberley Stewart? Did Andrew review her digoxin levels?' asked Lucinda a little later.

Sue pulled out Kimberley's file—it was twice the weight of the baby.

'Yes, she's in sinus rhythm at the moment. He's going to review her again this afternoon if everything remains stable. Did you want to examine her yourself?'

Lucinda shook her head and Sue gave a relieved smile. 'Good.' Minimal handling was the order of the day for babies as sick as this and Lucinda wasn't going to do anything to upset the apple cart.

'Where's Janine?' Lucinda asked. 'She started to talk to

me in the canteen but my pager went off. She seemed up-set.'

'She is. Mark goes back to work tomorrow—she's help-ing him pack now. Mark's upset because he feels that he's abandoning them and Janine's upset because she feels he's deserting them. It's like a tragic soap story. If only they'd sit down and talk they'd probably get somewhere.'

An idea was forming in Lucinda's mind and she sur-prised even herself as the white lie slipped easily from the mouth. 'I won a dinner for two at Surayan's Indian Restaurant, but it has to be used by this weekend. I'm on call, so that rules me out and, anyway, I've got plans. Perhaps you could persuade Janine and Mark to use it. After all, the distance to the restaurant isn't much further than the canteen. You can always ring them if there's any change.'

'That's really nice of you.' Sue gave her a quizzical look. 'Are you sure you don't mind? If I could persuade them to go, it could do a lot of good. I'd already suggested they go out tonight for their anniversary but money's very tight for them at the moment.'

Lucinda shrugged dismissively. 'It's no big deal. See what they say. I'll put a booking in their name for about eight. It's up to them whether they use it or not. You can only take the horse to water after all.'

After ringing Surayan's and letting Vijay in on the cha-rade, Lucinda took the chance to do some sightseeing. As she was on call she couldn't roam too far, but St Kilda beach was only a short tram ride away and if needed she could hail a taxi and be back at the hospital within minutes. It was totally unlike her more junior days where being on call had meant you had to stay in the hospital at all times so as to be immediately available for any emergency. Now it was the more junior doctors' turns and she would be called in only for emergency consults or operations.

It still didn't sit quite right with her, though, and invariably Lucinda never strayed too far and liked to pop in and out of the hospital, sometimes choosing to sleep there if worried about a particular patient.

She had been told about the street market St Kilda held on a Sunday and it was as enchanting as promised. Rows and rows of stalls lined the street the length of the beach. Wares were beautifully displayed, all hand-made originals in keeping with a by-law of the market. It was just the place to find a couple of one-offs to add some warmth to her apartment. The only problem was how to get things home, and Lucinda made a mental note to come better prepared next week. Wandering slowly from stall to stall, she settled on a couple of bright throw rugs and some hand-painted prints of the bay.

'I want an ice cream. I want an ice cream.' The piercing shrieks of a young child rose above the crowd. Lucinda turned and watched as two frazzled-looking parents made their way to the ice-cream vendor. 'Not that one.' Red in the face, the little boy flung the cone down onto the pavement and proceeded to cry loudly. His exasperated parents reluctantly bought another cone in a bid to quieten him.

What a terror, Lucinda thought to herself. Again she questioned the rationale behind pursuing a relationship with Seb. Her time off was precious enough without spending it with a child battling with her for his father's attention. There you go again, she thought, checking herself. You're only sharing a curry, not the rest of your lives. And anyway, she consoled herself, Billy was far too laid-back to throw a temper tantrum over an ice-cream cone—he only seemed to get upset about toilet rolls. A small chuckle escaped from her lips at the memory and Lucinda realised she was actually walking along, smiling just at the thought of him. What was it with Seb and Billy Carlisle? she wondered. And what on earth was happening to her?

Happy with her purchases, she started to make her way back to the tram stop, but a particular stall she had missed earlier caught her eye. Soft organza dresses hanging from the canopy fluttered gently in the breeze in a myriad shades from the palest lemon to a vibrant purple. They had all been tie-dyed. The colours gently ran into each other, adding a depth to the simply cut dresses.

They were completely different to anything she usually wore, but Lucinda was hooked and more so when she saw the price—about a tenth of what she usually paid for a dress, which made an impulse buy all the more irresistible. Settling on a pale lilac, she finally clambered onto the tram, her purchases taking up two seats, and settled back for the short journey home.

Her busy week, combined with the previous night's insomnia, made her unmade bed all too appealing. It was easier to climb in and rest awhile than bother making it. For once sleep came easily, and by the time Lucinda awoke it was well after seven. Cursing herself for not setting the alarm, she showered quickly and, pulling her new dress from the bag, slipped it on. It was stunning, gently ruched around the bust, its flowing length doing nothing to hide her curves and the lilac bringing colour to her face. She left her hair down and tied on some canvas espadrilles. A final glance in the mirror and she was ready.

The curry was delivered to her office promptly at eight and Lucinda set up the room for the meal. Candles would have been way over the top, of course, but her desk lamp provided a warm glow. Hastily she opened a file and started to write—she was supposed to be doing some paperwork after all. Just as she was starting to get nervous, wondering if it was actually going to be Seb that didn't turn up, he knocked on the door. Looking up from her desk, she tried to casually smile as her heart somersaulted. Even with his jeans and T-shirt crumpled from lying on Billy's bed, his sex appeal was overwhelming. His hair was as dishevelled as his clothes and she yearned to run her fingers through the wild raven locks.

'Sorry I'm late. Billy took a while to settle and, of course, I ended up dozing off. They've started playing this New-Age rainforest music at the children's settling time. Doesn't work a scrap on the children but it knocks me out like a light.'

Lucinda laughed at his explanation. 'I'll have to try it.' Her expression changed 'How is he?' she asked.

'Upset. It's starting to sink in that Gemma's going to Sydney. It's tough on the little guy.'

'And you, too?' she ventured.

But Seb wasn't going to be drawn. 'Oh, I'm all right—just starving. That curry smells marvellous.'

Lucinda smiled and closed the file she'd been pretending to read. 'Let's eat, then.'

'What work are you doing?' he asked as she spooned the rice onto the plates.

'Just compiling some research I was doing in Queensland. The paperwork it produces is horrific.'

'Tell me about it. I just finished a trial on PCA in paediatrics,' Seb said, referring to patient-controlled analgesia, a means of giving pain relief in an infusion which was controlled by the patient. A touch of a button meant the patient could administer more pain relief if desired. It was strictly controlled with a lock-out mechanism so patients couldn't overdose. Widely used with adults, it was becoming more common for some paediatric patients, and the trials were promising.

'I'm supposed to be presenting my findings next month at the medical conference in Queensland, though I'll struggle to have it all completed. Are you going?' he asked as they settled down to eat.

'Professor Hays did mention it. He said he had a wedding to attend but I rather think he's had enough of medical conferences. I'll probably be there but only for a couple of days over the weekend. We've got a lot of theatre cases the following week. It will be busy from then right up until Christmas.'

Seb nodded. 'The bulk of the conference is over the weekend anyway. The other days are more of an opportunity for a bit of a holiday. I'm only staying two nights as well. Gemma's going to be in Melbourne to see Billy as it will be too soon for him to fly to Sydney. Anyway, I've promised to cover for another consultant—Chris King—on the Sunday afternoon so he can go to a wedding, probably the same one as the prof. I owe a lot of favours,' he added. 'Now Billy's op is out of the way it's time to pay a few back.'

'I'm sure people don't want to be paid back. They understand how hard it is for you.'

'I doubt it,' he said. 'Anyway, I came here on the understanding we talked about you. So, tell me, what's it like, being the daughter of two famous cosmetic surgeons?'

'It's different,' Lucinda said cagily.

'And did your stunning looks come courtesy of your parents' genes or their scalpels?'

Lucinda laughed. 'A bit of both actually. Mum and Dad mostly, but nothing would stop my mother in the quest for a perfect daughter. I thank the heavens daily that I was born reasonably OK or I'd have been nipped, tucked and reshaped beyond recognition by now.'

'You're not serious?' Seb said incredulously.

Lucinda pulled back her hair. 'I had my ears pulled back when I was nine. I've seen old photos and they hardly stuck out at all.' She paused. 'Well, not that much. I had to wear this awful turban-like bandage for a week afterwards. I've had braces put on perfectly good teeth just so I could have a cover-girl smile, and my adolescent pimples were treated by a hysterical mother sending me off to dermatologists for antibiotics and creams.'

'Good heavens.'

'Fortunately I spent most of my teenage years at boarding school so most of the lumps and bumps and ugly stages all teenagers go through happened well out of the way of my parents or you could be sitting opposite quite a different-looking woman now.'

'How was it—boarding school?'

'I didn't mind it too much,' she hedged. 'What are your parents like?'

'Actually, they're both dead.'

'I'm sorry.'

'Don't be. I had a fabulous childhood. I'd love them to still be here, of course, but I know how lucky I've been when I hear stories like yours. I just can't imagine what it would have been like going to bed without giving your mum a kiss and Sunday dinners and all that sort of thing.'

'Well, there's the difference. I never had any of that, even when I was home on holidays. You can't miss what you don't know.'

'Oh, yes, you can.' He looked at her then, right into her eyes. Lucinda swallowed hard. He was right. She had missed so many things—the Sunday roasts, the unconditional love of a parent. With her parents it had all been about achieving. And now she missed intimacy even though she had never really known it.

'I worry that's what will happen to Billy. I can't keep

relying on my sister and nannies—he needs some stability. Boarding school might have to be an option.'

No, she wanted to shout. The idea of little Billy at boarding school was too awful to comprehend. He'd seen enough of institutions to last him a lifetime, she thought, but it wasn't her place to add to Seb's fears.

'I survived,' she said instead, her heart filled with an overwhelming sadness. No mum or dad to ask him how his day was at the dinner table or tuck him in at night. Limits on *Robot Savers*. That beautiful personality quietly stifled. Despite what she had said to Seb, though she had thought it all right at the time, with the benefit of hindsight it had been awful. It was there that she had learnt to hide her feelings, waving Mum and Dad off at the start of term. Kids needed their parents. She knew that now and was painfully aware of what she had missed out on.

The conversation flowed easily, and although they were only drinking diet cola Lucinda found herself telling Seb things she hadn't even thought about in years, letting him in on a side of herself she rarely if ever revealed. He was an amazingly good listener, and by the time the curry had been eaten and the remnants packed away there was only one thing they hadn't yet shared. Seb seemed to read her mind as the night came to a conclusion. For a moment the room was quiet, except for the hum of sexual tension, and then he gave her a small smile.

'You look beautiful tonight. I like you in that dress. It's very feminine, not that you need any help with that.

'I'm not all power suits and fitted dresses,' she lied, thinking this was the one garment she possessed that wasn't fully lined and dry-clean only.

Slowly, purposefully, Seb walked around the desk. Taking Lucinda's hands as she stood up, he pulled her towards him.

Lucinda was tall and in her espadrilles, despite Seb's height, her eyes were nearly level with his. He hardly had to bend his head to kiss her and their lips found each other easily. His hands, warm through the flimsy material, pulled her closer yet and she melted into his embrace. He was truly wonderful to kiss and Lucinda lost herself in the moment until he gently pulled away.

'I'd better go. It would be very easy to go and do something really silly here.'

Lucinda gave a little grumble and laid her head on his chest. He was right. She knew they shouldn't make love, not here and not so soon, but her resistance around this man was practically zero.

'Like what?' she said huskily, not wanting the evening to end, but his answer to her seductive question came as such a surprise that for once she was completely lost for words.

'Like fall in love.' He gently kissed the top of her head. 'I'd better get back.'

Dumbly she nodded, and stood quite still as he left. He felt it, too, it wasn't just her! How on earth she wondered, was she supposed to sleep after that?

CHAPTER FIVE

DESPITE the success of his surgery, Billy wasn't ready to go home by Monday. His asthma was still proving difficult to control and at the ward round it was decided to keep him in for a few more days to change his medication and continue with the aggressive physiotherapy. So far he hadn't developed a chest infection, but all the ingredients were there for one to manifest and it was safer to keep him in.

Seb's only concern was for his son and he ruffled his grumbling son's hair. Gemma, however, looked far from pleased by the news, but the round moved on before she had a chance to voice her objections. The rest of the round went fairly smoothly until they arrived at Bianca's bedside on PICU. Lucinda had to bite her tongue as Pete Hughes described his version of Saturday night's events.

'I popped into the ward in the evening to review the patients and Sister Benton seemed somewhat concerned about young Bianca. I reviewed her thoroughly but I couldn't find anything wrong. She seemed fine.'

'Very good.' Professor Hays nodded as he peered through the thick file that contained Bianca's notes. 'A lot of blood tests were done—excellent.' He carried on reading. 'I see you reviewed her as well, Miss Chambers?'

Lucinda gave a short nod, inwardly seething. Pete had let the professor assume it had been him that had taken Bianca's blood when in truth he hadn't even bothered to go anywhere near the patient. But to say anything here would be wrong. She would deal with Pete privately.

70

'That's right. I couldn't find anything significant either. She arrested just after I left.'

'Well, let's hope a donor becomes available soon for Bianca, though realistically I think we're getting past the hoping stage with Bianca. She really isn't a suitable candidate and the heart and lungs might be better suited to someone with a more realistic chance of survival.'

'No.' The words escaped from Lucinda's lips before she even realised she had spoken. Everyone turned and stared, surprised by her passionate outburst. But Lucinda knew that for Bianca her eleventh hour had come. She was fading fast and her life was governed now by the machines she so hated. Paralysed and sedated by drugs she had no chance to fight now, it was up to Lucinda to do it for her.

She recovered her composure quickly. 'I actually think Bianca will do very well, given the chance. Her strength is amazing—that's the only reason she's survived as long as she has and the reason that, despite the rapid progression of her disease, she was still deemed "too well" to be at the top of the list for a transplant.' Lucinda went on, her outburst quickly forgotten as she argued Bianca's case in an almost detached manner, relaying medical and technical details with such an air of authority that she knew as she concluded her persuasive speech she had won the argument—for now.

'Well, let's hope something comes up soon,' Professor Hays said, and Lucinda breathed an inward sigh of relief. He turned to Pete Hughes. 'Excellent work. It's good to be seen at the weekends. Patients are still sick. Perhaps you'd like to operate tomorrow, we've got a couple of interesting cases. Maybe it's time to see how much I've taught you. Miss Chambers and I will assist, of course.' Professor Hays marched off to his office as the entourage dispersed.

'Just a moment, Pete,' Lucinda called as he made his

way down the corridor. 'If I might have a brief word.' Pete gave a small nod and walked towards her, meeting her head on. She saw that his surly face had a look of defiance. 'In my office.'

She closed the door but didn't sit down. Dispensing with any niceties, she cut straight to the chase.

'You just popped in to check on the patients? You reviewed Bianca thoroughly? Are we talking about the same night here? How about you were hanging around the ward waiting to pick up your latest girlfriend and you had a cursory glance at her notes? That would be somewhat nearer the mark.'

'I had more than a "cursory glance" and Bianca was dozing. I thought it better to let her rest.'

'Oh, come on, Pete, that's no excuse and you damn well know it,' Lucinda snapped, furious at his indifference.

'You said yourself there was nothing abnormal to find. You're the great consultant. What makes you think that I, a mere registrar, would have found anything different? Why do you think that I might pick up something you missed?' So Seb had been right, that *was* what his problem was. Well, it was time to deal with it.

'Oh, that's the last thing I'm thinking, I can assure you of that. We both know you think this should be your office, that you should have got the job, but at the end of the day you didn't, and in my opinion the best doctor won. If it's a consultant's position you're after, Pete, you'd better start lifting your game. Next time a nurse is concerned, particularly one as senior as Ann Benton, try looking at the patient, not the notes.'

'Have you finished?' He spat the words through gritted teeth.

'For now.' She stood back as he brushed past and marched out of the office. Sitting at her desk, she put her head in her hands and took a deep breath. Lucinda had taken no pleasure in the confrontation, but Pete had to be brought in to line. She needed him and relied on him too much for him to be slacking off. If he missed something, then potentially so did she. But there wasn't time to dwell on her argument with Pete, for just as a watched kettle never boiled, the one time since Saturday night that she hadn't been consciously wishing it would go off, the shrill bleeps of her transplant pager broke the silence. Grabbing the phone, she dialled the numbers. Please, let it be for Bianca, please, let it be for Bianca, she prayed silently as she calmly went through the motions. Someone must have been listening. Bianca's ship had just come in—a near-perfect match!

All animosity with Pete was put firmly aside as the transplant team swung into action. More blood was taken from Bianca and the final checks were made that would determine if she was going to receive this precious chance. Flight teams were despatched to retrieve the organs, and in the hospital everyone came together. Each played their essential part, working alongside each other, from the professor down to the domestic staff who would prepare her post-operative room in the intensive care ward, meticulously cleaning and sterilising it to ensure the chance of post-operative infection was minimised. Each had a vital role to play and all did their best.

But finally when the arduous operation was completed it was left up to Bianca. The perfusionist weaned her off by-pass and all held their breath as the new heart and lungs perfused. No matter how many times this operation had been performed, for all the staff watching it was still like seeing a miracle take place. Before she had even left the theatre Bianca's colour was better than it had been in ages. Her oxygen readings reached new highs.

But her little body's reserves were woefully depleted. The last few days had taken their toll on her already fragile health and there wasn't much left to guard her for the long battle that lay ahead. Finally she was wheeled back to the huge sterile room in the intensive care unit, through the heavy double doors that would hopefully help to keep out infection which, along with rejection, was her biggest enemy.

Lucinda spoke with Bianca's parents, but she was guarded with her optimism. Bianca had been given a chance but there was still a very long way to go. And then it was back to Bianca's bedside where she spent the next few hours working alongside the anaesthetist and the nursing staff in the impossibly warm room, made worse by the gown, hat and mask she had to wear. Only when she was sure Bianca was stable did she leave her side and make her way to the on-call coffee-room.

Exhausted, she leant back on the sofa and closed her eyes for a moment, glad of the peace without the constant bleeping of monitors and hiss of the respirator, glad to be alone. But when she opened them, Seb was standing there like a beautiful mirage and Lucinda realised that she didn't really want to be alone, and Seb was the one person she wanted to see.

He understood how fatigued she was, that the day had taken its toll.

'You did a great job. I came and watched for a while from the viewing gallery.'

She gave a half-smile.

'I wish it had been a few days ago. Bianca would have been so much stronger then.'

'I know, but there's more takers than givers—we can only do our best with what's available. She's got a chance now.'

Lucinda didn't reply, she knew what he was saying was right. Bianca had received a precious gift, but in a perfect world she wouldn't have had to wait so long. But then again, she reflected, in a perfect world she wouldn't have been born with CF and the donor's family wouldn't be crying tonight, too, in agony over the death of a loved one. Lucinda's heart went out to these unknown people, who in the depths of despair had made the bravest and most generous of decisions, who had somehow managed to rise above their grief for a moment and give hope to another family.

'What are you thinking?' His words gently broke into her thoughts.

Normally she would have stiffened and given some vague reply about her workload or charts that need to be written, but under Seb's gaze she could only be honest. 'About the donor's family.'

Seb didn't say anything, he just walked quietly over to the coffee percolator and poured her a cup.

'How's Billy?'

'Good, thoroughly spoilt. I'll need a second mortgage to pay for all the Robot videos he's demanding.'

'How are you?'

He shrugged, his hand pausing a moment too long as he went to pour the milk. 'Getting there. Gemma went to Sydney this afternoon.'

'I thought she wasn't due to go for another week or so.'

Seb nodded. 'You know how much she hates the hospital. She's gone to get the move started and then she'll fly back once Billy's discharged. She's going to spend a couple of weeks with him once he's out of hospital. It works out better actually. Isabella will still come for a month but not so soon, so I don't have to worry for six weeks yet about babysitters. Still, it was hard for him, saying goodbye.'

And you? she wanted to ask. How did you take her going? There were so many questions buzzing in her head. Why had they broken up? Why did he have custody? And, most importantly, did he still have any feelings for Gemma? But instead of asking, she just sat there quietly, not wanting to intrude, not wanting to make things worse for him.

Seb looked at her melancholy face. 'What you need is chocolate.' He opened one of the on-call rooms and Lucinda followed him. 'I've got a stash here, Billy gets heaps and I've had to ration it.' Lucinda sat on the bed as he broke a bar in two and gave her half. In itself it was no big deal that she was in there with him. Doctors spent so much time together it was more like a firemen's dorm than a bedroom. No one would bat an eye if they walked in now and saw Lucinda perched on the bed. After all, the door was open and they were both fully dressed. But for Lucinda it was a huge deal. She had never been particularly chatty or friendly with any of her colleagues, not like this anyway. Her on-call nights in the mess had mainly been spent with her head in a book, studying for the next lot of exams.

'You're right—I did need chocolate.' She yawned suddenly. 'I had a bit of a confrontation with Pete Hughes this morning. It got pretty nasty.'

'I'm sure he deserved it. Pete needs bringing into line.'

'Still, it wasn't very pleasant.'

'Look, I know you adore the prof, but I'm sure you'd have to agree he's not hot on confronting people. He's too wrapped up in his medicine to deal with the frivolities of social interaction.'

Lucinda had to reluctantly agree. Professor Hays was easily the most skilled surgeon she had ever seen, but it was becoming all too apparent he wasn't a 'people person'. She thought back to the time he had avoided talking with

Seb and Gemma, how he had given Seb a blow-by-blow account of the surgery he had performed on his son without softening the details.

'Maybe it's a trait amongst cardiothoracic surgeons,' Lucinda said thoughtfully.

Seb looked at her, bemused. 'What on earth are you talking about?'

'Well, let's face it. With the best will in the world you could hardly call me a great communicator. Every time I try to show a bit of compassion I end up sounding like my mother—and if you'd met her you'd realise I wasn't paying myself a compliment. She's the most shallow person you're ever likely to meet.'

'But you're nothing like that,' he argued.

'It's how I come across—you've heard me.'

'Rubbish,' Seb said confidently. 'You're a warm, perceptive, caring woman. It's just that you're...' His voice trailed off.

She looked up. 'Go on, say what you were going to.'

Seb started to laugh. 'A *really* bad communicator.'

She had no choice but to laugh with him. 'OK, Mr Man of the People,' she said finally when Seb had finished laughing. 'What do you suggest I do about Pete?'

'Give it to him straight—he's got to be told he won't get anywhere until he tries harder because the prof will just let him carry on as he is until Pete misses the promotion boat again. You're better off laying down the law and hopefully Pete will start toeing the line.'

Lucinda by now was only half listening. At that moment she couldn't have cared less about Pete or the professor. The long day had finally caught up with her and the thought of sleeping held far more charm. She put up her hand to stifle a yawn. 'I'm exhausted.'

'Rest, then,' Seb said simply. He kicked the door shut

and, stretching out on the bed, pulled her into his arms. Too tired to resist and so tempted by his touch, she slipped off her shoes and lay back against him. And though he didn't kiss her or try anything—both knew it was neither the time nor place—Lucinda had never felt such an overwhelming feeling of rightness and peace as she lay there in his arms. Her eyes heavy, she glanced at the bedside clock. Eleven minutes past twelve—she wanted to remember the time and the day. After all it would go down in her history as the day that both Bianca and herself had been given a new beginning.

The smell of fresh coffee and a gentle kiss from Seb awoke her. Lucinda responded warmly but, suddenly aware she hadn't brushed her teeth for ages, then she pulled away and stretched luxuriously.

'What time is it?'

Seb smiled. 'Six. I thought you said you were an incurable insomniac? You snored all night.'

'I did not,' she said indignantly, glad of the darkened room as she felt herself blush.

'I'm only teasing, but you did sleep well. Chocolate for breakfast?'

'There'll be none left for Billy.' Lucinda laughed as she peeled off the wrapper. 'My mother would never forgive me if she saw me now.'

'In a strange man's room?' Seb said jokingly.

'Oh, no, she wouldn't give a hoot about that—it's the chocolate that would worry her. I'll need to go on a diet at this rate. Queensland's only a few weeks away and if I start putting on weight she'll never let me hear the last of it.'

'But you're perfect. What on earth would you need to go on a diet for?'

'As I said last night, you haven't met my mother. Nobody's perfect to her—there's always room for improvement.'

Seb's hand teasingly pulled her theatre top. 'The only improvement you need is to get rid of this,' he said huskily.

'I couldn't agree more, and that's exactly what I intend to do. But in the shower—alone,' she added laughingly. 'Is anyone out there?' Seb opened the door slightly and peered out.

'No, the coast is clear.' She brushed past him but he stopped her in the doorway and pulled her toward him. 'I'll see you later.' As he kissed her, so heady was his embrace she forgot about not brushing teeth and kissed him back.

'Now I know what they mean when they say, "Take a cold shower,"' she joked. 'You're not very good for my blood pressure, Doctor.'

But she didn't take a cold shower. Instead, she took her time relishing the warm water on her skin, recalling the tenderness she had felt wrapped in Seb's arms. Dropping a two-dollar coin in the honesty box, she unwrapped a toothbrush and, after rinsing her mouth, was tempted to go back and kiss him all over again, but common sense won. There would be time for all that later.

After a brief meeting with the professor and Pete, who was looking decidedly seedy, it was decided that Professor Hays would assist Pete in Theatre that morning, leaving Lucinda with the task of catching up on yesterday's work. Lucinda would also see the patients pre-operatively to assess any changes and answer any last minute questions that arose.

Despite wanting to see Bianca, Lucinda bypassed the PICU, knowing that once she went in there it would be a long time before she could get away. She arrived on the cardiac ward just as the nursing staff were changing over. Ann was looking more harassed than usual.

'I'll be right with you.' Ann finished checking the controlled drugs with another nurse and joined her. 'Sorry about that. We're two nurses down—one's rung in sick and heaven knows where Ellen is. Apparently we're over budget with agency staff so Admin has said we'll have to make do. I wonder if they'd be so pedantic about budgets if it was one of their children having cardiac surgery this morning.'

Her uniform dishevelled, her hair unbrushed, Ellen flew into the ward.

'Sorry I'm late, Sister.'

Ann gave a tight smile. 'You look as if you should be going off duty, not coming on, Ellen.'

'I know. I'm sorry. We had a late night. Pete—'

'I'm not interested,' Ann snapped. 'Go to the staffroom and get a cup of strong coffee, and while you're there how about you make yourself look a bit more professional?' She dismissed the young nurse and walked to the nurses' station with Lucinda. 'Silly girl,' she said huffily. 'She could go far if she put her head down. Too many parties and not enough early nights.'

For her boyfriend, too, Lucinda reflected, but didn't say anything. No wonder Pete was looking so awful. How could he? she wondered furiously. How could he be out on the tiles the night before his big break? If he carried on like this he might as well kiss his career goodbye. She would have to say something, Lucinda decided. As soon as Theatre was over she would have a strong word or two with Pete.

Bianca was doing incredibly well. After a long discussion with the staff, it was decided to attempt to extubate her that afternoon, a little bit earlier than the ideal, but she had already had an ET tube in since Saturday, and if she needed to be ventilated for much longer she would have to have a tracheostomy.

Lucinda's anger at Pete abated somewhat throughout the morning. The patients all returned from Theatre with their notes meticulously written up by Pete, and the word going around was that he had operated beautifully. Somewhat mollified and prepared to discuss things rationally, she made her way to the theatres at lunchtime to be told that Pete was in the coffee-room. Her good-will flew out of the window, though, at the site that confronted her. Pale and sweaty, he was hunched over the sink with the taps running.

'Next time take more water with it.'

Pete splashed his face with water and deliberately turned the taps off before slowly turning around to face her.

'What exactly do you mean by that?'

'You know very well. What on earth were you doing out till all hours at a party the night before you operate? The biggest break of your career and you almost blew it.'

'Ah, but I didn't blow it. Surgery actually went very well this morning, thank you for asking.'

Lucinda ignored his sarcasm.

'Thank God it did, Pete. These are children's lives we're dealing with. This isn't a motor repair garage. You make a mistake here and there might not be a chance to fix it.'

'You think I don't know that?' he shouted.

'Well, act like it, then, Pete. You've got a reputation around this hospital and if you want anyone to start taking you seriously you'd better get rid of it.'

'And you'd know all about reputations, wouldn't you, Miss Chambers? You unfeeling bitch.'

Lucinda stepped back as if she'd been hit.

'How dare you?'

'No, how dare you? You march in here and practically accuse me of being drunk on the job. You've had it in for me since Saturday. The great Miss Chambers examines a patient who promptly arrests. It's not Bianca you're upset about, just the fact you might have missed something. Well, don't take it out on me. Anyway, there was nothing to miss, there was nothing to find. Your excellent medical reputation remains unblemished. And just because you don't have a life outside this hospital doesn't mean the rest of us have to act like confirmed bachelors and spinsters.'

'Well, at least it means I can keep my mind on the job,' she retorted furiously. She was angry with him, of course, but also genuinely concerned. Pete *was* a good doctor, but he was going to lose everything. She needed to take Seb's advice and bring him into line. 'Sometimes you just have to be single-minded to get what you want. I didn't get to be a consultant by trying to juggle relationships with work. They just don't mix, and the sooner you see that the better you'll do.'

Pete shook his head, his eyes narrowing. 'I almost feel sorry for you. You're so hell-bent on your career, there's no room for anyone or anything else. But I tell you this much, I feel sorrier for any guy who tries to get too close to you—he'd need an ice-pick to get through the front door.'

He left smartly and as Lucinda's eyes followed him angrily she almost jumped out of her skin to see Seb standing at the door.

'How long have you been there?' she asked in a shaking voice.

He stared at her for what seemed an age. 'Long enough. I was down here to check on my annual leave and I could hear you two halfway down the corridor. When you give someone a piece of your mind, you certainly don't mince your words, do you, Lucinda?'

Lucinda paled. Still shaking with temper, she frantically

tried to remember exactly what she had said. 'I know I sounded harsh but I was just trying to make a point. It has nothing to do—'

But he cut short her pleas. 'You sounded very convincing to me.'

Before she could argue the point he had gone, leaving Lucinda standing white and thin-lipped. Trembling, she sat on one of the chairs. What a mess, what a sorry mess, and just when things had been going so well, too. But surely when Seb calmed down he would realise what he had overheard had been an argument? That the words she had spoken had been for Pete's benefit, not his? With a groan she placed her head in her hands. The truth was, it didn't matter at whom the words had been directed. Seb had heard her innermost fears today. How could she give Seb and Billy what they both needed? How could she juggle a readymade family with her work? They had already had one career-minded woman in their lives, and look how that had worked out. Why would Seb risk it again?

Reluctantly she replayed the argument in her mind. Pete had been right, she conceded, well, partly. Some of her anger with him *did* indeed stem from Bianca and her own guilt about Saturday night, but Pete had had no right to speak to her like that, no right at all.

He had every right, she soon found out. Back on the ward she found Ann and asked for a run-down on the postoperative patients.

'All stable. Ellen's looking after the high-dependency patients. I think she had a couple of IV orders but the resident's sorted them out.'

'Ellen's on the high-dependency unit?' Lucinda queried the wisdom behind this decision. But Ann didn't respond as the young nurse herself came over.

'All their obs are good. James White is on his second

unit of packed cells and when that's through the resident needs to review him. They want him to have some Lasix before we put up the third unit. I've handed over to the late staff. I thought I might go and grab a late lunch, if that's all right?'

'Why don't you go home, Ellen, grab an afternoon nap? I think you've more than earned it. We're pretty up to date and now the late shift are here I'm sure we can cover.'

Lucinda raised her eyebrows at Ann's maternal tones.

'Well, if you're sure…'

'Off you go, love,' Ann said kindly, and the young nurse gratefully departed.

'You've changed your tune,' Lucinda remarked once she was out of earshot.

'I had to eat a huge slice of humble pie for my morning coffee-break.' Ann gave an ashamed smile. 'Apparently, Pete had a bit of stage fright in the night. It would seem he's not as cool as he makes out. Poor Ellen spent the night "walking" through the operations with him. She said he went into such detail she feels she could have performed the surgery herself. So I let her put her newfound knowledge to the test and she passed with flying colours. Seems I misjudged her—Pete, too, for that matter. By all accounts he did a great job in Theatre this morning.' She turned and caught sight of Lucinda's worried frown. 'What's wrong?'

'That humble pie you ate this morning,' Lucinda said remorsefully. 'Is there any left?'

Pete, of course, wasn't anywhere to be seen, so Lucinda had to resort to leaving a message with the switchboard to page him and ask him to come to her office. He entered after a brief knock and his temper obviously hadn't abated.

'What's the problem? Hadn't you finished turning the knife?'

'Sit down, please, Pete,' she said calmly.

He did as he was asked and she took a deep breath. 'I owe you an apology, Pete—a big one. I just assumed you were out last night, partying. I had no right to infer that you had been drinking. I know now that I was wrong on both counts. You were also right about Bianca Moore. I was trying to somehow lessen the guilt I feel by dragging you into it when the truth is that no one was to blame. I truly am sorry for the things that I said.'

She held her breath, wondering what his reaction would be, and when she finally dared to look up at him she saw that he was smiling.

'Apology accepted.' He held out his hand over the table and Lucinda shook it.

'And now it's my turn. You were wrong about a lot of things but not all. I feel as guilty as hell about Bianca but, unlike you, I have reason to. Maybe there was nothing to be found but I still should have examined her. And in truth the only reason I was on the ward in the first place was because of Ellen. It's been a huge wake-up call.'

Lucinda relaxed back in the chair. 'So I've got a reputation as a sour old spinster?' Pete shifted uncomfortably. 'It's OK,' she said. 'I did know that was the general consensus of opinion.'

'You don't deserve it.'

'Why not?'

'Pizza and slushy films with Bianca, and I've been going to Suriyan's for years and never seen a competition running.'

'Who told you about that?' Lucinda asked.

'Janine Stewart has been telling everyone. It did her the world of good, and there's not been too many light moments in that woman's life recently, let me tell you.' He paused for a moment. 'So what about my reputation?'

'Pete, it's just a few things I heard, and from what I can

tell now it's totally unfounded, but it must have started somewhere.'

Pete nodded. 'I ran a bit wild when I was a medical student and then when I was an intern it went a bit to my head. But, hell, I was only in my twenties. Ellen and I have been together for two years now. We're deadly serious but everyone just seems to think it's just another fling. I want to get engaged—that would shut them up—but then I wonder if I would be getting engaged for the right reasons. I don't want the hospital to come into it. I want it to be about us.'

Lucinda pondered his dilemmas. 'What I said before about relationships and work not mixing—well, I was referring to the more transient kind. Heaven knows, this job would be a thousand times easier if there was a sympathetic ear to bend at the end of a long day. I'm presuming that's the case, of course. As you so well pointed out, I don't have a lot of experience where relationships are concerned.'

Pete squirmed in his seat and Lucinda gave him an amicable smile to show there were no hard feelings before she continued. 'Pete, you know as well as I do that mud sticks. You have to not only be careful but be seen to be careful. There's a lot of people watching.'

Pete shrugged. 'Not any more,' he said dejectedly. 'You were right about that as well. I did want this job, but at the end of the day you were the better doctor. I can see that now.'

Lucinda shook her head. 'Not better, just a bit more experienced. Your time will come.'

'But when?' he said gloomily.

'When you least expect it probably. Something will come up.'

There was a knock at the door and Pete stood up to leave.

'Friends?' He offered his hand again and Lucinda stood up and shook it warmly.

'Friends.'

As he left Seb entered. 'G'day, Pete, how's things?'

Pete grinned. 'Better. How's your son?'

'Better, too. I just popped in to pick your boss's brains about him, actually.'

'Well, I'll leave you to it.'

Pete closed the door behind him and as Seb turned to face Lucinda she felt her insides melt. The anger was gone from his eyes and she saw again the man who had gently woken her that morning.

'I'm sorry I walked out on you earlier,' he rasped, and as if he couldn't bear the distance between them he crossed the room and took her in his arms, his mouth fervently searching for hers. For a while their minds concentrated on the moment as their lips mingled sensually, the doubts that plagued them both temporarily a million miles away. But as the kiss slowly ended the world rushed in.

'You wanted to see me about Billy?' she asked, pulling away, her voice suddenly concerned. 'Is there anything wrong?'

Seb shook his head. 'Just an excuse. Billy's going great guns this morning. I see you've made up with Pete?' he added.

'Pete and I are fine now,' she said with a mischievous glint in her eye. 'And thanks for your advice by the way— it nearly landed me in court for defamation of character.'

'I never said you had to go that far,' he said contritely, but Lucinda just laughed.

'Enough about Pete. I'm more interested in Billy. How's he coping without Gemma?' Lucinda probed, then held her breath, worried she might have intruded too far. But Seb didn't seem concerned by her question.

'He's coping. Hopefully things are going to start picking up for him now, and not just with his health.' He paused a moment, his eyes narrowing as if he was weighing up whether or not to go any further. Lucinda held her breath until slowly Seb started to open up to her.

'Gemma and I had a long chat yesterday before she left, and for the first time in ages we actually got somewhere.'

Lucinda listened intently, hoping he would elaborate.

'I know it's hard to understand—it's taken me five years—but I finally think I'm starting to.' He sat down and then continued slowly, choosing his words carefully. 'She's not a terrible person. She's just not cut out for motherhood and, being here, she feels as if everyone's judging her, and for once even I can understand where she's coming from. I mean, it's hardly orthodox, a mother walking out on her own child. I was aghast when she decided to move so far away, but now…' He looked up at Lucinda. 'She's actually a better mother. Now the responsibility's gone, now that she can concentrate on her career and all that, she's actually got more to give Billy.'

Lucinda sat there quietly for a moment. 'It must be hard,' she said finally. 'She's made out to be the Wicked Witch of the West just because she's a woman. Nobody bats an eyelid when a man walks out on his children. I'm not condoning it, for either sex, but I guess it's just not as clear-cut as it seems.'

'There is something else I need to talk about, Lucinda.' He held her hands as he spoke. 'I know you were only talking in the heat of a row before, but what you said isn't that far off the mark.' She opened her mouth to protest but Seb held her hands tightly and shook his head. 'Let me finish.'

Nodding silently, she watched with growing trepidation

as he searched for the right words to say. 'We're not going to be able to see much of each other for a while.'

So she had blown it after all. Pulling her hands free, she went and sat down. Picking up a paperweight, Lucinda focussed on the prism of colours in a desperate attempt to keep her composure—there would be time for tears after he had gone. But as Seb continued to speak, hope surged in her again as she realised he wasn't giving up on them, just voicing the problems they both faced.

'As sure as I am of my feelings for you, we've got a lot to work out before we go public, so to speak. We *both* have to be sure before I introduce you into Billy's life. Not just sure of our feelings, but how we're going to work this. I don't want to sound chauvinist, and I honestly don't think I am, but I swore I'd never get involved with another career-minded woman, and look what I've gone and done.' He gave a small smile and Lucinda managed a wobbly one back.

'I'm not saying you're like Gemma...'

'I know,' she admitted, replacing the paperweight on her desk.

'But Billy's been through hell. I don't have the luxury of taking risks and following my heart. So while he's recovering I'm going to have to lie a bit low. We'll see each other at the hospital once I'm back at work, of course, and I can ring. I just think it's too early to be openly going out. You do understand, don't you?'

Lucinda nodded; it was something she had already thought long and hard about. Part of her wanted to tell him the truth, that she wasn't sure if she even wanted her career, but how could she? If she let her feelings be known and things didn't work out between them, she would have potentially committed career suicide, for even the vaguest hint that she wasn't devoted to her work would see her passed over for promotion—Pete Hughes was living proof of that. As private a person as Seb was, to tell him she was having doubts about her job could place her in a very vulnerable position. And anyway it was far too early to be making such huge declarations. It might scare him off.

She gave him a reassuring smile. 'Of course I understand,' she said honestly. 'It's difficult enough for us to comprehend the speed at which things have happened. I can only imagine how hard it would be for a child. There's no rush. Billy has to come first.' She saw the relief wash over his face. 'Look, Seb, I have to go over to PICU now. They're going to extubate Bianca and I'd like to be there.'

'Sure, and, Lucinda, thank you for understanding.' And as he pulled her into his arms and his lips met hers she knew she could hold on for as long as it was needed. Some things were worth waiting for.

And so they took it gently, very gently. Their work schedules hardly allowed for anything else. But they would grab a coffee in the canteen and sometimes breakfast and catch up on each other's lives until invariably one or the other was called away. The problems that had surfaced were still there, waiting in the wings, but they were put on hold for a while as Lucinda and Seb got to know each other better. And while the rest of the hospital remained oblivious to the scandal that was evolving—and by hospital standards this really was a plum piece of gossip—in Theatre she would check the whiteboard each morning and her heart would soar or sink depending upon which anaesthetist had been allocated to her.

Seb, Lucinda soon found out at first hand, was indeed a skilled and competent anaesthetist, and despite her desire to see him for more personal reasons, Lucinda also enjoyed working alongside him on professional grounds, secure in the knowledge her patients were receiving the best of attention.

As Professor Hays had pointed out on Lucinda's first day, Seb did indeed talk to his anaesthetised patients. In his pre-op checks he would find out their interests, and on Seb's operation notes you could always find a brief summary of a child's hobbies. She grew used to listening to Seb nattering away about the football scores or the latest pop groups. 'They can't hear you,' she pointed out during one long operation. 'And if they can, you're not doing your job properly.'

But Seb had just smiled and carried on chatting, his passion for the patient's individuality a constant reminder to all that they weren't just dealing with numbers here, but precious children.

And despite the restraints of work and his family, they somehow managed a few stolen kisses in her office, and late at night when Billy was asleep he would try to ring. As hard as it was, living in limbo, Lucinda was in a strange way grateful for the reprieve. The depth of her feelings enthralled and terrified her. She was considering taking on an awesome responsibility in Seb and Billy—it was a lot to think about.

CHAPTER SIX

PETE HUGHES, once the animosity had gone, over the next few weeks became a wonderful friend as well as colleague. Now Lucinda trusted him implicitly, and the more responsibility she gave him the better surgeon he became. They spent the time between theatre cases whiling the time away with idle chit-chat and Pete filled her in on the hospital gossip.

'Ellen's lingering a bit too long over the jewellery catalogues,' he mentioned one lunchtime.

'So why don't you go ahead? Lucinda asked.

Pete gave a shrug. 'I'm not against marriage as such. It's just, well, my parents are divorced and so is my brother. And working in this place, it's hardly an advertisement for the institution of marriage. Everyone seems to be playing the field—the divorce rate around here is terrifying.'

Lucinda mused over this. 'It is pretty scary.' She hesitated. 'Look at Seb and his ex-wife.' The chance to talk about him to gain some insight was too tempting to pass up. But Pete shook his head.

'That was one marriage that didn't end because of an affair—well, definitely not on Seb's part and I'm pretty sure Gemma didn't have one. That really would have been the last straw. Seb would never have put up with that and he put up with enough, let me tell you.'

'Like what?' Lucinda said casually, trying not to sound too interested.

'Well…' Pete had a brief look around the theatre coffee-room to be sure no one was listening. 'I think they were happy until Gemma got pregnant. Apparently she was devastated but Seb was pleased, I was only junior then but he bought everyone cigars and was grinning from ear to ear. Anyway, Gemma just didn't want to know. She'd never wanted children but everyone thought that once the baby came along she'd change her mind. But it only made her more adamant.'

'Maybe she had postnatal depression?' Lucinda ventured, but Pete shook his head.

'She just didn't want a child. She wanted her career. She's in advertising or something and the fact Billy was ill only made things worse.'

'But how do you know all this?' Lucinda asked. 'Seb strikes me as a really private person. How come everyone knows all the details?'

'Because poor Seb had no choice but to tell. Gemma just carried on as if she didn't have a baby. I was doing my surgical rotation when Billy was a baby, and most of my lunches in this room were taken with one of the nurses feeding Billy because the nanny had resigned or Billy was too unwell to go to day care. Billy was brought up here, and if it wasn't the theatre staff feeding him, he was tucked in a bassinet in Ann Benton's office. Everyone likes Seb and they were only too happy to help.

'Anyway, Seb finally drew the line, said it was ridiculous. He'd be better off on his own. At least he and Billy would know where they stood. Gemma was only to happy to relinquish any responsibility, and now she's living in Sydney.'

Lucinda took it all in, her face portraying only the usual interest she would have shown at any hospital gossip, but her heart sank. What Seb must have been through didn't bear thinking about. How, she tried to fathom, did he manage to be so civil to her? No wonder the nursing staff had been hostile towards Gemma.

'Not very pleasant, is it?' Pete concluded, then turned the subject back to work. 'Are you looking forward to the medical conference?'

She gave a half-smile and nodded, but inside her heart soared.

Queensland was only a few days away and Lucinda had already packed. Dashing out to the shops on her lunch-break, she had purchased some flattering clothes and the thought of two days with Seb made her toes curl. She knew they would be busy but still...

'Lucinda, there you are. I've been paging you?' Jack Wells popped his head around the door.

Lucinda gave a small frown as she checked her pager. 'My batteries are flat. I'd better call Switchboard.' She picked up the phone on the coffee-table. 'What did you want to see me about, Jack?'

'Billy Carlisle has been admitted from Casualty to the chest medical ward.'

Lucinda hastily replaced the telephone. 'He's what?' she said, alarmed. 'What's wrong?'

Pete's eyebrows shot up in surprise at her response as Jack filled her in on the details.

'A chest infection, and possibly gastro. He's all right, though. Vince Cole, the respiratory consultant, thought that we should have a look, though, given he's only a few weeks post-op. I thought I should let you know, what with his dad being a doctor here. It might be better if a consultant takes a look at Billy.'

Lucinda, realising she had completely overreacted, gave a casual smile, though her heart was racing. 'Sure, I'll be right down.' She picked up her stethoscope and went to leave.

'Shouldn't you let Switchboard know about your pager?' Pete asked.

'Of course. Could you ring the ward and get them to organise an echocardiogram?'

'He's already had one in Casualty—the results are up on the ward.'

By the time she had rung Switchboard and collected a new pager, Lucinda was nearly beside herself. She knew she was probably worrying unnecessarily but, still, with Billy's asthma she just had to see the little guy for herself. A nurse escorted her to the side room and she braced herself to remain professionally cool when she saw Seb, but it was just Billy, sitting by himself on the bed.

'He's not very happy,' the nurse warned her. 'He's completely hospitalised. He wants to go back to his old ward or "at the very least" be moved onto the main ward. It's probably not gastro. More than likely the antibiotics are giving him diarrhoea, but until we get his results from Path I don't want to risk him on the main ward.'

Lucinda gave a laugh. 'Fair enough. Hello, Billy.' His miserable face looked up and at the sight of a familiar face broke into a huge grin.

'Miss Chambers.'

'We'll be all right,' she said to the nurse, who nodded gratefully and made her way back to the busy ward.

After examining him thoroughly, Lucinda looked at his X-rays. He had some consolidation on the right lower lobe and his lungs were hyperinflated from the Ventolin. She scanned the echocardiogram results.

'Your heart's working beautifully.'

Billy gave a frown.

'What's wrong? You don't look very pleased. That's good news.'

'Not for me. I want to go back to my old ward, see Ann and my friends.'

'I know, but hopefully once these new antibiotics kick in and you've had some extra fluid through that drip, you'll be home again.'

Billy didn't look very appeased. 'Dad said Bianca's a lot better.'

'That's right. She went home on Monday.'

'Dad said that she got a whole new heart and lungs. That would have saved you a lot of work, I guess.'

'How's that?' she asked.

'Well, you said yourself it was too complicated to fix. I suppose it was much easier just to get a new one.'

His five-year-old logic brought a smile to her lips. 'Well, I'm going to write some notes up. I'll probably come and check on you tomorrow.'

His face fell.

'Dad's gone to the airport to get Mum. I can't get this stupid video to work.' He pushed at the remote control.

'You have to turn the television on first.' Lucinda fiddled with the switches and a huge silver robot appeared on screen.

And Lucinda was never quite sure how it happened, but before she knew it the film had ended and she was now well versed in the hierarchy of the Mega-Galaxy and the battles of the Robot Savers. Lucinda glanced at her watch, yelping when she saw the time.

'I really do have to go now and you, young man, should get some rest.'

He gave a big smile. 'Bye, Miss Chambers.'

'Would you prefer an aisle or window seat?'

'Window, please.'

The flight attendant tapped her request into the computer.

'Travelling alone?'

Lucinda tried to smile. 'I'm not sure. I was supposed to be meeting a colleague here. Has a Dr Sebastian Carlisle checked in yet?'

She continued tapping. 'Not yet. He'd better step on it, they're starting to board. I'll reserve the seat next to you for him if he makes it in time.' With a smile she handed Lucinda back her ticket and gave her her boarding card. 'Have a nice flight.'

Annoyingly, and most unusually, the flight boarded bang on time and with a sigh Lucinda clipped on her seat belt, glancing longingly at the empty seat beside her. All her hopes had been pinned on Queensland and now it looked like Seb wasn't going to make it. She had tried not to build her hopes up, but after the initial panic Billy had responded well to the antibiotics and had been discharged on the Wednesday. Seb, after a lot of thought, had decided to come. Gemma was going to stay with Billy. But he must have changed his mind.

Just as the cabin doors were about to close a flurry of activity made her look up. Seb, slightly breathless, made his way down the aisle, his eyes lighting up when he saw her.

'What happened? Is Billy all right?'

Seb slipped into the seat beside her, his thighs brushing against her as he put his hand luggage under the seat. 'He's great. He and Gemma are armed with videos and popcorn. Couldn't wait to get rid of me. I got stuck with a patient at the hospital.'

'Not one of mine, I hope?'

'Kimberley Stewart. She's had a cerebral bleed.'

'Oh, no, but she was doing so well.'

Seb shook his head. 'Not really, Lucinda. She's never really picked up.'

'How bad is it?'

Seb gave a heavy sigh. 'Bad enough, on top of every-thing else.'

'Poor Janine and Mark.'

The mood was subdued as the plane taxied along the runway.

'Lucinda, I know it's awful but there's nothing either of us can do from here. We'll be back at work on Monday. You've been working sixty-hour weeks and you need a break. You can't take it with you.'

She knew he was right—of course he was—but as the plane took off she offered a silent prayer for Kimberley and her family. Turning to Seb, she saw his eyes closed and knew he was doing the same.

After lunch had been served the chattering stopped as most of the passengers dozed, but the bliss of being able to talk uninterrupted by pagers and to sit in such close proximity meant that sleep was the last thing on either of their minds. Sipping their gin and tonics, they gradually left behind the world and its problems and concentrated on each other. And slowly Seb filled her in about Gemma. It was exactly as Pete had described it, but hearing it from Seb made her eyes fill with tears for what they had been through.

'But how do you manage to stay civil to her?' she asked.

'That took a while, but she is Billy's mother. It's not as easy as just washing your hands and saying that's it.' He looked at her confused face. 'Gemma's not a bad person, we had a happy marriage at first. We were young and apart from work there were no responsibilities. I guess it was easy to be happy then. She was so upset when she found out she was pregnant, but I just assumed she'd come round. I never really took her doubts seriously.'

'But she didn't come round.'

Seb took a sip of his drink. 'No,' he said sadly. 'She tried, I'll give her that, but it just wasn't her. I guess some women just shouldn't have children. As I said before, I don't consider myself a chauvinist, but a sixty-hour-a-week job and children just don't mix, to my mind anyway. Something has to give when you're a parent.'

'Why didn't you stop working?' Lucinda asked, playing devil's advocate. 'Become a house husband?'

His eyes narrowed as he considered her words, and Lucinda suddenly realised what he must be thinking—that she was suggesting *he* give up work if they were to ever get together.

'Because as high-flying as Gemma is now, it took a long time and a lot of work before the dollars started rolling in. Someone had to pay the mortgage.' He swirled an ice cube around his drink and Lucinda found herself holding her breath as he continued.

'Maybe I'm more of a chauvinist than I thought,' he admitted honestly. 'I don't know if I'd like to be a house husband. I was always brought up to believe a man worked for a living.'

Lucinda hesitated and then thought, To hell with it. She asked the question whose answer she dreaded the most.

'Do you miss her?'

Seb nearly choked on his drink. 'Hell, no. Look, Lucinda, I did love Gemma but that was a long time ago. I know I seem accepting of her but it's taken me a long time to get there, it's been a hellish five years. Now it's just me and Billy, things are better. Gemma does care and she does love him in her own way—she just isn't cut out for the school runs and tooth-fairy tales. Anyway, there's been too much water under the bridge to even think about giving it another go. All I want from Gemma is for her to treat Billy properly. If she can't be a full-time mother I have to accept that, and I won't make things worse for Billy by rowing with her, but I certainly don't love her any more.'

'But what if she changed?' Lucinda insisted. 'What if she decides she wants Billy and you later on?'

Seb's face darkened and it was the first time Lucinda had heard any animosity in his voice. It made the hairs on her neck stand up.

'She'll never get him back, I made sure of that when I got full custody, I won't have Billy messed around again. And as for me, how could I love her again after seeing the pain she's caused my son?'

He took another long drink and for a second stared beyond her out of the plane window, but Lucinda knew he wasn't taking in the view. He turned back to her and his face was smiling. That conversation was definitely over.

'Where do your parents live?' he asked.

'In Noosa. I'll probably take a taxi and meet them for lunch on Sunday before we head back.'

'How's your speech going?' Seb gave a grimace. 'Do you know John McClelland? He's the bald guy a few rows in front, works at Ballarat City.'

Lucinda shook her head.

'We've both been doing similar research and we're going to do the presentation together. We were supposed to brainstorm it this week, but with Billy being sick we didn't get round to it. I'm going to have to do a lot of work with him tonight.'

Lucinda felt a stab of disappointment.

'Which gives us most of Saturday. Once my speech is out of the way I'm all yours. Anyway, we can hardly hole ourselves up in our room the whole time.'

'Why not?' Lucinda grumbled, then smiled. 'OK, never let it be said I stood in the way of your career.' A look she couldn't interpret flashed over Seb's face and for a second Lucinda wondered what she had said wrong, but as she continued speaking his face broke into another smile. 'John can have you tonight but then it's my turn.'

If Lucinda had had any romantic ideas of a cosy weekend for the two of them, her illusions were hastily shattered when they arrived at the luxurious beachside hotel. After checking in, she was shown to her room. After reading the itinerary, she realised that all of their time there was pretty much accounted for.

The afternoon was taken up with formal lectures, followed by dinner and then back for a group discussion. The following morning was packed again, with a break after lunch for some leisure time and then more lectures. There were even lectures on Sunday morning, though only until eleven. The rest of the day was free with further conferences in the evening. However, that didn't apply to her and Seb as they were leaving. No wonder Professor Hays had seemed so delighted when he'd said he couldn't attend. Oh, well. Lucinda shrugged. It was her first medical conference as a consultant and she was determined to enjoy it.

A welcoming basket of tropical fruit was on the table and Lucinda helped herself to a pawpaw. There was also a small wicker basket containing shampoo and conditioner and various bath and body oils, even a few condoms. The Plaza, it seemed, catered for everyone.

Making her way down to the conference room, she stood at the door uneasily for a moment. Seb was nowhere to be seen and most of the faces were new to her. Assuming a confident pose, Lucinda hovered on the edge of the most familiar-looking group, desperately hoping to be included in the conversation. Seb was still nowhere in sight, she realised miserably, then kicked herself. The last thing she wanted was to look as if she needed rescuing.

'We haven't been introduced. The name's Jeremy Foster. I'm a consultant surgeon at Melbourne City.'

Lucinda turned grateful to have someone to talk to.

'Lucinda Chambers. I'm at the Women's and Children's.'

'I know. I've heard a lot about you and what I don't already know I intend to find out.'

Lucinda nearly choked. Well, he didn't waste any time. She took in the blond looks and sultry eyes. He was good-looking, but not to her taste. And he was about as subtle as a sledgehammer. Still, at least it was someone to talk to.

'Are you giving a talk here?' she asked politely.

'Not this time. I'm actually working on designing a new instrument but it's rather early days to be presenting it.' And he was off. Over the next fifteen minutes Jeremy Foster gave her an in-depth description of his idea, which to Lucinda's mind was nothing particularly new or exciting anyway. The only reason he would be doing it, she knew, was to put his name to something, but she listened politely or at least pretended to. The occasional 'hmm' or 'really' was all the encouragement he needed to talk about himself.

'Hello, there, Jeremy, Lucinda.' Seb greeted them both and Lucinda gave a relieved smile.

'Hello, there, Sebastian. Haven't seen you in ages, though I must make a point of following up a couple of the referrals I pass your way if your hospital's latest acquisition is anything to go by.' His eyes flicked knowingly to Lucinda.

Seb gave him a cool smile, 'And I thought we were here to discuss medicine.'

Thankfully Jeremy took his cue and left them to it.

'What did he want?' Seb asked, sounding irritated.

'To talk about himself,' Lucinda replied lightly, glad that Seb seemed rattled. 'How's your room?'

'Too far from yours. Hell, I hate these things. Everyone trying to outdo each other, full of their own self-importance. If you weren't here I'd be tempted to catch the next plane home.'

'You're speaking, remember.'

'How could I forget? John's getting worked up. Apparently a couple of the bigwigs from his hospital are here.'

'I don't blame him for being worked up. This is the big league here, real make-or-break stuff. Sorry. I'm probably not helping.'

Seb shook his head. 'I couldn't give a damn. I'm not out to impress, just to learn something and hopefully share what I've been researching.'

That was so like him, Lucinda thought. Seb was easily as knowledgeable as anyone in this room yet he didn't let it go to his head. His concern was always his patients. Resisting the urge to reach out and touch him, instead she took a sip of her drink. It was hell being so close and not able to do a thing about it.

'C'mon. You can show me your room. The lectures don't start for another half-hour.' He must have read her mind.

And finally they were alone, and those brief moments were all it took to convey the urgency of their feelings and sustain her until tomorrow. He took her hand and led her to the king-sized bed. Gently he laid her down and stretched out beside her, his hand gently exploring her body through her flimsy dress and coming to rest on her breast as he kissed her deeply, his hand becoming more insistent as her nipples swelled beneath his expert touch. With a low moan she arched her body towards him, and despite the unwelcome restraints of their clothes she could feel the solid weight of his desire against her trembling thighs.

'We're like a couple of teenagers,' Lucinda gasped a few moments later, 'creeping away for a necking session.'

Seb reluctantly pulled away. 'Shall we put the "Do Not Disturb" sign on the door and play a bit of hookey, then?'

It was tempting, very tempting, but they both knew it was impossible. Finally they stood up, straightening their clothes.

'Do you want to go down first? I'll follow in a couple of minutes.'

'I'm sick of playing games,' he said suddenly. 'We've nothing to be ashamed of and after this weekend the whole world's going to know anyway.' And purposefully he took her hand and walked out with her to the lift. They made their way down the stairs, their hands entwined. Never had she felt more proud or confident.

The stolen moments in her room and the public display of affection made the rest of the day more bearable. Oh, she longed to be near him, longed to whisk him away from John McClelland and upstairs, but she had waited this long so she could wait a bit more.

And when on Saturday morning he stood up with John to deliver the lecture she knew she had been right to be patient. They were superb. Seb, being the more senior, went into considerable depth about their subject while John backed it up with the statistics and results. But it was Seb who somehow delivered a human touch, allowing the personalities of his subjects to shine through, which made for riveting listening. Suddenly he held the room in the palm of his hand as he spoke of the reduced pain, the increased mobility, fewer chest infections.

Lucinda knew he had done what he had to set out to do. Knew that everyone in this room would go back to their various roles and see where paediatric pain-controlled analgesia could be implemented. The thunderous applause that followed made her heart swell with pride. Seb and John were the men of the moment and Lucinda was more than happy to take a back seat.

Throughout the day various doctors accosted him, and though he spoke to them politely Lucinda was ever aware of his hungry eyes on her.

Finally, though, the lectures were over. Seeing Seb holed up with John and a few cronies, she escaped to the pool to do some laps.

'We meet again.' She surfaced, pushing her hair out of her eyes. Jeremy Foster gave her the benefit of a very wide smile.

'Well, as we're staying at the same hotel it's hardly much of a surprise.' Lucinda said, somewhat irritated.

'Do you fancy a drink?'

Lucinda shook her head. 'If I have to look at that bar again, I think I'll go,' she said truthfully, then kicked herself as she realised she had given him an opening and men like Jeremy rarely missed a chance.

'Who said anything about going to the bar?' He gave her a seductive smile. 'I've got a well-stocked mini-bar in my room just waiting to be raided.'

Lucinda was used to being chatted up, and normally she could brush unwelcome advances off easily, but this man had skin as thick as rhino's hide. Suddenly she became angry. Just what did he take her for? Did he really think she would go upstairs with him?

'Well, you'd better get used to drinking alone,' she snapped, and in one lithe movement she hauled herself out of the pool. Wrapping her sarong tightly around her, she made her way to her room.

Gibbering with rage at his unwelcome advances, she peeled off her bathers, only to hear a firm rap on the door.

'Go away,' she shouted.

'Lucinda?' Hearing Seb's voice, she grabbed her sarong and tied it around her waist, before opening the door.

'What's wrong?' he demanded. 'I'm sorry I couldn't get away sooner but I'm here now.'

'It's not you,' she said, pulling him in. After having a brief look down the corridor, she closed the door.

'I thought we weren't in hiding any more?'

'We're not, just me. That Jeremy Foster really is insatiable.'

'Has he been giving you a hard time?' Seb frowned. He was wearing only a beach towel draped around his waist. 'Do you want me to have a word?'

'I can take care of myself, thanks. I just gave him an extremely cold shoulder. For a moment, though, I thought he'd followed me up here.'

'Wouldn't put it past him—that guy has broken more hearts than you've fixed. I saw him eyeing you up. Bloody lech.'

'Seb.' Lucinda laughed. 'You weren't jealous, were you?'

'No,' he said, then shrugged. 'Well, maybe a little bit, I guess. I was just coming down to the pool to join you for a swim. I've spent the last twenty-four hours with you looking completely stunning and haven't been able to do a thing about it.'

'Until now,' she said huskily.

'Until now.' he replied, his eyes glazing over with lust. 'Come here.'

Seductively she undid her sarong and it slithered to the ground. His eyes travelled searchingly over her body, melting her with his gaze. Slowly she walked over to him, her hands reaching out and touching his broad chest, her long nails dragging teasingly around his nipples then slowly working their way down. She undid the towel and purposefully she slipped off his bathers with one hand as the other boldly explored the delicious beauty of his malehood.

His lips nuzzled her shoulders, soft hot kisses, her satin skin fragrant with the scent of desire, mingling with the pool's chlorine. Moving downwards, ever downwards, his searching mouth found her glorious heavy breasts and with a low moan he buried his head in their velvet softness.

'Lucinda, oh, Lucinda,' he rasped, his voice deep and breathless. Scooping her up in his strong arms, he carried her over to the bed, his mouth never leaving hers. As he tenderly laid her down they both trembled violently. His mouth hadn't finished exploring her yet and he searched relentlessly as she lay beneath him, squirming in ecstasy until she could take it no more.

Gasping with pleasure, she leant over and with shaking hands she wrestled with the foil package that was their final obstacle. Achingly slowly, firm and then gentle, she unravelled the thin latex along the long length of him, and then there was nothing that could stop them and he dived into her depths.

Like two lost souls that had always belonged together, they began their journey, each knowing instinctively the way to go, pushing each other on, pulling each other back, climbing slowly with sudden bursts of energy that brought them nearer. Until finally, exhausted and gasping, they reached the peak in perfect unison, holding each other tightly as the world rushed by around them.

'I've wanted you for so long,' he said finally as they lay in each other's arms, their long limbs entwined. As she gazed into his loving eyes Lucinda finally knew what it felt to be loved.

Later as they bathed together in the huge spa and he slowly soaped her thighs, the dispersing bubbles displayed her breasts so invitingly that Seb seductively moved his hand slowly higher and to her gasps of surprise and delight he took her there and then in the water.

Drying her slowly, his strong hands massaging her through the soft towel, Seb laughed as he caught sight of the empty basket 'We've exhausted the hotel's supplies.'

'Well, I'm not ringing housekeeping to ask for more condoms.' Lucinda said, blushing at the thought.

'We'll just have to move up to my room, then.'

As good as they were, the evening's lectures were wasted on Lucinda and Seb. Trying hard to concentrate, she was all too aware of Seb next to her. She could smell his newly washed hair, feel his thighs next to hers, and she was tempted to take him by the hand and run back up to her room. But they got through and finally when the meal was over and they had stayed for one drink to be polite, they escaped back upstairs, ordering breakfast to be delivered before she succumbed again to his rapturous love-making.

'You're a great cure for my insomnia,' she said finally as she lay completely spent beside him.

He kissed her goodnight slowly, then tucked himself behind her with one arm protectively wrapped around her until she drifted off. And it felt so right he stayed like that all night, not wanting to ever let her go.

CHAPTER SEVEN

AS THE Queensland sun streamed through the window, Lucinda felt the delicious glow on her face. In their haste to be together they hadn't drawn the curtains and she lay there half-asleep, feeling the sun on her skin and the warmth of Seb so close next to her. She felt him stir slightly and she nuzzled against him, feeling him rising against her as welcome as the new day, their bodies instinctively reaching out for each other. Effortlessly he slipped inside her and they rocked together. Like a surreal dream, drugged on sleep and lust, they made hazy love.

'What a gorgeous way to wake up,' she said much later, stretching like a cat on the bed.

He ran a warm hand over her breast. 'You look good enough to eat.' He bent his head and tenderly nuzzled at her breasts, but a sharp knock on the door halted him.

'Looks like the real thing's here.' Lucinda laughed as they hastily covered themselves with the sheet.

Without even a glance, the housemaid delivered the breakfast trolley, wheeling it in and with painstaking slowness proceeding to pour the juice.

'We'll take it from here, thanks,' Seb said finally. 'Do you think I was supposed to tip her?' he asked when she'd gone.

'She'd have got a pretty big tip if you'd got out of bed like that,' Lucinda remarked as he stood up.

They feasted on eggs Benedict and guava juice and fed each other strawberries and melon like two newly-weds.

'Let's skip the morning's lectures,' Seb said as they read the papers.

Lucinda gave a shrug. 'All right, but if Professor Hays finds out I'm going to say you corrupted me.'

'I corrupted you?' He laughed. 'I think it was the other way around.' The ringing of the telephone interrupted their cheerful banter. Lucinda answered it and listened carefully as Seb carried on reading.

'We're not going to be missing the lectures,' she said eventually when she replaced the receiver.

'How come?'

'This morning's speaker has gone down with gastro and they've asked me to do it.'

'What's it on?' he asked gently, seeing how pale she had gone.

'Micro-prems.'

'You'll walk it,' he said confidently, but they both knew it was a tough task. Lectures like these took weeks of preparation, but an opportunity to be seen on this floor was just too good to pass up.

Lucinda was an excellent public speaker. Years at a top boarding school and her time at uni on the debating team had seen to that, but as she took the stage she realised this was her toughest audience yet. Although the presenter had thanked her profusely for stepping in at such short notice, and had told the guests the same, the room was packed with the best medical brains and her hastily written notes were sketchy. The only statistics she had to back her up were the ones in her head. She had no slides, no graphs to work with.

Clearing her throat, she started. Seb gave her a reassuring smile and she smiled back hesitantly. Then, like a baby bird stretching its wings, she hopped off the branch and realised she was flying.

'Initially I was sceptical. These babies are barely viable. We put them and their families thorough hell and more often than not to no avail.' She went into the various ailments these babies faced, speaking briefly of cortical blindness from too much oxygen, necrotising encolitis and then in more depth about cardiac defects, arrhythmias and lung immaturity, recalling statistics that had stuck in her head from when she had pondered this subject long into the night. Her depth of knowledge was truly amazing and she held the audience in the palm of her hand as she spoke with wisdom and passion on this most difficult subject.

As she concluded she looked around the room, her eyes staring directly into the enthralled audience. 'Micro-prems aren't my speciality, but neither are they the exclusive property of the neonatologist. It takes a huge combination of skill and experience, involving practically the whole spectrum of specialties, to care for these infants, and each plays a vital role. Pain, too, plays a big part. Are we subjecting these babies to too much pain? A lot of research is being done but we'll never know the complete answer. We heard yesterday from Drs Carlisle and McClelland about the problems of interpreting pain in infants. How must it be for these the tiniest of babies? It is something we must all consider when we subject them to endless procedures in the quest for life.

'As I said, I used to be sceptical, and it used to worry me. I like to know my own opinions, be able to give an assured answer, but I have now realised that on this subject no one can. We are right to be sceptical—the answers to the ethical and medical debates thrown up by these micro-prems remain equivocal. But, like it or not, medical research is advancing and these tiny babies pave the way for ones that come later.' She paused. 'So we will soldier on until such time as a law is passed which dictates a viable delivery age. But we have to tread carefully, we have to inform the parents each step of the way.' She thought of Kimberley, of Janine and Mark.

'Some will say enough is enough and we have to respect that, others will want us to do all we can. We have to respect that, too. But our first priority once a baby is born must be to that child. We, as doctors, have to be their advocates first and foremost, no matter how tough the going gets.'

She took her seat, the applause continued, and Lucinda let out a huge sigh of relief. The presenter thanked her once again for stepping in and then called an end to the morning lectures.

As Lucinda made her way to the bar her peers shook her hand and congratulated her but it was only Seb she wanted to see. Jeremy Foster, ever the optimist, appeared suddenly with two glasses of champagne.

'You were fabulous. I thought you might like to celebrate.'

And then Seb was beside her.

'She was, wasn't she?' He kissed her cheek and, taking the glasses from a furious Jeremy, he handed one to Lucinda. 'How thoughtful of you, Jeremy. Cheers.'

They were still laughing about it as Lucinda waited in the foyer for her taxi.

'You look nervous,' Seb commented. 'I thought you'd be relieved now it's over.'

'They…' she gestured to the bar '…were a piece of cake compared to my parents.'

Seb laughed. 'They can't be all that bad.'

'You don't know them.'

Seb took a deep breath 'Well, that's easily solved.'

'You mean…' Her heart soared at the prospect of him joining her.

'It will take me two minutes to pack. Tell the taxi to wait.'

As the porter loaded their suitcases into the boot John McClelland came to say goodbye and congratulate Lucinda on her speech.

'In all I would say it's been a successful weekend,' he said in a friendly voice as he shook her hand. 'I'll catch you later, Seb, and think seriously about what I said.'

Seb gave him a brief nod and shook his hand. As they climbed into the taxi all thoughts of her lecture vanished as Lucinda contemplated the meeting ahead.

'Don't worry.' Seb squeezed her thigh reassuringly as she sat tensely next to him on the back seat. 'It will only be for a couple of hours—our plane's at two.'

She turned her troubled eyes to him. 'Don't say I didn't warn you.'

Despite Lucinda's hesitancy at introducing Seb to her parents, the initial meeting went well. Seb played along when Abigail insisted on kissing him on both cheeks and Richard patted him on the back like a long-lost son. He also didn't look remotely embarrassed when Abigail kicked up the most terrible fuss at an extremely smart restaurant because she didn't like the table, but Lucinda inwardly cringed.

'*Lucindah*, what on earth have they been feeding you down there? My baby's grown so big, hasn't she, Richard?'

Seb leant back in his chair. 'Your ''baby'' has just delivered the most marvellous speech on micro-prems with only an hour's notice. She was very impressive.'

Abigail turned to Lucinda.

'Where was the conference held again?'

Lucinda felt her irritation rise—she had already told her mother three times in the hope they'd come and see her. 'The Plaza.'

'That's right, I remember you telling me now. It's *very* nice there. They have a new head chef there, poached from Romeo's. The Merringtons are having their Christmas do there, I'm looking forward to it.'

Lucinda felt her spirits sink. If she was so looking forward to testing the menu why couldn't she have come down this weekend? Lucinda wondered, but, then, the Merringtons were important people, Lucinda reflected, while she was only their daughter.

'So you're an anaesthetist?' Richard finally spoke.

'That's right.'

'Excellent. Where would we all be without a gas man?' He laughed heartily at his stale joke, but Seb joined in.

Abigail studied the menu carefully. 'Everything's fried, or with cream sauce,' she said impatiently. 'I'll have to speak with the chef myself.' She clicked her fingers at a passing waiter.

'Mum, please, there's plenty of choice. What about the barramundi in lime sauce? It sounds delicious.'

'Is that what you're having?'

Lucinda nodded reluctantly, replacing the menu on the table.

'Well, I'm going to have a huge roast with all the trimmings,' Seb said loudly. 'It is Sunday after all.'

Richard chose a grilled flake and after the waiter had received his strict instruction about the salad dressing there was a sticky moment as Richard ordered the drinks.

'We'd better make it two bottles. Is sparkling all right with you, Seb?'

Seb nodded amicably. 'Whatever everyone else is having.'

'We'll have two bottles of sparkling mineral water,' Richard said to the waiter as he finally handed him back the menus.

Seb called the waiter back as he gratefully departed from the difficult table.

'I'll have a beer, thanks,' Seb said pointedly.

Abigail again turned her attention to Lucinda.

'Next time your professor has to go to a wedding and wants you to attend a conference, make sure it's an international one. You need more exposure, Lucinda. You really ought to be pushing for some international experience. London would be good. Have you asked about a secondment yet?'

'Mum, I've only been there five minutes, for goodness' sake.'

'Doesn't matter. This is no time to be resting on your laurels. Amanda Merrington has just been made Associate Professor, and she was in your year at medical school. Why do you think they've booked the Plaza for their Christmas do? So Phillip and Celeste can ram the happy news down everybody's throats, that's why. Mind you, she's a dermatologist.' She turned to Seb and shuddered visibly. 'I couldn't think of anything worse, could you? What a frightful job, looking at all those ugly skin rashes. Yuk.'

To his credit Seb laughed. 'I expect you see a few unpleasant sights in your job,' he said with good humour, attempting to divert the conversation.

But Abigail wasn't going to be deflected. 'Ah, but not for long. By the time I've finished with them they're perfect. Now, Lucinda, as I was saying, you mustn't let the grass grow under your feet. You need to get a few articles published—put your name to something, make a bit of noise.'

Thankfully the meals arrived, which managed to stop Abigail's attack as she scrutinised her plate. Lucinda poked at her salad with a fork.

'What are you doing?' Seb said quietly. 'Trying to find

a calorie?' Lucinda gave a small laugh and watched hungrily as Seb tucked unashamedly into his roast. And slowly she started to relax. Her parents were as obnoxious and pretentious as ever throughout the meal, but somehow with Seb here beside her, deflecting the blows, adding a dry touch of humour, her parents didn't seem quite so poisonous. She was actually almost enjoying herself.

'Lucinda,' Abigail said sharply as the dessert trolley was wheeled before them. 'Remember the saying—a moment on the lips, a lifetime on the hips.'

Seb started to laugh. 'You could always give her a free session of liposuction. I'm going to have a huge slice of mud cake. Billy would never forgive me if he found out I passed on dessert. Billy's my son,' he added as Abigail gave him a questioning look.

'You've got a son?' she asked in a horrified voice.

'Seb's divorced. His ex-wife lives in Sydney,' Lucinda hastily explained, and Abigail seemed placated.

'That's all right, then. I expect it's nice when you get up there to see him,' she said in friendlier tones, but her face turned purple when she heard Seb's reply.

'Actually, I've got full custody. It's my ex-wife who does the visiting.'

'I'm just going to the powder room,' Lucinda said, excusing herself and rushing off. Once there she splashed her face with water. She had known Seb would never hide Billy—he was fiercely proud of his son. And after all, she was hardly in her early twenties. Most men of her age had some history. In a funny way she actually felt relieved now everything was out in the open. There was never going to be a good time to tell them and now at least they could move on. Feeling better, she made her way back to the table where her mother was examining her face in her compact mirror.

'Where's Dad and Seb?' Lucinda asked.

'They've gone to the bar.'

'Why didn't they ask the waiter?'

Abigail shrugged and carried on admiring her reflection.

'What do you think of Seb?' Lucinda asked gingerly.

'He seems a bit wrapped up in his son,' Abigail said nastily.

'He mentioned him once,' Lucinda replied, exasperated. 'Please, Mum, what do you really think? This is important to me.'

With an angry snap Abigail shut the powder compact. 'Oh, come on, Lucinda, you're not serious. He may be a perfectly nice man but he's got a child, for heaven's sake. You're hardly stepmother material. He's probably just testing his wings after his divorce. It's just a fling, I can tell he's not serious about you.'

'But how?' Lucinda asked.

'I just can, that's all.' Her tone softened somewhat and she reached over and patted Lucinda's hand, which Lucinda thought was probably the tenderest thing she had done to her in years. 'Don't go reading too much into it, you'll only get hurt.'

Seb and her father returned, minus drinks.

'I thought you went to the bar?' Lucinda asked in a falsely cheerful voice.

'I just settled the bill. I didn't realise the time. We'd better be off if we want to catch that flight.' He looked tense and Lucinda, with a sinking feeling, realised what a terrible time he'd probably had. It was hardly the most pleasant end to a perfect weekend after all.

They said their goodbyes and, slipping into the taxi, Lucinda let out a huge sigh of relief as they drove off.

'I told you they were awful,' she said after a few moments, trying to lighten the mood.

Seb didn't say anything for a moment. His face was lined with tension and suddenly he looked tired. 'They love you, Lucinda,' he said finally. 'They just want what's best for you.' But his voice was pensive instead of reassuring and his words did nothing to comfort her.

As the plane touched down somewhat bumpily in Melbourne, Lucinda reflected that the flight had only been marginally less turbulent than her emotions. Seb, though kind and pleasant, seemed lost in his thoughts and Lucinda could almost feel him slipping away from her. It was as if everything good had been left at the Plaza and now it was back to the real world.

Stepping off the plane and into the arrival lounge, the air of tension was broken by the unexpected sight of Billy and Isabella.

'G'day, sport, this is a surprise.' Swinging him up in his arms, Seb listened attentively as Billy chattered excitedly.

'We watched your plane land. I saw it come right along the runway and up to the window. I could see the captain and everything. Can I watch the bags be unloaded?'

'OK, but don't go wandering.' Seb waited until Billy was safely out of earshot. His little face was pushed up against the glass, watching as the ground staff unloaded the bags. 'What happened this time?' he said wearily to Isabella.

'For once she had a genuine excuse, Seb,' Isabella said in a placating voice. 'Gemma's mum has had a fall and probably fractured her hip. She had to fly back, of course. It was pointless ringing you as you were probably on your way, so I met her at the airport. You only just missed her.'

'Is she all right, apart from the hip, I mean? No other injuries?' His voice was concerned.

'I think it's just her hip.'

'I'm sorry, Bell, you always seem to be bailing us out.'

Isabella gave her brother a friendly smile. 'I don't mind a bit. I wanted to see Billy anyway after the scare he gave us last week. But I do have to rush off. By the time I get home it will be late and I need to sort out the kids' uniforms and everything for tomorrow—they're still sitting in the laundry basket. And the kids haven't even started their homework. Dave's useless, he's probably playing footy with them in the garden as we speak.'

Seb laughed. 'Probably. Look, thanks, Bell.' Isabella made her way over to Billy to say goodbye.

'You've got to cover for Chris King,' Lucinda said.

'I know. I'll just have to take Billy in with me, I guess. Hopefully it will be quiet.'

'You can't do that,' Lucinda reasoned. 'What if there's an emergency? Look, why don't I take him back to my flat? I know Billy and he knows me. I'm sure he'd be all right about it.'

Seb didn't look too keen. 'Go on,' Lucinda insisted. 'It will be fine. You really can't take him and you can't let Chris down.'

Seb eventually agreed, and although Lucinda could tell he was reluctant she was grateful for the chance to extend the weekend and hopefully end it on a somewhat happier note. Maybe he had only agreed for her to look after Billy because he didn't have any other choice, but Lucinda was determined that this twist of fate would be the chance she wanted to show him how things could work out for them. Her mother's cruel words rang in her ears. 'Hardly stepmother material.' Well, she'd show them!

And Billy, despite his father's apparent hesitation, was delighted at the prospect of an evening with Lucinda.

'Now, you've got all your pumps?' Seb asked as he checked Billy's backpack. 'He needs the Becloforte at eight, and if there's any sign of a wheeze he's to have two puffs of the Ventolin, the blue one.'

'Seb.' Lucinda put her hand over his as he held up the pump. 'I prescribed it—remember?'

Seb looked sheepish. 'I know, and I know you can manage an asthma attack. It's just…'

'That you're his dad,' she finished the sentence for him. 'Go on, we'll be fine.'

At the car park they said their farewells and Billy climbed into the car with hardly a backward glance.

'Shouldn't you be in the back?' she asked.

'Dad always lets me go in the front,' he said.

Lucinda gave him a questioning look. 'Always?'

Billy gave a small shrug. 'Sometimes,' he admitted reluctantly.

'Well, I'd rather you sat in the back.'

Lucinda waited for an argument but Billy accepted her decision with a happy 'OK'. And he clambered into the back, clipping in his seat belt without prompting. 'Can we stop at the video shop?'

'I don't know where it is,' Lucinda replied honestly, grinning to herself at Billy's incredulous look in the rearview mirror. 'Anyway, you can have lots of fun without watching a video.'

To Billy's remarks of 'cool' and 'what's this for?' as he wandered around her apartment, Lucinda rummaged through her hallway cupboard.

'Is that a present for me?' he asked excitedly as she brought out a huge wrapped parcel.

'It was actually for my godson,' Lucinda answered truthfully as he tore at the paper, 'but I can get him something else for Christmas.' It was probably just as well, she reflected. The wooden bagatelle set she had seen in a craft shop had evoked memories of the 'den' at boarding school where she had whiled away many an evening playing bagatelle. Children seemed so much more advanced now. Her godson was into computers and the like. A bagatelle board probably wasn't the best gift idea she'd had.

But Billy loved it. The silver ballbearings raced around the board and they laughed and laughed as Lucinda showed him the tricks she had learnt of old. And Billy with a child's enthusiasm clasped his hands in a victory salute when finally he beat her.

Lucinda, stopping to put on the overhead light, suddenly noticed the time.

'Come on, Billy, it's time for your puffers. Do you want something to eat?' Her fridge contents didn't hold much attraction for a five-year-old so she made Vegemite on toast and poured two long glasses of orange juice.

'What did you and Dad do in Queensland?' he asked as they settled on the sofa to eat.

'We were at a medical conference.'

'Boring,' declared Billy.

'Probably to you. I saw my parents today, though. They live in Queensland.'

Billy took a bite of his toast. 'My mum lives in Sydney,' he said, without swallowing what he had eaten. 'She didn't want me to live with her.'

'But your dad did,' Lucinda replied.

'I heard Mum say once I was an accident.'

Lucinda took a swig of her juice. Billy, she decided, was playing to his audience and, awful as the truth was, she wasn't going to give him the satisfaction of a shocked look. 'So was I.'

It was Billy who looked shocked. 'Really? How did you know?'

'Same as you. I heard my mum tell someone.' Billy seemed pleased with this information, and they chatted a while. He really was the cutest kid. Terribly spoilt, Lucinda decided, probably from Seb trying to overcompensate and a multitude of nurses won over by that smile, but there was also a really great person there, a fun little man who was kind and good and clever, not unlike his father. The evening they'd spent had, in fact, Lucinda thought as she tucked a blanket round him, been probably one of the best she'd ever had. It had certainly been the funniest.

Once Billy was asleep she rang Surayan's and ordered a curry. It had been ages since she and Seb had shared that first night together. It was a calculated move and she knew it. A happy, contented child asleep, a gorgeous meal—all that was left was for her to put on some make-up and Seb would realise what a great mum she could be.

Her plans were to no avail, though. The intercom buzzed and she had time only to run a quick comb through her hair.

'You're back already?'

Seb gave a small smile. 'Chris said the wedding was awful and he was glad of the excuse to get away. Still, he was there long enough to hear about your lecture.'

'My lecture? But how?'

'News has filtered back that a star is born. Apparently Professor Hays, buoyed by a couple of glasses of champagne, is walking around singing your praises. How's Billy been?'

Lucinda gestured to the sleeping child. 'He's been fine, we had a great night. He fell asleep about fifteen minutes ago. He had all his pumps,' she said before Seb had a chance to ask. 'Any news at the hospital? How's Kimberley?'

Seb shook his head. 'Not good, I'm afraid. I didn't see her but apparently there's an NFR order.'

Lucinda turned away and busied herself, wiping the

bench, so that Seb couldn't see her face. Hastily she wiped away a tear. An NFR order meant 'not for resuscitation'. For Janine and Mark to have agreed to that, it must mean there was no hope. It was awful news, and by now she should be used to it, but...

'Anything else?' she asked in a strangely high voice.

'I met up with Vince Cole on his way home—he'd been in with a patient. We had a long chat about Billy and his asthma—he's quite good at straight talking.'

Her composure restored, Lucinda turned and made her way over to him.

'Speaking of straight talking, Seb, is something wrong? We've hardly exchanged a word since we left my parents.'

He ran a hand through his hair and Lucinda felt her heart plummet as his eyes avoided hers.

'I've been doing some thinking.' He paused and Lucinda knew what was coming. 'There's something worrying me, I just don't know how to say it.'

She swallowed hard. Her mother had been right after all, it had all just been a fling. Longing for him to put her mind at rest, to somehow reassure her that she was mistaken, her heart sank further as he tentatively continued struggling with his words.

'We really need to talk. I just don't see how this is going to work. You've got so much going for you, I just can't imagine...' Seb's voice trailed off and finally he gestured to Billy, asleep on the sofa.

'It's just that I can't... You're not...'

Lucinda finished the sentence for him. 'Not stepmum material.'

'I didn't say that,' he said fiercely.

As the world crashed around her, the Lucinda who was good at hiding her feelings, of staying in control, came to the fore. Somehow she managed a smile, determined to escape with some dignity. If Seb wanted to end things, she damn well wasn't going to let him think it was solely his decision. She had some pride. 'You didn't have to. I'd actually started to realise that myself.'

Seb looked at her, his eyes full of confusion. 'You had?'

'Having him here tonight. I mean, we had fun and everything, but…well, look, you're right. I don't see how it could work. It's just not for me. It's no big deal. We're consenting adults after all. We had a good time, no one got hurt, we can still be friends.'

Seb gave a small nod. 'Of course.'

He made his way over to Billy who stirred gently as Seb lifted him. The love in his eyes when he gazed at his son made her want to weep. She was so sure she had seen it there before, but for her.

'Hold on a moment,' she called as he made his way to the lift. Grabbing a bag, she stuffed the bagatelle set into it. 'I said he could have it.'

'You don't have to, Lucinda.'

'Please.' She gave a small laugh. 'What am I going to do with it?'

She stood there watching the numbers go down on the lift lights, watching as the two males she loved walk out of her life. She was still standing there when the lift returned and Vijay's son arrived with the curry. Somehow she paid him and chatted about the weather. Somehow she made it back into her apartment.

Numb, shocked, she made her way into the shower, standing quite still until eventually the water ran cold. And even then she didn't notice. 'No one got hurt,' she'd said. That had been the biggest lie of her life, for the pain that she was feeling now was utterly indescribable. Finally, shivering, she made her way to bed, the curry having long since gone cold. There she lay alone and waited for morning.

Monday was easily the blackest day of Lucinda's life. Somehow she had thought to set the alarm and had awoken to the smell of cold curry and the painful memories of the previous night. It seemed impossible to believe that only twenty-four hours ago she had woken in Seb's arms and made love. How, she wrestled with herself, could she have been so wrong? How could she have misread him so badly? 'A fling', her mother had said, and she had been right, it seemed.

The ward round was painfully slow and when they finally walked into NICU the sight of Janine and Mark at Kimberley's incubator was almost too much to take.

'How's Kimberley?' Lucinda asked Andrew Doran.

He shook his head. 'Her parents want another CT scan, but it's pointless.'

'Will you do one?'

Andrew nodded. 'I think it's merited if it helps Janine and Mark. She's going down soon.'

Making her way across to the catheter suite, Lucinda checked the whiteboard. Seb was the anaesthetist on. Bracing herself, she walked in, only to find Chris King checking his equipment.

'Good morning, Lucinda, or should I say good afternoon?'

Lucinda managed a cheery greeting as Chris explained he was filling in for Seb who was stuck on the wards. His excuse was plausible enough but Lucinda felt it was rather more convenient than facing her today of all days.

They were busy for the next few hours and Lucinda was more than happy to concentrate on others' hearts. Her own was in a mess.

When the last of the patients had been dealt with, she made her way to the canteen. Lunch orders had finished so there were only sandwiches available from the machine. The canteen was relatively quiet but, longing for some peace, she made her way up to her office. As she reached the top of the stairwell she was met by the grief-stricken faces of Janine and Mark.

'Has Kimberley gone for her scan?' she asked, full of concern.

Mark shook his head and pulled the sobbing Janine towards him.

'We decided not to send her, she'd been through enough. Seb came and extubated her. She died soon after...' His voice broke. 'We were both holding her.'

Lucinda stood there, frozen. She had seen raw grief so many—too many—times, but it was something she knew she would never get used to. 'I'm so very sorry,' she said, her voice thick with emotion.

'We're just going to the hospital chapel and then we're going to go back and spend some time with her.'

Lucinda nodded.

Janine looked up and Lucinda couldn't bear to see the pain in her eyes.

'Thank you for all you did. Everyone's been wonderful.'

'I just wish we could have done more.'

Mark shook her hand and guided his wife gently towards the chapel. Numb, Lucinda walked the few steps to her office. Taking off her white coat, she sat at her desk and stared at her hands for a few moments. Then the tears came, rolling out of her eyes, splashing onto her hands, and she did nothing to stop them. It took a moment or two before she realised someone was knocking on her door.

'One moment.' Hastily she wiped her tears away and blew her nose. 'Come in.'

It was Seb. 'Sorry to disturb you.'

'No problem.' She forced a smile.

'I didn't want you to think I was avoiding you this morning, not that it would be possible in a place like this even if I wanted to, which I don't.'

'Like I said, we're adults. It's not as if we were married or anything. We can all make mistakes.'

'You've been crying?'

She was about to deny it, but what was the point? Her face was probably bright red. 'I just saw Janine and Mark Stewart.'

'It's awful, isn't it? That's where I've been. I've had a fair bit to do with them over the last couple of months and I wanted to see things through.'

Which was so like him, Lucinda thought, taking the hard road when he didn't have to, giving that bit more. She could read the concern for her in his eyes, and she knew if she started to cry again she wouldn't be able to stop. She couldn't let him see her like that. They had made a deal. Friends, remember?

'You had a bit to do with Janine. Is that why this one's hit you so hard?' Seb asked gently.

How could she tell him? Yesterday maybe, but yesterday they had been a couple. Today he was a colleague. How could she tell him that they all hit her like this? That the name of each child that had died was etched on her heart? That right now she would love to grab her bag and run? Put as much distance as she could from this place and never come back? Instead, she gave a tight smile, the persona of cool.

'That must be it. She seemed like a nice woman. It was to be expected, of course. Twenty-four weeks is barely viable and Kimberley had a lot of problems besides immaturity.' She picked up a file and reached for her Dictaphone. Miss Chambers was back!

But Seb seemed to see through her bravado. 'Lucinda, are you sure you're all right?'

She longed to tell him she wasn't, that Kimberley's death, him leaving, they had both devastated her, but instead her face remained impassive. 'Of course. I'm fine. It's sad and all that but, well, it comes with the job.' And clicking on her Dictaphone, she opened the file in front of her and flashed Seb a cool smile. 'I'll catch up with you later. I really am snowed under.'

Seb raised his eyebrows at her reaction, but didn't comment. Without another word he turned and left, closing the door behind him. She heard his footsteps fading down the corridor and only when she was safely alone did she put her head down on the desk and weep. She wept for them all—for Kimberley and Janine and Mark and then for herself. In a few short hours everything had changed and life for them all would never be the same again.

CHAPTER EIGHT

As Seb had pointed out, if they had wanted to avoid each other they couldn't, and in the weeks that followed they were thrown together often.

Lucinda coped by day. They had polite conversations when she asked about Billy and he asked about her work, but it wasn't enough. From answering 'better' and 'fine' to her questions his answers had become 'not bad' and 'getting there'. She had heard from her peers that Billy's asthma was worsening and she yearned for more information and deep down she ached to see him for herself.

At least workwise things had never been better. November turned into December and the operation lists were overflowing as they tried to get the numbers down before scheduled operations ceased over Christmas. It was a blessing in disguise as the days flew by and Lucinda could bury herself in work and forget about her own problems.

It was a different question at night, though. Exhausted, she would collapse on the sofa. Not even hungry, she would have a couple of slices of toast or a biscuit if there were any, before collapsing on the bed. There she would lie and wait for sleep, trying to block all thoughts of Seb out of her mind, determined not to cry herself to sleep again. But eventually the tears would win and she would awake puffy-eyed and tired, only to start another weary day all over again.

Sitting at her desk one morning, she dunked a teabag in a cup of hot water and decided to tackle the mountain of internal mail that had piled up. Most were Christmas cards, and she made a mental note to stop at the shops on the way home and buy a couple more boxes. Everywhere in the hospital was decorated with tinsel and flashing lights. The children's ward was abuzz with excitement and nurses walked around with flashing Christmas-tree earrings.

Lucinda, at Ann's insistence, had stuck a piece of tinsel around her name badge but that was as far as her festive preparations went. It seemed like a lifetime since she had been happy but it had, in fact, only been eight weeks. Eight weeks of hell. She felt like she had forgotten how to smile naturally and could hear herself barking at the staff. So much for festive cheer. She was living right up to her reputation and decided to try and brighten up.

It was to no avail, though, for as she opened a yellow envelope a memo greeted her, and as she read the words about the recent resignation of Dr Carlisle, it was as if a knife were being plunged straight into her heart. She sat there, trying to make sense of the words blurring before her, but before she had time to digest the contents her emergency page went off and she rushed across to CGU.

'What's the story?'

The little girl sitting on the bed, was struggling with her breathing.

Jack Wells gave her a worried look. 'Pre-op for removal of a cyst on the right lung. She's developed sudden onset of shortness of breath, with reduced air sounds on the right.'

'Has she had an X-ray?'

Jack handed the films to her. 'We just got them back after I put the page out. She's got a tension pneumothorax.'

Lucinda had a brief look at the films, confirming Jack's diagnosis.

'Ann set up for a chest drain. Put her oxygen up, Jack, to one hundred per cent. What's her sats?'

Jack checked the saturation machine.

'Ninety per cent on one hundred per cent oxygen.'

'OK. Let's put a tube in now. Right, Jack, you can do this one.'

She saw the anxiety on his face and she knew he was nervous, but he had done this procedure before, albeit not in an emergency.

'Come on, Jack, you can do this.' She watched his trembling hands.

'That's right—between fourth and fifth intercostal spaces. Now inject your local.'

Ellen spoke to the young girl who was concentrating too hard on her breathing to be scared, while Ann assisted the doctors.

'Now push till you feel it give. That's it—further. You're in. OK, now remove the guide.' The bottle by the bed connected to the chest tube bubbled merrily with each breath. 'Now stitch the chest tube firmly in place.' She listened to the girl's chest. 'Much better. Good air entry. When you've finished stitching her she'll need a repeat chest X-ray.'

Lucinda watched closely as Jack, his confidence up now, deftly stitched the tube in place. The ward was very warm and Lucinda felt the beads of sweat rising on her forehead and trickling between her breasts. Suddenly she felt quite dizzy. 'All right, Jack, you carry on from here.' With the ward spinning, she made her way to the office and sat on the nearest chair, taking some deep breaths. Serve her right for skipping breakfast and lunch, too, for that matter. She really had to start taking better care of herself. Ann came in quietly and closed the door.

'Are you all right, Lucinda?'

'Just felt a bit hot in there. The air-conditioning in this place leaves a lot to be desired.

'When did you last eat?'

Lucinda gave a small shrug.

'Yesterday, I think.'

Ann tutted loudly. 'I actually saved you some mince pies.' She pushed the plate toward her. Lucinda took a look at the curling pastry and shook her head.

'A rum ball, then?'

Lucinda gave her a smile. 'I'm fine, Ann, really. I think I'll grab some sandwiches from the machine.'

'How about some cornflakes? We've got some on the ward. Save you going down to the canteen.'

'I guess I did miss breakfast—that sounds good.'

Ann scuttled off and returned a few moments later with two small boxes and a carton of milk. She set about preparing them and poured on some sugar.

Lucinda tucked in, realising how hungry she was.

Ann hovered, ensuring Lucinda cleared the bowl. 'You certainly enjoyed them,' she said cheerfully, then her tone changed and Lucinda listened as she continued in a searching voice. 'Cornflakes were all I could manage myself when I was pregnant.' And Lucinda knew Ann's words had been carefully chosen. With a clatter Lucinda dropped the spoon back into the bowl and stared at the empty plate, not saying a word.

'Didn't you realise?' Ann asked gently.

Lucinda sat for a while before answering. 'Not really,' she replied quietly.

Ann, bless her, didn't bat an eyelid. 'So you haven't done a test yet?'

Lucinda shook her head, trying to blink back tears.

'I take it this isn't a planned pregnancy.'

It was all Lucinda could do to shake her head.

'I'm sure you're worrying about nothing, it could be a false alarm.'

Lucinda gave a hollow laugh. 'I don't need to do a test.

I've had it at the back of my mind for the last few weeks. I guess I was trying to avoid facing up to it.'

'Ignoring it won't make it go away.'

'How did you guess?' Lucinda asked. 'Is it that obvious?'

'Only to me. I had terrible morning sickness with my boys, couldn't eat a thing. For someone like you who loves their tucker to suddenly be eating like a sparrow, well, I had a good inkling. Then seeing you go faint when Jack put in the chest drain. Cardiothoracic surgeons don't normally have weak stomachs. It all added up. Do you want to talk about it, Lucinda, or do you want me to mind my own business?'

Lucinda thought for a moment. Ann was the one person she knew who wouldn't be remotely offended if she told her to butt out. But she needed to talk, she needed some help badly.

'You don't mind me dumping this on you?'

Ann gave a big smile. 'See these shoulders? They're wide for a reason. Now, you take this.' She rummaged in her drawer and pulled out a specimen bottle. 'I don't need to tell you what to do with this. I'll pop over to the gynae ward and grab a pregnancy test. I'll have a check on the ward as well and then I'll tell Ellen we don't want to be disturbed. She'll just think we're going over a patient or the budget or something.'

Lucinda nodded. 'Ann,' she called to her departing back.

The woman swung around. 'You don't have to say it— I won't breathe a word.'

Lucinda shook her head. 'I know that already. I was going to say thanks for being here, for helping.'

Ann came over and gave her a warm hug. 'I haven't started yet.'

Waiting for Ann to return, Lucinda paced the floor. How,

she tried to fathom, could she have let this happen? Of all the stupid mistakes to make. She was a doctor and so was Seb for that matter. They should both have known better. But that beautiful Sunday morning as she had lain so warm in bed next to him, had felt his male urges stirring, their bodies awakening together, consequences and ramifications had seemed a million miles away. Even at the memory of his touch she felt a stirring within. It had all seemed so right then. She'd thought they'd had all the time in the world. How could she have known that it had all been about to end, barely before it had started?

Ann returned, putting the 'Knock and Wait' sign on the door.

'Are you ready?' she asked as she unwrapped the package which would determine her fate.

Lucinda shook her head. 'No, but do it anyway.'

Those two minutes were probably the longest of her life. She thought of the niggling worry, pushed to the back of her mind over the past few weeks, growing as the days passed and her symptoms became more apparent. At first she had put the exhaustion down to stress, lack of sleep, and they were both good reasons. Since Seb had gone from her life she felt as if she were living two lives, by day the consummate professional but by night a child lost. The nausea she had blamed on gastro, a bad take-away—anything but this. Lucinda wasn't a woman who wrote her cycles in her diary, like she never filled out her cheque stubs, so she'd had no idea when she'd been due. But as the weeks had dragged on and nothing had happened, she had known her fears were with good foundation and now she was about to have it confirmed. The result was a foregone conclusion.

Ann glanced at the indicator. 'Well, I don't think that leaves any room for doubt.' She pushed the test over the desk and Lucinda stared at the dark pink cross that had formed on the blotting paper. It felt strange. Nothing had changed from two minutes ago—she was still a doctor a woman—yet *everything* had changed. She was now pregnant. Growing inside her was a baby, a person in its own right, a permanent legacy of when her life had been perfect.

'Oh, God,' she groaned. 'Ann what am I going to do?'

Ann was over in a flash. 'You'll be fine,' she reassured. 'You'll do whatever has to be done. I take it this isn't the news you were hoping for?'

Lucinda shook her head.

'Then you're going to have to make some decisions.'

Lucinda stared at the pregnancy test for a moment and then looked up at Ann.

'I can't end the pregnancy, Ann, it just isn't me.'

Ann gave her a smile. 'Well, as strange as it might seem, I'm going to say it anyway—congratulations, Lucinda. It might not feel it now but this is going to be the best thing that's ever happened to you, and you hold on to that thought through all the difficult times. When you hold your baby in your arms all the problems you've had getting there will seem minute, I promise you that.' She gave her a hug.

'Do you want to tell me who the father is?'

Lucinda thought for a moment and took a deep breath. 'Seb,' she said quietly.

Again Ann managed not to look remotely surprised. 'I thought that was the way the wind was blowing for a while, and then it all seemed to die down. I'm glad I'm not losing my touch.'

Lucinda managed a small smile.

'Seb's a wonderful man,' Ann enthused. 'He'll be delighted. He'll take care of you.'

Lucinda angrily wiped away a tell-tale tear that had escaped down her cheek. 'It's not that straightforward. He's already had one failed marriage, remember. He's not going in to bat again unless the pitch is perfect—he said as much.'

'Maybe this will give him the push he needs. I'm an expert where Seb's concerned. Seb would never have slept with you if he wasn't serious. That man has had loads of women after him before, during and after his marriage, and he's never looked twice. He would never have let things get this far if he didn't think you were pretty special.'

'I think he does love me in some way, but there's Billy to consider. He doesn't think I'm stepmum material, he said so.'

'Seb said that?' Ann exclaimed, this time failing to keep the shock from her voice. 'I can't believe that—are you sure?'

'I was there, remember. He doesn't think I'm up to the job of being a stepmother. What on earth's he going to say when he finds out I'm actually having his baby? What if he's right? What if I'm not up to it.'

'Now, we'll have none of that talk,' Ann said firmly. 'Lucinda, you'll be a wonderful mother—don't you ever doubt that. And when Seb hears I'm sure, once the shock wears off, he'll be delighted, too.'

'I'm not going to tell him.' Lucinda said firmly.

Ann stood up. 'Lucinda I know I'm a mere nurse and you're the one with the medical degree but, without meaning to state the obvious, it's going to become pretty clear to everyone that you're pregnant. You said yourself that you're going to keep the baby and you're hardly going to leave work now and get a new job. Seb's going to have to be told.'

'No, he isn't.' With a shaking hand she retrieved the screwed-up memo from her pocket and handed it to Ann, who read it silently. 'He's handed in his notice,' Lucinda said wearily 'He's taking up a Chief of Anaesthetics position in Ballarat. He's leaving next month.'

'But he'll still hear about the baby—you know how word spreads.'

'By the time he hears he'll just assume I've met someone else.'

'Lucinda, he has a right to know,' Ann said, exasperated.

'No, Ann,' Lucinda said firmly 'He had a right when we were together. I'm not going to go to him with a begging bowl for a few dollars and some access visits I'd rather manage on my own. And, please, Ann, promise not to breathe a word.'

Ann nodded. 'You don't have to worry about that, it's not my place to tell him.' She sat down again. 'Right, let's deal with the practicalities. Have you managed to find a GP since you moved here?'

'No, there's been no need till now.'

'Right, I'll ring mine for you. I'll do it now. She's ever so good. Is that all right?'

Lucinda nodded her consent as Ann made the call.

'She can fit you in at two o'clock tomorrow—can you get away?'

Lucinda nodded her agreement. She had to get seen after all. This was going to be the first of many doctors' visits her schedule would have to accommodate.

'Ann, I haven't taken folate or been sleeping or eating properly. What if I've done the baby some harm?'

'Well, considering the way you ate before you got pregnant one could safely assume that you've got enough iron stores to open a mine, but welcome to motherhood.' Ann smiled. 'You never stop worrying.'

'How are you feeling?' Ann gave Lucinda a smile as she walked on the ward for the Christmas party.

'Terrified. It's a bit like getting ready for a date. I've spent an hour in the shower, shaved my legs, checked my bag a million times.'

'What for?' Ann laughed.

'Clean underpants, specimen jar, medicare card, private health cover card.'

'You wait till the baby gets here, you'll need a juggernaut to carry your bag then.'

Everyone gathered around the tree. Past patients and their parents, doctors, nurses. All the children's beds and cots had been moved and formed a huge arc around the tree, and the children's faces were expectant. Lucinda concentrated on the tree, trying not to catch Seb's eye as he held for dear life onto a thoroughly over-excited Billy.

Ann stepped forward. 'Now, we all know Christmas is a few days off but for very special children, which you all are, special things happen so Father Christmas has taken some time out of his busy schedule to pay you all a visit.' She put her hands up to her ears as the sound of bells filled the corridor.

'What's that noise?' she asked the grinning faces.

The children cheered and even the most unwell managed to sit up in their beds.

'*Ho! Ho! Ho!*' The doors swung open and Professor Hays, hardly needing any stuffing in his outfit, burst in as the place erupted. The next twenty minutes were mayhem as the children gathered round, extracting their gifts, all painstakingly chosen by Ann and beautifully wrapped. And finally when each child had opened their present and were chewing on the surprises in their lolly bags or tucking into cherries and mandarins if they were diabetic, the carols started.

Lucinda joined in with 'We Wish You A Merry Christmas', but as the cassette started to play 'Away In a

Manger' and the little voices joined in, it was too much. Stealing a look around the ward at the little faces covered by oxygen masks, the drips and monitors, she felt a huge lump in her throat. As happy as the ward was, it was tinged with sadness because they all knew for some it would be their last Christmas, and she thought of the ones like baby Kimberley who never even got to see one. Quietly she slipped away to the privacy of Ann's office. She wasn't alone. Ann had beaten her to it, sitting at her desk, with shaking shoulders.

'That hymn gets me every time,' she said with great tears pouring down her face as Lucinda entered.

Lucinda managed a smile, determined not to break down in front of anyone. 'I'll get you a tissue.'

'There aren't any—the kids all used them to have a snowball fight this morning,' Ann said through her tears, and as she held up a toilet roll it reminded Lucinda so much of that morning with Billy that there was nothing else to do but have a good cry.

With a sob she took the roll from Ann and tore off a few sheets. 'At least I can blame it on my hormones.'

Neither heard at first as Seb and Billy entered.

'Sorry to barge in, but Billy wanted to see you both,' Seb explained, his gaze not quite reaching Lucinda's eyes.

Billy handed them both a small parcel and Lucinda opened hers somewhat shakily.

A tiny gold robot stared back at her, and she swallowed hard a couple of times as she looked at it.

'Thank you, Billy, it's beautiful.' Ann had the same.

'It's to go on your necklace, I bought it with my own pocket money. They're solid gold,' Billy said importantly.

'Solid gold-*coloured*, Billy. You can't be too careful in these days of litigation. Billy managed to find a robot tie-

pin for Professor Hays, which I know he's going to love.'
Seb gave the women a wink.

'We can't find him anywhere, but guess what?'

'What's that?' Lucinda asked.

'I think the professor looks a bit like Father Christmas.
Dad said it's because they're both magic.'

'Notice anything different about me?' a theatrical voice
boomed from the open door. Bianca stood there with a huge
smile.

'Your braces are gone!' Lucinda exclaimed.

'Yes, yes,' Bianca said dismissively. 'But there's something else, can't you see?'

They all stared for a moment as Bianca stood there impatiently waiting. 'I'm wearing a bra!'

'So you are, and don't you look just gorgeous?' Ann
exclaimed.

Seb managed a small blush. 'Well, we'll leave you ladies
to discuss your secret women's business.' He laughed. 'Say
goodbye and thank you, Billy.'

As they left the office it took every ounce of self-control
she could muster to stop herself from running after the two
most important people in her life. Instead, she clung onto
the tiny metallic robot as Bianca handed Ann a present and
spoke at length about her recent growth spurt.

'I got something for you, too.'

'For me? How lovely you didn't need to do that.'
Lucinda opened the parcel to reveal the video of the film
they had been watching the night Bianca had arrested.

Lucinda was touched and told her so.

'See, you said there'd be a happy ending, and here I am.'
She gave Lucinda and Ann a small thumbs-up.

Lucinda gave Bianca a hug. 'That's true, but since that
night I've never been able to eat pizza.'

Bianca gave a laugh. 'Actually, neither have I.'

Once they were alone again, the room fell silent.

'This will be my last Christmas here. I think it's time to hang up my apron,' Ann said suddenly.

Lucinda looked at her, aghast. 'You can't be serious. This place would collapse without you.'

'No, it wouldn't, it would manage just fine. It gets harder each year, thinking about all the ones we've lost. I'm thinking of getting a nice job in a nursing home. At least when someone dies there you know they've had a fair crack.'

Lucinda thought for a moment. 'But you seem to cope so well with it all.'

'"Seem to" is right. It takes its toll on all of us, Lucinda, even you, I'm sure.'

Lucinda gave a small shrug. If she confided this to Ann she knew she would be lost. 'I just look at the bigger picture. Look at Billy, look at Bianca—there's more wins than losses.'

Ann gave her a quizzical look. 'Well, the wins are great but the losses are just too hard to take sometimes. You'd better go if you want to make your appointment.'

Lucinda made her way out of the hospital and took a tram to the address Ann had given her. She had been tempted to confide in Ann about her own feelings about work, too, but what good would it do? Even if she wanted to she couldn't leave now; she was hardly in the position for a career change. She was going to need her salary now more than ever.

CHAPTER NINE

DR INNES went over to the sink and washed her hands as Lucinda stood up and got dressed.

The GP got out a daisy wheel and started fiddling with it.

'So you don't know the date of your last menstrual period?'

'Er, no, but my dates are definitely right. You see, it could only have been then.'

Dr Innes gave her a small smile and reached for a pad.

'I think we might arrange for an ultrasound. Mr Field is an excellent obstetrician and he does his own ultrasounds. He's very nice to talk to, especially for first-time mums. I know you're a doctor but you'll still have a lot of questions.'

'I thought you didn't do routine scans until eighteen weeks. Is there a problem?'

Dr Innes hesitated for a moment. 'There's no problem, but your uterus seems rather larger than I'd expect at this stage, and if you're sure about your dates...' She carried on writing.

Lucinda felt as if the chair had been whipped from beneath her. She'd already had enough shocks in the last twenty-four hours, but now this! Her voice came out in an unsteady rasp. 'You're not thinking it could be twins?'

'Let's just wait and see, shall we?'

How many times had she herself said that to an anxious mother when she'd organised a test? But sitting on the other side of the fence, well, it was a whole new experience. 'How long till he'll be able to see me?'

Dr Innes reached for her phone. 'He's very popular but I know him well and, with you being a doctor, I'll see what I can do. I'm sure he'll squeeze you in. I must admit I'd want to know myself.'

Twins. Twins! It didn't bear thinking about. How on earth was she going to tell Seb this? And her mother!

'He'll see you in half an hour. Have you been to the loo recently?'

Lucinda shook her head.

'Good.' She went over to the sink and filled a glass with water. 'Drink this— all of it—so he gets a good view. I expect you need a glass of water anyway. It might be a false alarm. It will be nice to have a scan anyway. Sometimes it helps you get used to the idea of being pregnant if it wasn't planned.'

Bursting for the loo, she waited anxiously in the waiting room, trying and failing not to think about the impossibilities of raising two children. So much for her career. Single parents didn't make the best cardiothoracic consultants or so she thought. It wasn't as if she could think of one who had tried, but as a single parent of twins, it seemed impossible.

'Miss Chambers?' Expecting to see the receptionist, Lucinda reached for her bag and stood up.

'Just coming.' She was stunned when she saw the smiling face of Janine Stewart.

'I bet you weren't expecting to see me here. Are you here to review a patient?'

Lucinda gave a noncommittal shrug. 'Something like that. How are you, Janine? How are you and Mark coping?'

'It's been awful,' she admitted honestly. 'It still is. I expect it's going to take a long time. We've both been walking around like a couple of zombies, we just miss her so.' She wiped away a tear with the back of her hand. 'Christmas is going to be hard but, then, every day is. Mark was worried about me so he took me back for a check-up, and guess what?'

Lucinda didn't know what to say. They were in an obstetrician's waiting room after all, but what if she was wrong? Maybe they were here to give IVF another go.

'It's all right,' Janine said. 'We can't believe it either, but I really am. The one time in ten years we're not trying for a baby I go and get pregnant. The doctors don't know what to make of it, but I am having a baby, and it's all down to you.'

'Me? But how?'

'That "competition" you pretended to win. I don't know what they put in the curry but it worked. We only did it the once. Still, I guess that's all it takes.'

Lucinda gave Janine a wide smile. 'That's fantastic, but how are you coping with it, after all you've been through?'

'I'm trying not to get my hopes up, but I've just got a feeling it's meant to be. I even *feel* pregnant this time. With Kimberley I never did. Mr Field says I'm pumping with hormones and it all looks great on the ultrasound. After all the emotion of the past few weeks and me not knowing, I haven't been making allowances. Well, the fact I'm still pregnant is amazing in itself. In some ways I didn't want to be if that makes any sense. I felt this baby was sort of intruding on my grief for Kimberley, but I'm getting there.'

'It's a lot for you to deal with, but it's the most fantastic news. Where's Mark? He must be thrilled.'

'He's the same as me, just taking it one day at a time. But we're together and we're happy so we've got a lot to be grateful for, whatever happens.' A car tooted noisily outside, 'That will be Mark, we couldn't get a parking space nearer. Look, I won't be coming back to the Women's and Children's with this one. Obviously, if there's a problem I'll have no choice, but we kind of wanted to go somewhere else this time—not that you weren't all fantastic,' Janine added hastily.

'I understand. I'd feel exactly the same.'

'I know you won't want to give out your address so I won't ask, but can I drop you a line at the hospital and let you know how things go?'

'Don't be silly. Here.' Lucinda scribbled her home address on a piece of paper and handed it to Janine. 'Give me yours. It will be nice to keep in touch.'

The car tooted again and Janine wrote quickly.

'Good luck,' Lucinda called as Janine went out to her husband.

'Miss Chambers.' This time there was no mistaking the summons.

Straightening her shoulders, Lucinda turned and smiled.

'Just coming,' she said, and, following the receptionist, made her way down to the ultrasound room, wondering what fate held for her.

Mr Field was, as promised, a lovely doctor, chatty but professional. He introduced himself and asked a few questions.

'Well, I won't keep you in suspense. We'll go over everything thoroughly in your first antenatal appointment. Let's find out, shall we?'

He helped her onto the examination couch and placed the blanket over her as Lucinda lifted her gown. He squirted cold jelly onto her abdomen and Lucinda lay there, rigid.

'Do you want to see the screen?'

Lucinda thought for a moment. 'Not yet.'

He placed the probe on her abdomen and pushed against her full bladder. Lucinda listened to the familiar crackling as the machine zoned in. And then she heard it, loud and regular, her baby's heartbeat.

'Well, there's definitely one in there,' Mr Field stated. 'I'll do the measurements in a minute.' He moved the probe slightly and in just a few seconds Lucinda heard the same rapid sound. 'And there's number two.'

She lay there for a moment as the news sank in. Somehow hearing the heartbeats made it all seem a bit better—it was a sound she heard every day. But these were her own babies' heartbeats she was hearing, and it really was like music to her ears. She thought of Janine who had lain here before her, desperate for a child. Though this wasn't what she herself had planned, never in a million years, Lucinda there and then accepted that this was just the way it was. Lady fate had stepped in and given her not one but two babies and now she had to deal with the situation head on. Somehow she would.

'There's not another one hiding in there?' she asked nervously.

'No, just the two,' Mr Field said cheerfully.

'Can I see now?' He turned the screen and Lucinda gazed in increasing wonder at the tiny hearts beating, scarcely able to comprehend that there were two babies tumbling inside her.

Mr Field clicked away, taking measurements. 'Two placentas so they're not identical. Of course, too early to tell the sex—will you want to know?'

Lucinda shook her head. 'I'm getting used to surprises—why spoil it?'

And then it was over. Clutching her photo, she said her goodbyes, gratefully went to the loo and paid the bill. The afternoon sun was bright after the darkness of the ultrasound room. Catching the tram, she sat by a window and fished the picture from her bag. Looking up, she saw an old woman smiling at her.

'Is that your baby?' she asked, offering Lucinda a toffee.

Lucinda took the toffee with a smile. 'Actually, I'm having twins—see.' She showed her the photo.

'Looks like a map of the moon to me, but congratulations, love. Here, you'd better have another one.' She offered Lucinda another toffee. 'You'll be needing to keep your sugar up.'

Back at the hospital, unlocking her office, she paled as she saw Seb making his way out of PICU.

'Lucinda.' He gave her a smile.

'Where's Billy?'

'There's a Christmas party on Chest Med which he "had" to go to. Little devil. He's cleaned Father Christmas out already and it isn't even the twenty-fifth.' Though he was smiling, she could see the tiredness on his face.

'You're leaving,' she said simply.

Seb nodded. 'Seems my speech went down well. John told me at the conference about this job. I was only half listening but, well, things just aren't working out here. I don't want Billy to go to boarding school and I'm sick of nannies. This job's practically nine to five. It's a promotion, I know, but leaving a hospital like this for the country, some would see it as a bit of a side step. All the same, it's what I want.'

'Is it?'

Seb stared at her for a long time. Oh, she wanted so badly to put her hand up and touch his face but she just stood there. 'Sure, it's more admin than I'd like but Billy has to come first. His asthma is getting worse, and the country air will improve it. We'll be near Bella. As she pointed out, she's got four kids already so what's another one in the school holidays? Billy will have to go to after-school care a couple of nights or to Bella's but I'll be able to take him most mornings. He'll have his dad around, and Bella can be a constant feminine role model. He needs that, Lucinda. Gemma is being good but she's not going to provide what he needs.'

And it all made perfect sense. Seb was right—he did have to go. But it didn't stop her heart from aching as she listened.

'When are you leaving?'

'Two weeks. I'm just covering over Christmas and New Year. Billy's going to spend it in Sydney with Gemma and her parents. I can finish up here and do the big move myself. I think it would be all a bit much for him otherwise. I want to get Billy settled into his new home before he starts school. We've found a house.'

'Nice?'

'Too big, but it's got stables and Billy is desperate for a horse. We've done the allergy tests and unfortunately for me that's the one thing he's not allergic to, so it's going to be up at the crack of dawn for me, mucking out stables.'

Lucinda managed a smile. The vision of Seb and Billy riding together made her want to cry. He had got his life all sorted—how could she tell him now? Surely it was better this way?

'Sounds fun,' she replied lightly, but it came out all wrong, as if she was being sarcastic. Seb gave her a strange look

'It probably sounds awful to you, but I'm kind of looking forward to it.'

She gave a nod, terrified her voice might betray her again.

'You'll come to my leaving party.'

'Of course.'

And that was it. Lucinda lingered a moment, watching

him walk smartly along the ward. How she longed to call him back, to explain her apparent indifference. But how could she? That would mean telling him about the twins. How could she ruin his life just when he had it on track? She simply couldn't do it to him and to Billy.

And so she retreated back to where she was safe. Back to the days of old before Billy and Seb had spun her life around. She smiled less and worked ever harder, if that was possible.

Christmas Eve came and the hospital was in a frenzy of excitement. Although the theatres were only open for emergencies, Lucinda was kept busy with outpatients and ward work. Finally she made her way over to CGU.

'Anything for me?'

'Of course.' Ann gave her a smile. The ward was more than half-empty. 'Robert Good is doing amazingly well.' She nodded her head to the bed where a pale young boy lay. Lucinda had performed cardiac mesh repair on him only two days previously. 'I know it's a bit soon but his parents have asked, as he's doing so well, could you consider him for day leave tomorrow? Jack had a look, but said it was your call.'

Lucinda nodded. 'Yes, he mentioned it. What do you think?'

Ann gave a small shrug. 'He seems all right but, to be honest, if it was my son who had just had cardiac surgery I wouldn't want him home yet. I tried telling the parents, but you know what some people are like. They don't think we're doing much for him and think I'm just being pedantic.'

'OK, I'll take a look.' She walked over to the young patient. 'Good afternoon, Robert. How are you feeling?'

'Great. I just want to go home.'

Lucinda gave him a smile. 'Well, let's have a look at you.'

His parents hovered anxiously, obviously keen to have their son home.

'He feels a bit warm. What was his temp?'

Ann checked the chart. 'Thirty-seven at four o'clock.'

'Could you just check it again, please?'

Ann put the tympanic thermometer into the young boy's ear.

'Thirty-seven four.'

Lucinda finished her examination.

'Could I have a word, please?' She called the parents over to the office.

'I'm not happy for Robert to have day leave,' she said.

'But why not? Is something wrong?' Mr Good asked tersely.

'He has a low-grade temperature that I'd like to keep an eye on. It's probably nothing to worry about but I'd rather he stayed here.'

Mr Good stiffened his shoulders. 'Well, if his temperature's normal tomorrow, can he go home?'

'I'd really rather he stayed.'

'What's a couple of hours?' Mr Good demanded. 'It's not as if you're doing anything for him now. Just a couple of pills here and there. The kid should be home for Christmas.'

Lucinda began to feel irritated but kept her voice even.

'Mr and Mrs Good, I explained to you in Outpatients that if the operation was done on the twenty-second it would mean your son would have to spend Christmas in hospital, to which you agreed.'

'Yes,' Mr Good admitted. 'But he's done better than expected. Surely there's room for a bit of leniency? We've bought him a new computer game and he's desperate to try it out. What's he going to do here all day?'

Lucinda stiffened. 'Here skilled nursing staff will monitor him. If he develops a temperature, bloods will be taken promptly and if, heaven forbid, he develops any of a multitude of post-operative complications there will be staff immediately on hand to deal with them. As much as I can understand your desire to have your son home for Christmas, even allowing for leniency, I cannot in good faith allow him to go.'

Mr Good huffed and puffed a bit longer but Lucinda stood firm and finally they retreated to Robert's bed.

'Well, that told them. Good for you,' Ann remarked.

'Goodness, you perform open heart surgery and they moan you're not doing enough. If something untoward happened, they'd be the first to blame us for letting him go home. You'd think they'd just be grateful Robert's well. So much for Christmas spirit.'

'Speaking of Christmas spirit, where's yours?' Ann asked. 'I hear you're snapping at everyone.'

Lucinda pursed her lips. 'I am not,' she stated firmly, then relented. 'Well, maybe I am. I don't know, the nice me didn't seem to get very far.'

'Oh, yes, it did. It got you pregnant with twins,' Ann joked.

'Exactly. Oh, I don't know, Ann, maybe once Seb's gone it will be a bit easier. It's agony, seeing him every day and not being able to tell him.' She sat there glumly. 'On second thoughts, who am I kidding? It's going to be hell when he leaves. As much as I avoid him, it's nice knowing he's around. I just can't imagine not seeing him.'

Ann gave her a knowing look. 'Well, you'd better do something about it. Have you told your parents yet?'

Lucinda shook her head. 'There never seems a good

time. I'll probably get Christmas out of the way first. I don't want to ruin it for them.'

'They're not children, Lucinda. It's not as if you're telling them Father Christmas isn't real. I think now would be an excellent time. From what you've told me, their lives will be one big party over Christmas. It might be just the time to slip in the news, when they're not going to be sitting dwelling over things.'

Lucinda laughed at the idea. 'I don't think so. Can you just imagine? ''Well, happy Christmas for tomorrow. You enjoy your party tonight, and by the way your prodigy is about to become a single parent and you're going to be grandparents to twins. Say hi to the Merringtons for me.''' Lucinda shook her head. 'I'll probably fly up there in the new year once the prof is back. I'll have a couple of annual leave days by then.'

Ann gave her a dry smile. 'Oh, well, it's up to you, but you're going to have to let people know soon. You're starting to show.'

'Surely not,' Lucinda said, shocked. 'I thought that didn't happen for ages yet!' Standing up, she pulled her dress against her stomach. 'I just look a bit bloated.'

Ann laughed. 'I meant a bit higher up. You look as if you've had breast implants.'

'Awful, aren't they? I think I'm going to have to take myself off to Bianca's bra shop for a fitting,' Lucinda joked, but suddenly Ann shivered, and her face paled. 'Are you all right, Ann?'' Lucinda asked, concerned.

Ann gave her a worried look. 'I think so. I just went all cold, as if someone walked over my grave.'

'You're not getting one of your hunches, are you?' Lucinda asked, genuinely concerned.

Ann shook her head. 'I hope not. Still, I'll check the

patients carefully. It'd be awful to have one go off over Christmas.'

'I'll let you get on, then.' Lucinda stood up. 'Are you on in the morning?'

'Yes, just till one.'

'I'll say happy Christmas tomorrow, then.'

The evening stretched out before her. Home didn't sound tempting, but if she went to the doctors' mess she'd probably end up seeing Seb. Suddenly, for the first time in weeks she actually felt hungry. An evening at Suriyan's sounded good and then she could head home to watch 'Carols by Candlelight'. She made her way to the office to collect her bag, but typically now she had decided what to do with herself a spanner was thrown into the works as her emergency pager went off and the overhead system crackled.

'Cardithoracics to Emergency Department. ETA five minutes.'

Lucinda made her way across the hospital. ETA meant the expected arrival time so the paramedics must be bringing someone in. These were the patients she dreaded most. Usually desperately ill and requiring urgent intervention, in the emergency department more than anywhere you had to think on your feet.

She headed straight for the resuscitation room where a collection of staff was waiting around the empty resuscitation bed. Jack Wells greeted her.

'MVA with a penetrating chest injury. Paramedics said it was pretty bad.'

Lucinda nodded. 'Set up for a chest drain and have an emergency thoracotomy tray ready,' she said to the charge nurse.

'Done.'

Lucinda gave a small nod. Here the staff were incredibly

efficient. They made idle chit-chat, used to the drama, but Lucinda didn't join in. Instead, she focussed on the job ahead, aware that to the rest of the staff she probably looked aloof. The charge nurse handed her a lead gown to wear during the resuscitation so that X-rays could be taken without all the staff having to leave the patient.

'G'day, guys. What's the story?'

Seb, breathless from the run, took his place at the head of the bed, slipping on a lead gown while the charge nurse gave him the available details.

Seb listened intently as he set up his equipment. 'Fifteen years old, you said?' He started to pull up some drugs, carefully strapping the ampoules to the syringes so he would have all he needed easily to hand. 'Just the one coming in?'

The charge nurse nodded. 'Just the one. He's the passenger. The driver died at the scene.'

Lucinda felt the usual butterflies around Seb, but as soon as the paramedics wheeled in the teenager all of that was put to one side as she concentrated solely on the patient.

The accident and emergency consultant took the lead. 'On my count.'

The patient was deftly lifted onto the resuscitation bed and a swift assessment was made. Seb checked the airway and sucked out the secretions then introduced an endotracheal tube. Lucinda examined the chest while listening to the paramedics.

'It wasn't a penetrating wound, as we first thought, just a branch, very superficial. But he's got decreased breath sounds on the left.' Lucinda nodded.

'He's tight,' Seb said.

'X-ray.' The radiographer called his warning and everyone not in lead gowns made their way briefly out of the examination room. Lucinda hesitated, torn for a moment.

She knew the lead gown protected her but she didn't want to expose the babies unnecessarily. Once her pregnancy was out in the open there would be no question of her staying, but to leave now could raise a few eyebrows. But now was such a vital stage in the pregnancy and the babies had to come first.

She made her way outside and grabbed the arm of one of the paramedics that had brought the boy in.

'Was it a parent with him that died?'

The paramedic shook his head. 'No, another kid. Wayne Blackwell. He had his licence on him. Only got his P Plates last week. Such a bloody waste.'

The resuscitation doors slid open.

'All clear.'

Lucinda stepped inside and Jack looked up from the patient.

'Where did you disappear to?'

She could feel Seb's eyes on her.

'I just wanted to check something with the paramedics.' It was a bit of a feeble excuse but Jack just nodded.

'He's tight,' Seb stated again.

'I'll put a chest tube in. Here are the films now.'

The films confirmed her suspicions—a massive haemo-pneumothorax.

It took Lucinda only seconds to insert the chest tube. There was no time for local anaesthetic and no need as the patient was deeply unconscious. Fresh blood poured down the tube.

They all worked together, each with his or her own skills and specialities but united in their efforts to save this young life. 'I'd like him up in Theatre as soon as possible,' Lucinda said, examining the films more closely.

'Sure,' the accident and emergency consultant said. 'The surgeons are happy with his abdomen, but his pelvis is shattered. Neuro want a quick CAT scan before he goes up. Is that all right?'

Lucinda nodded. 'I'll go ahead and scrub.'

She raced ahead up to the theatres where the staff were already setting up.

Once her hands were scrubbed the theatre sister helped her into a gown. 'He's on his way up, no name as yet. Apparently he's got a large subdural haematoma—he just blew a pupil.'

'What a mess.' But there was no time to dwell on it. Seconds later the young boy was wheeled in and together they continued their efforts to save him. The neurosurgeons performed an urgent craniotomy to evacuate the blood clot that was pressing on his brain. Lucinda performed a thoracotomy and repaired a large laceration on his pulmonary vein. Seb monitored his vital signs closely, relaying his messages clearly to the theatre nurses and surgeons, yet he still managed to find the time to talk soothingly to his patient.

Finally the mammoth operation was over and wearily Lucinda made her way to the recovery area, where Seb was still with the patient before his transfer to PICU.

'Have we got a name yet?' she asked the nurse.

'Humpty Dumpty for now, but the police are apparently coming up. They've got some details.'

'All right. When they get hold of the parents, page me. I'm going to have a quick shower.'

Aiming the hot water onto her neck, Lucinda felt the tension in her shoulders start to melt.

Stupid kid, she thought, but not unkindly. She tried to put aside the image of the police knocking on his parents' door on Christmas Eve of all nights. Replacing the soap, she closed her eyes as she thought of the other boy, the one that hadn't even made it to casualty. Wrapping a towel around her, she stepped out of the shower, to find Seb standing there. The showers were unisex but she couldn't help feeling embarrassed to see him, yet one look at his angst-ridden face and she knew the sight of her half-naked was the furthermost thing from his mind.

'What's wrong?' she asked, feeling the hairs stand up on the back of her neck. 'It's not Billy?' she begged.

Seb shook his head slowly. 'No, it's not Billy, thank God. Lucinda, that boy we just operated on—his name is Jake. Jake Benton. He's Ann's son.'

Lucinda's hands flew to her face and she covered her eyes. This was the worst nightmare for all hospital personnel—that it might be a member of your family wheeled in. For Lucinda, having her family in Queensland had allayed that fear, but she had felt a stab of it that day when Billy had been readmitted and he wasn't even her son. How on earth would Ann be feeling?

'No, oh, no. Poor Ann. Does she know?' The towel she had wrapped around her started to slip and Seb gently pulled it tight, covering her. She was vaguely aware of feeling grateful to him for protecting her dignity. He steered her to the little wooden bench where she shakingly sat down.

'Not yet. She's still on the ward. We only just found out. I'm going to go across now. I thought I'd better warn you.'

Lucinda gulped. 'She had a sort of premonition something was wrong. I just assumed it was one of the patients. I never dreamt…'

'How could you have?' he said gently.

Lucinda took a deep breath. 'I'll come with you. You don't want to do that on your own.'

Seb looked into her eyes. 'Are you sure? It's not going to be very pleasant.'

Lucinda stared back. She longed to rest her head on his

chest, longed for him to put his arms around her, but instead she nodded simply. 'Ann's my friend. I should be there for her. She'd do the same for me.'

Seb stood up and, opening the linen cupboard, pulled out a pair of theatre greens and politely turned his back. 'Get dressed quickly, then. You know how gossip spreads. I don't want her finding out by accident.'

They made their way across the hospital to CGU, Lucinda with her hair dripping down her back. There was no small talk, no planned speeches. They arrived on the ward and with relief saw that Ann was alone in her office.

She smiled when she saw them together, a questioning look crossing her face. Lucinda guessed she must be assuming they were finally together. But when she saw their worried faces, her smile faded.

'What's wrong?' The air hung heavy and Seb cleared his throat.

'There's no easy way to say this, Ann, but I've got some bad news for you.'

Ann stood there, her face paling as she prepared herself for the news.

Seb continued gently. 'Jake has been involved in a motor vehicle accident.'

'Is he…?'

'He's not dead, Ann, but he's been very badly hurt.'

'How badly?' Gently Seb sat her down and, dragging another chair over, sat directly opposite her, taking both her hands in his.

'He was brought in a couple of hours ago. We only just found out it was your son.'

'Seb, tell me what his injuries are.'

He nodded and in the gentlest way possible he went through Jake's horrific injuries. Afterwards he sat there silently, letting the news sink in—not moving, just tenderly holding Ann's hands.

Finally Ann spoke. 'I have to see him.'

'We'll take you there now. The police have gone over to tell Tod.'

She stood up and smoothed her dress, but as she started to walk her legs gave way and Lucinda dashed to help her. 'It's all right, Ann. You lean on us we'll take you to Jake now.'

'The ward,' Ann said vaguely.

'The ward will be fine.' They all looked up as Heather Gibbs, the nurse co-ordinator, arrived, her face a picture of concern. 'You go and see your son.'

They walked with Ann to the theatre recovery area. Normally relatives weren't allowed in there when patients were so critical, but in this case no one was going to make a fuss.

Seb took control and managed to say all the right things, and Lucinda realised he could empathise to some extent with what Ann was feeling for he, too, had stood there, looking at his own son. Lucinda busied herself, checking the monitors and drug sheets and IV orders.

'We're going to transfer him over to PICU now,' the theatre sister said, and Ann nodded.

'I'll go and see if Tod's here.' She bent and gave Jake a gentle kiss on his cheek.

'Hang in there, Jake,' she said through her tears, and looked over to where Seb and Lucinda stood. 'I'm glad you two were on tonight. How long are you on, Seb?'

'All night.'

Ann gave a worried look. 'But you're not supposed to be. I've seen the roster. What about Billy?'

'Ann, Billy's with Gemma, and I'm only doing what you did for me. I couldn't be anywhere else.' He gave her a brief hug. 'Now, you go with Lucinda and find Tod. I'll stay with Jake. I promise I won't leave his side. We're going to get you through this, Ann. Stop worrying about everybody else.'

As a doctor, once Theatre was over there wasn't much more Lucinda could do for the time being, but as a friend there was plenty. Seb, as good as his word, parked himself on a stool by Jake's bedside and stayed there all night while Lucinda helped Ann. Dialling phone numbers when her hand was shaking too much, fetching her coffee, and Panadol when she developed the most awful migraine. Taking her husband Tod out onto the roof for a cigarette when it all became too much. And somehow together they made it through the endless night.

'Thought you could use this.' Lucinda stirred from a light doze.

Seb handed her a steaming cup and Lucinda took a grateful sip.

'Yum. Where did you get a cappuccino on Christmas morning? Is the canteen having a party?'

'I bunged one of the orderlies a few dollars and he headed over to Southbank. A lot of the restaurants are doing Christmas lunch so they're open.'

'You should have bunged him a bit more and got some muffins,' Lucinda said in a grumbling voice, but Seb knew she was only joking.

'Lucindah, have you any idea the damage a single muffin can do to your thighs?'

It was a perfect impersonation of her mother and Lucinda managed a smile. 'How's Jake? Any change?'

Seb shrugged. 'No change, but I guess no news is good news at the moment. We're just going to have to play the waiting game. Are you going to go home and have a rest? You look exhausted, Lucinda.' He sounded concerned.

'I'll stay. I can always go to one of the on-call rooms if I'm getting in the way.'

'That's the last thing you're doing. You've been a great help to Ann. You two are really close, aren't you?'

'She's hard not to like.'

He picked up the cardboard tray with the coffees. 'I guess it's not really appropriate to say merry Christmas, given the circumstances, but you know what I mean.'

'I know,' she said softly. 'But it is a time for miracles.'

'Let's hope so,' Seb said solemnly, and made his way back onto PICU.

She sat there awhile, drinking her coffee, and though her thoughts were with Ann her mind drifted to Seb. His had been the first face she had woken up to on Christmas morning and the only face she ever wanted to wake up to, but their time had been and gone. It might be a time for miracles, she thought sadly, but it would be selfish to wish for two, and of them both, Jake was probably the safer bet.

CHAPTER TEN

DESPITE the sweltering weather, it was the bleakest of Christmases. Lucinda duly rang home and tried but failed miserably to inject any enthusiasm into her voice. Not that Abigail appeared to notice.

'Guess what your father got me for Christmas?'

'I have no idea.'

'No, go on, try and guess.'

'Just tell me, Mum,' Lucinda said wearily, her mind on far more important things.

'Spoilsport. Well, you'd never have guessed anyway. We're going skiing in Europe—doesn't that sound so-o glamorous? It was a huge surprise. Your father got our secretary involved and together they've rigged it so we've got a full three weeks off. I can't wait.'

'You're going skiing? Mum, you've never even seen snow.'

'Goodness, no, Lucinda. I may be going skiing but I certainly won't be doing any, perish the thought. Could you imagine the havoc a fall could wreak at my age? Not that I look it, of course. I went for a check-up last month and my darling GP said I had the body of a thirty-year-old.'

'Which one?' Lucinda tried to joke, but her mother wasn't listening.

'Anyway, apparently the après-ski is simply *très bien*, so France, here I come.'

Lucinda managed a laugh. 'No doubt your winter wardrobe will cost more than the plane tickets.'

'Of course, darling, you have to look the part. Lucinda,

you are all right, aren't you?' her mother asked suddenly. 'You're not feeling homesick or anything?'

Lucinda paused, momentarily stunned that her mother had even noticed. 'I'm fine, Mum. We had some bad news at the hospital overnight.'

Abigail seemed to accept her explanation. 'Oh, dear. I was actually just thinking this morning, do you realise this is the first Christmas that we haven't seen each other? Not that we're a turkey-and-singing-round-the-tree-type family, but we've always managed at least a glass of champers together. I suppose you were too busy to notice. It was just a thought, that's all.'

Lucinda found herself smiling into the telephone. 'I was actually thinking just the same thing.'

After hanging up, she sat for a few moments, just staring at the telephone. It took a few seconds to register that Seb had come into the room.

'Are you all right?'

Lucinda looked up. 'I was just talking to my mum. Funny, she actually sounded as if she was missing me. I must be going soft or something. I'm actually missing them.'

Seb smiled. 'That's what families do to you. Can't live with them, can't live without them. I just spoke to Billy.'

'How is he? Did you manage to get a word in?'

Seb gave a small shrug 'He told me everything Santa had bought him and all that, but he was a bit teary.'

'Is it your first Christmas apart?'

Seb gave a small nod. 'I'm normally on call more often than not, but it's very different to being thousands of kilometres away. Not that the last few years have been particularly joyous occasions, but we at least managed to put on a united front for Billy's sake.'

She ventured a little further, she simply had to know more. 'How are things going now with Billy and Gemma?'

'Good, touch wood.' He reached over to the small coffee-table. 'Now she doesn't have the daily grind, as she called it, she actually seems to be enjoying motherhood—in small portions, mind. She'll soon have had enough but at least this way Billy feels like he's got a mum who cares, even if it is only in short bursts.'

Lucinda stood up. She had wanted to know but it simply hurt too much. 'I'm going to have a shower.'

'Lucinda?'

She turned.

'I couldn't help but notice yesterday when I came and got you from the theatre showers.' Lucinda held her breath. Surely he hadn't noticed anything. But she had to think on her feet when Seb continued, 'You were wearing the robot Billy bought you on your necklace.' Seb's eyes searched her face for a reaction and Lucinda opened her eyes wide, feigning surprise.

'Was I really?' She pulled her chain out from inside her theatre top. 'So I am. I must have forgotten to take it off after he gave it to me.'

'It'll turn your chest green.'

As she walked to the showers she let out a sigh. That had been a bit too close. What would Seb have said if he'd known the truth? That she'd actually gone to a jewellers and had had the tiny little robot heavily gold plated the same day Billy had given it to her, after it had indeed left a large dirty green streak in her cleavage. Lucinda had probably spent a hundred times its original price but it had been worth every last cent. Somehow, wearing it, she felt closer to them both. Silly maybe, but who ever said love was sensible?

After her shower she made her way back to PICU, just

in time to see Ann coming out. 'I was just coming to see you. How's things?'

Ann looked grey. Her uniform had been replaced by some theatre greens and her eyes were swollen and puffy.

'No change,' she said wearily. 'Tod wants me to go and lie down but I don't want to leave Jake.'

'I know you don't,' Lucinda said sympathetically. 'But Tod's right. You haven't slept in over twenty-four hours, Ann. You have to get some rest.'

'I couldn't sleep. Every time I close my eyes I see his face…' Her voice was rising and Lucinda could hear the note of hysteria creeping in.

'I'll get you something to help you sleep.'

'I don't want to be knocked out. What if I don't hear? What if there's any change?'

'Ann.' Lucinda's voice was firm without being unkind. 'I'm not going to give you a general anaesthetic, just 10 mg of temazepam. It's only light, it will just help you to rest. Now, Jake's going to need you to be strong—Tod, too. We can't have you fainting all over the place. What help will that be to Jake?'

Ann seemed to accept this and Lucinda led her to one of the on-call rooms where Ann, calmer now, lay on the bed.

'Just wait here. I'll be back in five.'

She walked to CGU where Ellen was on the telephone. Hastily she finished her call. 'What can I do for you, Miss Chambers?'

'Can you give me 10 mg of temazepam? Ann needs to sleep. I'll sign for it.'

Ellen got her keys out of her pocket and opened the drug cupboard.

'There you go. Tell her that we're all thinking of her. If there's anything we can do, you will let us know?'

Lucinda nodded as she signed the drug book. 'At this stage all we can do is wait and hope, but thanks for this. If she can get a couple of hours rest it will be a big help.'

Lucinda filled a polystyrene cup from the sink and Ann swallowed the pill meekly.

'Now, once you're resting I'll go and tell the PICU staff and Tod what room you're in. Of course they'll come and get you if anything changes, but Jake's stable at the moment, Ann. Tomorrow or the day after, when they extubate him, we'll know a lot more. You need to keep your strength up for then. Now, close your eyes.'

But she didn't. She lay there and with brimming eyes stared directly at Lucinda. 'One minute they're babies and the next... I don't know where the time goes. Before you know it they're teenagers and they think they're invincible. I know he did the wrong thing but he's still my baby. He didn't deserve this. What if it had been Jake that died? I don't think I could have gone on.'

'Shh,' Lucinda soothed. 'It wasn't Jake. You just have to be grateful for that.'

The pill was starting to take effect and Ann's eyes grew heavy. 'Don't let Seb go without knowing, Lucinda. Your babies deserve a father. I couldn't do this without Tod. You'd be so good together, I just know.'

Lucinda sat there with tears rolling down her cheeks but Ann was too out of it to notice. 'Don't worry about that now, Ann,' she said in a shaking voice. 'You sleep now.'

Finally Ann drifted off and Lucinda sat there until she was sure Ann wasn't about to wake up. Tiptoeing out of the room, she gently closed the door and made her way over to PICU. Seb was checking Jake's pupil reaction. Tod was holding his son's hand. Carols were belting merrily from the radio, but not loud enough to drown the hiss of the ventilators and the bleeping of the monitors. 'Joy To The World'.

What joy? she thought angrily, and then checked herself. The last thing she wanted to become was bitter. Yet it was the most ironic of scenes—sad because Jake and the other children here were so desperately ill on Christmas day of all days. Sad because Seb was without his son today, and unaware of the twins she was carrying.

But in some ways if it wasn't happy exactly, there was an air of hope. A feeling of quiet efficiency, guarded optimism for these young lives surrounded by dedicated staff and family that cared. There was joy, too, for her, and Lucinda acknowledged that next Christmas, God willing, she would be spending it with her babies. Seb looked up as she stood there and Lucinda managed a small smile.

'Ann's asleep. She's in on-call 2.'

Seb nodded. 'Why don't you go home, too, Lucinda? Grab some shut-eye. You look completely worn out.'

'I'd rather be here,' she said.

'Take your own advice, Lucinda. Who knows what's going to come through the doors of A and E? You need to rest while you can.'

Lucinda nodded. He was right, of course. And so she collected her bag and without bothering even to change she walked back to her flat, still dressed in her theatre gear. As she wearily let herself in she headed straight for her bed. Too tired to even pull back the covers, she lay on the top and, closing her eyes, for once she went straight to sleep.

The ringing of the telephone broke into her dreamless sleep. Fuddled, she reached for the receiver.

'Lucinda, darling.'

'Mum?' She sat up. 'What time is it?'

'About eight. Your father's had too much brandy and is

snoring away. Such a revolting sight. I thought I'd ring you.'

'Is everything all right?' Lucinda asked cautiously. Never in living memory had she been on the phone to her mother twice in the same week, let alone twice on the same day!

'That's what I was about to ask you. I know you said things had been a bit grim at the hospital, but I can't help thinking there's something else wrong. You can talk to me, you know. I am your mother.'

Abigail's concern caught Lucinda completely off guard and she sat silently on the bed, holding the telephone.

'Lucinda, are you still there? Say something,' her mother demanded.

'I'm pregnant, Mum.'

It was Abigail's turn to be silent. Lucinda heard her intake of breath and found she was holding her breath as well.

'You're what?' Abigail gasped a moment later, and Lucinda could hear the absolute horror in her mother's voice. 'You are joking, I hope.'

Lucinda didn't reply but it didn't matter. Her mother had plenty to say. 'So who's the father—that anaesthetist you brought to lunch?'

'Yes, Mum, but we're not together any more. He's moving to the country with his son.'

'Oh, he is, is he? Well, we'll soon see about that. You're not going to have it, are you?'

'Of course I am,' Lucinda cried.

'My goodness. This sort of thing happens to teenage girls, not women in their thirties. You're both doctors, for heaven's sake. Didn't you learn about birth control in medical school? How,' she asked, 'do you expect to look after it? It's simply not feasible. You've got your career to think of.'

They were the same questions Lucinda had been battling with. She fought back her tears. Oh, well, she might as well tell her all of it.

'I'm having twins, Mum.'

'My God, Lucinda. Well, this just gets better and better. Twins! What is Seb—some sort of hippy guru that goes around impregnating women? Can't he take the twins to the country with him and his precious son, and they can all live in their commune together?'

'Mum, you're being silly,' Lucinda said, but Abigail hadn't finished yet.

'No, you're being silly, Lucinda. All those years at the best private schools, *the* top medical school and a career going somewhere, and you're about to throw it all away— for what? If you think I'm going to babysit, think again. I've done my child-rearing. What am I going to tell everyone? It's just so, well, embarrassing.'

Lucinda had listened to enough. Anger rose within her. Hell, she hadn't expected an easy ride when she told her mother but a little bit of encouragement wouldn't have gone amiss.

'You can tell your friends what ever you like. I really couldn't care less what they think. And don't worry. I wasn't counting on you to be around to help. It's not as if you've much experience with babies.'

'What's that supposed to mean?' Abigail interrupted furiously.

'Well, how many of my nappies did you change, Mum? You certainly didn't put your career on hold for me. Why would you do it for your grandchildren?'

'How dare you speak to your mother like that?'

'Mum, I have to go.' Lucinda said.

'I haven't finished yet.'

'Well, I have.' She put down the phone and then, after

checking her pager was working, took the telephone off the hook. With a sigh she lay back on the bed. Her hands instinctively reached down and gently she massaged her stomach.

She'd told her mother and, as expected, Abigail had signed herself off the help roster. Ann, however much she might have wanted to help, wasn't going to be able to now. And Seb, well, he had to get his life sorted with Billy.

'Don't worry,' she said in a trembling voice to the babies inside her. 'We'll manage.' Her voice wavered. 'We'll do fine by ourselves.'

Jake was gradually weaned off the ventilator. It took longer than had been hoped and he was still disorientated and confused from his head injury, but the neurosurgeons were cautiously optimistic that this would resolve over the coming days and there would be no residual brain damage. His chest drain was removed and finally he was transferred to the orthopaedic ward where his shattered pelvis would keep him in bed for the next few weeks.

For Ann and Tod the days were endless the nights even longer. They had the unenviable task of going to the other boy's funeral, and when Lucinda saw Ann when she returned from the service she was shocked by how much Ann seemed to have aged.

'They'll turn you grey,' Lucinda remembered her joking to Seb. It seemed that Ann, yet again, had been proved right.

For Lucinda, too, the days were torture. Seb's departure grew ever more imminent and she felt a growing panic. Was she doing the wrong thing in not telling him? Billy's robot still hung around her neck. Not only was she depriving Seb of his children but Billy of his half-brothers or -sisters. What right did she have to do that? The agony of indecision weighed heavily on her. So many times she was tempted to tell him, but it never seemed the right time. Her throat would go dry and Seb would give her a quizzical look until she made some excuse as to why she had said she needed to see him.

New Year's Eve found her sitting alone in her flat with the balcony doors open. She could hear the trams clattering by, carrying revellers to their various parties, hear the joyous calls of partygoers. It only served to make her feel even more alone. With a sigh she pulled the balcony door closed. The intercom buzzing caught her unawares. With a surge of hope she thought it might be Seb and then checked herself. It was probably just the neighbours to warn her of a noisy party. Never did it enter her head that it might be Abigail.

'Mum, what on earth are you doing here?'

Abigail brushed past her. 'Before the big speeches I simply must lie down.' She made her way dramatically over to the sofa. 'Get me some pillows—quickly, Lucinda,' she ordered.

Lucinda rushed to her bed and grabbed the pillows. Whatever was wrong? Anxiously she tucked the pillows behind her mother's head.

'Not there, Lucinda. Put them under my legs.'

'But why?' Lucinda demanded. 'Mum, what on earth's wrong?'

'My ankles have swollen. Look at the size of them. I have to elevate them. If a few hours on a plane from Queensland can do this, what am I going to be like when we go to France?' Lucinda hid a smile as her mother continued. 'Mind you, we'll be flying first class so I can keep my legs up all the way. I had to slum it in economy to get here. All the decent seats were taken—can you imagine?'

'I've only ever flown economy,' Lucinda said truthfully, 'and I've never had a problem.'

Abigail screwed up her nose.

'But, Mum, what are you doing here, on New Year's Eve of all nights? I thought you were going on a cruise on the river.'

Abigail waved her hand. 'Never mind about some silly cruise. I've come to apologise to my baby.'

Lucinda's jaw dropped.

'Don't look so shocked—I can admit when I'm wrong.'

'I'm sorry too, Mum,' Lucinda said graciously. 'It must have been an awful shock.'

'You can say that again. Your poor father's still on the brandy.'

'Is he very upset?' Lucinda asked nervously.

'No. Isn't that the strangest thing? He's completely stunned, but aren't we all? Your father, once he got over the initial surprise, is actually delighted, keeps wanting to celebrate. I'm not quite there yet but I'm coming along. It will just take some getting used to. I actually read an article on the plane about supermodels who deliberately have a baby without a man, well, not completely—you know, a one-night stand or IVF. It's apparently quite trendy.'

Lucinda tried not to laugh. 'Mum, I'm not a supermodel.'

'Well, you could have been if you'd wanted to. I got you a present. Pass me my bag.'

Lucinda did as she was told and Abigail handed her a huge jar of cream.

'You have to massage it in three times a day—religiously, mind. It will help to prevent stretch marks.'

'Mum, you know as well as I do that nothing can prevent stretch marks.'

'Well, it's worth a try and, let's face it, you need all the help you can get. Have you any idea the havoc twins will wreak on your body? But don't worry, darling. I couldn't operate on my own baby but I'm sure Malcolm will give you a free abdominoplasty. He's a great surgeon. He's done a few things for me but that's my little secret.'

All Lucinda could do was laugh. 'Mum, you're completely crazy, do you know that?'

'I know. You've obviously had an ultrasound?'

Lucinda unpinned the photo from the fridge and handed it to Abigail.

'Golly,' she said as she stared at the photo. 'There really are two in there. But that's just like us Chambers, isn't it? We don't do anything by halves. Look at you, Lucinda, good-looking, clever and incredibly fertile.' She gave Lucinda a wink and patted the sofa beside her. 'Come and sit down and tell me all about it.'

And so she did, telling her all. Abigail surprised even herself by actually listening for once, and when the clock struck midnight they stood on the balcony together, watching the fireworks light up the Melbourne sky line.

'Happy New Year, Mum.'

Happy New Year, Lucinda. It's going to be a big year for you, for all of us really. I can't believe I'm going to be a grandmother.'

Lucinda nodded, watching as a rocket soared upwards. 'I'm scared, Mum.'

'Lucinda Chambers!' her mother barked. 'Stand up straight and take a deep breath. You can handle anything.' It was the same line she had used over and over when it had been time to go back to boarding school or Lucinda's exams had been about to begin, but this time Abigail reached out and took hold of her daughter's hand, her voice softening as she continued, 'I'm here now. We'll get there.'

Those few days with her mother were precious. Instead of reminding Lucinda of the calorific value of each mouth-

ful she ate, Abigail went and bought a blender and mag-
icked up wicked mango and banana smoothies, adding huge
dollops of ice cream to welcome Lucinda's returning appetite. But all too soon it was time for her to leave. Lucinda
sat on the bed, watching as her mother packed with military
precision, separating each carefully folded article with layer
upon layer of tissue paper. Even her undies were individ-
ually wrapped.

'I really feel awful, leaving you,' Abigail said as she
collected up her numerous creams from the dressing-table.
'Are you sure you don't want me to ring your father and
cancel the skiing? We can go any time.'

Lucinda shook her head. 'Please, don't, Mum.'

'But it's Seb's leaving party tonight. I should be here for
you.'

'I'll be fine. You go and have a great time.'

'I might head off to Paris while I'm there—see what I
can get for the twins. The French are so chic. Their babies
must be, too.' She turned then, her face suddenly serious.

'Seb has to know, Lucinda. I agree it might be better to
let him get settled into his new home but you'll have to
tell him soon.'

'I know, Mum. Just let me get tonight over with and then
I'll work something out.'

'Do you really have to go tonight? It might be a bit much
for you.'

'I'll be fine and, anyway, I've got no choice. I'm expected to be there. I'll just go for a couple of drinks to be
seen.'

Abigail closed her case and checked the straps. 'You're
sure you don't want me to stay.'

'Positive.'

Despite her declarations, Lucinda was anything but fine.
Seb had served the hospital well over the years and in re-

turn he was being given a big send-off. The party was being held in the doctors' mess and everyone had chipped in. All the guests had a list of what bottle to bring so cocktails could be mixed.

Lucinda made her way up the steps. Despite the warm night, she shivered in her flimsy dress, a grey chiffon with shoestring straps that flowed gently and covered the tell-tale bulge that was definitely, despite what the books said, starting to show already. It was the only dress in her ward-robe that fitted well, and she just hoped the thin straps held up against the weight of her ever-increasing bosom.

Handing over her bottle, she looked anxiously around the room.

'Lucinda.' Pete marched over. 'Have you heard?'

'What?'

Pete was grinning like a Cheshire cat. 'Mr Felix isn't coming back and the prof has had a quiet word to me. He's going to speak to you, too.'

Lucinda stared back at him. 'You mean...'

'That's right,' Pete said triumphantly, 'I've finally made it. And wait until you hear what they've got in store for you. I hope your passport's up to date.'

Lucinda managed to smile but inside her heart sunk. It meant she was going to have to tell the professor sooner rather that later. It was just another thing to worry about on top of everything else.

'It's supposed to be hush-hush,' Pete carried on, 'but everyone knows. I've already had four champagnes thrust at me.'

Lucinda smiled, genuinely this time. 'You deserve it, Pete. Now, what are you going to do about that woman of yours?'

Pete smiled. 'Well, now, I might just have to make an honest woman of her.'

Lucinda leant over and gave him a kiss on the cheek. 'I want an invitation to the wedding, remember. I love wearing a hat.'

'The speeches are about to start. I must go and find Ellen. Come over and sit with us.'

'I'll just stand here and listen, thanks, Pete. I'll be over in a bit.'

'You're sure? Can I get you a drink, then?'

Lucinda gave him a smile. 'I'm fine, Pete. Go and find Ellen.' He made his way across the room as the lights dimmed and everyone hushed. She wanted to be alone for this and she listened with tears sparkling in her eyes as colleague after colleague spoke about Seb. Everyone here had known him for longer than her, and she couldn't help but feel a stab of jealousy as they recounted stories about him, tales from his past where she didn't belong. She listened quietly as they wished him well for the future where she didn't fit in either. All the speeches came down to the same thing—Seb was a rare blend indeed, compassionate and caring but funny, too, a wonderful man, a brilliant doctor, and everyone would miss him. She could second that.

And then it was Seb's turn to speak. Taking the microphone, he looked his usual confident self, but she could hear the emotion in his voice as he thanked everyone for coming.

'You've been a great team to work with over the years. But it's been so much more than just work with you guys. You've all been there for me through all the ups and downs with Billy, and I know there's been more than enough drama there. Hopefully now things can settle down for both of us but, rest assured, we'll come back and visit often. We're going to miss you all, too.'

For a second Lucinda thought his eyes met hers but his gaze travelled past her. She stood there quite still, memorising every detail of his beautiful face, the face that might be apparent in the features of his children. How could she stand here and watch him leave? How could she just stand there and let him walk out of her life when there was so much that needed to be said?

And then it hit her. It was because she loved him and Billy, too, that she was letting them go, letting them have this time to get their lives together before she complicated things yet again for them. Letting them have a breathing space to settle in before she turned their worlds upside down. Seb didn't love her enough, didn't think she was up to being a stepmother to Billy. When she saw him again she would have things worked out, be able to give him the news without breaking down, without telling him how much she loved him, leaving him free to get on with his own life.

She held onto that thought and when Seb replaced the microphone in its stand and left the stage it was the only thing that stopped her rushing over to him.

'We should be here waving the two of you off together. You're not just going to let him go, are you?'

Lucinda swung around and there was Ann. 'I have to, Ann, but I am going to tell him.'

'When?'

'In a couple of months or so. By then I'll be more sure of how I'm going to cope. It will be easier telling him if I at least know what my plans are.' She swallowed hard a couple of times and then managed a smile. 'I didn't expect to see you here.'

'I couldn't let Seb go without a proper goodbye, and nor should you.'

'It's just not that simple,' Lucinda argued, but Ann wasn't giving in.

'It's as simple as you want it to be. You're having his

babies, Lucinda. I know what he said, but I'm sure he didn't mean it, not Seb. He's special and—'

But Lucinda cut her off. 'Just leave it, Ann, please.' Ann nodded but Lucinda could tell there was plenty more she wanted to say. 'How's Jake?' Lucinda asked, glad to be able to change the subject.

'Sore and sorry. He's got a long road ahead of him but he'll be all right. I'm just waiting for him to get a bit more strength back and then I can kill him,' she said dryly.

'And how are you coping with it all?'

Ann gave a small shrug. 'Every time it gets too hard, I just think of Wayne's parents and think what they're going through. I know then that I'm the lucky one. It's made me do a bit of thinking, though. I've taken long-service leave, I had twelve weeks owing, but after that I think I'll hand my notice in.'

Lucinda had half expected to hear it. Ann had already hinted she'd had enough at the Christmas party and now, given all that had happened, she wasn't surprised.

'The ward will really miss you, Ann. Me, too.'

'I'll miss them as well, but sometimes family just has to come first, as you're no doubt about to find out. I'm not against working mums. I'm one myself. And although we've needed my wage, I've also loved my career, but sometimes you have to stop and smell the roses. Some things just have to give when you have children. Anyway, with the way Jake is, I'll be around the hospital for a while yet so you're not going to get a chance to miss me. And that means I can keep an eye on you, make sure you do tell him.'

'You don't give up, do you?' Lucinda smiled.

'Only when it's a lost cause, and I certainly don't think that about you and Seb. Speaking of which, I'd better go and find him—I want to get back up to Jake.'

Ann made her way over and Lucinda watched as Seb, who was chatting away, stopped and greeted his friend, obviously touched and delighted she'd made the effort to come. He put his arm casually around Ann's shoulders and drew her into the group. The hospital was losing two of its finest.

Lucinda lingered a moment, not wanting to leave, but how could she stay? She had made an appearance—that was enough. If she had to speak to him, had to go over and say goodbye, she knew she couldn't do it. Turning on her heel, she slipped from the room, unnoticed, and walked out of the party and out of Seb's life. It was the hardest thing she had ever done.

Lucinda didn't go straight home. Instead, she wandered aimlessly along the Yarra, staring into the murky waters, tears streaming unchecked down her cheeks. No one paid her any attention. The riverbank was bursting with couples and groups. The theatres had come out and theatre-goers were walking past, clutching their programmes, stopping for a drink, prolonging the night, so that they could relive the play they had just seen.

She put her hand up to her necklace and clutched the tiny robot, reliving scenes of her own—that weekend in Queensland where no scripts had been needed, when it had all flowed so beautifully. Who could have predicted then how the final scene would have played out? Slowly she made her way across the bridge.

On Monday she would be back at work, but this time there would be no Ann and, more poignantly, no Seb. She would tell Mr Hays that she couldn't accept the promotion Pete had hinted at. It simply wouldn't be fair to take it, knowing that she was going to be taking maternity leave. Maybe she could work part time for a while, and if that didn't work out she could always go into research. What was that saying? Nine to five and no one died. It sounds pretty good from here, she thought wearily as she pushed the revolving doors to her apartment block.

'Lucinda.' Standing in her lobby was Seb.

She blinked a couple of times. 'What are you doing here?' she finally managed to ask.

'I've just been speaking to Ann. We need to talk.'

She nodded, her heart in her mouth. Seb pushed the lift button and they stepped inside, Seb watching her as she busied herself retrieving her keys from the depths of her bag.

She let them in and, flicking the lights on, found her voice.

'What did Ann say?' she asked nervously as she set about getting glasses from the kitchen cupboard.

'That I was mad to leave you.'

Ann, it would seem, had been busy.

'Anything else?'

'That I should tell you how I feel.'

She finally looked over to where he stood. For once he didn't look his usual confident self, and Lucinda was reminded of that morning in the annexe after Billy's operation.

'You've already told me how you feel, Seb, right over there by the door, remember, the same door you walked out of a couple of months ago.'

Seb shook his head 'That wasn't how I felt. Walking out that night was the worse thing I've ever had to do, you have to believe me.'

'Then why did you?' She stood there, her back straight, and took a deep breath. Abigail would have been proud.

Seb walked over and took the glasses out of her hands. Placing them on the kitchen bench, he took her hand and guided her over to the couch.

'Can we sit down and talk properly?'

She gave a small nod and sat down, staring ahead as Seb sat beside her. She was terrified her eyes might betray her and he would realise how much she loved him.

'I knew you were a great doctor even before I met you,' he started unsteadily. 'Then, after seeing you work, I knew that you weren't just good, you're probably the best surgeon I've ever seen. You can go as far as you like.'

Lucinda shook her head, and started to stand up. 'What on earth has that got to do with anything?'

'Please, Lucinda.' He pulled her back down beside him. 'Let me finish.

'When you made that speech in Queensland I knew you were going to be huge. Then when I met your parents, heard about your dreams, well, I just don't belong in that world.'

'Nor do I, and what dreams are you talking about?' she interrupted, then stopped as Seb continued.

'When you went to the loo your dad took me to one side. He told me that even from when you were little all you ever wanted to be was the world's best heart surgeon.'

'That was all *they* ever wanted me to be. Why would you listen to what my father says without discussing it with me?'

Seb stood up. 'Maybe I will have that drink'. He went over to the bench and poured out two glasses of wine. Putting down the bottle, he looked across at her.

'It got me thinking. At the conference John McClelland had told me about a chief of anaesthetics position coming up in Ballarat. When I went to the hospital that night, I told you that I'd spoken with Vince about Billy's asthma.'

Lucinda nodded.

'Well, he spelt it out for me. He said Billy needed a lot more stability. It just seemed all the signs were pointing against us. Then when Chris got back from the wedding he said that the prof had been blabbing. Lucinda, I've known since that day that Mr Felix was never coming back, that you were going to make at the very least Senior Consultant, and from the way the prof had been talking he was thinking of sending you to the UK. The hospital felt you were worth the investment, don't you see? You'll be a professor one day.'

'But what's that got to do with us?'

He slammed the glass down on the bench, exasperated.

'Don't be so naïve, Lucinda. It has everything to do with us. In a different place and time maybe we could work things out, survive the distance, work around each other's schedules. But there's Billy to think of. I can't put him through that.'

'Ah, yes,' said Lucinda nastily. 'As you said, I'm not exactly stepmum material.'

'I never said that, Lucinda. They were your words, remember?'

Lucinda swallowed. He was right. It had been her that had said that, but what was the difference? He had been about to finish things.

'Like I said, Billy has to come first,' Seb continued. 'He already adored you. How could I let him get to know you, let him get to love you, knowing it was useless, that you'd go off to the UK, get on with your life. I couldn't put him through that.'

'So why are you here, then? It seems you've already decided I'm not up to the job,' Lucinda said defensively.

'Because I don't think I can do this without you,' came his honest reply. 'I don't think I can get through the next fifty years without you. Ann finally had a go at me. She told me that me and Billy were about to lose the best thing that had ever happened to us if I didn't at least give you the option of coming with us. Look, Lucinda, when you said you weren't up to being a stepmum…'

'I was just saving face,' Lucinda admitted. 'I thought you were trying to end things.'

'Hell, no,' Seb rasped. 'I was just trying to be realistic. I knew we needed to have a long talk.' He took a long drink. 'I've had one failed marriage because of my wife's career, and I was terrified of making a mistake, yet with you I was sure things could be different, that we could somehow work something out. My God, I even considered giving up my work to let you carry on with yours. Have you any idea how that felt? The thought of giving up my career and having you supporting Billy and me! It goes against everything I've been brought up to believe, but if it meant keeping you… Doesn't that show how desperate I was to make things work?

'But when you said it wasn't for you, that it wasn't what you wanted, well, it just seemed pointless. The other stuff we could have worked out in time, but if you didn't, as you said, want Billy…well, he's not an optional item. You had to want both of us.' He looked across at her, his eyes searching her face. 'You really didn't mean what you said?' His voice was tentative at first, but she heard the surge of optimism as he spoke.

She shook her head 'Not a word of it. I adore Billy and I love you,' she gasped. 'I always have.'

'I have to take this job, Lucinda. I have to give Billy this chance.'

'I know you do.'

'And I know I'm mad even asking, I know there's a million reasons why you can't come with me, but I have to ask you. Lucinda, if you can't come I'll understand, and we'll work something out.'

She gazed into Seb's troubled eyes. Here he was, this

beautiful, proud man, putting his son's happiness before his own and in his own jumbled way telling her just how much he loved her, wanted her, needed her.

'So you're asking me to move to the country with you and Billy? To juggle the school runs and packed lunches...'

'Together, we'd work it out together.'

A smile started to flicker across her face. The news she'd been so dreading telling him was now a pleasure.

'There is one small problem—two, actually.'

Seb's face had a pained dignity as he waited for her to deliver the reasons why she couldn't come with him.

'Billy's going to have to get used to sharing me, and I hope that house you told me about has lots of bedrooms. We're going to need them when the twins are born.'

'The twins?' Seb asked, his voice bewildered.

'Our twins,' she said softly. 'They're due in July.'

And as he looked at her glowing, radiant face, gradually realisation dawned and a smile crept across his weary, strained features. With an incredulous laugh he pulled her towards him, running a tender hand over her swollen, heavy breasts and down to her gently rounded stomach.

'Hey, you really are,' he said in wonder. 'You really are.'

'No, Seb,' Lucinda whispered as he wrapped his arms tightly around her. '*We* are.'

EPILOGUE

'WHAT'S burning?'

'Shh.' Lucinda gave a pained look as Seb walked into the kitchen and, putting down his briefcase, gave her a long kiss.

'Mum's *attempting* to bake Billy a birthday cake,' she said finally. 'It's her third go.'

'Why doesn't she just buy one?'

'Because the local baker's range didn't stretch to robots,' Lucinda said matter-of-factly.

Seb ruffled her hair as she pulled off the scarf she had been using to tie it back.

'Any post?'

Lucinda handed him a couple of snapshots. 'Ricky Stewart. Isn't he gorgeous? Janine's beside herself—doesn't even mind the sleepless nights.'

Seb smiled as he looked at the photos. 'He is a cute baby.' He looked back at Lucinda. 'You've been doing some painting?'

'Just the fretwork on the veranda. I'm saving the big jobs for you. I'll come up with you and get changed.'

'Mum, watch the children,' she called as she made her way up the stairs, with Seb following. 'I'm just going to get out of these work clothes.'

Watching her peel off her paint-splattered dungarees, Seb felt weak in the knees with longing as he admired her full breasts encased in cream lace. Her body, always gorgeous, was softer now and more curvaceous despite Lucinda's heroic but sporadic post-pregnancy dieting attempts.

185

'Come here,' he said huskily, pulling her towards him.

Lucinda, laughing, wriggled out of his embrace. 'Mum's downstairs.'

'She won't even notice we're gone with the kids about. Have you told her yet?'

Lucinda nodded. The local GP had offered her a position at his practice. Very part time for now—alternate Saturday or Sunday mornings and one evening clinic a week. The hours would increase in later years as he wound down with a view to retirement. Lucinda had jumped at the chance. Though more fulfilled than she had ever been in her life, the chance to use her brain again, practising medicine, *and* still have heaps of time for the children had been accepted like a gift from the gods. But telling her mother had proved difficult. 'She wasn't too keen.'

Seb's face sank. 'I guess it is a big step down from consultant cardiothoracic surgeon to GP.'

'No, silly.' Lucinda threw a pillow at him. 'She had the gall to tell me I should spend more time with the children. "They're only young for five minutes, Lucinda, you should enjoy this precious time."' She mimicked her mother's voice. 'You'd think that she'd won the Mother of the Year award for raising me. I was tempted to point out that she'd barely delivered the placenta before she went back to work.'

'Maybe she realises what she missed out on,' Seb said gently. 'She's really changed, hasn't she?'

'Changed?' Lucinda said incredulously. 'I hardly recognise her.'

'It doesn't upset you?'

'Not a scrap,' she assured him. 'I'm delighted, even if it is over thirty years late.'

Seb's voice was suddenly serious. 'I know what you've given up.'

'Seb, we've been over this. I've never been happier.'

'But still…'

She silenced his doubts with a kiss, and with her soft, fragrant skin pressing against him his uncertainties slowly vanished.

'Look at everything I've gained,' she whispered into his ear. 'You, Billy, Molly and Harry, even Mum.' She kissed him again, deeply this time, until all that was on Seb's mind was how quickly they could get the children and mother-in-law off to bed.

'Someone's coming,' he gasped, pulling away.

Delighted at the effect she had on him, Lucinda laughingly pulled on her bathrobe as Billy entered the bedroom.

'Nanna's taking us to the shop. We need some silver sugar balls for the robot cake's buttons.'

Seb winked at Lucinda. Maybe they wouldn't have to wait till bedtime after all.

'Does she really have to go back to Queensland on Friday?' Billy asked, his big eyes filling with tears.

Seb pulled Billy onto his knee. 'She'll come again soon,' he said comfortingly.

'Honest?' sniffed Billy.

Seb rolled his eyes but his voice was light and Lucinda knew he was only teasing her.

'Oh, you can count on it, sport, you can count on it.'

MILLS & BOON®

Live the emotion

Modern
r o m a n c e ™

THE MEDITERRANEAN PRINCE'S PASSION
by Sharon Kendrick

He was like the hero of a film. He had rescued her, made
love to her... But now Ella had discovered who he was:
Nicolo, daredevil Prince of the Mediterranean island of
Mardivino! Nico was used to getting what he wanted –
and he wanted Ella...

THE SPANIARD'S INCONVENIENT WIFE *by Kate Walker*

Ramon Dario desperately wants the Medrano company –
but there is a condition: he must marry the notorious
Estrella Medrano! Ramon will not be forced into marriage,
but when he sees the gorgeous Estrella, he starts to
change his mind...

THE ITALIAN COUNT'S COMMAND *by Sara Wood*

Miranda still loves her estranged husband, Count Dante
Severini, and misses him and their son. Dante wants to be
rid of Miranda, but their son misses her. Dante issues
Miranda with a command: she must live with him and act
as the perfect wife...

HER HUSBAND'S CHRISTMAS BARGAIN *by Margaret Mayo*

When Italian businessman Luigi Costanzo discovers that
his beautiful estranged wife is the mother of his child, he is
furious! How dare Megan keep his daughter from him?
Megan is unimpressed when Luigi turns up, just before
Christmas – but he is hard to resist...

Don't miss out...

On sale 3rd December 2004

*Available at most branches of WHSmith, Tesco, ASDA, Martins,
Borders, Eason, Sainsbury's and all good paperback bookshops.*

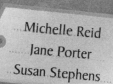

MILLS & BOON

**Volume 6
on sale from
3rd December
2004**

Lynne
Graham

International Playboys

*The Winter
Bride*

*Available at most branches of WHSmith, Tesco, Martins, Borders,
Eason, Sainsbury's and all good paperback bookshops.*

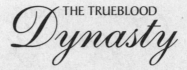

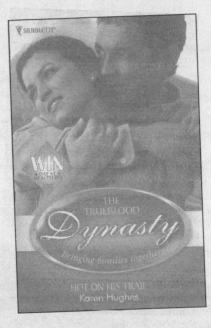

MILLS & BOON®

Live the emotion

Tender romance™

TO WIN HIS HEART by Rebecca Winters

(The Husband Fund)

Bubbly blonde heiress Olivia Duchess is attracted to gorgeous Frenchman Luc de Falcon, and he's attracted to her – but his famous racing driver brother is infatuated with her. Luc is an honourable man, but Olivia has the Husband Fund at her disposal, and is determined to win his heart…

THE MONTE CARLO PROPOSAL by Lucy Gordon

Multimillionaire Jack Bullen has a proposal for Della Martin: pose as his girlfriend in Monte Carlo so he can avoid an unwanted marriage. Della agrees, only to find that kissing and flirting with Jack when it's all 'pretend' is hard. She wants it for real…

THE LAST-MINUTE MARRIAGE by Marion Lennox

(Contract Brides)

Peta and Marcus had a wonderful wedding – but it's a sham. Theirs is a marriage of convenience. Yet Marcus is showering his bride with gifts and offering a life of luxury – but Peta wants *Marcus* not money…

THE CATTLEMAN'S ENGLISH ROSE by Barbara Hannay

(Southern Cross)

An Outback cattle station is the last place Charity Denham thought she'd end up searching for her brother – she won't leave until she finds him. Kane McKinnon lives for the Outback, but he harbours a secret – one that Charity is close to discovering…

On sale 3rd December 2004

Available at most branches of WHSmith, Tesco, ASDA, Martins, Borders, Eason, Sainsbury's and all good paperback bookshops.

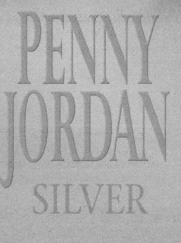

*A story of passions and betrayals...
and the dangerous obsessions they spawn*

PENNY JORDAN

SILVER